N.G. Peltier is an anime-watching, book-reading, video-game playing, story-writing kinda girl.

A devourer of words and books from a young age, she enjoys writing romance and creeping people out with the Caribbean folklore stories she grew up hearing.

A Trinidadian born and raised, she currently lives in Trinidad with her mountain of ideas and characters battling each other for whose story gets told next.

Read more at ngpeltier.com

You can also find her on Twitter @trinielf

ALSO BY N.G. PELTIER

The Dating Countdown

ISLAND BITES

N.G. PELTIER

PIATKUS

PIATKUS

First published in the US in 2024 by N.G. Peltier
First published in Great Britain in 2024 by Piatkus

1 3 5 7 9 10 8 6 4 2

A CIP catalogue record for this book
is available from the British Library.

ISBN 978-0-349-44321-8

Typeset by Hewer Text UK Ltd, Edinburgh
Printed and bound in Great Britain by Clays Ltd, Elcograf S.p.A.

Papers used by Piatkus are from well-managed forests
and other responsible sources.

Piatkus
An imprint of
Little, Brown Book Group
Carmelite House
50 Victoria Embankment
London EC4Y 0DZ

An Hachette UK Company
www.hachette.co.uk

www.littlebrown.co.uk

To all those who are questioning. I see you.
I love you. You are valid! 😊🖤

CHAPTER ONE

MAXINE

NOVEMBER

THE WALL OF BODIES PRESSED INTO HER AS SOON AS SHE MADE HER way inside. Maxine hadn't been to a party like this in ages. Actually, in ever. What was she doing at this strictly invite-only gathering for the queer community on the island? She didn't even know the host, Laney something or other—her surname eluded her—but her friend, Victoria, had insisted it was fine. It would be fine. This was just what they both needed.

Maxine wasn't so sure of that. She felt like someone would point an accusing finger at her at any moment and demand to know why she was here. Did questioning everything she thought she knew about herself mean she belonged here?

You made out with Remi in that Bootleggers bathroom, and in the bathroom at the wedding, remember? I'd say it counts.

She brushed off the voice of reason and scanned the crowd for Victoria. Now wasn't the time to have a full-on crisis about her sexuality. She'd already been doing that since she came back to Trinidad and ran into Remi Daniels.

No thinking about Remi. Not tonight. Maybe not ever.

An impossible feat considering her brother was now dating Remi's best friend. Now, they were back in each other's circles.

It was different when they were teenagers. Then, they'd been fierce competitors about everything. Until the moment that changed it all.

Great, now I'm taking a trip down memory lane. That isn't what tonight is about.

Jesus, this house was packed. There'd been people scattered about the pool, mingling, drinking, laughing, even some with their feet in the water, but the difference between outside the house and inside was stark.

Inside was where the fun was happening. Music pumped through the sound system as the DJ did her thing. Colourful strobe lights pulsed on and off, bringing a club vibe to the house party. It should have clashed with the Christmas décor the host had going on, but somehow it worked. The twinkle lights, tinsel, and giant Christmas tree didn't take away from the vibe at all.

The end of November had crept up on her. As far as Maxine was concerned, it was a bit early to pull out this décor, but malls were already decorated and maybe the host was one of those people who liked putting their stuff up early. She was used to her mother waiting until December to dig out the Christmas stuff. Either way, the partiers didn't seem to care. She caught a glimpse of a couple actually grinding against the tree, which shook with their exuberant dancing. Hopefully, the thing was sturdy enough not to topple over.

Maxine stood on the edges of the crowded space swaying along with the music. When music played, her body took on a life of its own. Even as the nervousness did a little dance in her stomach, she kept on grooving, hoping to spot Victoria making her way back to her.

Victoria had gone to the bathroom a while ago and Maxine had grown tired of waiting. She'd killed some of the time gaping at familiar public faces—discreet gaping, or so she hoped. The last thing she wanted was to make someone feel uncomfortable. She'd thought she'd spied a popular local athlete but couldn't be sure. From where she'd been standing, only his profile had been visible as he'd draped his arm across his companion's shoulder. The two men's faces so close, one move forward and the athlete would have brushed the man's cheek.

The mandatory rule of handing over all electronic devices before anyone could enter the party made sense now. Maxine hadn't protested when she and Victoria had been told to hand them in to be tagged and stored away until they were ready to present their numbered chit and leave. It was a smart move. This private party *was* queer friendly, but some of the people she'd seen were high profile and definitely weren't out. It would only take one compromising shot for scandal to rear its head across the island.

She considered squeezing through the crowd in search of Victoria, figuring at some point she'd stumble upon the bathroom. But she'd have to shimmy through the sweaty bodies and she wasn't sure she was up for that. Instead, she stayed on the fringes and continued to people watch.

Two women dancing a short distance away swung heated looks her way, a clear invitation to join in. Maxine swallowed, the swirls in her belly intensifying as she tried to look anywhere but at the two women.

"Hey, there you are!"

A bottle was pressed into her hand and Maxine relished the feel of the cool glass against her palm.

"You were supposed to stay outside." Victoria wagged a finger at her.

Maxine shrugged. "Got tired waiting."

Her gaze fixed on the two women again. They were still staring, their lips quirked up in similar smirks. Victoria nudged Maxine's shoulder with her own.

"Well, well, somebody's picking up." Victoria sipped her drink, lifting her silky black hair off her neck with her other hand. The accumulated body heat *was* a bit much. It had been far cooler out by the pool.

"Doubtful," Maxine said, not willing to let on that her brain and dreams were filled with another woman. "Maybe they can smell the imposter on me."

Victoria frowned. "C'mon, you know that's not true. You have every right to be here."

Maxine didn't feel like that at all.

When Victoria had mentioned the party, Maxine had been torn. They'd slowly been reconnecting since Maxine had moved back to Trinidad. Friends in secondary school, they'd drifted apart when Maxine had moved abroad to pursue her degree in Music Management. Sure, they'd sort of kept in touch through social media, but there hadn't been constant communication. Maxine had been thrilled that they were slowly getting back to the friendship they'd had. Even though they'd been sort of catty mean girls during their time at school, it was interesting to see how they'd both grown. They'd cringed over some of the shit they'd done back then.

Maxine had been excited to go out, but hesitant to attend *this* party. She'd only given in because Victoria had convinced Maxine that she needed her – to drown Victoria's recent break-up woes with hot women and ice-cold drinks. But Maxine had only recently got divorced from her husband and still felt unsure about relationships. She'd blabbed to Victoria about her spontaneous make-out session with a girl in the Bootleggers bathroom a few months ago, how everything had been building in her since. Maxine had needed to talk to someone other than Keiran. Her brother was a good listener, but . . .

She hadn't mentioned any names. Victoria knew Remi from back in their school days, but she hadn't known about their fooling around during that last holiday period before they got their exam results. After all, she and Remi had been hardcore rivals, fighting about everything. Who got top spot in their class? Who would be captain of the netball team? Who would replace the captain of the women's cricket team when the former captain went off to school? That last one had led to the night of fooling around, at the cricket retreat that changed the entire dynamic of their relationship and launched the few months of secret hooking up.

She'd wanted to keep Remi's identity to herself, unsure of Victoria's reaction. She *wanted* too much, that was the problem.

Maxine sipped her Smirnoff Black slowly. She didn't drink often, so was all about pacing herself tonight. If she went past drink number two, she'd be a giggling, oversharing mess. She wasn't about to be careless in someone else's house, surrounded by strangers. No matter if she had Victoria to look out for her. Maxine preferred not to leave her wellbeing in anyone's hands.

"I just don't know what I'm doing with all this." *This* being feelings she'd locked away and not looked at for years. *This* being Remi. Dammit. There she went again.

"You're figuring yourself out. Nothing wrong with that. You belong here." Victoria patted Maxine's arm. "No one's going to demand to see your queer card. It's all good. And if they do, I'll kick their asses." Victoria still didn't reach Maxine's height of five-nine, even though she was rocking these sky-high heels. Without them, she was barely five-one.

"Now." Her gaze swept the crowd. "Find me a hottie to grind on. You're slacking off on your wing-woman skills. Get with it, girl!"

Maxine snorted. Her, a wing woman? Victoria could do *so* much better, but she'd try. She pointed at the same two women from earlier. "What about them? They're stunning."

That was an understatement. The taller of the two was stacked. Hips and breasts for days. More than a handful. Long braids brushed her ass. Victoria had made it quite clear that she loved her women thick. The woman's dance partner was curvy as hell too, her mini skirt rode up on her thighs as she ground her ass back onto Ms. Thickie Number One. Maxine caught a flash of underwear, realised she was staring and averted her eyes.

Victoria took another swig of her drink. "Sexy as hell for sure, but one woman is enough of a handful. I can't handle those two. Not even ashamed to admit that. Besides, they weren't looking at me like they wanted to eat me out *oh so good.*" She winked and heat crept up Maxine's neck.

Subtle, her friend was not. Maxine couldn't handle anything these two women were eager to dish out. She'd get eaten alive for sure. She'd only ever fooled around with one woman and . . . *God.* She pressed her thighs together. Do. Not. Go. There.

"You did say you wanted to drown in hot women tonight. Your exact words," Maxine pointed out, pressing the cold bottle against her neck. Why did all her thoughts always flow back to Remi?

"Hmm, I did, didn't I?" Victoria drummed her fingers against her mouth. "They do say the best way to get over someone is to get under someone else, right? Maybe two someones will help me get over Zia faster."

"Sounds logical to me." But Maxine continued to scan the crowd.

Victoria needed some options. Thus far, she'd put up a good front, but her friend had been devastated over the breakup. When you'd been with someone so long, you figured the happily ever after was a given. Since her divorce, Maxine could relate to that all too well.

The music switched from the sexy-slow-grinding-required dancehall song to a fast-paced trance beat and the crowd's mood changed along with it. People started jumping around and pretending to whirl imaginary glow sticks in their hands. One group of ladies were especially raucous, their drinks pumping in the air as they sang along with Sonique's "Sky". One of the women twirled on the spot, her long black curly hair swishing around her, and Maxine's heart stuttered in her chest.

No. No way. Lots of women had curly hair almost down to their ass like this. It didn't mean . . .

She caught sight of the woman's face. Those lips curved into a wide smile as she tossed her head back. All that luscious hair spilling down her back. Ah shit.

"Wait a minute. Is that Remi?" Victoria shouted in her ear, arm outstretched as she pointed at the group of women.

"I don't know." Like hell she didn't. Her brain was trained to recognise Remi from a distance now. The woman she was still pretending wasn't Remi tucked a bunch of hair behind her ear and Maxine zeroed in on the slightly pointy tip of that ear.

"I think it might be," Victoria insisted.

Maxine seriously considered excusing herself, running outside, anything but standing here waiting to be seen. She wasn't prepared to face Remi in general. Coming face to face with a Remi dressed in tiny black leather shorts that drew the eyes to her long brown legs and a lacy black top that . . . *God* . . . revealed enough to send Maxine right to the bathroom to sort out this tangle of emotions, was too much.

"I don't think it's her," Maxine tried weakly.

Victoria gestured to the woman again. "I wouldn't mistake that hair anywhere. When you used to dream about how that hair'd feel on your skin, you sure as shit don't forget it."

Maxine blinked at Victoria. "*W-what?*"

Victoria grinned. "Oh, yeah, right, you didn't know about my crush on Remi." She shrugged. "I wasn't exactly out to our crew back then, so I kept the lusting to myself."

Well, this was awkward. Maxine couldn't mention now that Remi was the woman she'd been randomly, kinda, sort of, hooking up with.

Victoria peered at her. "Does that weird you out? I know you two were always fighting, but I figure we're all adults now and we've outgrown that, so saying hi shouldn't be odd. Right?"

"Are you tryna make Remi your rebound woman or something?" Maxine cringed at her caustic tone. Could she sound any more like a jealous lover?

Victoria laughed. "I mean, stranger things have happened, but no. I was just going to say hello, but you seem weirded out about it."

"I'm not. I just . . ." Maxine shook her head. She should just come clean, at least partially. "Remi and I have actually been talking. Sort of. We were both in that wedding party. For Ava? Cherisse's sister?"

"Oh right. True. So what's the problem?" Victoria pointed at Maxine with her almost-empty beer bottle. "You're being sketchy about this."

She was, and she didn't want Victoria to probe further. She had to get it together. Prove to herself she could act casual around Remi. Unaffected. She mustered a smile. "It's all good. Let's go say hi."

Victoria hooked their arms together as she danced them over to where Remi and crew were still having a good time. They got to the women just as Remi spun around to grind her ass back against another woman's front, giving Maxine an eyeful of her breasts as her top dipped low.

"Remi Daniels! Small world, eh?" Victoria shouted.

Remi's eyes rose to meet Victoria's, hips pausing mid dance, but her gaze quickly shifted to collide with Maxine's. She barely moved as Remi's eyes roved over her. She'd worn a simple, little black dress with thin straps and a strip of see-through fabric across her stomach for a peekaboo effect. It clung. Everywhere. She'd gone braless—tonight was the night to be daring apparently—and in spite of the heat building with all the bodies in the room, she felt her nipples pebble under that heated stare.

"You're here," Remi said to her, ignoring Victoria's greeting completely.

Maxine licked her dry lips, tried not to stare at Remi's neck, which was encased with several chokers. What would she do if Maxine just slipped a finger beneath the silky fabric around her neck and tugged her closer? As if she'd ever go through with it. Maxine wasn't brave enough for that move, so she managed a weak, "Hi."

Next to her, she noticed Victoria's head swivelling back and forth between them. Behind Remi, the woman she'd been dancing with also watched them, curiosity gleaming in her dark eyes. Maxine wondered if she was Remi's date, then chided herself for even thinking that. It wasn't her business. This crashing together, fooling around, didn't mean they were exclusive by any means. They didn't talk about that.

But the tiny voice in her head pestered, chanting: "What if she *is* her date?"

Maxine tried to think of something witty to say. A "fancy meeting you here" quip. Anything. Instead, she stared. Her body was too aware of Remi, and even though they had an audience, Remi's stare down was also too intense for her. Maxine couldn't conjure anything else to add to her pathetic "Hi."

"*So.*" The woman who'd been behind Remi stepped around to stand at Remi's side. "This the one you've been pining over this whole time?"

Maxine's mouth hung open. Next to her, Victoria snorted and turned to face her, brow raised. "You got some explaining to do, missy."

CHAPTER TWO

REMI

REMI HAD HAD A PLAN FOR TONIGHT'S PARTY. GRIND ON HER FRIENDS' asses. *Check.* They'd all been dancing together since they'd arrived. Get all up on some unknown behinds. *In progress.* She'd spied some prospects earlier, but their group had gotten into the music so much they hadn't really paid anyone outside of it any mind.

Laney's parties were the best kept secret on the island— except if you moved in certain circles in the island's queer community; then it was well known. Remi had been attending these for years, never one to pass up a chance to dance, drink free booze and just be herself. She hadn't been prepared to see Maxine. Why would she ever consider running into her? Here of all places?

Remi realised this was a pattern—not being prepared to see Maxine. Their teenage hook-up had been fuelled by too-strong homemade liquor some brave classmate had smuggled into the retreat, and probably curiosity on Maxine's part. They had never spoken about it. The fact they'd kept hooking up for the entire holiday period was still mind boggling. It had been the best vacation of her life, truly – until reality had set in when

Maxine had to leave for school and Remi had gone into asshole mode, said some hurtful shit. God, she'd been a hot mess at that age.

Maxine's return to the island recently had been unexpected. Remi hadn't expected divorce would be the reason. Their reconnecting hadn't been a consideration. She figured they would run into each other randomly, on the rare occasion their friend group collided. But then the wedding happened, which brought them quite literally into each other's space.

She sure as fuck hadn't been ready to see Maxine in her groom person's gear at the wedding. She still had fantasies of the way the suspenders had curved over Maxine's generous breasts. Then they'd ended up fooling around. It kept happening, and she wasn't sure how much longer her luck would hold out where Maxine was concerned, but she was embracing it all the way until it all fizzled or blew up in their faces.

They hadn't been face to face since their last bathroom encounter, all communication happening via texts, and those had stayed clear of any mentions of hooking up. They'd been bland conversation about innocuous things – akin to talking about the weather.

Remi ignored her friend Sanaa's joke about pining—she *wasn't*. Her eyes were firmly fixed on the way Maxine's dress moulded to her body. Fuck! Maxine had curves for days and Remi was all about them.

Her eyes shifted from Maxine to the tiny Chinese woman next to her. Victoria Chow. Another person she hadn't expected to see here. Victoria looked basically the same. Long black hair worn stick straight with the ever-present side part. She hadn't gotten a single inkling that Victoria was queer, but then again, when you attended an all-girls Catholic school, you kept that under lock. Didn't advertise. Discreet became your middle name.

Back in school, Victoria and Maxine had been tight. Now, it seemed they were still on friendly terms, and Remi wondered if they were more than that. Was Maxine here as Victoria's date? The idea seemed ludicrous. Maxine was one twitch away from bolting anytime they got too close to each other. The two occasions she and Maxine had made out, Maxine had been the one to pump the brakes on it going any further. She was figuring things out, so Remi didn't think she would have gone from nervousness to full-on out on a date with another woman, but what the hell did she know?

She'd gone from questioning her attractions in university to screwing Sanaa in someone's dorm room. It had been freeing just to give in, not worry about anyone but herself, and the desire of finally being with someone who wasn't ashamed of what they'd done. She and Sanaa hadn't lasted as a couple for various reasons, but they remained friends.

"What are you doing here?" she asked, eyes back to Maxine.

Sanaa draped an arm around Remi's waist. "Same as us I expect." Remi didn't have to look at Sanaa to know she was flashing her trademark panty-dropping grin. The way Victoria was suddenly biting her lip signalled that it was working. Sanaa strikes again.

"I uh . . . V invited me." Maxine's gaze dipped to Sanaa's arm around Remi's waist, lingered for a bit before snapping back up to her face. Interesting.

"She's my wing woman for the night," Victoria supplied cheerfully. "I'm single and ready to mingle."

"And what about you Sexy Black Dress?" Sanaa asked. "You ready to mingle?"

Okay, they weren't doing this. Sanaa was a big flirt and Remi wasn't about to let her set her sights on Maxine. No damn way.

"She's not for you," Remi blurted, regretting it immediately. Now, she just looked like some jealous weirdo. Awesome.

Maxine's brow winged up, the "oh really?" heavily implied by the sharp curve.

"Sorry, I didn't mean it like that. Just . . ."

How exactly could Remi explain what she meant? It wasn't her place to spill Maxine's business to her friends. She could picture Sanaa's interest tripling the minute she found out Maxine was new to this whole queer scene. Her friend just didn't know how to deploy tact. She'd make it her mission to help Maxine navigate the tricky waters that was this community sometimes, all while dropping her best seduction moves.

All of that was liable to scare Maxine off than bring her any sort of comfort.

Luckily, Victoria saved her by closing the distance between herself and Sanaa. "Let's dance, gorgeous," she purred, snapping Sanaa's glittery suspenders. "These two seem to have some catching up to do."

Sanaa pointed towards the crowd. "Lead the way."

Remi rolled her eyes. Sanaa wasn't even being coy about wanting to ogle Victoria's ass encased in that short skirt. Victoria didn't seem to mind; she threw a smile over her shoulder, adding a little more swing to her hips.

"Sorry," Remi said again, once they were alone. Well, alone-ish.

"What'd you mean by that?" Maxine's nose wrinkled and Remi found it the cutest thing. "Your friend's not for me?"

"You're not ready for Sanaa. She's intense."

Maxine looked over to where Sanaa towered over Victoria's smaller frame. The DJ had switched to some old-school dancehall again, the kind that brought out the slow bumping and grinding. Perfect songs for getting up close and personal with someone on the dance floor. Jesus, the way those hips were moving, those two needed to get to a room soon.

"Yeah, maybe I'm not," Maxine admitted when her focus came back to Remi. "I'm definitely not ready for that."

Remi wasn't certain which "that" she meant. Dancing with a woman in public, Sanaa specifically, or any of it? Being with a woman in general?

"Victoria might be able to handle her. I sure wasn't."

"Are you and her?" Maxine's eyes grew wider. "I mean, it's not my business. Sorry, forget I asked. I didn't mean—"

"Hey." Remi placed her hand on Maxine's shoulder before she went further into over-apologising panic mode. "It's cool. Really." She might as well get this out of the way. She *had* brought them here with her slip about Sanaa.

"She was my first serious-ish relationship with a woman. We met at UWI where she was doing part-time classes for her degree. She'd always wanted to get it but said marriage and kids sort of derailed that, so after her divorce she went for it. And we uh, yeah, sort of fell into this intense thing where um, it was more physical at first." Damn, this was awkward. Spilling her guts like this when she should be making like Victoria and Sanaa and asking Maxine to dance, instead of spewing this babbling mess that was her and Sanaa's complicated relationship.

"So, lots of sex?" Maxine asked, flat out, teeth pressed into her bottom lip, eyes darting out to the crowd and back to Remi. In the semi darkness of the dance floor, Remi couldn't tell if Maxine was blushing, but her actions indicated she hadn't meant to outright ask that.

Remi coughed. "Uh, yeah. That. Long story short, Sanaa was ten years older and I was in awe that this gorgeous older woman wanted me, you know? But she was ready for settling down again and I just wasn't. We remained good friends and

Sanaa likes to trot out the claim I broke her heart ever so often, so now she's a giant flirt who doesn't do relationships."

"It's cool you remained friends," Maxine said.

"Yeah. Sanaa's fun." Remi glanced over to where Sanaa had last been seen grinding on Victoria. They weren't so much dancing now as making out.

"Oh."

That one word, exhaled on a hitched breath, brought Remi's gaze right back where she wanted it anyway. Maxine's teeth were fiddling with her bottom lip again, and her eyes were locked on the two women in the heated embrace. "She looks good at that." Maxine cleared her throat.

"She is, but I'd like to think I'm better."

Maxine's head snapped back to her, and Remi grinned. Maxine's eyes dropped down to Remi's lips, no subtly whatsoever. Did she realise she wore everything on her face? The kisses they'd shared all those years ago as teens had been great, but the ones they'd shared as adults were electric. Remi wanted to do it again, and again, and again. They hadn't done more than make out and some light groping – well, not since cricket camp all those years ago. They'd done some serious heavy petting and touching then.

But she wasn't pushing it. Not with Maxine being skittish right now. They could get their start with a dance at least.

"Wanna dance?" Nice, easy, calm.

Maxine looked down at Remi's outstretched hand like she didn't have a clue what to do with it. Remi braced to be hardcore rejected.

"Not trying to pressure you, but just know what happens at these parties usually stays here." She tried to reassure. "Laney and Mira make sure of that."

"Dancing," Maxine muttered like it was a foreign concept. She inhaled deeply. "Yeah. I can do that. Dancing is easy."

Oh, the poor soul. Easy? Not the way Remi danced, but Remi revelled in the feel of Maxine's soft palm in hers as she led them away from her posse. Remi ignored the teasing whistles that followed them into the thicker part of the crowd. She shot a middle finger behind her, then reeled Maxine in, but not too close. Not yet. She was already so jumpy.

They'd been trying to be lowkey about this thing. Cherisse and Reba, Remi's friends, were aware. But Remi didn't know if Maxine had told her twin, Keiran. Tonight, though, they didn't have to dial anything down if they didn't want to. Remi chose the goofy path and twirled Maxine instead. Maxine laughed as they kept that up, but eventually Remi reeled her in until those lush curves were pressed along her front.

"You okay with this?" Remi asked. Maxine's arms wound around Remi's neck as if she couldn't resist the contact.

Maxine nodded. "Yeah, of course. I've danced with my girl-friends before."

"But not me. Are we friends, Maxi?"

They hadn't danced at all at the wedding, at least not one on one. They'd done it in a group, and when they'd broken away for the bathroom, that had been a different sort of inter-action all together.

Remi wet her lips. The fruity scent of Maxine's perfume tickled her nose and the urge to nuzzle at the curve where Maxine's neck and shoulder met was strong.

"I'd like us to be friends."

Remi's hands slipped down to Maxine's waist. "Sure thing. I love showing my friends a good time." She spun Maxine around, that plump ass pressed against her front, and she didn't have to say a word. Maxine's hips moved along to the music. The slow roll was almost Remi's undoing.

"You're absolutely killing me." She didn't know where this teasing Maxine was coming from, but she was going to revel in it for as long as she was allowed.

Maxine spun around, looping her arms around Remi's neck again, hips never ceasing their slow roll. This time Remi's hands slipped down to right above Maxine's ass. *Sweet, Jesus.*

Maxine leaned in. "I want." She paused, tongue poking out as Remi's hand slipped a bit further to boldly caress an ass cheek. She hummed low, but they were close enough for Remi to hear that little sound of delight. "I want to kiss you," she rushed out.

Remi wasn't one to waste opportunity. "Yes, please."

The kiss was tentative. Never mind it wasn't the first occasion . The other times had been hot, ravenous, as if they had limited time and had to get in as much of each other as they could. Considering they always ended up in some bathroom, the possibility of being caught had been high, so yeah, limited time had been no joke.

This time, they went slow. Remi savoured Maxine's lips. Mmm, whatever her gloss was it actually tasted good. Or maybe that was all Maxine. This very second she didn't care enough to ask.

Their hips bumped up against each other and Maxine made a sound into Remi's mouth, not quite a moan, but it spurred her on to deepen the kiss.

"Get a room!" someone shouted jokingly, and Maxine jerked back, eyes wide, panic beginning to fill in where there had been heat before. She looked around, dazed, clearly having forgotten she was among other people. Remi could relate. She'd zoned out everything but the feel of Maxine's tongue against hers.

Maxine touched her mouth and stepped back. "I shouldn't have done that. Shit, I'm sorry. I—"

"Hey, it's okay. I promise. It really is."

That didn't seem to soothe. If anything, she looked more panicky, head whipping around, probably looking for Victoria so they could make a quick exit out of here. Remi knew Sanaa well enough that she figured she'd taken Victoria somewhere less crowded for some more fun activities.

"I need to go. To the bathroom. Sorry." Maxine dashed off leaving Remi achy and staring after her retreating form.

CHAPTER THREE

MAXINE

BY SOME MIRACLE, THERE WASN'T A LINE TO THE BATHROOM. AS SHE pushed through the door, there was, however, Victoria splayed out on the couch, dress hiked up to her waist and Sanaa's head planted right between Victoria's thighs.

"Oh, *fuck*. Yeah that's . . . just . . . don't fucking stop." Victoria's voice was strained as she gripped Sanaa's head.

"Shit!" Maxine clapped her hand to her mouth. She definitely hadn't wanted to hear her friend sound like *that*. Or see her like this. She could've just backed the hell out, not alerted anyone to her presence, but the surprise had her mouth moving before her brain could tell her to shut the hell up.

Sanaa turned towards her, tongue swiping out to lick her lips. Holy shit. Maxine was too stunned to do anything but watch. She stayed focused on Sanaa, who rose to her feet, wicked smile curving her lips.

"Well, hey there." She pulled Victoria up. "We'll just get right out of your hair."

"Sorry," Maxine said, weakly.

Victoria's cheeks were pink, but she didn't seem embarrassed, not the way she was smiling like that.

"Whoops," she giggled tugging her dress down. "Sorry you had to see, and, well, hear me. Our bad."

"It's fine. Really." Maxine had barely gotten that out when Sanaa pressed Victoria against the sinks and full-on kissed her, hand kneading her ass as if Maxine wasn't even there. Victoria's leg came up to wrap around Sanaa's waist. Oh my God, why did she find that so hot?

Sanaa pulled back. "Come on sweets, let's stop scandalising your poor friend and go finish our business elsewhere." She steered Victoria towards the door, threw Maxine a dirty smile and left.

Well, damn.

If Maxine had been revved up before dancing with Remi, and then that kiss. Lord, help her. Seeing Victoria like that. God, *hearing* her . . .

She pressed her palms against the sink and squeezed her legs together. *Hold it together.* She was unravelling. Ducking into a stall to take care of this heat that was engulfing her body would be so easy. One touch of her finger and she'd probably just explode.

What the hell had she been thinking? That kiss was a bad idea, because now she wanted more.

She stared at her reflection in the mirror, considered splashing water on her over-heating face. Then she thought better of it. Victoria had done her make-up and Maxine wasn't about to ruin her masterful work. She'd done some light contouring magic that Maxine would never be able to replicate if she tried.

Just, breathe. Just breathe.

The door swung open and Maxine jumped. Dammit. Remi stood there with her hand pressed to her chest.

Maxine tried not to let her eyes slip down to the V of Remi's lace top. Here, in the harsh light, it was so clear Remi wasn't wearing a bra. Her small breasts pressed against the top, playing a peekaboo game with that lace, making you question whether you were indeed catching a glimpse of nipple or not.

"You okay?" Remi asked.

"Yeah." A damn lie because, as they faced each other, the thumping in her chest grew louder to her ears. "I ran into V and Sanaa. They were occupied." Now why'd she think bringing that up was a good idea?

Remi laughed. "I don't even need to ask if they were in a compromising position. I know Sanaa well enough."

And she certainly had to know how talented Sanaa was with her tongue. Maxine didn't say *that* out loud. She could picture Remi and Sanaa together. They'd look so good. Remi and Sanaa were both tall, beautiful women. She could easily picture all that brown skin sliding against each other. Jesus. She had to stop her overactive imagination.

"Yeah, I wasn't prepared at all. That was something."

"A good something?" Remi's lips twitched and Maxine's grip on the counter tightened. Remi's lipstick was slightly smudged. Maxine had done that—in her need to taste.

"Yes, good. Very good. Better than those videos I watched."

"Why Ms. King," Remi drawled. "You been watchin' porn? Do elaborate."

Maxine covered her face with her hands.

"Nothing to be ashamed of." The tentative touch against the back of Maxine's hand drew her to spread her fingers and peek at Remi. "But I *am* curious. If you want to tell me, that is." Remi smiled back at her, encouragingly.

Maxine slid her hands away from her face. She could do this. She could talk about how she'd wanted to satisfy her curiosity about the different ways women could have sex with each other. What that would look like. She could casually discuss that she had bitten down on her own fist to keep quiet while watching wide-eyed in her bedroom.

"I mean you and I were so young when we . . ." She absolutely could not finish that sentence. What they had done back at that cricket camp had been a fumbled, frenzied moment. Both of them inexperienced. Maxine was still inexperienced, having only been with Leo after Remi. "I was curious," she admitted.

Remi stepped closer and Maxine's breath caught in her throat. She swallowed hard and stared at those damn chokers encasing Remi's long neck. Her previous fantasy of slipping one finger beneath them and pulling Remi close was back with a vengeance.

"Nothing wrong with being curious, but you know what's best? Experiencing it for yourself. Learning what you like." Remi cocked her head. "You have no idea how you look when you're like this, do you?"

"Like what?"

"Turned on."

"H—how do you know I am?" She was. She so was.

"Well." Remi swung her heavy curls over her shoulder. "That look in your eyes. The way you're looking at me like you want to take the plunge again. You keep biting your lip and your nipples are just saying a hearty hello right now." Remi grinned. "They're begging to be sucked, among other things."

Oh geez, the nipples in question tightened further. She'd chosen to go bra-less with this dress. Something she rarely did, but the dress supported her chest more than most she owned, so she'd gone for it.

"God, Remi. I don't know what I'm doing here. I really don't."

"It's alright. I can help you. If that's what you want."

She did want and it scared her—scared her to know she wasn't who she thought she was her entire life. After everything had gone down with Remi in their teens, she'd pushed all those feelings to the back of her mind when she'd married Leo. She hadn't looked too closely at the fact that she maybe wasn't as straight as she'd always thought. Even after the cricket camp moment that started all this. She had simply considered it a moment that stood all on its own. A one-time thing that didn't mean anything, really. Except, even as she had made a life with Leo, she couldn't deny that way in the back of her mind she sometimes thought about that, and Remi.

"This is a safe space, I promise you. I know you're worried about the kiss out there but trust me, everyone here has a reason to keep quiet about these parties. And not just anyone can get in. You have to be personally invited and have people vouch for you. The hosts take their guests' safety pretty seriously. And I'm not saying this just to get into your panties."

"But you *do* want in my panties?" Maxine smiled at Remi's snort.

"Well yeah, obviously. No pressure or anything. I just wanted to make sure you were okay."

Maxine shook her head. "I'm not okay." Remi's eyes immediately reflected concern and Maxine didn't let herself chicken out. She soldiered on. "There's this ache between my legs, you see. I don't know if you can help me with that."

"Oh."

The look on Remi's face was priceless. Stunned, with a healthy dose of aroused. Maxine didn't give either of them time to back out. She tangled her hand in Remi's hair and drew her in that last step, bringing their faces so close together, within kissing range.

"Can you help me or not?" she asked. No idea where this bravery was coming from. She couldn't even blame the alcohol;

she'd only had the one drink. She just waited. Almost certain Remi wouldn't turn her down, but the small, pesky voice came at her again.

You keep doing this to her and then running away. Maybe she's tired of your shit.

She never meant to start anything with Remi, but when they were around each other all her intentions just fled.

"Hell, yeah, I can." Remi removed the hand in her hair and held up a finger. "Hold that thought." She turned back to the door and pressed in the lock. When she faced Maxine again the heat in her eyes was back in full force. "No interruptions. There's more than one bathroom in this place."

She pressed Maxine back into the marble counter. "Just lemme know if you want to stop. At any time."

Maxine nodded. "Please kiss me."

Remi winked. "As you wish."

Maxine squeaked as Remi lifted her up onto the counter. Whoa. She knew Remi was strong. She'd seen the muscles bunch in her biceps enough times. Remi was a regular gym buff, but she hadn't expected that at all.

"All this gyming pays off," she said while Maxine tried to catch her wits, but it was hopeless, because Remi's lips found hers and all coherent thoughts fled. She concentrated on the feel of Remi's mouth on hers, the tentative press of her tongue, the hand sliding up her thigh that pushed the hem of her dress further up her leg.

Maxine clenched in anticipation of that touch, but Remi's hand stopped right at the edge of her panties. She groaned in frustration as that finger toyed with the edge of her thong, just as the tongue in her mouth toyed with her.

"Remi," she gasped. "Please."

"I love when you say my name like that." She pulled back and Maxine made a frustrated noise in her throat. "I wanna see you when I do this."

Maxine bit her lip as Remi pushed her thong aside and nudged her sensitive flesh with just the tip of her finger. Her entire face was on fire as Remi watched her closely. Oh God, she couldn't do this. Not with Remi watching her like that. She was practically squirming on the counter as Remi's finger moved in and out of her slowly. So damn slow.

"Have you been wet like this the entire time?" Remi asked.

Maxine nodded. The pleasure was too much. What were words at this point? She should feel embarrassed the way her hips shamelessly chased that finger, but damn if she cared.

Remi pulled her finger away then slowly drew it into her mouth and sucked. Maxine didn't know how she didn't detonate right then. She was holding on by a thread as it was already.

"Mmm." Remi gave her finger one last lick. "Let's get on the couch. I'm gonna taste you right from the source."

"Oh, shit." Maxine wobbled as Remi helped her down and led her to the couch. She dropped down onto the soft material, groaned when Remi didn't give her a chance to catch a single breath before she was back at her mouth again with heated kisses.

Remi smattered kissed down her neck and Maxine arched into it. Yes. God, that was so good. Remi kneaded at her breasts and Maxine needed her touch there. She didn't wait for Remi to make a move, instead tugged the top of her dress down to expose her breasts to the chilly bathroom.

The first suck on her nipple shot pleasure right to her core and Maxine was grateful the damn door was closed. She hoped it was sound proof in here too because she was loud. But how could she be anything but vocal when Remi nipped at her nipple then soothed with a slow lick of her tongue.

"You're killing me," she uttered.

Remi smiled up at her. "Don't die yet. Not before the best part."

Maxine shivered. She wondered what she looked like to Remi in this moment. Heavy breasts just out there on display, her dress rucked up around her thighs. Remi's gaze was pure hunger and Maxine felt wanton, sexy and wanted. It had been a while since she'd felt anything like that—that she was someone somebody could want with such intensity.

That it was Remi was mind blowing, and she wouldn't let her worry creep in. Not now. Not here when she was about to have her fantasies fulfilled. But she couldn't help the smidge of nervousness when Remi moved between her legs and tugged at her underwear. Maxine wasn't exactly waxed all pretty down there, so when Rem drew her underwear down her legs she stiffened.

Remi paused. "You okay? We can stop if this is too much."

"I . . ." She cleared her throat, heat rising up her neck. "I'm not waxed or anything. It's been a while. I just didn't think about it. I didn't want you to be like 'Whoa! Jungle attack!'."

This was embarrassing. After her divorce, she hadn't dated or been intimate with anyone like that. It had been the last thing on her mind. She had only been thinking about her daughter and how she would adjust to the big changes. The making out and small touches with Remi, when she had gotten back to Trinidad, had been the closest she'd come in a year. So trimming or waxing hadn't been high on her list. Things had sort of gotten out of control down there.

She hadn't thought of what would, or could, come next with Remi. Her brain had only allowed her to be in the moment. Not that the feeling lasted for very long because the time they hadn't seen each other, after the wedding, had her spiralling a bit. And now . . . here they were.

Remi chuckled. "I don't give a shit about that. But I'll stop if *you* want me to."

For the briefest second, she thought about it—just getting up and halting everything. But her horny brain said *fuck that,* so instead she said, "No, I want you to go down on me." How she was able to say that so bluntly she didn't know. But there it was.

It had been too long. She didn't want to think about the consequences right then. Just wanted to *feel*. She wasn't going to let a little hair stop her if Remi was cool with it.

Remi's smile was so filthy she wanted to press her legs together, but then she wouldn't get what she really wanted. She spread her legs, urging Remi to take her thong all the way off. Remi didn't hesitate once her underwear was out of the way.

The first touch of Remi's tongue between her legs had her grabbing onto Remi's curls. Heat suffused her entire body as she remembered this. Those secret, stolen moments between two teenage girls. Both inexperienced, but one who *seemed* to know exactly what to do, while the other fumbled along to follow the lead.

"Remi." She pushed against Remi's tongue, urging it deeper into her body. She was so close. Then Remi sucked on her clit while inserting her finger and Maxine just lost it. She bit down hard on her lip to keep her moan in as she came, but that was a complete failure.

She flopped back against the couch, breathing hard. Jesus Christ. Her heart was hammering so hard in her chest. Was this how she died for real?

"Hey, you good?" The tender touch of Remi's fingertips on her cheeks roused Maxine enough to open her eyes and focus on Remi, who—oh God—was licking her lips. Licking her taste off her lips. They'd really done that. "Maxi?" Remi nudged her again. Right, she hadn't replied to her first question, but how did she even form words right now?

"I'm . . ." She struggled to sit up while tugging her skirt down and her top up over her chest. Where were her panties? "I'm good. Yes, good. Great."

Remi smiled. "Okay, good. We should get back out there."

"Wait, what about you?"

Remi hauled her to her feet. "I'll survive. Next time you can do me if you're so inclined."

Was she inclined? Maxine *had* thought about it. She'd be lying if she pretended otherwise. But could she reciprocate right this second? She didn't know.

Remi held out her hand, the missing thong dangling from her fingertip. "No pressure. You got time to think about it. We'll probably see each other in Tobago?"

Right. That trip. They were all heading to Tobago, the weekend after Christmas, and would be staying to ring in the new year. Maxine's entire family was going. Well, everyone except her father, who was no longer really part of their circle after their parents' divorce.

And Remi would be there too.

"Thanks," she said retrieving the thong, and only mildly flushing as Remi watched her slip it back on. "And yeah, Tobago. I'll see you."

"Or, you know, we'll talk before then."

Maxine nodded. "Yeah." She would be with her family on Christmas and Boxing Day, but she didn't plan to ignore Remi until the trip.

It might actually help her take her mind off the fact that Leo was flying in on Christmas Eve to take Leah back to Atlanta for a few days with his family. He would bring her back to Tobago in time to ring in the New Year. This was their solution for now. From next year, they would rotate who she spent the entire Christmas with.

She didn't say any of that to Remi, not wanting to bring down the vibe of the moment. Leah needed to spend time with her father too, so Maxine couldn't begrudge the plan he had come up with, even as she silently pouted about it. Leah was excited, which was all that mattered. It was only a few days.

Remi unlocked the door and Maxine's wariness surged back in. Would everyone know what they'd done in here? She hadn't heard anyone trying to get in by rattling the door knob, but that didn't mean they hadn't. She'd been too wrapped up in the feel of Remi's tongue to notice anything.

Remi turned back to her, gaze intense. "Damn, you look fine." She shook her head. "Pleasure looks good on you. I'll head out first. Follow when you're ready."

She sagged against the counter as Remi slipped out. She had to collect herself before she went back out there, and somehow mentally prepare for that trip.

CHAPTER FOUR

REMI

DECEMBER

HER STOMACH GAVE ANOTHER LURCH AND REMI CLUNG TO THE SIDE of the table, eyes squeezed shut. *Don't puke, don't puke.* The boat hit another rough patch of sea and Remi groaned and breathed in deeply, then immediately regretted it as the combination of food smells and the gross "we tried to get rid of the throw-up smell on the seats but didn't quite succeed" scent of the entire inter-island ferry invaded her nostrils.

The seasick pill she'd taken before they'd come on the ferry seemed to be doing nothing for her. God, she hated taking the boat over to Tobago. Hated. It. She'd been tempted just to take the short flight instead of this almost three hours of torture, but multiple people were taking their vehicles over, including her, and you couldn't do that by plane.

Coupled with trying to not expel the remnants of the sandwiches she'd had hours ago, she was trying her best not to stare at Maxine, who was wearing a dress with a halter-style top. Maxine clearly wasn't wearing a bra. Again. Just like at Laney's party.

Remi spent way too long stealing covert glances, but damn, her stomach was making it hard to focus on not throwing up.

She groaned and used her arms like a pillow, pressing her head into them as the boat lurched again.

This was the first time seeing Maxine since the party—although they had texted and spoken on the phone. Maxine had been preoccupied with preparing Leah for spending Christmas with her dad in Atlanta. Remi had been busy with her family for Christmas. While her mom's side was predominantly Hindu, she did have some relatives who embraced the festivities by putting up a tree and decorating.

Her dad's side went all out, and Remi had been paranging multiple houses, especially since she had some family who flew in for a warmer Christmas this year. She had checked up on Maxine on Christmas Day, knowing she must be missing Leah a lot. Maxine had seemed fine, but tone was hard to read over text.

Apparently, Leo was meeting them in Tobago, with Leah, so that should be interesting. Maxine did look a bit antsy, but Remi supposed it was based on that rather than her stomach feeling like Remi's did.

The rest of the crew seemed fine too. Cherisse had offered another Gravol, but what was even the point? The pill that was supposed to help with that queasy, seasick feeling was doing nothing. So her bestie had left her to her misery, after Remi assured her she was fine. Remi had last seen her making eyes at Keiran. Those two together were annoyingly adorable, even if it was still a shock to see them as a couple. She was so used to them always snarking at each other, this cuteness was weird. But they did look good together. And happy.

"Hey, Remi."

Remi lifted her head and got an eyeful of delicious cleavage. This close, she could see tiny moles strategically sprayed over that plump brown flesh. She blinked as Maxine sank into the seat across from her.

"Oh, hey." *Get your mind out of the gutter Daniels, sheesh.*

"Still feeling queasy?"

"That obvious, huh?" she joked, even as she prayed her stomach wouldn't choose now to give up entirely and just bring those cheese paste sandwiches back up. She'd never live down throwing up in front the woman she was crushing on, hard.

She had told Sanaa she wasn't pining, but maybe that had been a teeny lie. Who could blame her? Maxine looked like a goddess with those blunt-cut bangs and that voluptuous body. Remi itched to capture her with her camera. Her mind whirred with a possibility.

She hadn't told many people about it, but her boss at the magazine she worked for, *Island Bites,* had secured her a showing for her photos at a local gallery. Remi had been quietly working away at her portfolio, since they were looking to present the exhibition in May. She had been reaching out to specific persons in her circle, but Maxine would be so perfect for it. Her entire idea was to make the series organic and not too staged—capture some element of her subjects that they were comfortable with revealing.

"I wanted to talk to you about something," Maxine said, bringing Remi out of her musing. She could talk to Maxine about the idea some other time.

"Okay, sure."

"I know Sanaa's your friend, but I just wanna ask. Can you tell her not to say anything? You know, make any jokes or tease you about us? I'm not . . . you know. I mean I don't know how my family would be about that stuff, and you know I'm still working all this out."

Remi hadn't told Sanaa anything about their bathroom hook up, but Sanaa was no fool. She'd already suspected, even if Remi refused to confirm or deny. Sanaa had been teasing her mercilessly since then. She'd smirked in Maxine's direction when they'd boarded but hadn't said anything outright. Maxine had clearly picked up on Sanaa being the type of person to tease about this, which she was. So even though she hadn't said anything out loud yet, her worry about it was founded. Sanaa just didn't know when to filter herself sometimes.

"Yeah, I'll talk to her. No worries."

"But will she listen?"

A legitimate question. "Sanaa's a lot of things, but once I explain the situation to her, she won't say anything. You got my word on that, alright?"

"You can't be sure what anyone will do in any given situation." Maxine scrubbed her hand over her face. "I'm sorry. I know this sounds like I'm ashamed of what we did. I'm not." She bit her bottom lip again and ducked her head, but Remi could tell she was blushing. It was adorable, and sick stomach or not she wished she could kiss Maxine right now, maybe help that blush along so it spread everywhere. "I'm just trying to work this all out."

"Hey, I get it, okay. You really don't gotta explain anything to me. I'm aware of where we live."

"Right, obviously. You've been through this. Maybe?" Maxine raised her head, a hopeful look in her eyes.

Remi had realised in secondary school that gender didn't play into who she was attracted to, and yeah, that had been disconcerting. When you lived in the Caribbean, proudly proclaiming your queer status was ill-advised. She'd been nervous about even admitting it to herself for a bit. But over time she'd decided she didn't give a shit about what people thought. She advertised her sexuality, subtly, with a few pansexual button pins and bracelets in her flag colours.

"Uh, yeah, sorta? I mean, my parents and brother are aware. Obviously, Cherisse has known since the beginning, when I realised, and I do have Sanaa and the friends from the party. All queer. Some out, some on the DL. But people at work don't exactly know. It's not really their business who I like." She shrugged. "And it's really your choice if you want to tell anyone, about anything. Don't let anyone pressure you, okay?"

"There's nothing much to tell right now, I guess. I kissed a girl and I liked it, and all that jazz."

Remi wondered if Maxine had thought about the implications of that when they had been teens. They hadn't exactly discussed it, then once the holidays were over Maxine was off to school, never looking back. That was a conversation for when they were alone. Bringing up all those messy emotions now would ruin the vibe of the boat ride.

"Well." Remi smirked, leaning in close. Even as she promised herself not to touch on the past, she really couldn't help but tease Maxine. "You did more than kiss a girl."

Maxine fiddled with her bottom lip even more. "Right, yeah. So just, don't forget to talk to Sanaa please." She paused. "You sure you don't want me to get you some crackers or something?"

Remi chuckled. "Do I look that bad?" Eating anything right now did not sound like a good idea. She'd stick to her tried and true method. "And nah, I'm good. I never eat on the boat. When we reach Tobago I'll eat everything in sight, though."

"Okay."

"You good otherwise?" Remi asked.

Maxine sighed. "I don't know. Leo bringing Leah over to the villa later is making me nervous. My family's pretty protective and I don't want them to be annoying about him."

Remi totally got her concern. She had never met Leo—although she had seen him a few times on Maxine's social media—and she was already preparing to size him up. Not in any obvious way, because she didn't want to make Maxine uncomfortable.

"I'm sure they'll be on their best behaviour." Remi wasn't sure at all. Maxine's twin, Keiran, and her other brother Devon, could both be intimidating. Leo would have met them during the time he was married to Maxine, but coming face to face again after a messy divorce? That shit was bound to be awkward.

She could picture Devon dialling up the attitude to one hundred, especially since Reba had had to do some convincing getting him to agree to join the trip in the first place. His grumpy mode was on full right now, although the way he was giving his full attention to Reba as they sat in their own little world away from everyone else, he might act as if Leo didn't exist.

Reba and Devon had also been an unexpected match, but it was cute how Devon acted as if he wasn't already smitten. Poor man. These King men were absolute goners for their girl-friends. Remi wondered if Maxine was the type to fall hard too. She had no context for how she would be in a relationship, but she wanted to know so badly.

Maxine laughed. "I highly doubt it, but if I ask them to chill, they may dial it down a bit. I'm heading outside to take in some fresh air. You wanna come? Might do you some good."

Hanging with Maxine in any capacity always sounded great, but she wasn't sure about going outside. She usually stuck to inside the boat, holding on to her stomach until they docked. But maybe taking in the view of the sea might help.

"Lemme go talk to Sanaa first, and I might think about meeting you out there."

Maxine smiled. "Okay."

Remi tried desperately not to stare too hard at the way the material of Maxine's dress clung to her shapely ass as she headed for the doors that led out to the deck. Obviously, she failed, because Sanaa slipped in next to her, grin huge and mischievous. She toyed with one long Senegalese twist braid as her smirk grew wider. At least Remi didn't have to go looking for her.

"She's wearing the hell out of that dress, isn't she?" Sanaa waggled her brows and Remi rolled her eyes.

"Shush. I want to talk to you about comments like that."

Sanaa's brow winged up. "What do you mean, exactly?"

"I need you to dial back on the teasing where Maxi's concerned, even if you're talking to *me* about her. She's not out, and you never know who might be around to hear you. I don't want to cause problems for her with her family and it's just a plain shitty thing to tease someone who's very much not out about stuff like this, in general."

Sanaa stared at her a few minutes. "Wow, okay."

"I'm being serious here, so I need you to promise me you won't say anything."

"Do you really think *I'd* out someone?" Sanaa leaned back, arms folded, lips pursed.

"No. I don't think you'd intentionally do it, but we both know sometimes you can take jokes too far, and not realise the things you just blurt out can hurt people."

That might have been a tad harsh, but the truth sometimes was.

"Yeah, you're right. I hate that by the way," Sanaa said pointedly. "But you don't have to worry about this. I won't out your girl. I promise. I would never want to do that to a fellow queer."

"Not my girl."

But how she wished she was. God, she'd really gone and done it hadn't she? Caught feelings for someone who *was* definitely attracted to her, but anything further remained up in the air. She'd just have to keep check on all the other feelings that threatened to spill out her mouth anytime she was around Maxine. Not push Maxine in any way. Let her come to Remi if she wanted.

It also occurred to her she'd see Maxine in swimwear at some point and she just wasn't ready for that.

"Who you really tryna fool, Rems?" Sanaa nudged her with an elbow. "Yourself or me? Either way, you're doing a shitty job of it."

Remi fiddled with the end of hair, tugging the curl down then letting it go. "Am I that obvious?" she groaned.

"To me, yes. To Maxine? Doubtful. Girl doesn't seem to know you're basically two steps away from serenading her under moonlight or some other ridiculous romantic shit."

Remi shot Sanaa her best death stare. Sanaa chuckled, but was right on all counts. Not that Remi would be doing any serenading. She couldn't sing for shit. Now dancing, yeah that was more her speed. Besides, Maxine had enough going on as it was to even care about their hook-ups being anything more than that.

"Just enjoy the sexy times and stop thinking too hard about it," Sanaa suggested, which actually sounded like good advice. "Too bad her sexy friend couldn't make it. She was fun."

Right. Victoria. "I thought you were doing the no repeats thing these days?"

Sanaa shrugged. "Barely got to scratch the surface there. I wouldn't mind a wheel and come again."

"I'm sure you'll find some unsuspecting Tobagonian to seduce."

Sanaa winked. "I'm sure I will. Lots of lonely singles out and about around the holidays."

All that sounded exhausting to Remi, just like dating did. She had given her best effort after Sanaa but no one seemed to stick. And she didn't have the energy to do all these hookups, like Sanaa, who insisted she was making up for lost time.

After all those years of trying to be someone she wasn't, she claimed she was quite happy being a player. Breaking hearts all over the damn island. Which was *so* going to bite Sanaa in the ass someday. The island wasn't that big.

For Remi, casual wasn't for her. To be fair, the few relationships Remi had tried *had* started that way, leading with sex then trying for more. When those didn't go anywhere, there was just nothing. Before Maxine came along, she hadn't been intimate with anyone for about two years.

"Anyhoo, I'm heading outside." Remi got to her feet. Less shaky. Good.

"You're going outside?" Sanaa's dark eyes reflected the incredulity of Remi's statement. Her friends knew her well enough when it came to the inter-island ferry.

"Yes, Maxi suggested it, okay. Shush. I don't wanna hear it."

Sanaa laughed and shook her head. "Girl, you a goner."

Didn't she know it? She ignored Sanaa's chuckling and carefully made her way to the doors that led out to the deck.

Maxine and her mother were taking selfies with the water and skyline as their background. Remi tried not to focus too much on the churning water behind them, instead taking several deep breaths and focussing on them hamming it up for the camera. Cute. Ms King seemed to be glowing these days. Good for her.

"Hi! Do you want me to take a picture of the both of you?" Ms King gestured for Remi to get close to Maxine. "Come on, scooch in there."

"Uh . . ." Remi didn't think Ms. King knew anything about her and Maxine. Her request seemed innocent enough and yet she hesitated, not wanting to make Maxine feel weird about it.

"It's alright if you don't want to," Maxine said.

"No, no, it's fine. Really. Here, can you take one with my phone too?"

Remi stood beside Maxine. At five-eleven, Remi was about two inches taller than Maxine, so their faces weren't that far apart.

"Maxi can you move a little bit that way? I want to get the sun in the photo too."

Remi chuckled. "Looks like your mom knows a thing or two about photography."

Maxine turned and Remi realised just how close they'd been standing. Maxine's mouth was just . . . there. "Not really. Leah might be into it, though. She always wants to use my phone to take a pic of something. She'll definitely get excited if she sees you in photographer mode."

"I don't mind showing her some things."

"Okay, ready? Say cheese!" Ms. King called out.

They both obeyed, plastering on huge grins. Remi resisted the urge to slip an arm around Maxine's waist. If they were together, it would've made for the perfect couple photo. In her mind, she'd frame up the shot with the sun's rays angled just right behind them so they'd look all glowy and happy with big cheesy smiles. Remi loved a sunset shot as much as the next photographer, but she loved playing around with bright sunlight too.

"I like this one. You two look great!" Ms. King showed them the results and Remi had to admit, yeah, they did look good together. Not that it was ever in question for her.

"Thanks Ms. King," Remi said as she pocketed her phone.

Maxine tucked the hair behind her ear. "Did you mean what you said? About showing Leah some photography stuff?"

"Yeah. I brought my camera, too, so it's not a problem. I can even teach her after this trip."

"Great. She'd adore you forever."

Remi beamed at that. Impressing her crush's daughter hadn't been in her plans, but it couldn't hurt—not that she would ever use Leah's interest in photography as an excuse to get closer to Maxine. But she genuinely liked the kid, and she loved her job. Teaching Leah wouldn't be a hardship at all, especially if she got to see Maxine more often as a perk.

Remi gripped the railing, staring out at the water being tossed up by the boat's engine's before shooting a glance at Maxine. "We'll sort out the details. I might be starting back dance classes, so I'll have to work out a schedule. We can start some basics when we get to Tobago, then work from there."

Maxine cocked her head. "Dance?"

"Oh yeah. I used to be a backup dancer for Machel and some other soca artistes. You really didn't know this?"

"Uh, no. We never really talked about each other's' interests like that. Except sports and well . . . we didn't really keep in touch after I left." She looked a little guilty after admitting that, but it was a fact. They hadn't kept in touch, which had made Remi feel like shit, but she had said some harsh stuff the day Maxine was leaving so she didn't blame her for not reaching out. If anyone should feel guilty it should be her.

Maxine brought them back to the topic. "But are you serious, though? You danced for Machel? As in Montano? Machel Montano?" Maxine looked genuinely surprised.

She had gotten those gigs after Maxine had left, and it had kept her mind off of their messy situation for a bit. "Guess you never stalked my socials, huh?" She tried to make light of their communication being non-existent. "I can't say the same. You looked happy over there."

Maxine looked out at the water. "I was. I had all these masterplans about getting that degree and proving to my dad that I was serious about working at King Kong. Didn't quite work out that way."

It sure hadn't. Remi had recalled the very real shock when the news about Maxine being pregnant and engaged had reached her. She had truly felt then that any sliver of hope that something could happen with Maxine when she got back had disintegrated.

"Maybe not, but life is like that," she added. "Because I never expected to dance for Machel, ever. My friend convinced me to audition and the next thing I know I'm dancing at a few of his Alternative Concept shows, then the Machel Monday ones. We even got to tour with him regionally for a bit. I also did an international show, which was so cool too. Fun times."

"I had no idea. That's amazing!"

Remi had been out of the professional dancer game for a few years, deciding to focus on photography instead, but her old dance buddies had been trying to lure her back into it in the form of running a beginner's class. She was pretty certain her days on stage were over.

She'd promised them she'd ease back into dance by dropping by their old dance studio soon, or checking out one of the dancercise classes her friends taught. She needed to know just how rusty she was or if she could fall back into it easily. These days, the only dancing she did was either in her apartment while cleaning or when she went out to a bar, club or Carnival fetes.

"It was fun. I'm looking forward to meeting up with the old crew. I'll show you some pics from the shows if you want."

"I want."

She was talking about seeing the photos, obviously, but Remi liked the sound of that way too much.

CHAPTER FIVE

MAXINE

THE VILLAS WERE GORGEOUS. PAINTED IN BRIGHT BLUE AND SUNNY yellow, they both had the works: kitchen, living room, one room and bathroom downstairs, a couple more upstairs and the pool outside. Her mother, Remi's and Cherisse's parents were all in the villa next to theirs. Her mother kept teasing that the older folks' villa was going to be the party house, when in reality Maxine knew her mother was eager to babysit Leah when the rest of them decided to go check out the night life.

For now, everyone was either settling into their rooms, by the pool, or trying to come up with a game plan for later. Maxine was nervously waiting for Leo to show up with Leah while trying not to think about Remi. Their rooms were both upstairs, right across the hall from each other. They had played rock, paper, scissors to see who would secure the coveted downstairs bedroom. Devon and Reba had won.

Remi had bounced back spectacularly from her sea sickness on the boat and was already sunbathing out by the pool in the tiniest bathing suit Maxine had ever seen. Maxine told herself she kept glancing out her bedroom window because the view of the water was calling to her, not because Remi was splayed out on a lounge chair, her mass of curly hair fanned out behind her. That bathing suit bottom barely covered her ass, and Maxine tried her best to not let her eyes drop when Remi had burst out of her room to race Cherisse out to the pool.

She was the last one to make it downstairs. She'd been texting with Leo and had been plagued with indecision about which suit to wear. She'd finally chosen her fuchsia pink one piece that had a lower neckline than she'd worn in a while. It had been tucked away in her drawer for years. Her chest was definitely out there, the plunging neckline showing ample cleavage, but whatever, she was on vacation, and if a tiny voice in the back of her head wondered at Remi's reaction, then so what? She was single and not exactly on the prowl, but didn't she deserve to feel sexy after a full year of feeling like shit? After realising her marriage was officially over?

Moving back to Trinidad had been a hard decision, but the best for everyone. Living in the house while separated and then the divorce being finalised was awkward. Moving Leah away from her friends had been tough, and every so often the guilt would try to claw free. But she needed her support system and family. Besides, this was a second chance for her to have the career at King Kong Entertainment that she had dreamed of as a child. Also, Leah seemed finally to be adjusting.

She checked the last message from Leo before heading downstairs, music and chatter from outside growing louder the closer she got. Sanaa stood in the kitchen, bag of Doritos in hand. She smiled, her gaze sweeping Maxine from head to toe.

"Nice suit. The colour really works for you."

"Thanks."

Sanaa was in an orange bikini, one leg crossed over the other. Her thick thighs were bunching with muscle as she leaned against the counter, rooting around in the chips bag, then lazily popping a handful in her mouth. Her bikini was showing a lot of smooth dark skin and Maxine was again struck by how good Sanaa and Remi would look together. The thought of Remi's long brown limbs and sleek muscles bunching against Sanaa's thicker frame gave her pause. Sanaa looked like she wanted to say something else but didn't. Instead, she stood there eating and smirking.

Maxine walked on, allowing herself a small smile as Sanaa muttered, "Dat ass though, damn."

She pulled her sunglasses from the top of her head and slipped them on. *The better to watch Remi all stretched out on that lounge chair without anyone knowing, my dear.* She mentally shook her head at herself, but it wasn't a lie. Remi's brown skin was getting toastier as she lay there basking in the sun and Maxi wondered if it was hot to the touch. It glistened under the sunlight, and an all-too-vivid image of her rubbing sunscreen lotion over her exposed skin had Maxine biting her lip. Jesus. Nope. She needed to get herself in that pool ASAP. Stave off her heated thoughts.

"Hey sis!" Keiran interrupted her sly gaping. He was in the pool with Cherisse, Reba and Devon. "You coming in or what?"

"Obviously!" She made her way over to the steps that led into the water.

"Is it safe to splash you?" Keiran asked.

"I came vacation ready, so yeah." Maxine pointed at her pinned-back bangs and hair pulled up in a messy bun.

"Looks like you trained him well," Cherisse said. "Thanks for that."

Keiran rolled his eyes. "I had to listen to years of 'If you wet my hair I'll end you' speeches. So better safe than sorry."

Maxine eased into the water and splashed her twin for trying to mimic her with that high-pitched tone. Any other time she'd worry about getting her hair wet, but while on vacation she didn't much care. She'd brought her shampoo, conditioner, blow dryer and a flat iron to deal with the aftermath of the pool and the salt water when they went to the beach. And with Leah's hair to comb as well, Maxine didn't want to expend anymore energy on her own hair than she needed to. Maybe she should have gotten some braids in. Oh well, too late now.

"He's a quick learner," she told Cherisse as she swam out to meet them and commandeered one of the donut-shaped floaties.

She stretched out her limbs and turned her face up to the sun. She needed to focus on relaxing, on ensuring Leah had fun, and the other things happening in her life besides Remi, whose presence she felt like the sun beating down on her exposed skin. She needed time to think about the talk she'd planned to have with her mother about her working for her father's company, King Kong Entertainment. It wasn't exactly a relaxing thought, but it was a conversation they should have sooner rather than later.

Her mother had barely had anything to say when Maxine had let her know her plans. Working at her mother's dental practice did nothing for her—she just wasn't interested in dentistry.

When she'd left the island, it had been to pursue a degree in Music Management and she'd never really gotten the chance to use it like she had wanted. Her entire plan to return to Trinidad had been derailed by Leo, which hadn't been a problem at the time, obviously. She'd been working her ass off at a studio as a production assistant—hoping to gather some experience before she headed back home—when she'd met Leo. She hadn't planned on falling in love, getting pregnant, then getting married and becoming a stay-at-home mom.

She'd always meant to return to work after she'd had Leah, but Leo had basically guilted her into scrapping that idea. He had made her feel bad for wanting to be both a mom and have a career, as if she was incapable of it. He made it seem as if going back to work at all made her a terrible mother, and she'd internalised that for so long, until she'd seen through his subtle manipulations. Having a baby and getting married at twenty-three had been a lot. Adding a crumbling marriage on top of that? She had basically been hanging on by a thread by the time she'd decided she couldn't do it anymore.

Her father was offering a chance to work in the field she'd wanted to since he'd started his company. Keiran had zero interest in working at KKE, even as he immersed himself in the music world via his own production company with his friend Dale. But Maxine wanted it, wanted her father to bring her into the fold, leave it all to her someday. It was her legacy, dammit and why should she feel bad for wanting to learn everything she could about it? Besides, it would also be a big "eff you" to her father once she succeeded where he'd always thought she'd fail.

She'd been at KKE for a few months now and loved it, even as some of the employees were wary of her, being the boss's daughter and all. They weren't outright rude, more cautious and sort of standoffish.

Her mother wasn't pleased. Her zero commentary on the matter was proof. Her parents' divorce hadn't been amicable and yeah, Maxine's relationship with her father was still rocky, so it was awkward, for her at least, to be working there. But getting the hands-on experience at the company she planned to take over someday was exciting.

Of course, she couldn't say for sure her father was going to leave it to her when he was ready to step back, but she had to show him she was serious about it.

As if she'd conjured her mother by thought alone, Sheryl King sauntered through the open doors that led from the kitchen out to the pool. She wore a colourful kaftan over her plain black bathing suit. Her newly dyed Copper Sunset curls shone in the sun. Her mother had recently decided to transition back to her natural hair, doing a big chop and forgoing her relaxer. Maxine thought it suited her, and by the way Sanaa was currently gaping at her mother, she thought so too.

It was funny. Her mother turned heads wherever she went—young men were always hitting on her—but the idea of her actually dating again wasn't something Maxine could fathom. Not that she had any say in that, her mother didn't owe any of them any explanations. In fact, Maxine often wondered if her mother was already dating. Recently, she'd been hitting them with the "Just going out for a bit" line more often than usual, and Maxine wasn't totally sold on Keiran's notion that she was just hanging out with her church lady friends.

"Aye mummy, you joining us in here?" Keiran called out, and Sanaa did a double take. *That* reaction never failed to amuse Maxine. Lots of people never guessed her mother's age. She kept herself on point, always, especially after her divorce.

"That's her mother? Well damn. Dem genes are good," Sanaa said, loudly.

"Inside voice, Sanaa," Remi chided, but she was snickering.

Maxine didn't want to look over at Remi, but how could she not? She was sitting up on the lounge chair, one leg stretched out, the other pulled up so she could rest her elbow on her knee. Deliciously sun browned skin just there.

Her mother walked over, cell phone waving in her hand. "Tried calling both of you. Food's ready."

"Thanks, mummy. Last one to the villa gets nothing, cuz I'm hungry enough to eat a whole cow," Keiran joked as he raced out the pool.

Cherisse and Devon rolled their eyes.

"Hey!" Maxine exclaimed as Keiran splashed them all in his haste to get out.

"Having second thoughts?" Reba asked, the question directed at Cherisse.

Maxine tore her gaze away from that crease of skin right at Remi's bikini line, swiping water from her face.

Cherisse grinned. "Not at all."

"Good, because he's yours to deal with now. No take backs," Maxine joked.

"Thanks," Cherisse said drily. "Better get to the food before there's none left and I have to murder your brother." She hauled herself out of the water and Sanaa whistled as Cherisse walked by them. She grabbed up her towel and winked at Sanaa.

She was probably used to Sanaa's shenanigans by now. Maxine looked up at her mother to gauge her reaction to Sanaa, but she had none. She was busy scolding Keiran, who was trying to pull her into a wet hug, so she'd possibly missed Sanaa's antics.

"Boy, if you don't stop playing." She dodged Keiran, flinging a towel at him. "Don't come over there dripping everywhere or no food for you!"

Keiran wrapped himself in the giant towel. "Fine. I'll go change."

It was ridiculous to be this on edge when Sanaa hadn't even been flirting with her, but Maxine didn't want to see any negative reaction from her mother at even the hint of queerness from Sanaa. Keiran was bi, but not out to their parents either.

Relax.

Way easier said than done, especially with Remi rising from her chair to do a full body stretch. Every bit of muscle moved deliciously beneath her skin and, oh shit. She needed to turn her gaze elsewhere because the minute Remi turned around, she'd get an eyeful of her ass in those skimpy yellow bikini bottoms. She wasn't wearing a full-on thong, but there was enough skin for Maxine to think about ducking under the water to cool off.

A splash of water to her face left her sputtering and washed away her lascivious thoughts.

"W—what the heck?"

"Sorry," Reba grinned. "Your mom was talking to you. Didn't you hear?"

She blinked up at her mother, who shook her head. "What were you so lost in thought about? I asked if you're coming over too. Keiran might seriously eat everything in sight. I swear that child has a bottomless pit."

I was daydreaming about another woman's ass.

She wasn't brave enough to say that, so she lied. "Nothing."

She swished around in the water, directing the donut closer to the edge so she could hop out the pool. It was probably best to remove herself from the zone of temptation and go over to the other villa for food.

"Is it Leo?" her mother asked. "He's supposed to come any time now with Leah, right?"

"Yeah." That was the easier topic to go with. It wasn't a lie either. She was still feeling anxious about him showing up here.

"Don't worry, we'll behave."

"Seriously, please don't say anything weird," she begged. She couldn't blame her family for not being overly friendly with Leo. They hadn't ended their marriage on the best of terms, but she needed everyone to remain civil. And this would be the first time they would be interacting with him since the divorce had been official.

They had liked him enough when they had all gathered before for family events. Of course, she hadn't revealed her struggles after her maternity leave had been drawing to an end.

She had kept up the front of being on the same page as him and wanting to be a stay-at-home mom when inside she had been close to screaming.

"*I* won't," her mother promised. "I can't control your brothers, though."

She glanced over at Devon who was still in the pool with Reba and Cherisse. Keiran would quicker say something snarky. Devon would stand there, saying nothing, but looking like he would be ready to beat somebody's ass.

"I know, but can you just ask everyone to chill before he gets here?"

"Sure, sweetie. See you over there." Her mother waved at the others in the pool, calling out, "Don't stay in too long or you'll get nada."

Maxine needed to get a move on as well. She had to run upstairs to grab a cover-up to throw over her suit before they walked over to the next villa.

Remi stepped in front of her. "Hey, you alright?"

"Yeah, of course." She patted her stomach. "Just hungry."

"I can stick around to wait with you for Leah. If you want?"

Sanaa was hovering, obviously waiting to hear her response. Last thing she wanted to do was spill her business. She forced out a smile she didn't feel.

"It's all good, really."

Remi didn't seem to buy that, but she stepped back. "Okay, after you then."

"Why Ms. Daniels, are you trying to look at my behind?"

"Well, I mean, the opportunity's right there."

"Get a room already," Sanaa piped up softly from behind them. "I can make up an excuse to the others if you need a quickie."

Remi spun around. "Sanaa."

"Alright fine, okay, I promised. Sorry, that one slipped out." Hands out, she backed away into the kitchen.

Remi sighed. "Sorry."

"It's cool." And she meant it. Not like she'd done it when everyone else was around. Besides, she and Remi *had* been skirting the line of flirtation.

"We should go," Remi suggested.

"After you." Maxine deployed her brightest smirk. Why waste a good opportunity indeed. It was easier to be bold when it was just the two of them. "Hate to watch you go, but love to watch you leave."

"You surprise me every damn time," Remi said, but she walked away, an extra swish in her hips.

Maxine bit her lip, eyes glued to Remi's ass. That quickie was sounding better and better by the minute. She shook herself out of it. Not the place. Not the time.

CHAPTER SIX

REMI

REMI HADN'T PLANNED TO BE THE ONE TO OPEN THE DOOR WHEN Maxine's ex showed up. Maxine had gone to her room to grab her cover-up and Remi had needed to duck into the downstairs bathroom before she did the same. She'd been heading there when the knock sounded and debated between ignoring the door and relieving her bladder, but she opted for the door. The others were still chilling outside by the pool so the likelihood of them hearing the knock was slim.

Maxine's ex, Leo, peered down at her as she opened the door, Leah at his side. Damn, he was tall. And good looking. That shouldn't have irritated Remi in any way, it wasn't a competition, but she'd never claimed to be a rational individual. His photos on Maxine's social media had not done the man justice at all.

"Hi, I'm here to see Maxine," he said, in what sounded like a Southern accent to Remi. She remembered he was from Atlanta, Georgia.

Remi sized him up without, hopefully, appearing obviously to do so. He was dressed casually in a white t-shirt and cargo shorts. Jaw clean shaven, hair trimmed close to his scalp.

Brown eyes observing her as closely as she was doing to him. She needed to rein this in before she did something ridiculous like ask his skin care regimen. Dude had some flawless sandy brown skin that was annoying as heck.

"Maxi went upstairs to get something. I'm Remi, by the way."

"Nice to meet you." Polite, and obviously had no idea who she was. She didn't offer her hand and he didn't seem to care either way.

Not that he should know her. Remi wasn't certain how much Maxine and Leo kept in contact these days, what type of conversations they shared—she assumed it was always Leah-related—so it wasn't too weird for him not to have an inkling of who Remi was.

Why would he? Maxine wouldn't be forthcoming about the extent of their relationship. That would be strange considering Remi didn't know if Leo supported the community like that. He would probably be shocked if he found out his ex-wife had been hooking up with a woman.

Remi stepped aside as Leah bounced in waving at her. "Hi, Auntie Remi!"

"Hey, kiddo."

Leah was already dressed in her bathing suit and some denim shorts, looking cute as ever.

Remi gestured for Leo to come in and pushed the door close. She should really get to the bathroom, but Maxine came down the stairs, freezing at the bottom when she saw them.

"Oh, you're here."

"Yeah."

Yikes. They could cut the awkwardness with a knife. Now would be a great time for Remi to do what she'd come out here to do. Pee and get herself ready to head over to the other villa too.

"You've met Remi," Maxine said, right hand reaching down to the hem of her cover-up to pluck at the fabric.

"I did," Leo replied.

Okaaaaay . . . She needed to leave this room immediately. Remi pointed a thumb in the direction of the bathroom. "I need to go pee, so . . ."

Not her classiest exit, but she wasn't sticking around for this. Maxine obviously wasn't after support; she barely gave Remi a glance.

Finished with her business, Remi headed back outside where Leah was wrapped around her father. Maxine stood close by, fingers still working at that hem.

"We should head over to the other villa. You know, before your brother inhales everything," Remi suggested, trying to move this along because she had no desire just to stand here with all this tension.

Her time could be put to better use covertly checking Maxine out in her bathing suit. The netted cover-up wasn't doing much to stop Remi's wayward thoughts. Besides, she was sort of hungry, too.

"Yup, we should," Maxine said.

"Mummy, can daddy come with us?" Leah looked all excited and adorable.

Maxine glanced at Leo, face unreadable, which meant she was trying hard not to show her true reaction to Leah's curveball. "If daddy wants to, then sure."

Leo shrugged like he didn't care either way. "If your granny doesn't mind. I wouldn't want to just invite myself over."

"She knows you were dropping Leah off, so I'm sure it'll be fine. It's really up to you."

Geez, they could be here all day if this kept going around in this weird-ass circle.

Remi clapped her hands. "Okay, well, Leah and I will head on over if it's alright with you? Your brothers really can eat a person out of house and home." She waited for Maxine's nod before she reached for Leah's hand. She hoped that would jolt Maxine into getting a move on too, without making it too obvious that's what she was doing, because Remi sensed she would not want to be stuck over here with Leo alone.

Maxine nodded, took Leah's other hand, maybe without even realising how cute they both looked with Leah between them. "Yes, let's head over. Leo?"

"Sure, lead the way."

Remi happily swung Leah between them as Leo followed behind. There was no way in hell she was going to let this ruin Maxine's day. She bumped Maxine's shoulder and mouthed, "You good?"

Maxine nodded, gave her a small smile and mouthed back, "Yeah."

Remi wasn't quite sure she believed that, but she hoped Maxine knew she had her back if needed because the minute they walked in with Leo behind them, the constant chatter that had been going on around the table dramatically died away.

Remi swung Leah around and loudly announced, "The party is here!"

Leah giggled and that weird-ass tension broke as Ms. King got up to give her granddaughter a big hug.

"Hellooo, my heart," she said, giving Leah big cheek kisses that had her giggling even more.

Perfect. Who could resist Leah's infectious laughter? No one, because everyone focused on her instead of the tall, ex-shaped elephant in the room. Well, almost everyone. Devon wore his typical frown as he munched on his food and Remi's father was watching everything with his usual eagle-eyed gaze.

"How was the trip, Leah?" Cherisse asked. Remi noticed the slight arm pat she gave Keiran. He wasn't giving Leo the death stare like Devon, but he kept clenching and unclenching his hand.

"It was *so* fun, Auntie Cherry! Daddy's friend was nice and gave me a present," Leah chattered. "Maybe mummy can come next time too?"

Oh lawd. Remi turned to look at Maxine who had on that struggle smile.

"We'll talk about it, okay, hon?"

Leah nodded, bouncing over to where Reba sat next to the still-scowling Devon.

"We have a lot of food, so feel free to help yourself." Remi's mother swept her hand across the self-service spread on the side table. She had been sitting next to Ms. King when they'd walked in and had just been observing everything.

She wasn't surprised her mother was the one to make the offer. Ever the mediator, she wouldn't sit there and just let things get strained. Not on Shala Daniels' watch.

"Thanks, but I'm good. We had breakfast before we came over."

Ms. King re-took her place at the table. "We're heading to the beach later if you want to join."

Maxine's head whipped around to her mother as if to ask *what the hell?*

As far as Remi was concerned, Leo had done his part by dropping Leah off. They didn't need to hang out with him. Ms. King was probably trying to be nice.

"I'm sure Leo has things to do." Devon's deep voice filled the quiet left by his mother's comment.

Reba snickered and Remi pressed her lips together because she almost busted out laughing herself. She didn't think Maxine would find that amusing at all.

Leo's gaze swung to Devon who was casually sipping from his drink like he hadn't just basically told the man to leave.

"Right." Leo cleared his throat. "I have to get back to my friend anyhow. We have plans as well. One more hug before I go?"

Leah came over and gave her father a big warm hug. "Tell Sheralee I said bye again."

"Uh, yes. Will do."

Well, that confirmed for all the adults in the room that "friend" had been code for "lady friend".

"Maybe I'll see you all before ringing in the new year," Leo said.

Remi doubted that. No one here, except Leah, cared to come into the New Year with him.

Devon got to his feet, empty plate in hand. "No need to put yourself out. I'm sure you and your *friend* would have fun doing that together."

Leo's gaze lingered on Devon for a heartbeat before he waved and left.

"Seriously?" Maxine said as soon as the door closed.

Devon didn't look the least bit apologetic "What? Did you actually want to take him up on that offer?"

Maxine glanced over at Leah, who was busy chatting with Reba and Cherisse. "No, but c'mon. None of that was necessary."

"I don't like him."

"You don't like anyone," Maxine countered, shaking her head all while scrubbing her hand over her face.

Remi wanted to go over and give her a hug, but she wasn't sure how it would be received just then. Maxine didn't look pleased with Devon at the moment.

"Not true, he loves meeeee," Reba sang out, which made everyone laugh as Devon shot Reba an exasperated look.

She simply blew him a kiss and went back to listening to Leah's story about her trip.

Remi chuckled. Devon could look put off by Reba's comment, but she was just speaking facts. That big grump was whipped.

Maxine folded her arms. "I told you all to be civil, didn't I?"

Devon shrugged "That *was* me being civil."

"Anyhoo, you two get some food and then let's get ready to head out to the beach." Ms. King waved Remi and Maxine over. "C'mon, let's not dwell on any of that, okay?"

"And why did you invite him with us?" Maxine demanded as she started putting food on her plate.

Remi watched her slap down a pastelle next to her ham. Oh yeah, she was not happy about any of this.

"You just said for us to be civil, didn't you?" Ms. King pointed out.

"I meant don't throw passive-aggressive barbs." She glared at her brother. "Not ask him to tag along with us." Maxine sighed. "You know what? Just . . . Whatever. You're right. Let's forget it. Should've known they couldn't even keep it together for a few minutes." She muttered that last part, but Remi was next to her filling her own plate, so she heard.

"Hey, sorry that turned out like it did."

Maxine shook her head. "It's whatever, really. I should have told Leah no. It's just . . . I'm trying to strike that balance between having clear boundaries and not making it seem like it's a problem for him to join us for things."

"Yeah, that's tough to manage." Remi gave into her urge and squeezed Maxine's arm lightly. "You're doing great. Don't forget that."

She gave Remi a small smile. "I think you're a lil' biased, but thanks. Means a lot. Let's just eat and get ready for the beach."

Remi tried not to shoot heart eyes over Maxine saying her comment meant a lot. She wasn't sure what her face was doing at the moment, but she looked down as she kept adding more stuff to her plate. Just in case. She was trying to take it easy, not overwhelm Maxine, but damn, she was a whole lost cause with this woman.

She just had to make it through this short vacation without throwing herself at Maxine's feet and begging her to be hers. Yeah, that should be easy enough.

REMI WAS IN STRUGGLE MODE. EASY ENOUGH? WHY THE HELL HAD she ever thought anything would be easy when it came to Maxine?

She was trying to distract herself by teaching Leah about exposure and demonstrating with some shots of the sky and the waves crashing on the beach.

Leah was eager to learn about photography and Remi was excited to teach. She'd never done that—taught anyone about anything—but she liked how Leah was actually listening, being attentive and asking lots of questions as Remi showed her some basics after they'd had lunch at the parents' villa. Who knew she'd even be into teaching, or have the patience for it?

Everyone was full and sitting around, basking in the sun's rays for now, allowing their food to digest. But just smelling the salt and letting the sea air waft around them was a great feeling. They'd even booked a glass-bottom boat tour to the Nylon Pool for the next day after being bombarded by a bunch of the boat operators the minute they'd driven through the entrance to Store Bay Beach. The guy they'd gone with promised snacks, drinks, and music on his boat.

Leah had never been, and she was extra excited and spewing facts she'd found online. The kid had done her research.

"It looks really nice in the picture," Leah said, forehead creased as she got deep in thought. "I wonder if it's really like that."

"Oh, it is," Remi said. She'd been a few times in the past. Seeing it for yourself was always an awesome experience. A shallow pool in the middle of the ocean wasn't exactly something you saw every day.

"You've been there before?" she asked Remi, eyes wide.

"Oh yeah. It's really amazing. You'll see. I have a waterproof camera we can practice with there too."

Leah grinned. "Yay! Mummy said we can go snorkel too!"

Remi glanced over to where Maxine had been watching their lessons. She sat cross-legged under the umbrella one of the parents had the foresight to bring—the rented chair and umbrella combo was ridiculously priced so luckily they had their own—a small smile playing about her lips.

"That sounds fun," Remi replied, eyes still on Maxine who looked away after a while, as if their eye contact was just too much to hold.

Remi could relate. She took a deep breath and refocused on her student, briefly wondering what bathing suit Maxine would wear tomorrow. Would she go with another one-piece or grace them with a two-piece? Remi might actually die. Seeing more of that luscious brown skin and those curves may very well be her undoing. And acting like she didn't care either way? That would be a challenge.

It already *was* a challenge.

"Hey."

Remi looked up as her mother sat next to them, smiling at Leah who was practicing working with exposure, small hands grasping the camera firmly just as Remi had shown her. This Canon was one of her precious babies, so she had told Leah to be extra careful with it.

"Hey."

"There's a cricket game about to start, you in?"

Remi was all for physical activity and she hadn't played cricket in years. Not since her time on the team in secondary school though. Her mother couldn't know it, but just the mere mention of cricket was dragging up all sorts of memories better left in the dark.

The cricket camp. The moment when her relationship with Maxine changed forever. They'd been bitter rivals up to that point and then . . . someone had smuggled in homemade wine and brought it out after Coach had gone to sleep.

She and Maxine had been arguing—nothing unusual for them, they were competitive about everything—about who would get the captain spot after the previous captain went off to college abroad. It was a ridiculous argument because they were both graduating the following year and should let the spot go to someone else. The spot *had* gone to someone else after all that, which was funny now that Remi thought about it.

But they'd been going at it, hard. Everyone else had grown tired of their bickering and left, and then Remi wasn't even sure how they'd gone from that fight to kissing, but before she could even figure out what the fuck was going on, they'd made their way back to the room they'd been forced to share, making out the entire way.

"Remina, are you even listening?"

Her mother's use of her full name and that hand waving in front her face jolted her back to reality.

"Ugh, no full names please." She glanced over at Leah and sure enough she was looking over all curious now that her mother had dropped her whole name in public. Great.

"It's the name I gave you and it's what I'll call you."

Remi just hated the way all the extra syllables had been drawn out when she was a child and her mother was scolding her for some mischief she'd done. Besides, telling people to call her Remi gave them fewer ways to massacre her name or say it in a taunting sing-songy way that only children, intent on being mean, could do. She'd never told her parents about that last part.

Just hearing it made her freeze, and her heart raced same as back then. She had to get over that reaction whenever her entire name was deployed. She wasn't in trouble, nor was she about to be teased. It was silly, but what could she do? The reaction was just too damn ingrained.

She put just enough impudence into rolling her eyes that her mother grinned and patted Remi's cheek. "You in for the cricket game or not? Your father and I are on opposite sides and I need you to help me kick his behind."

Remi chuckled at the gleam in her mother's dark brown eyes. Her parents really were too cute and clearly she'd gotten her competitive streak from both of them. She looked over to where her father, a tall, strapping black guy, was making windmill motions with his arms. His idea of a warm up.

"Oh, we so got this."

Her mother grinned evilly. It was time to kick butt.

When they walked over, it turned out that Maxine had opted to play for her dad's team.

"Seriously?"

She shrugged. "He asked me first."

"Mummy, I want to field please," Leah said, bouncing up and down in the sand. She had safely returned the camera.

"She knows how to play?"

"Are you kidding?" Maxine scoffed. "You think I wouldn't teach my daughter how to play cricket? Me? The best player on our secondary school team?"

Oh, those were fighting words and Maxine damn well knew it. Her smirk said as much.

Remi leaned in, careful not to let her lips brush Maxine's ear, but just barely. "Oh, you're going down, and not in the fun way."

Maxine made a choking sound, which she tried to cover up with a laugh, but Remi's work was done here. She walked away smiling. She wasn't above playing dirty for her team to win. It was already going to be some work running in the sand. She'd grab any advantage she could. Besides, it was fun to distract Maxine, knock her off her game. She couldn't be the only one fighting for some sort of control on her emotions out here.

Cherisse and Keiran ended up on opposing teams too which was going to be hilarious to watch. Apparently, Keiran sucked at cricket, judging from the teasing he was getting from Maxine. Cherisse *definitely* sucked. Remi knew that for a fact. But they couldn't put all the best players on one team, that wouldn't be fair.

"I'll be fielding," Cherisse piped up when they were deciding on positions. "It's the best thing for the team. You do *not* want me behind that bat."

Damn right they didn't. They wouldn't make a single score. Remi loved her best friend, but she was terrible at this game.

"I'm sitting this one out!" Sanaa called out. "I'm not big on balls flying at my face."

Remi shook her head as laughter erupted around them. It worked out in their favour, because with Sanaa lounging just watching the game, they had five players on each team now.

Remi and her mother were up first to bat, while her father was bowling for the opposing team. The game soon turned rowdy with cries of "Run! Run!" which Remi ignored.

She and her mother were pretty in sync, knowing when to take the chance to run to the opposite wicket and when it was too risky. Even Sanaa was trying to give instructions from the sidelines, which, no. She wasn't even in this game.

After holding strong against her father's swinging throws for a couple of runs Remi could admit she'd gotten cocky, because when they switched to Maxine to bowl, she almost got her wicket knocked down. If Remi had been any slower swinging her bat, she would've been out of the game.

"Holy shit," she muttered as Maxine threw her the most self-satisfied smile Remi had ever seen. And why was that so hot?

"Stay focused!" her mother shouted. She'd pulled back her short black bob into a stubby ponytail when the game had started, and her eyes were narrowed at Maxine.

Right. Stay focused while Maxine was currently bouncing on her bare feet in the sand, which made her ample chest bounce too. Well that was unfair.

Maxine's team hollered and hooted at the almost out. Keiran threw in some mild trash talk and high fived his twin. Oh no, Remi wasn't having any of this. Her reputation was at stake here. Also, her mother would *not* let her hear the end of this if they lost to the other team.

In the end, Maxine was just that good and Remi watched as her bat didn't make it to crease before the ball shattered her wicket. She stared in shock as Maxine whooped and her team erupted in happy shouts. Dammit.

"Who's going down now, huh?" Maxine whispered as she strutted past Remi.

Remi didn't think it was possible to be irritated and aroused at the same time, but here she was. In that moment, she wanted to drag Maxine off somewhere and kiss that mischievous grin off her mouth.

The game ended with her father's team wining. Her father strolled over to where her mother was glaring.

"Victory kiss, my love?" he asked, smiling.

Her mother rolled her eyes but planted one on his cheek

anyway. "There will be a rematch," she stated, poking him in the side with one long nail.

"Maybe not so soon, eh? Wouldn't want to destroy you again after that sorry display."

Remi giggled as her mother poked him in his side again, right in the dreaded tickle spot if the way he jerked away was any indication.

"No fair!" he shouted, taking off down the beach as her mother chased him. Seriously, those two were *too* cute. Even after all these years.

Remi wanted something like what her parents had. She didn't know if she would ever have it, but she hoped.

"That was fun." Remi turned to find Maxine standing next to her.

"I suppose." She pursed her lips in a full-on pout. She wasn't upset at the loss, but she silently patted herself on the back when Maxine's eyes dropped to her mouth.

"Never took you for a sore loser."

"I'm not."

Maxine rubbed at her bare thigh and Remi wondered if she was playing dirty, the way Remi had tried. Or was Maxine just busting a casual move and Remi was the only one perving here?

"Damn. It was fun, but it made me realise I gotta get back into some sort of exercise routine. That was a good little work-out." Maxine moved down to her calves and Remi allowed herself a quick look as those fingers worked at her flesh. *Be cool be cool be cool.*

Maxine had always had strong, thick thighs that had almost made Remi fumble the ball back in the day when they used to play netball in the school courtyard. Those short skirts didn't help at all. It had been a struggle to stay focused and not stare too hard, even as she couldn't stand her back then. It didn't stop her from appreciating her amazing legs.

And now here they were.

"You okay there?" she asked. Anything to distract from the daydreaming about those legs wrapped around her head as she . . .

"Yeah, mostly."

"Good. If you're interested in a workout routine, I can help. Maybe."

Maxine let up on her thigh and calf kneading—thank God—and looked Remi's way.

"I'm not a certified fitness instructor or anything, but I know people who are. As I mentioned before, I'm also going to check out one of my old dance buddy's dancercise classes. It's for beginners. If you'd be into that."

"Hmm. That does sound fun. Dance might be a good starting point."

"Yeah," Remi agreed. "I also have another friend who does pole exercise classes, if you'd wanna try too."

"Oh. That sounds like something I don't think I'm ready for. Yet."

Remi could totally picture it though. She'd be so sexy. Maxine would be hesitant at first, but she had a competitive nature just like Remi did. She suspected Maxine would work her ass off to get good at it, even if she'd be wary about it at first. Most people felt like the pole dancing classes weren't for them, but Remi had seen, the few times she'd dropped by, how as the class progressed people got more confident.

"My friend also does aerial fitness with silks and hoops."

"Now you really want me to bust my ass."

Remi chuckled. "Okay, I hear you on that one." She'd never tried the aerial stuff either. "Let me know about the dance class."

"Sure." Maxine smiled and turned to walk back to where Remi's parents were still mildly trash talking each other over the cricket game.

It looked like the others were ready to take a dip. Remi definitely needed to cool down. The way Maxine's hips swayed as she walked over to Leah. Jesus, save her.

She could easily picture Maxine in that dance class. The movement of her body, those hips shaking and shimmying. As soon as they got back to the villa she was sending her all the information she had on the dance class. She needed to be real convincing, because she realised how much she wanted this to happen.

She was merely being a good friend, right? Helping a sister out on her fitness path. That was all.

She watched Maxine as she clasped Leah's hand and giggled as they ran down to the water, the muscles in Maxine's thighs moving in distracting ways.

Yup. She was being such a good friend. So altruistic. Zero ulterior motives.

CHAPTER SEVEN

MAXINE

"Aye, sleepy head! You getting ready or wha'?"

Maxine peered up at her brother. He stood in her doorway dressed in jeans and a crisp blue, short-sleeved shirt.

"Uh." She looked around her bed for her phone. "What time is it?"

She'd crashed hard when they'd returned from the beach. They'd spent most of the afternoon on Store Bay, frolicking in the water after the cricket game, and Maxine had decided on a short nap to recover before they went out to Shade, a popular nightclub.

She found her phone next to her, blinked down at the time. It was after eight. "Oh, shit." She jumped up. "Why didn't someone wake me? Is everyone already ready? Where's Leah?"

Leah had been curled up with her when she'd dozed off hours ago.

"She's over at mummy's villa already," Keiran said. "You still have lots of time to get ready."

Maxine got off the bed. Luckily, she was always organised and had already sorted out her outfit for tonight. She just had to shower, change, do her makeup and . . . shit. She patted her head. Her hair! She hadn't washed or flat-ironed it when they'd come back to the villa. She stared at herself in the dresser mirror.

It was the furthest thing from her signature straight look, but she could work with this. It was all curly and sort of frizzy from the sea water, but whatever, she was on vacation, and it really wasn't that serious.

The crease marks from the pillow were another story entirely.

Keiran cleared his throat. "I know I said we have time, and no one goes to Shade too early, but maybe don't take forever to get ready either?"

Maxine grabbed a pillow from the bed and tossed it after her twin. He ducked and the pillow sailed over his head. They both turned at the not so muffled, "Hey!"

Remi stood a little way outside the door clutching the pillow to her chest. "This is what I get for coming to see what the holdup was?"

Her hair fell like a black silky curtain down her back, no curls in sight. Maxine didn't think she'd ever seen Remi with her hair flat ironed. God *damn.*

"Your hair." She hadn't meant to say that out loud. "It looks nice," she added hastily. It did look nice and shiny.

"Thanks. It took forever. This is why I rarely bother doing this." She ran her hand through her hair and it flowed over her palm. "I didn't even get a good nap in because I wanted to get this done, but good to switch up the look sometimes."

"Yes. Definitely."

Keiran, who was back to facing Maxine, rolled his eyes. She not so politely told him with a glare to get out. He shook his head and left, calling over his shoulder. "We're leaving at nine-thirty."

With Keiran out of the way, Maxine was treated to the entirety of Remi's outfit, and it was a chore to keep a neutral expression when face to face with that dress. Why was she even trying? There wasn't anyone to see her except Remi who, if her smug smile was anything to go by, knew Maxine was trying hard not to react.

So she let herself drink it all in.

The dress was short, tight and shimmery. Maxine thought the colour was called rose gold, but she couldn't be sure. She didn't much care. The colour looked amazing against Remi's warm brown skin. Remi's shoulders and neck were bare of any jewellery, and she didn't need any. That dress was eye-catching enough. It was basically a short tube of rosy gold that Remi was poured into. She wore simple strappy sandals on her feet.

"The way you're looking at me right now. A girl could get ideas."

Maxine blinked. "Sorry." She really should be getting ready and not gaping rudely.

Remi's grin was equal parts pleased and naughty. "No need to be. I like when you look at me like that. Would make my panties wet. If I were wearing any." She winked and tossed the pillow onto the bed and turned away, pausing at the door, giving Maxine a good view of her backside in that dress. "Better go get ready." Remi tossed a small wave over her shoulder then disappeared.

"Oh my fucking God," Maxine whispered. A cold shower it was then.

By the time she made her way downstairs, she was a ball of nerves, wondering if something would happen between her and Remi tonight. Did she want it to? They were surrounded by family and friends, but Leah was spending the night over at her mother's villa and she was alone in her room, so if she wanted something to happen, it definitely could.

She shook away those thoughts and focused on the others who were sitting around the living room chatting.

"Finally she emerges. So glad you decided to grace us with

your presence, your highness." Keiran executed a sweeping bow and Maxine rolled with it.

"Perfection can't be rushed," she said striking a regal pose. She didn't know of any queen who would greet her subjects wearing a tube top and a long high-waisted swishy skirt, but she felt pretty damn royal in her outfit. "But seriously, sorry for over sleeping."

"No worries." Cherisse waved away her concerns. As usual, she looked put together in her black sleeveless top, tucked into her pink shorts and heels. A giant clutch under her arm.

Reba was decked out in her short pink wig and a white romper tonight, with Devon at her side, eyes down in his phone. It was a miracle Reba had even gotten him to agree to come out, but Devon couldn't resist her charm.

As Cherisse and Keiran led the way out the house, Remi swept in beside Maxine. "You do look like a queen," she said. "Your hair looks nice, wavy like that."

Maxine felt heat rise up her neck and face. "Thanks."

She kept her cool as much as she could on their ride to Shade. It didn't take long, the nightclub was about fifteen minutes away by car and Sanaa had called the middle seat, which Maxine was somewhat grateful for. Fifteen minutes sitting next to Remi in that dress, her bare leg brushing up against her, would've been pure torture. Her entire body felt like a live wire, wound too tight, ready to go off at the slightest thing. The simplest touch or look from Remi might be her undoing.

God, this was terrible, yet exhilarating at the same time.

Maxine hadn't felt this "I'm attracted to you and it's making me nervous and trying so hard not to act a fool around you" feeling in so long. Definitely not since her divorce from Leo. But now there was the whole added anxiety of it being Remi. A woman. And what did that mean for her? She wasn't sure she was ready to deal with *that*.

She'd pushed what had happened between them as

teenagers so far down that she'd basically cut ties with Remi completely. She had glanced at Remi's social media briefly for those first few months in school, but eventually had made herself focus on why she was abroad and not think too much about what they had done. Now, everything was just so much. She had no idea how to process or deal with this. She only knew she wanted it, and it was making her incredibly on edge.

Maybe she needed to talk to Keiran. Her brother had confessed his crush to Scott. It hadn't ended how he'd wanted it to back then—Scott hadn't returned his feelings—but he wasn't out to anyone but his close friends and her. So why did she have to be? And what the hell was she going to be out about anyways. She didn't know what, or if, she and Remi would be anything beyond this flirtation and fooling around. And there was no way she was brave enough to bring that up with Remi.

They were two adults having occasional consenting fun and it was no one's business.

The bubble of anxiousness sitting in the pit of her stomach only grew as the night wore on. Not that anyone noticed, so at least that meant she was keeping up her façade. It wasn't that she wasn't having fun, but every look Remi threw her way had Maxine's heart racing.

Shade filled up with people the later it got and Maxine sang along with the music pumping through the club, like everyone else. She watched Remi dancing with Sanaa. It was so easy to see the chemistry they had. Still had? They looked good together. Comfortable. Dancing with another woman wasn't a big deal. Most women she knew did it. Everyone just assumed they were friends.

But she felt that if she danced with Remi the way she was feeling right now, with her emotions so close to the surface, everyone would know this wasn't just two friends having fun. And that was scary.

She drained the rest of her drink and discarded the bottle on the bar, still watching Remi and Sanaa.

"Hey, you good?"

Maxine jumped at the voice so close to her ear. When the hell had Keiran come over here? She'd been so busy staring at Remi and Sanaa she hadn't noticed.

"Yeah."

"You look ready to jump out your skin so I'm calling bullshit."

She didn't need this twin bond thing to be working overtime right now. She wanted to talk to Keiran, but not here. The loud music wasn't conducive to having any sort of serious conversation. Besides, spilling her guts in Shade wasn't what she wanted to do. She wanted to have fun, like everyone else, go home and not think too hard about any of this until she worked up the nerve to talk to Keiran.

"I'm just in my head a lot tonight and I'll talk to you about it soon, okay? Just not now."

He looked over to where Sanaa and Remi had roped Cherisse into dancing with them, then back at her. "Alright. I'm holding you to that. You just look," he shook his head. "I don't know. Not happy."

That shocked her. Did she truly look unhappy? She wasn't. Not really. She was getting herself back after her marriage fell apart and yes Leah had been her priority the entire time of that. She had to be. Change was hard. She had to ensure her daughter wasn't falling apart at the seams the way she'd been. So she'd let her own self-care fall to the wayside a bit—but she was working on that more. But unhappy? She hadn't thought she was since coming back home.

"I'm not unhappy," she said. "I'm just trying my best to get *me* back. But it's kind of hard when you're not really sure who that is anymore."

Dammit. She hadn't meant to admit that. The prickly feeling in her eyes wasn't a good sign. Those emotions close to the surface were trying their best to spill out. Nope. She wasn't doing this.

"I gotta go pee." She tossed Keiran a wobbly smile and took off towards the bathrooms.

The bathroom was empty, the stall doors all ajar. Was this her thing now? Running off to bathrooms when she didn't want to deal with people?

Seriously, get a grip.

She was so out of it, she jumped when her phone vibrated in the pocket of her skirt. No matter how much she wanted to ignore it right now she wouldn't. When you had a child and they weren't with you, ringing phones and incoming messages became a source of anxiety, especially past a certain hour. Her first thought was Leah.

She let herself breathe properly again when she saw it was Victoria.

Victoria: *lady I hope you're having fun for me* 😢

Victoria had been pissed she couldn't get vacation time off for the trip. She had mentioned possibly flying over for the weekend but hadn't confirmed that.

Maxi: *Sanaa's here. Just FYI.*

It was easier to deflect than let her friend know she was in the bathroom potentially losing it.

Victoria: *I bet she looks hot. Of course she does. Curse this job.*
Maxi: *might wanna get a drink for that thirst there*

Victoria: hell yeah I'm thirsty. Sanaa knows how to do me
right 😊

Maxi: we are not discussing your sex life!! I want to be able
to look Sanaa in the face for the rest to this trip!!

Victoria: why bother? She'll only be looking at your tits,
hips and ass anyways. I'm seriously thinking of coming
over. Gotta have that kiss to ring in the New Year right 😊

Maxine chuckled aloud. Rekindling their friendship had been
the best idea. Maxine had her friends back in Atlanta and she
kept in touch with a few of them, but there were some who had
taken to gossiping gleefully after everyone learned about the
divorce. She didn't understand why people she'd thought of as
her friends would take joy in discussing her broken marriage
like that, but whatever. It made her all the more grateful for
Victoria.

Maxi: hey. I just wanna say thanks for being awesome.

Victoria: oh no. what's wrong?

Maxi: nothing. Just freaking out in a bathroom cuz I don't
know how to be around Remi. Pathetic right? 😬

She waited for Victoria's reply. Heart in her throat. Those
bouncing dots adding to her anxiety. Would Victoria call her a
fool for making a big deal out of this when she could just be
flirting, having fun with Remi and not take any of this so
seriously?

Victoria: not pathetic at all. Give yourself a break okay?
This can't be an easy thing. To realise you're queer? I don't
want to put words in your mouth since I don't know if
you've settled on an ID or anything and frankly? You don't
need to unless you want to. Alright? And if anyone gives

you a hard time I will fight them. I'm small but you know
how I do.

She did know. Victoria had never been the type to let anyone
walk over her. She had gotten into enough verbal fights that
had almost turned physical because she would not back down.
Girl was scrappy.

Maxi: *thanks. I wish you were here too.*
Victoria: *just go fool around with Remi to make me feel*
better.

Maxine smiled down at her phone. Victoria's teasing did make
her feel a bit less like she was drowning, until the door swung
open and Remi waltzed in. The fluorescent lights bouncing off
her dress made it shine even more. Her hair was up in a messy
bun and had already gone from straight to slightly wavy. Not
surprising. It had gotten hot out on that dance floor.

"We've got to stop meeting like this." Remi's smile was
tentative, like she was dealing with a skittish animal and didn't
want to make any sudden moments. Apt really, because Maxine
was so close to running, but didn't move a muscle.

"We're not making out in this bathroom," she blurted out.

Remi's eyebrow rose and Maxine truly wanted to bolt, but
then she'd have more explaining to do than she wanted to.

Relax. You got this. It's fine. Don't be weird. Well, weirder . . .

"Okay, noted. No making out in the bathroom. Got it."

Remi didn't look too serious about that. Maxine hoped she
wasn't. She liked kissing Remi. She was good at it. She just
wasn't about to do it again now when anyone could walk in on
them. It was a lot harder just to lock a bathroom door at a club
and not have someone pound it down to get in than at a private
party where there were multiple bathrooms anyway. But she

had jumped ahead of everything, hadn't she? Remi hadn't mentioned kissing right this second or anything of such a nature.

"You okay? I just wanted to check on you, but if you want me to leave?"

Maxine didn't know what she wanted. That much was clear. Her confusion was messing with her and she hated that. Not knowing how to deal with any of the creeping anxiety. Adults were supposed to have everything figured out, right? Her phone kept buzzing in her hand. She'd ended her chat with Victoria abruptly. Perhaps she could use that as an excuse for why she'd run off in here but it wasn't like she was on a phone call where she needed some quiet time away from the music outside.

"I'm good, really."

"Okay. Just so you know, I'm not buying that for a second but I won't push." Remi shrugged. "You wanna talk, I'm here. You wanna go back out there and dance, I'm more than here for that. The crew's doing shots and I'm not sure if you're down for it, but I did tell them I'd come check on you."

"Thanks for that. I'll be out in a bit. Promise."

Remi seemed like she wanted to say more but nodded and left. Maxine shot off a quick *talk to you later* to Victoria and steeled herself for heading back out. She could channel her anxiety into dancing. She couldn't come to Tobago and get in her head so much that she bombed the entire vacation.

The new year was also right around the corner, three days away to be exact. That meant a fresh start, right?

"Where were you?" Sanaa sang out as soon as Maxine rejoined the crew.

Keiran's look was silently asking if she was okay, so Maxine mustered a smile for everyone. She wasn't fooling her brother, or Remi, who was watching her over the rim of her shot glass, but she didn't need all of them worried about her. Not that she thought Sanaa would even notice. They didn't know each other that well. Plus, Sanaa was too busy on the prowl to care about anything else, especially not something that would put a damper on her fun.

"Bathroom break. I was talking to Victoria, too."

Sanaa's smile brightened. "Oh yeah? How's that little minx, hmm? Shame she couldn't make it. Would've made this vacation all the more pleasurable."

"Oh, she wishes she were here too. She might try to come over. Maybe. But you should talk to her about that."

Success. The crew took to harassing Sanaa about Victoria. Well, Cherisse and Keiran did. Remi was still watching her without saying a word.

It was unnerving and exhilarating. She wished she knew what Remi was thinking. She could find out. Asking was always an option, but Maxine was too on edge to think clearly.

You know how to take that edge off.

She did know, but the thought of doing more with Remi, again, was one of the things making her anxious, so did it make sense to use the very thing to calm her racing mind? Why was she thinking so hard about this? Everyone else was having fun and she was here over pondering this thing to death.

Remi, as if finally coming to a decision, started walking over, but before she could get there a guy stepped in front of Maxine.

"Hi there, wanna dance?"

Maxine gaped up at the guy. He was tall, good looking, nice smile too and had actually asked her to dance rather than just backed up on her and expecting her to go with it. Sometimes if she was already dancing, and depending on her mood, she didn't mind reciprocating, but there had been times when guys had turned to spewing nasty words when she moved away from their gyrating hips. That hadn't happened in a long time because of Leo. Well, before their divorce.

When she went out with Leo, guys stayed clear. When she had her girls' night out, she refused, knowing that even an innocent dance could be twisted by some. Anything to fuel the gossip fodder.

Maxine stared past the man at Remi, who was waiting. "Sorry," she mouthed and turned back to the guy. This was easier. "Sure," she said mustering a cheery smile she didn't feel at all.

She didn't look at Remi. Didn't want to see any hurt reflected there. She would understand. Wouldn't she?

REMI

Watching Maxine dance with someone else was fine. Totally *fine*. She didn't control anyone's movements and Maxine was free to do as she pleased. She'd been dancing with Sanaa earlier, so this wasn't any different right?

But as she watched Maxine dance with this guy, whoever the hell he was, she felt that snub like a hastily ripped-off Band-Aid. The ones that stuck to your not-fully-healed cut and ripped off a little bit of skin. It hurt like a bitch.

This was foolish. Standing here like this. She kept on walking, like she'd been heading to the bar the entire time. A drink, yeah. Great plan. She tried to get the bartender's attention, but it was crowded up here at the moment, so she'd have a bit of a wait. Not that she cared. It forced her to keep her back to everything else going on behind her. Forced her not to replay that little scene, frame by frame, in slow mo. Nope, not doing it. Definitely not wondering what her face did when Maxine had mouthed that quiet "sorry" and gone off with that guy. She didn't care about that at all.

"Hey."

Remi tossed a look over at Cherisse who squeezed in next to her. "Wow, almost didn't recognise you without Keiran next to you," she quipped, then realised how bitchy that sounded, like she was jealous of the time Cherisse and Keiran spent together.

Which she wasn't, right?

Cherisse's brow went up. "Do we need to have a discussion or . . .?"

"Sorry. I'm just. Hang on." She turned away as the bartender came over to take her order. "Want anything?"

"No." Cherisse was frowning at her and Remi wished she'd just held her damn tongue. She didn't need to take her frustrations out on her bestie. "Love life problems?" Cherisse inquired, a knowing look in her eyes. She turned, her back pressed against the bar and looked out at the dance floor.

Remi knew Cherisse well enough to know she was watching Maxine dance with that guy. Remi still refused to turn all the way around.

"Just me being silly. She can dance with whoever she wants."

"Obviously, but you still feel some kinda way about it. Which doesn't make you a bad person. Now, if you acted on it and got all up in her face like a jealous weirdo, then . . ."

"I know." No matter how strong the urge was to roll up on this guy and shout "mine!" it wouldn't go over well. She'd embarrass Maxine and that was the last thing she wanted.

"But I get it. I wanted to throttle my cousin at my birthday party when she was all up on Keiran." She gave Remi a wry grin. "I don't know what I was playing at with trying a FWB situation with him."

Remi chuckled. "That was a failure from the beginning. You know you, always catching feelings."

"Him too, though."

"Clearly." Remi was thrilled Cherisse and Keiran had gotten over themselves and had sorted all that out. Yeah, she'd always had Cherisse's back where her mini feud with Keiran was concerned but she wished them all the best. Cherisse deserved to be happy.

And Remi wanted that too, with Maxine. A foolish thought perhaps, but a girl could dream, right? And a girl could get over herself and stop acting like the mere act of watching Maxine dance with someone else would literally kill her. It wouldn't. It would suck, but she could be cool about this.

Her drink arrived and with payment made she turned around, mimicked Cherisse's stance, pressed her back against the bar.

Watching Maxine dance was a beautiful thing, regardless of who she was with. The DJ had jumped to some retro tunes—and if she was silently thanking him for switching from bump and grind music so what?—and Maxine and this guy were having fun, her black and white striped skirt swished around her as she danced along to "Oh, What A Night". She and the guy were mouthing along to the words and God, Maxine's smile was the most gorgeous thing.

Shit, she was in some deep trouble here.

"I hate that guy right now," she muttered.

"You're way cuter. Taller too. Come to think of it, too tall maybe. Like share some of that with the rest of us. Don't be selfish," Cherisse said, face serious, but she pressed her lips together, clearly holding back a laugh.

"You're ridiculous and I love you."

Cherisse's mouth twitched. "I know."

Remi sipped her drink, gaze back on Maxine, locked on the arm that the guy had on Maxine's hip. Her tube top showed off a bit of her soft tummy and Remi wished she was the one getting to touch that sliver of skin. She took a bigger gulp of her vodka and cranberry juice.

"Maybe we should go dance," she suggested.

"Sure." She offered Cherisse an arm. "My lady."

Cherisse linked their arms. "Let's do this."

Remi felt Maxine's eyes on them the entire time, but she didn't look at her when she returned from dancing with the guy. She *was* aware of Maxine swaying from side to side, her skirt swishing about her legs. Sometimes, the fabric would brush against Remi, the club had gotten so packed. The spacious area had turned into a sweat box, which was fine by Remi, but it was getting harder and harder to ignore Maxine. She wished she could dance with her like she wanted. Like they had at the private party. As brief as that had been before that person had made the "get a room" comment and shattered their little bubble.

There was no way to be discreet here, so the thought was pointless. It wasn't happening.

By two in the morning, they agreed it was time to bail. They'd planned a fun-filled packed day tomorrow and Remi wanted to enjoy every minute of it, not over sleep from partying too hard. Sanaa, Cherisse and Keiran filled the car with chatter on the way back to the villa. Remi stole quick glances at Maxine who was once again on the other side of the car. Sanaa had claimed the middle position in the back seat. Remi doubted Sanaa had noticed a weird vibe between her and Maxine and had taken the spot to act as a buffer. Sanaa was too busy texting whoever, giant smile on her face. Remi assumed it was one of the women whose numbers Sanaa had scored tonight. Or maybe it was Victoria. With Sanaa, there would be too many possibilities, and she wasn't noticing a damn thing, other than her latest potential conquest.

Either way, Remi was glad Maxine wasn't next to her.

Although, that was short lived. The moment they filed out the car, Maxine placed a hand on Remi's arm as the others walked inside.

"Can I talk to you?" she asked, softly.

"Sure." Remi's reply was immediate. She should have said she just wanted to get to bed, but if there was a way to say no to that pleading look in Maxine's eyes, Remi hadn't figured it out yet.

Maxine's eyes darted around the kitchen where the others were busy grabbing water and stuff from the fridge to munch on, as if they had no intentions of going to bed right now.

"Dip in the pool anyone?" Sanaa asked, taking a healthy swig of her water before resting it on the kitchen counter to tie up her braids. "No one? Alrighty then?" She started discarding her clothes right there, and Remi hoped she was actually wearing underwear this time.

Sanaa didn't have a shy bone in her body, which she and Cherisse were used to. Judging from Keiran's raised brow and Maxine's open mouth, they sure as hell weren't. Down to her bra and panties, Sanaa grabbed her water, walking backwards toward the doors that led to the pool.

"Come on, live a little," she called out before turning and running through the doors. A big splash followed soon after.

Cherisse and Keiran exchanged amused looks.

"YOLO!" Keiran shouted, reaching for his shoes.

There was no way in hell Cherisse was doing this, except she grinned and slipped off her heels, giggling. Remi and Maxine watched, stunned, as they dashed out the doors too. What the hell was happening?

"Uh, I don't suppose you want to—" Maxine shook her head and Remi nodded. "Me either. You wanted to talk to me? We can do that."

"Can we go upstairs?" Maxine asked.

"Yeah."

Remi had no idea how long this random pool dipping would last, and it was clear Maxine wanted privacy for their discussion. The squeals of delight from the pool followed them upstairs to Maxine's room. Remi was sharing a room with Sanaa, so it made sense they talk about whatever in Maxine's room. With Leah sleeping over at the other villa, Maxine had the room all to herself tonight. Remi forced herself not to focus too hard on that. Maxine wanted to talk, nothing else.

"I'm sorry," Maxine rushed out. "For ignoring you like that when that guy asked me to dance. I'm sorry."

"You have nothing to apologise for." As much as that moment had stung, she couldn't fault her for it.

"It's just . . . I want. So much. You. I want you. And it's making me *so* anxious."

"Oh."

"Which isn't your fault, but I wish I could've danced with you tonight. I do. I wish I . . . no, I want to do a lot of things with you. I just want so much," she whispered that last part.

Remi closed the space between them and Maxine's breathing changed. Grew faster, and there went that lip biting. Well damn, she wasn't kidding. "I want those things too, which I'm sure you know. Fuck, in this light I can see your nipples through that top."

"Vacations make me go bold and braless I guess." Some of the worry in Maxine's eyes disappeared, replaced by amusement and heat.

So much heat. She wanted Remi. The way they kept crashing together should've been evidence enough of that but hearing those words never got old.

"What else do you want?" Remi asked, eyes fixed on the press of those nipples against that tube top.

It wouldn't take much to free Maxine's breasts. A single tug down and they'd be bared for Remi's hungry eyes and mouth.

Maxine's outfit had been driving Remi wild all night. The strip of bare flesh between her top and skirt begged to be touched.

"Whatever it is you're thinking right now. That. I want that." Maxine exhaled loudly, eyes locked on Remi, tongue darting out to wet her lips.

The lipstick Maxine wore was a peachy pink and what Remi wanted was to smudge it a little, but first that tube top. She wanted that more, and Remi always considered herself an accommodating person.

She traced Maxine's skin, right above her top, revelled in the way Maxine's teeth pressed into her bottom lip. It was her tell. She was anticipating what Remi was going to do. The kick of Maxine's heartbeat against Remi's fingers said a lot too. She forged on, fingers trailing down the front of the slash of fabric that covered Maxine's chest. She rubbed her thumb against a tight nipple.

Maxine's chest rose and fell. "What else, Remi. Show me."

"Patience will get you everything." She tugged at the bottom of the tube top. "Can I take this off?"

"I told you, whatever you're thinking."

"Yeah, but tell me anyways?"

Maxine nodded. "Yes. You can."

Remi didn't wait another minute. She moved her hands back up, moulding them to Maxine's breasts before swiftly yanking the top down to Maxine's waist. Her breasts fell softly against her chest and, oh yeah. Remi went right for one of her dark nipples, pressing her thumb to the bud, rolling it between her fingers, prepping it for her tongue, but she needed to see more of Maxine first.

"Turn around and take off the skirt."

Maxine turned, reaching back to unzip her skirt. It fell in a soft pool of fabric at her feet and Remi couldn't stop the harsh curse that blew past her lip.

"Jesus fuck, Maxi."

The back of the lacy thong Maxine wore disappeared between her plump ass cheeks. Remi's goal had been to tease and play with Maxine's breasts until she was wet and begging, but now, presented with that ass, her initial idea would have to wait a bit. She wanted to explore every dimple.

She wished she had her strap-on, even though she figured that was a big step for Maxine. They hadn't even discussed penetration like that. She didn't know if Maxine would be into it, but the fantasy of driving into Maxine from behind was front and centre. So vivid, Remi could picture Maxine's ass jiggling with each thrust.

Yeah, they were going to need to have that discussion at some point. She needed to know what Maxine was comfortable with trying, but right now . . . Remi sank to her knees and palmed Maxine's ass.

"Spread your legs for me," she urged.

Maxine obeyed and Remi rubbed at the centre of her thong. Maxine pressed back, chasing Remi's finger. She loved that. Loved how responsive Maxine was. She couldn't wait to get her tongue all up in that wet heat. And she knew Maxine was wet, and getting wetter and more turned on with the way she was squirming.

She needed this thong gone. She reached for the sides of the panties and eased them down Maxine's legs. Which was when she realised Maxine was still wearing her shoes. Easy enough to deal with. The sandal unzipped in the back. She got those out of the way, then lightly pressed on Maxine's lower back.

"Bend over."

Fucking beautiful. That's how Maxine looked right now. Her breasts hanging in front of her, ass in Remi's face, everything she wanted just right there and ready to be feasted on. Remi was so fucking turned on.

Maxine jerked at the first touch of Remi's fingers inside her thigh. Remi's ears devoured the next sound out of Maxine's mouth when she eased her finger inside. A moan. She pumped the finger in and out while Maxine slowly followed the movement, her back arching.

Now was time to amp things up.

Remi's tongue joined her finger and Maxine gasped.

"Remi." Her name fell from Maxine's lips as those hips kept going. Fuck, yes. Remi rubbed at Maxine's clit while she licked and flicked her tongue deep inside.

Giggles from outside reminded Remi that the others were still awake, which meant they should be quiet, but fuck that. She wanted the noises Maxine made. Revelled in them. She leaned back and Maxine looked over her shoulder.

"Don't stop."

Remi got to her feet. "Trust me, I'm not. Just slight location change." She motioned for Maxine to get on the bed and nearly bit her tongue hard enough to draw blood when Maxine scooted back on the bed, using her elbows to prop her up. She planted her feet on the sheet, letting her legs fall open. It was a brazen move and Remi discarded her heels and dress in record time.

Then they were kissing, which they should have done first, but Remi had been so eager to get her mouth and hands on Maxi. Their bare skin slid and pressed against each other, the same way their mouths did. Remi lifted Maxine's thigh to hook around her waist, lining up their hips right where she wanted them, thrusting forward slowly at first, watching the line of Maxine's throat as she threw her head back and pushed her hips up, matching Remi's thrusts.

Their slick flesh rubbed against each other and Remi leaned down. "You can touch me if you want," she panted. "Only if you want. No pressure, okay?"

She'd possibly detonate if Maxine touched her anywhere, but she wanted that. If Maxine was comfortable with it. She didn't need her to reciprocate. Their lower halves were already touching, their grinding was driving her out of her mind, but she wanted Maxine to touch the rest of her too.

Maxine bit her lips as her hands slid up Remi's stomach to her breasts, cupping them, tugging at her nipples *Yes! God.* She felt that pull right between her legs.

"You like that?" Maxine asked.

"Mmm, yeah." She rolled them to their sides, yanked Maxine's leg further up, spreading her wider, pressing their bodies closer. Their breasts rubbed, sweet lord every part of Maxine was pressed against her now, her movements growing frantic. Remi was chasing that sweet relief. It was right there.

She pulled Maxine to her, taking her mouth in a hot kiss, their tongues thrusting against each other the same way their hips were. Remi's hand snaked down between their bodies and she pressed a finger to Maxine's wetness.

"Please," Maxine begged against her mouth. "Please, Remi."

"Please what?"

"Fuck me."

Oh yeah.

She pumped her fingers into Maxine and Maxine licked at her mouth, her hips grinding down on Remi's fingers. She was so going to taste them after she was done blowing Maxine's mind. The urge was great.

"Fuck, fuck," she chanted against Maxine's lips. She felt Maxine clench around her fingers and her groan was loud as Maxine came. Remi pulled her fingers from Maxine's body. "Watch me," she commanded.

Maxine's eyes widened when Remi touched herself with the fingers wet from Maxine's release.

"Oh shit you're not gonna . . .?"

"Yes. Watch me."

It was the hottest thing ever. Maxine watching Remi finger fuck herself, teeth once again pressed into her bottom lip. "Can I?"

Remi didn't bother to ask Maxine if she was sure. "Yes, please."

Maxine drew her fingers down to where Remi's fingers were, her thumb rubbed lightly at Remi's clit and *Jesus.* Remi fell back on the bed, legs spread wide. She didn't give a shit how shameless she probably looked, hips pumping, her fingers moving faster as Maxine's intense stare speared her, her thumb still rubbing up and down.

Remi came and nearly blacked the fuck out. She blinked away the spots behind her eyes and turned her head to stare at Maxine.

"Suck your fingers clean."

Oh fuck. She had *not* expected that at all, but she didn't need Maxine to tell her twice. She did it. Slowly. Savouring the mix of Maxine and her own taste.

They stared at each other, chests heaving, and Remi wanted Maxine's mouth on her. Everywhere. But baby steps. She didn't want to scare her off. So they just laid there, breathing in each other and trying to recover.

CHAPTER EIGHT

MAXINE

The sea breeze soothed her burning cheeks as the glass-bottom boat pulled away from Store Bay beach. Trying to act like she and Remi hadn't been intimate last night was a bit more difficult in the bright light of the day.

Suck your fingers clean.

She didn't know who that woman was who'd uttered those words but just remembering them tumbling from her lips suffused her entire body with heat.

She was so aware of Remi on the opposite side of the boat, but she refused to look. Instead, she spilt her attention between the glass that covered a portion of the bottom of the boat and Leah's excitement as she pointed out the water beneath it. She also tried to focus on the boat operator as he talked about the reef and the Nylon Pool. Interesting stuff. If only she could keep her mind on that.

But her night with Remi kept replaying in her mind like a film reel.

She'd woken up to the bustle of the villa as the others got ready for their day of adventure. Naked. Alone in her bed. Of course, Remi wouldn't have stayed. There'd be too many questions in the morning if she'd been found in Maxine's room. None of which, Maxine was ready to answer.

She wasn't clueless. She knew her friends suspected there was something between her and Remi, but knowing and coming face to face with hardcore proof by finding them together in bed was something entirely different.

"Mummy, I saw a fish!" Leah said excitedly, pointing to the glass. Whatever she'd seen had already swum away by the time Maxine brought herself back to the moment. There was only the dark ocean visible through the glass.

"Oh, that's pretty cool."

"Yeah. It was pretty!" Leah looked over at Remi. "Can I go by Auntie Remi now? She said she'd show me more things with her camera."

Maxine glanced over to Remi's side. She was busy snapping scenery shots with her camera. Maxine took the opportunity to enjoy the sight of Remi's long legs in her denim shorts.

"Sure honey, just be careful walking over there."

The boat was small and, even though the sea had no waves to speak of, who knew if that glass was slippery.

Remi watched Leah as she walked carefully over. Her gaze flicked over to Maxine before coming back to Leah, her smile bright as she instructed her to look through the camera. She was good with Leah. Patient. Didn't talk down to her or use any annoying baby talk that some people did with children, no matter their age.

That did something to Maxine's insides that she didn't want to focus on.

Keiran sat down next to her. "So, I got up to use the bathroom last night. I was pretty sleepy so I could be wrong here, but I could've sworn I saw Remi leaving your room?"

"You want to ask this now?"

"We're stuck on a boat, you can't run, so I figure it's the perfect time to be the annoyingly nosy bro." Keiran chuckled and Maxine was tempted to throw him over board.

"Not taking this bait."

"C'mon."

She glared at him. "Nope."

He nodded at Remi and Leah. "Well, that's just cute."

He wasn't slick. She wasn't taking *that* bait either, even if she'd been thinking that same thing a moment ago. They *were* adorable together, which didn't make any of Maxine's worries any less. What did she think would come of this? They'd be something more than a hookup? How would that even work out?

There were no answers coming to her and she didn't have time to linger on it for much longer when the boat operator announced they'd be arriving at the pool shortly. He gestured to the bottom of the boat for everyone to watch the dark bottomless water change to the shallow sea floor. That never failed to create a buzz.

Keiran shot her a look that said their discussion was tabled for now. Maxine was too busy trying not to stare at Remi as she shimmied her shorts down her legs to give a damn about her brother being annoying right now. All she saw was Remi's bright yellow bikini.

Maxine had chosen to wear her blue bikini under her cover-up. She tossed off the flimsy fabric and tucked it away in her bag. People were already stepping off the boat into the clear waters of the pool.

"This never gets old," her mother said as she led Leah down the steps.

Remi was standing there gaping at her, and jolted when Sanaa tapped her on the forehead. Maxine allowed herself a small, satisfied smile. They claimed a spot for their group as the other tour boats around them blasted their music, creating a jumble of songs as everyone frolicked in the water.

Maxine scooped up some of the white sand and scrubbed it into her skin. The sand was supposed to be a natural exfoliant. This place was stunning. She pointed out the darker-tinged water around them to Leah who was spouting facts she learned from online.

"Yes, mummy I know. Where it's dark it means the water is deep, so we have to stay here where it's clear."

"She really did her homework," Remi said as she casually scrubbed some sand on her already gorgeous skin.

"Her first time here. She wanted to make sure she was prepared."

Remi kept scrubbing the sand onto her arms as she watched Maxine. "I'm trying to be good here, but that bikini . . ."

Maxine tried not to be smug about the obvious affect her swimwear was having on Remi, but it was only fair since Remi's was doing the same to her. "Yeah? What about it?" She was playing with fire here, but in spite of her reservations earlier she just couldn't help herself when Remi looked at her like that. Like something delicious to devour.

"You're a wicked woman, Maxine King, and I had no idea of your evil ways."

Maxine batted her eyelashes in a ridiculous manner. "Who me? No idea what you mean."

Remi closed the space between them, and the warm water rippled towards Maxine. "You like being naughty, huh? I got some ideas about what to do to naughty girls."

Maxine swallowed. Eyes wide, she looked around for the rest of their group. Her mother was busy helping Leah take photos with Remi's waterproof camera. Cherisse and Keiran were off being cute and Sanaa was chatting up some small blonde woman who was either turning red from the sun or whatever pickup lines Sanaa was dropping on her.

They were away from prying eyes and ears. The other people around them were strangers. She and Remi weren't even touching in any way, but Maxine was on high alert. So aware they were in public, but flirting with Remi was fun, and hot. And was it so wrong to indulge while on vacation? Reality would set in soon.

"What would you do?" she asked, gaze fixed on Remi's mouth as it curved up.

Remi swished her hand through the water. "Oh, nothing much, just put you on your knees, taste you, touch you until you're just right at the brink. Then, if it's something you'd be curious about," she leaned in close, lips inches away from Maxine's ear, "make use of my favourite strap-on."

"Oh." That was all Maxine could manage right now, throat suddenly dry. She could visualise that. It wasn't too hard to imagine Remi behind her, getting ready to . . .

"Mummy, look at this shot!"

Leah's enthusiastic shout and her loud splashes as she came over was like a bucket of cold water dumped on her head. Maxine spun away from Remi and those thoughts.

"Oh, those are great!" She beamed down at Leah who grinned back up at her and Maxine's heart swelled. That smile never failed to elicit one from her as well. Every so often she got these little zaps of shock that she was a mother. She was responsible for raising this tiny human. The pressure not to screw up was real.

"Great job," Remi agreed. "We can do some more lessons later, or tomorrow if you want."

"Yes please!" Leah grinned. "Can daddy come with us tomorrow?"

They had planned a trip up to Castara and Maxine had no

intentions of including Leo in that. In fact, she wasn't sure when he was leaving. She knew he was still here but wasn't privy to his schedule. It wasn't her business as long as Leah was back with her.

"Uh, honey, I don't know. He might be busy," she said. Considering he had his friend with him too, she wasn't about to ask him or her to tag along.

It had been awkward enough yesterday.

"Okay." Leah didn't look disappointed with her response, but Maxine knew she had to be careful not to act as if she didn't want him there. "Can I go show granny more stuff with the camera?" Leah asked Remi, who nodded.

Maxine watched Leah splash back over to her grandmother. Her phone was stashed in her bag on the boat. She could reach out and ask Leo, but did she want to ruin her day like that?

"It's not really my business, and please tell me to fuck off if I'm overstepping, but are you really going to ask him to come along?" Remi asked.

"No, it's not worth the tension. Besides, he had her for Christmas. This is my time," she said firmly, in spite of her brief moment of wanting to extend the invitation. "Just because he chose to stay here doesn't mean I should feel obligated to include him and . . . his friend."

"I'm guessing you haven't met this friend. Did you even know about her?"

"No." She didn't actually care if Leo had a girlfriend, but she should have at least been told since she had been around Leah on their trip. "Maybe I'll bring it up casually. I don't want it to seem like it's an issue. It's not. I just prefer to know since if it's serious she may be around Leah when he has her. It makes sense to at least meet her, right?"

Remi nodded. "Yeah."

The sun was still high in the sky when the boat operator corralled everyone back on the boat. Leah slid in next to Remi to chat her up some more about photography. The parents were all together further down the boat cooing over the photos Remi's mom had taken with her fancy waterproof phone. Cherisse and Keiran were busy taking selfies. Which left Sanaa free to slide in next to her.

Maxine ignored her and reached for her phone to see if she had any messages. There was an unexpected one from Leo.

> **Leo:** *hey Leah left one of the souvenirs Julia bought for her. Can I drop it off sometime later or tomorrow morning?*
> **Maxine:** *Julia? Your friend?*
> **Leo:** *Yes. You two should probably meet?*

She frowned down at the message. Did she want to do that now? Even if she said yes, she didn't think that should happen at the villa. That poor woman wouldn't even know what she was walking into.

> **Maxine:** *so it's serious?*

She sent that before she could stop herself, fingers drumming against her thigh as she waited.

> **Leo:** *yes. We're officially dating and all that. Also just fyi, we fly out after the 1st. So if you wanted to meet her . . .*

Which meant they would also be ringing in the New Year on the island. Leo was giving her the chance to meet Julia before the celebrations. It was obvious they wouldn't be seeing each other for Old Years' Night. That was family time and Leo was definitely not invited to their little get together at the villa.

Maxine chewed on her bottom lip. God, why was this so hard? She either had to say yes or no.

"Baby daddy drama?" Sanaa suddenly asked.

Maxine rolled her eyes. "It's rude to read other people's messages. Mind your damn business."

"Ooh sexy and feisty? I like."

Maxine turned her back on Sanaa and went back to replying to Leo.

> **Maxi:** *We have plans tomorrow so later you can drop off the souvenir. I'll let you know what time is best and if you can bring Julia.*

She tossed her phone back into her bag, deciding that she would make up her mind when they got back.

She turned to face Sanaa who had gone back to her phone after bugging her. "Listen, I don't know you and you sure as hell don't know me. So, we're not at that level where you get to joke around about my shit. And I know Remi already spoke to you."

Sanaa looked up, raised a brow. "Okay I . . ."

"No, *don't* interrupt me."

"Well damn, why is that so hot?" Sanaa grinned. "Never wanted to be put in my place more."

Maxine shook her head. "If I was strong enough, I'd seriously throw you overboard right now. Can you listen, please?"

Sanaa mimed zipping her mouth shut.

"We can be cool. Just stop with the teasing shit. I don't like it." She narrowed her eyes. "And I don't think Victoria will like it either."

"Wow, you would seriously mess with my play with Tiny like that?" Sanaa pursed her lips. "Okay, fine, I'll stop for real. I don't want to get on Remi's bad side either. And she *is* strong enough to throw me overboard."

"Good."

"I'm sorry. I know I play around too much sometimes and you're right. We don't have that kind of relationship. Yet." Sanaa winked. "But when you two get your shit together and we do become friends like that, all bets are off."

Maxine said nothing to that. Who knew what them getting their shit together even looked like? What did she even want? She stole a glance in Remi's direction. She was still showing Leah more things with the camera. She didn't know where they were going with any of this fooling around. All she knew was her heart did a little thump at how cute Remi and Leah were, heads together as they both looked at the camera. Their giggles mingling with the different conversations floating around the boat.

She turned away, stared out at the water as they approached Store Bay. Vacation Maxine didn't want to think too deeply about anything. She just wanted to get her sexy on and get off.

She'd figure out all the rest outside of her paradise bubble.

CHAPTER NINE

REMI

"WE'RE GOING TO VISIT ONE OF GRANNY'S FRIENDS TODAY IN –" LEAH frowned as she tried to remember the name of the place.

"Castara," Maxine reminded her and Leah bounced excitedly.

"Yes! There! I looked it up online."

Seriously, Leah was too sweet. How did Maxine get anything done with all that adorableness around her?

Sanaa came to stand next to Remi. "So, your girl handed me my ass yesterday and gotta say it made her ten times hotter."

Remi had no idea what the hell Sanaa was going on about. "Um, what?"

Sanaa chuckled. "I was doing exactly what you told me not to and she told me off. Didn't mince any words."

Remi frowned. "What did you say to her?"

"Okay, chill, don't fight me. I already got my buff from her, okay? I was teasing about baby daddy and yeah, I know before you cuss me out, I shouldn't have."

Remi took a deep breath, released it through her nose. She loved Sanaa, really, she did, but she had been telling her for years that her teasing would rub people wrong. Especially if they weren't used to her like Remi was. "Why won't you ever listen to me?"

Sanaa laughed. "Cuz it's more fun to annoy you? But sexy told me to mind my damn business, so message received. She threatened to turn Tiny against me and, yeah know, we can't have that."

"Are you telling me you actually listened because she was going to cock block you with Victoria?" Remi shook her head. "Unfuckingbelieveable."

It was ridiculous, but so like Sanaa to not want her booty call to be messed with. Good on Maxine for telling Sanaa off though. Remi didn't want anything causing her discomfort. Especially not after last night when Leo showed up to drop off something for Leah, with his new woman in tow.

Maxine had told Remi about her decision to meet Julia, but she hadn't said anything else when she'd returned inside. Remi didn't want to press her. She would talk about it when she was ready. She just wanted everyone to enjoy their trip.

The van arrived fifteen minutes later, and Remi secured a seat across the aisle from Maxine, who was seated next to Leah. They had opted for a hired vehicle since Castara was a bit far from where they were staying and no one wanted to drive today. They preferred just to sit back and enjoy the ride.

Sanaa stopped before she slid in next to Remi to throw Maxine a salute. Maxine nodded like the goddamn regal queen she was before turning back to Leah.

"Wow," was all Remi could get out.

She wished she had been there for the call out. Maxine probably did look super-hot telling Sanaa off. Damn, she was down so bad if even the thought of Maxine angry made her want to squirm in her seat.

"Yeah, girl," Sanaa added. "I told you, didn't I?"

She sure had. Maybe *she* should get on Maxine's nerves so she could be put in her place too. She reached across the short aisle space and tapped Maxine's shoulder. She waved her phone at her, indicating she wanted Maxine to pick hers up. This conversation wasn't for others' ears.

> **Remi:** *that was so damn hot*
> **Maxine:** 🙁 *what?*
> **Remi:** *you with Sanaa just now. she told me you called her out. And yeah she was right . . . fucking hot judging from the small taste I just got.*

Maxine stared down at her phone, the corner of her mouth kicked up in a small smile.

> **Maxine:** *thanks* 😊
> **Remi:** *I only speak the truth* 😉

Maxine's cheeks bunched as her smile grew wider. She cast Remi a sidelong glance but didn't say anything. Her smile said it all for Remi.

There wasn't much conversation after that as Leah kept Maxine busy pointing out the passing scenery and chattering a mile a minute.

The house where they were spending the day overlooked a beach and Remi took a big whiff of the salty air as soon as they piled out the van. Nothing beat that smell—except, maybe, the light coconut scent of Maxine's skin. Remi had to ask her about what lotion she used. That scent was intoxicating.

The house had a lovely, wide gallery that was perfect for grabbing scenery shots. Remi wasted no time getting her camera out. Leah left her mother's side to come over and take her own shots with her grandmother's camera. She beamed as she showed Remi her photo.

"Nice angles you got there!" Remi said excitedly, and she meant it. Leah was picking up her lessons already.

"Mummy! Can I take a pic of you over here?"

Maxine's smile was radiant as she leaned against the wooden banister in whatever pose Leah positioned her. Leah was having fun with it as she told Maxine to pout more.

Leah looked down at the shot she had just taken before glancing back up at her model. "Mummy, more ducky lips please."

Remi couldn't help the giggle that broke free at Maxine's raised brow.

"And what do you know about duck lips, young lady?" Maxine asked.

Leah shrugged. "Terry does it in her photos a lot."

"Of course she does." Maxine shook her head, but her smile remained bright and beautiful. She was having fun and it showed. Whatever conversation she'd had with Leo and his girlfriend last night had thankfully not soured her mood today. "Terry's one of her older cousins," she explained to Remi.

Maxine pursed her lips just as Leah asked and threw up a peace sign along with it.

Remi reached for her phone to take a shot too, and Maxine immediately focused on her. "Eyes on your photographer, madam. Just act like I'm not here."

Maxine opened her mouth to say something but their host came out onto the deck.

"I hope allyuh came ready to eat cuz is rel food," the short dark-skinned woman announced. Keisha Williams was all smiles as she surveyed the group. "But I know you want to tackle the beach first. So a dip in the salt then bellies fed."

"I mean we could eat first too." Keiran piped up and Cherisse and Maxine rolled their eyes.

Cherisse tugged Keiran close and whispered something in his ear that made his smile grow wider. "Okay, beach now, food later," he amended. Cherisse's grin was full of satisfaction.

Remi chuckled, certain her bestie had reminded Keiran of the bikini she was wearing under her cover-up. Keiran would never pass up the opportunity to see his girlfriend in the multitude of sexy swim wear she'd brought for this trip. Remi had been highly amused at each reveal, and Keiran's reaction to it.

Her eyes casually swept over to Maxine and she wondered what type of swim wear she was wearing today. She'd been enjoying every single one Maxine had worn so far. Was she sporting a new one? Or wearing one she'd already worn?

Remi had tossed all of hers in her luggage, so she'd have multiple options. Waiting for swim wear to dry for the next day was a hassle. They would be heading back to Trinidad on Tuesday afternoon as they wanted to enjoy the New Years' morning before they left, and Remi was going to have as many swim wear changes as possible. Besides, having Maxine's gaze linger on her while wearing a bikini didn't hurt one bit.

Maxine's cover-up skimmed her upper thigh and Remi used the excited chatter with Keisha and her husband Kyle, who had strolled outside a few moments ago, to trace her gaze up Maxine's legs. She couldn't see it with the fabric in the way but that dimpled skin right beneath Maxine's ass was the stuff fantasies were made of. She wanted to kiss right there, see the reaction she'd get out of Maxine.

Her eyes skimmed right up and clashed with Devon's who was watching her, a curious expression on his usually serious face, like he was trying to figure something out. Shit. Was he wondering why the fuck she was eating his sister up with her eyes like that?

Remi waved and his brow went up, but he said nothing, so she just turned away to where her parents were suggesting everyone get changed to head down to the beach.

Fine by her. She'd rather covertly stare at Maxine from behind her sunglasses as she soaked up the sun's rays.

"He totally saw you checking her out. Seriously, can you be any more obvious?" Sanaa asked from her side.

"Devon *may* be wondering about my intentions, but he's not like Keiran. He won't care enough to ask. That man will avoid an awkward conversation at all costs."

Sanaa laughed. "Sexy pink hair seems to have his attention anyhow."

She sure did. Devon's gaze was fixed on Reba, who was doing some sort of dance in front of him. Remi had no idea why, but did it even matter when it came to Reba? She did what she wanted, when she wanted. Devon looked like he had no idea what was going on either but the small twitch at the corner of his mouth was a giveaway that he was loving it.

Sanaa nudged her suddenly. "Heads up, yah girl's about to remove that cover-up."

Maxine didn't bother to go inside to change, and Remi hoped her whispered "Fuck" was as soft as she'd thought, because *Fuuuuck*. She hadn't seen this bathing suit yet and holy hell it was a struggle to act natural.

The cotton-candy-pink bikini boasted high-waisted bottoms with little patches cut out on the front that provided teasing glimpses of stomach and pelvis. The top fully covered Maxine's breasts and was held up by some elaborately crossed straps. It was the cutest, sexiest suit Remi had ever seen and when Maxine bent down to grab up Leah's book bag Remi almost wept. The bikini bottoms hugged Maxine's ass and there were the lovely dimples right under that crease.

"That's such a cute suit, Maxi!" Ms. King called out. "Haven't seen it before."

"Thanks mummy. Been waiting a while to wear it." Her cheeks grew rosy as everyone agreed with Ms. King.

"Girl, you in danger," Sanaa quipped, clearly amused.

It was the hard truth. She was in danger of falling for Maxine, was already halfway there, with no idea whether Maxine would ever feel the same.

CHAPTER TEN

MAXINE

"ARE WE GONNA MAKE IT OUT OF THIS WEEKEND ALIVE?" KEIRAN'S whisper was loud enough to reach Maxine across the grocery aisle and she chuckled.

She had been wondering the same thing as she watched her mother, Remi's parents, and Reba put more bottles of wine into the cart.

"I didn't come here to be sober. I came to ring in the new year and have a good time!" Ms. King declared.

They'd decided to make their grocery run for the Old Years' Night party on their way back from Castara. Fine by Maxine, but she didn't know what sort of debauchery the parents were planning with all this liquor in the cart. She raised her brow as Reba added a bottle of tequila to the mix.

"Good lord, we *are* gonna die." Keiran turned to Maxine. "I haven't lived a full life yet. I just convinced Cherisse to put up with me. We still have the Sweethand store opening. I have to see her fulfil her dream."

"Stop being dramatic." Reba grinned at Keiran. "No one's making you drink anything. Besides, tequila loosens everyone up. It's gonna be so great!"

Maxine needed to stay far away from that tequila. She didn't need to be any looser around Remi. There was no telling what she would do, and with her family around she preferred to be discreet.

Today had already been a struggle while fully sober.

She recalled Remi's eyes on her the entire Castara trip. It had been exhilarating to know the reaction she had. Maxine had relished the sneaky glances. It was exciting, but scary too. Her anxiety at the club hadn't been a fleeting thing. It was lying in wait to smack her in the face again.

Hooking up was fun—when she wasn't spiralling about it— but could she keep that up with Remi for some undetermined time that neither of them wanted to talk about? Without it going anywhere? Should she even be thinking about it going somewhere other than sex? Ugh, she hated this.

She'd caught Devon watching her a few times. She had no idea if he'd noticed something between Remi and her. She was *not* ready to have that conversation.

Not that she expected him to come ask her anything. Her brother tended to be a silent observer not wanting to be a part of people and their many dramas. He didn't care to get into their personal business because he didn't want them in his.

Maxine had ignored him, trying to dial back on her thirsting. But damn, Remi in that white bikini was a dream. Toasty brown skin looking even more delicious than usual. The top had been lined, so sadly there'd been a serious lack of nipple action. She'd been slammed with an all-too vivid image of her peeling that top away to reveal the slightly lighter skin underneath, untouched by the sun.

How would Remi sound if Maxine licked at her skin, laved her tongue around her nipple? Would she try to hold it in? Or be loud, let Maxine drink up every single moan?

"Should we get these?" Remi's question made her jerk out

of her naughty thoughts. Shit. When had Remi come back from the other aisle? How long had Maxine been standing here just fantasising like this?

"Uh, what?"

Remi was shaking a pack of something in front her face. Maxine blinked, urged her brain to focus. She couldn't be getting turned on in the middle of a grocery store for fucks sake.

But presented with Remi in that bikini, even if she wore a thin strapped top and tiny shorts over it now, wasn't helping. Maxine's self-control was hanging on by a thread.

"It's got some New Years' crowns and noise makers in here. Figured it could be fun."

"Oh, yeah sure. Leah would love it."

"Cool." Remi placed the packs in the cart that wasn't over-flowing with drinks before turning back to give her a long, assessing look. "You good? You looked a bit spaced out there when I came back."

"Yup. Great. Just tired from the beach, I guess." And super fucking horny apparently.

"Well, we can do whatever we want when we get back before we have to prep for the party tomorrow. You can sleep if you like."

Or lock my door and take care of my little problem.

She nodded. "Yep. A nap is probably needed."

"Yeah, I didn't want to pry or anything but yesterday must have been stressful?"

"Yesterday?" Maxine had no clue what Remi meant.

"With Leo and Julia?"

"Oh, right, that." She'd been so consumed in her thoughts about Remi, her mind hadn't run on Leo or her talk with Julia at all. "It was weird for sure, but . . ." she shook her head. She didn't actually want to talk about this now.

She felt like it would ruin this buzz she had running along her skin from her sexy daydream.

"We can talk about that later."

Remi nodded. "Okay."

"Alright party people, let's roll!" Reba's voice echoed down the aisle as she shimmied over to them. "I need to decide which wig and outfit I'm wearing tomorrow." She swept her hand down her body. "Gotta make sure I have maximum seduction vibes going."

"You do know you don't have to do much with Devon, right?" Remi pointed out.

Facts. Her brother was head over heels for Reba. It was cute and hilarious to see how hard he tried to hide it.

"I mean I know that, but I like to keep him on his toes as much as possible." Reba winked. She wiggled in between the both of them, linking arms. "Now, if you two need any relationship advice . . ."

"From you?" Remi laughed. "No thanks."

"Hey!" Reba pouted. "I'm in a committed relationship. I know things."

"Weren't you the same person who was brakesing from a relationship a few months ago, though? Who didn't even know they were being wooed by my brother?" Maxine joined in.

"In my defence, I was distracted by his pipe game, okay? That man knows how to work his d—"

"Nope, stop right there!" Maxine unlinked their arms, placing her hands over her ears. She did not want to hear anything about her brother's pipe game. Hell no.

"Sorry." Reba didn't look the least bit remorseful. Not with that big grin on her face.

"Let's just get to the cashier and get out of here." She grabbed onto one of the carts that actually had some food stuff in it—thank God because they needed fortification with all that liquor—and went to find the others, ignoring Reba and Remi's laughter behind her.

By the time they got back to the villas and packed away the groceries and copious amounts of alcohol—seriously, were they even going to be able to drink all of this?—everyone had decided to do their own thing. Her mom and Mrs. Daniels had gone into party planner mode with Keiran giving his input about music choices.

Leah was busy in the pool with Cherisse. Reba had taken Devon's hand and dragged him away, which meant they were definitely getting some sexy time in, no doubt about it, with that cheeky smirk on Reba's face.

Maxine had taken the opportunity when Remi and Sanaa had been deep in conversation to head to her room. She just needed some time to herself. To catch her breath because she seemed not to be able to do that around Remi at all. It was . . . concerning. Because she had no clue how to deal with this.

She had to figure herself out. Remi seemed fine going with the flow, but underneath the teasing and flirting Maxine sensed she wanted more. She hadn't come out and said so, and Maxine had definitely not asked, but . . . why did this have to be so hard? Why did she have to make it that way? Couldn't she just enjoy her vacation without all this worrying about everything?

The fact was, *she* had too much at stake with this. She might not want to dissect this to death, but she couldn't continue like this indefinitely. Not with Leah involved. God, she didn't know what to do.

She flopped back on the bed, decided to send Victoria a text. They hadn't really spoken since her mini bathroom meltdown.

Maxi: SOS
Victoria: *what's happening? Who do I need to fight?*

Maxi: *ok Rocky, stand down. I'm just having a Remi-related crisis which seems to be my life now . . . sigh*
Victoria: *this is too funny to me. Sorry but you two couldn't even stand each other in school and now* 🖤
Maxi: *I got horny in the damn grocery V . . .*
Victoria: *w h a t??? okkk. don't worry I got you. I'll help you with this*
Maxi: *how??? You're not here and I don't know what I'm doing*
Victoria: *pretty sure you're fine. You're just panicking cuz this is new to you but trust your gut ok?*
Maxi: *my gut isn't leading the show at the moment. I literally had a flash of licking Remi's uh . . . yeah . . . god I can't even type that . . .* 😳
Victoria: *ooh la la. Just don't worry like I said. Hey I gotta go but I'll talk to you soon k. just go lick whatever you wanna lick. I'm suuuure Remi won't mind* 😉 🙈

Of course Victoria would be all for her giving into her urges. She had literally walked in on her getting eaten out by Sanaa in a bathroom. She wasn't shy about doing what she felt like in the moment. But she also didn't have a daughter to think about. Or an identity crisis to deal with.

In spite of her swirling thoughts, Maxine felt a throb between her legs at the memory of the bathroom moment. Nope, do not think about *that*. She needed to go take a shower or just . . .

She rested her hand on her stomach. Or she could give herself some relief. Who would even know? It would be better than suffering here with all this pent-up energy. She slid her hand down inside her bikini, aiming for right where she needed it, her teeth digging into her bottom lip as she imagined Remi's hand . . .

The knock on her door jolted her and she yanked her hand away, neck heating up as if the person on the other side of the door would know what she was doing.

"Hey, can I come in?"

Shit, of course it was Remi. She squeezed her eyes shut, considered pretending to be asleep. They had talked about her taking a nap when she got back; she could easily not respond. Just let Remi think she had come up here to do just that.

"Yeah," she called out because she was a glutton for punishment apparently.

The door opened and Remi walked in, sans the top that covered that damn bikini. Why hadn't she just kept her damn mouth shut?

"Do you want some company? If you don't feel like coming down." She pushed the door closed, kept her back to it, like she was waiting for permission to come closer. Maxine realised she was still laying down and got off the bed, rising to her feet.

"Company?" She raised a brow.

"Yeah, Maxi. Like, just to hang out. I didn't mean sex or anything."

"I wasn't implying . . ." Or was she? Every time they'd been alone that's what it had ultimately led to. Hell, she had been up here about to get herself off because she couldn't act normal around Remi in that fucking white bikini. Or in general, it seemed.

"Not sure if you came up here to nap like you said, but wanted to check on you."

"Why? I'm a whole adult. I can take care of myself. I'm not gonna have meltdown after a talk with my ex and my replacement."

Okay, she sounded so bitter right now.

"Never said that." Remi shook her head. "Maybe I should go . . ."

"Wait! How're your hugging skills?"

Remi eyed her like she'd been out in the sun too long before she broke into a smile.

"Are you just trying to make excuses to rub up on me? Cuz you don't need to. You can just ask." The corner of her mouth kicked up into a sly grin.

"That's not what . . . I just . . ." She glared at Remi. "You enjoy teasing me."

Remi nodded. "Yup." She pressed her back to the closed door, one leg crossed over the other, as she stared at Maxine expectedly. "I'll do whatever you want."

There were so many things Maxine wanted, especially given her aborted masturbation attempt, but she reached for the safest thing. "I'd really like a hug, please."

Maybe she wasn't about to have a meltdown after meeting Julia, but it had been strange to know Leo was really moving on. As for the hug request . . . was she out her damn mind? Safest thing and she chose a hug? If she was thinking right, she'd tell Remi to leave. Hugging Remi could never be safe. That body pressed against hers wasn't a good idea. Not when she was wound up this tight. Who was she fooling?

Remi moved forward—no, that wasn't right, she prowled—until she was right in front of Maxine. "On three."

"What?"

"I'm giving you time to back out if you want. One."

Maxine didn't move.

"Two."

Her breath quickened.

"Three."

And then she was in Remi's arms, enveloped in her embrace.

"I'm really tempted to palm your ass right now. These damn bikini bottoms have been tempting me all day." A laugh burst out of Maxine because she could so relate, and Remi chuckled along. "Sorry, can't help it. Those cheeks are barely contained in these things."

Remi's hands didn't dip down to Maxine's ass, though. They remained firmly secured around her waist. Maxine just listened to the sounds of Remi's breaths near her ear, the feel of Remi's chest rising and falling against hers. This felt nice. Every inch of Remi was pressed against her, but her thoughts weren't just on naughty things. She allowed herself to wonder if she could have this. This moment. Outside of their vacation bubble. But what would that even look like?

"Feel better?" Remi asked.

"Lil' bit."

"Wanna talk about it now?"

"Meh."

Remi's laugh washed against her skin and Maxine held in her shiver. "Okay."

She hadn't wanted to, but she found herself spilling anyways. It was somehow easier to voice everything while she and Remi were pressed cheek to cheek and not actually looking directly at each other.

"I know I'm over Leo. Our relationship has been over for a while, but it's just strange knowing he's moved on. Do I even have the right to feel that? *I* asked for the divorce. Sometimes I feel like I ruined everything by asking for that."

Maxine braced for judgement. It was all she'd gotten from her supposed friends back in Atlanta. They'd turned on her after she'd got the courage to tell them she'd planned to ask Leo for a divorce. They were quite fine gossiping about the drama in others' lives, but she'd apparently broken some unspoken rule about never letting anyone onto the fact that your life wasn't perfection.

One had even suggested just screwing the pool guy if she wasn't satisfied with Leo anymore, which hadn't been the reason for their declining marriage. After their comments, she hadn't felt inclined to share any real details.

Besides, she hadn't wanted to repeat how Leo had basically tried to gaslight her. Sniping at her about what sort of mother wanted to abandon her child to go back to work, when he could provide for them.

Maxine had internalised that for years. The guilt slowly growing, eating away at her. Her mom crew hadn't exactly been helpful on that front either, throwing their own remarks about the mothers in the neighbourhood who worked.

Maxine admired stay-at-home parents so much. It was an entire job in itself, but it wasn't what she'd wanted for herself and Leo had known that from the start. His total 180 had thrown her completely.

"Hey." Remi's hand on her face brought her back. "I'm not gonna judge you for that. You're allowed to feel what you feel."

"I know that." Didn't change the fact that she was still ridden with guilt. Why did she care about Julia? She was doing things with Remi so it didn't make sense at all.

"Listen, I've never been married, but you two did build a whole life together. You have a kid. That sort of links people, right? It's going to be awkward to see him getting serious with someone else, even if you don't want to get back together."

Remi's hand rested on Maxine's, and Maxine's were on Remi's shoulders. She slowly disengaged until her hand met Remi's. She tugged Remi towards the bed.

Remi's brow rose. "Are you gonna have your way with me Ms. King?"

"No, just lay down with me? If you want to."

"I do want. I always want."

Maxine ignored the intense look in Remi's eyes and drew them to the bed. She positioned them so Remi was behind her. She just needed to be held a while. Just for a bit, then they would go down to join the others before someone else came looking for them.

"Cuddle buddies. I can get behind that. And, well, you. Behind you isn't a bad place to be at all."

"You're the worst." Maxine chuckled.

"So, those videos you watched? Any of it include strap-ons?" Remi's breath tickled her ear and Maxine wasn't sure if the question or that sensation on her skin made her shiver and press her legs closer together.

Fine, it was both. She had watched videos with women fucking other women while wearing a strap-on. It had intrigued her and turned her on.

"W-why do you ask?"

She felt Remi's shrug. "No reason."

"You can't just ask me a thing like that for no reason!"

"Shh, nap time now." Remi snuggled into her more until she was wrapped around her like a koala. "We can discuss later how you'd feel about getting fucked like that. If you'd be into trying it. Or fucking me if you'd like. I'm good with either."

"Oh my God. I can't with you," Maxine whispered into her pillow, but she pressed her thighs together as the throbbing intensified between her legs. They *would* revisit this, because her body was definitely curious.

For now, she enjoyed the feel of Remi's body against her and dozed off, thinking about how things would be when they left their vacation cocoon and returned home.

CHAPTER ELEVEN

REMI

REMI WOKE UP TO A WHOLE COMMOTION COMING FROM DOWNSTAIRS
and the softness of Maxine in her arms.

She blinked, rubbing the sleep from her eyes. How long
had they been up here? She'd left her phone somewhere downstairs when she'd come up to see how Maxine was doing.

She needed to go see what all the happy chatter was about.
She could barely make out any actual words, but something
was definitely going on. Yet moving meant possibly causing
Maxine to wake up. She didn't want to disturb her yet.

Maxine shifted, rolling over, which brought her face so
close to Remi's.

"Hi," she said, smiling.

"Hey."

"What's going on downstairs? I didn't imagine all that
noise, did I? Someone sounded pretty happy. Sounded like
Sanaa actually."

"Yeah. We should go check that out."

Maxine stretched, but rolled right back onto her side, hand
tucked under chin, eyes roaming over Remi's face. Remi
wondered what Maxine was thinking in that moment.

"Maxine, get your sexy ass down here!" Sanaa's shout was clear as day now.

Remi frowned. "What the heck is going on down there?"

"Maybe they got into the tequila early." Maxine yawned and rolled onto her back. "You go on down. I want to take a quick shower and change."

"Okay." She got up and watched as Maxine stretched the entire length of her body. She really needed to get out of here because that was way too enticing a move and Maxine hadn't meant it like that at all. "I'll see you down there."

She turned away from Maxine, closing the door behind her. She headed to the bathroom first to splash some of that sleep out of her face, then waltzed down the steps to see what chaos was transpiring.

She'd barely made it all the way down before she spotted their visitor. Oh, so Sanaa's loud-ass exclamations made sense now.

"Look who came to grace me with her sexy presence." Sanaa grinned, waving her hands at the woman standing there with a smug smile on her face.

Victoria stuck her tongue out at Sanaa. "I didn't come here for you. It's a surprise for Maxi."

"Yeah, keep telling yourself that." Sanaa licked her lips, eyes drinking up Victoria in her white shorts and crop top. "We have unfinished business."

"Hmmm," Victoria hummed. "Besties before breasties, my friend."

Remi laughed. "That was terrible."

Victoria shrugged. "Now where's my girl?"

"She'll be down soon."

"She needs some recovery time? I feel that." Sanaa smirked and Remi rolled her eyes.

"It's not like that."

Sanaa winked. "Remember I'm intimately familiar with how much it's not like that."

Remi didn't bother touching that one. She and Sanaa had been friends long enough that a little teasing about their past sex life wasn't a big deal, but she looked over at Victoria. Those two were having some casual fun – it didn't mean Victoria would necessarily want to hear any of this. She seemed unbothered, though.

"I bet you two were *so* damn hot together," Victoria said and, oh well, Remi guessed she was more than fine with it. Victoria swung her hair over her shoulder as she leaned against the counter.

Sanaa leaned into Victoria's space. "Baby, you don't know the half of it."

Jesus, where was Maxine? These two were going to start making out any moment. As if she heard her silent plea, Maxine finally came down, looking casually gorgeous in teal shorts and a white strappy top.

She stopped at the bottom of the stairs and blinked at Victoria, who wiggled her fingers.

"Surprise!"

"Wha—?"

Victoria ran over and launched herself at Maxine like a tiny spider monkey. Maxine received the hug but still looked stunned.

"What are you doing here?"

"Told you I'd see you soon. I couldn't let you all ring in a new year without me. So, what's the plan? Sanaa told me your mom is about to get everybody drunk? I'm down." Victoria prattled on as she untangled herself from Maxine. "Work has been extra annoying, so I'm here to let loose, babyyyy."

Maxine's eyes slid over to Sanaa, then back to Victoria. "Did you seriously come here for some vacay booty?"

"I'm offended that everybody thinks that's all I came for when I could literally just wait til Sanaa got back."

"But it *is* on the agenda now, right?" Sanaa piped up

Remi shook her head as Victoria shushed Sanaa, but she knew those two would be getting up to no good in no time at all.

Victoria linked her arm with Maxine. "Right now, the only thing on my agenda is stealing her away, so bye. We'll chat later." She tossed a wink Sanaa's way and sashayed away with a bemused-looking Maxine, leading her outside to the pool.

Sanaa shook her head. "Damn, she's a tiny terror, for real, and she's staying not too far from here." Sanaa rubbed her hands together. "Which means I can loudly get up to no good."

"Weren't you chatting up some tourist a few hours ago?" Remi asked. Before she had made her way upstairs, Sanaa was busting her moves over the phone on one of the women she had collected numbers from.

Sanaa shrugged. "So? That's not a sure thing. But V is."

Watching Sanaa be a whole player was still weird to Remi. She'd been super romantic when they'd been together, but now she was set on this Casanova act. It all looked exhausting to Remi who had never liked that sort of chase. She wanted Maxi and would do what it took to show her that. Without making her uncomfortable of course. This was new territory for both of them. Remi had never been with anyone who was questioning and on the DL like this.

"Let's go see what's going on next door," Remi suggested, suspecting Victoria and Maxine had a lot to catch up on. She wouldn't be surprised if she was the topic of discussion.

She and Sanaa walked over to the bright pink villa and into what could only be described as chaos.

"Uh . . ." Remi blinked at Keiran who was passionately

arguing with his mother over the party playlist while Ms. King was busy untangling a string of lights.

"We have to include a mix. We can't listen to oldies the whole night!"

Ms. King rolled her eyes at her son. "I don't wanna just hear whatever rab music you young people listen to these days. Just make sure it have some classics on there."

"You don't trust my taste all of a sudden? When have I ever failed you on this?"

Remi pointed to the lights in Ms. King's hands. "I can get these set up if you like." Anything to get away from this mini music battle.

"No, I got this. I have a vision I need to see through." Ms King waved her off. "You can go help your dad with the balloon set up. Or, actually, go make sure whatever punch Reba's doing a test run of isn't going to have us jumping off the roof or something." She turned back to Keiran. "Now, we *have* to have Auld Lang Syne."

Kerian sighed. "Mummy, you feel I don't know that?"

Sanaa and Remi looked at each other and walked briskly towards the kitchen where Ms. King had pointed. She would see what her dad was up to with those balloons after.

They both entered the kitchen in time to see her mother sputtering after a big sip from her cup. "Wow, okay hmm that's . . ."

Reba grinned. "Good, right?"

Remi eyed the various bottles of opened liquor on the kitchen counter and the small glass jug filled with red liquid.

"Are you drunkening my mother in here?" Remi asked, taking the cup from her mother's hand.

"I'm fine. It's good. Just strong." Her mother smiled over at Reba who preened at the compliment and waved her hand at the jug.

"Try it."

Remi wasn't too sure she wanted to, but Sanaa didn't miss a beat. Taking one of the clear plastic cups from the opened pack, she poured herself some of Reba's concoction and took a sip.

"Damn, girl, that's potent but oh so good. What you got in here?"

"My Passion Punch has everything to make all your inhibitions go out the window."

"Oh lord," Remi muttered.

"C'mon Rems, try it." Reba poured some in a cup for her and pushed it into her hands.

She sniffed it, the scent of alcohol and juice hitting her before she took a tiny sip. Damn was right. There was no mistaking this punch had liquor in it. But it wasn't bad either, just liable to have you wasted after one too many glasses.

"Okay, it's good," she admitted.

Reba clapped. "Great! And now to work on my Hot Lips shots."

"Say what now?"

Reba's grin was mischievous as hell. "These are gonna be pink-coloured shots with some tequila in there so ... stay tuned."

That was Remi's cue to leave. She couldn't be tipsy because she stuck around to taste test Reba's deadly mixes. Sanaa didn't look inclined to leave. Neither did her mother, so she decided to exit and go check on her dad. That seemed a safer place to be.

She didn't need to be high while she had Maxi on the brain. No way. Waking up next to her already had her mind racing.

If they hadn't been interrupted by Victoria's arrival they would probably have still been cuddling upstairs, which was a little too damn domestic for Remi's fragile emotions. Maybe she needed to talk to Cherisse. Get all this mess off her chest so she wouldn't spill her emotions everywhere.

She found her father outside blowing up the balloons and Cherisse was with him.

"Hey, sweetie," her father called out as she came over. "Right on time. We really could use another set of lungs over here."

"Agreed. Who knew my lung capacity was this shit?" Cherisse huffed. "I'm waiting on Reba to vacate the kitchen so I can prep my desserts for tomorrow night."

Remi picked up a gold balloon. "She's working on shots now."

"Devon had the right idea exiting the scene early. All this taste testing will have us a mess before the actual party." Cherisse tied off her balloon and added it to the half-filled garbage bag. "We'll leave a few to blow up in the morning just in case some of these pop."

Remi puffed into her balloon, nodding. The repetitive motion of blowing the balloons helped keep her mind off of Maxine.

"So how are we using these for décor?" she asked.

Her father pointed to the pool. "Some in the water. Some bunches inside. Nothing too fancy." He gathered up the garbage bag that was already full. "I'm going to put these inside. We probably just need a couple more, then we're good to go."

"Thank God." Cherisse stuck another balloon in the smaller garbage bag. "I'm itching to get in the kitchen right now."

"Need help?" Remi asked.

"Yes, you can taste test everything as usual." Cherisse knew what a fan of her desserts Remi always was.

"I'm actually asking if you need an assistant since yours is off trying to give everyone alcohol poisoning."

Cherisse squinted at Remi. "You only like the end result of baking. What's going on?"

"I . . ." Remi tied her last balloon and placed it in the bag. "I just need to talk to you I guess. The club wasn't really the best place to try to have that convo."

Cherisse tied off the bag. "Has there been any progress with Maxi?"

"I don't know. Is cuddling upstairs and then falling asleep together before I came over here progress?"

"Aww, that's cute."

"Yeah," Remi agreed. "But . . ." she tugged on one of her curls. "I feel weird asking her serious questions about what we're doing because I don't want to seem like I'm pressuring her for answers. I've been through this before. This whole figuring myself out. I know who I am, but she's . . . you know."

"Hmm, I hear you."

"And on the other hand, I just want to enjoy what we're doing while on vacation here and not stress. Sort it out when we get back to Trinidad. Let future Remi deal with that shit. If that makes me a wuss then so be it."

Cherisse tugged on the same curl she was yanking at. "Hey, don't call my bestie a wuss."

"But what if she is?"

"Does future Remi have plans to get a midnight kiss from Maxi?"

"How the hell did you know that? God, you know me too damn well," she grumbled, ignoring Cherisse's chuckle.

Cherisse released her hair. "Just go with the flow, buddy. It'll work out."

Remi picked up the pack with the extra balloons. "Just cuz it worked out for you and Reba doesn't mean it will for me, but I'll try not to be a loser about it, alright?"

Cherisse slung her arm around Remi's shoulder. "Now let's go reclaim the kitchen from Reba and your mom, who's probably, definitely, tipsy by now."

"Oh God, I forgot I left Sanaa with them too." Sanaa could hold her liquor, but she was also too damn persuasive. Her mother could be dancing on the kitchen counter by now. Jesus, they needed to get a move on to see what chaos was transpiring.

CHAPTER TWELVE

MAXINE

"IT'S TOO MUCH."

"It's perfect."

Maxine eyed herself in the mirror as she moved to the side. "My boobs are gonna fall out."

Victoria smirked from her place on Maxine's bed. "Remi would love that."

"What was I thinking with this? I'll wear one of my other options."

"Tonight isn't the time to bring out a boring dress. It's the night of new possibilities. You wanna make that woman lose her mind."

Is that what she wanted when she decided to pack this strappy short, gold dress that would flash the entire world if she bent over too far? It had been a total impulse buy and an even more impulsive decision to wear it.

She looked amazing in it, there was no denying that. She felt sexy. Desirable. But it was so far out of her usual comfortable attire that she wasn't sure about it at all. It definitely sent a message, that was for damn sure— *Look at me.*

Victoria got to her feet. She hadn't been privy to the glitz and glam theme since they didn't know she would be here, so her outfit was actually a blue romper with billowy sleeves and a plunging neckline which still worked for the occasion.

"Look, you're *so* sexy in this. I also have boob tape that will help if you need it."

Boob tape. Right. Why hadn't she thought of that. It would be fine. She wasn't going to have a wardrobe malfunction of any kind. She was more worried about her reaction to however Remi was going to react to this dress. There was no denying there would *be* a reaction.

Maxine grinned to herself. If she didn't wear this, she would miss out on that, wouldn't she?

"Alright, let's secure the girls and then let's go." Victoria winked.

"Not yet." Maxine plopped down on the bed. "I need to ask you something first."

"What's on your mind?"

"Remi and I were cuddling upstairs before you came, and it was nice. I've been so in my head about everything, I just don't know how to navigate this."

"Well, that's cute. The cuddling part." She folded her arms. "Have you two talked about this beyond sex?"

"God, no." That was terrifying. She did want to know if they were going to take this outside of the bedroom, but she didn't have the courage to ask that. Wasn't it too soon even to bring up serious shit like that? "I'm still trying to figure me out. Should I even go there?"

"Well, you're not just going to keep this sexy times forever, right?" Victoria asked.

Maxine had obviously been thinking about what a relationship with Remi would be like, but she didn't know. She had no context for that.

"I don't know," she admitted. "I've never been in a

relationship with a woman. How would we manoeuvre this? Can we even do it?"

Victoria came to sit next to her. "You're asking the right questions, but answer this. How well do you two know each other? You know you've got the chemistry part, but outside of that? Maybe you need to figure out the part without the sex. What that would look like. Dating?"

"I . . ." Damn. Victoria was making sense. She and Remi truly hadn't taken the time to know each other after she had come back. Their entire relationship had revolved around sex and still did now as adults. "You nailed it," she murmured in awe.

Victoria patted her arm. "I know things. Here's a wild thought. Why don't you two try friend dates?"

"Friend dates?" Maxine wrinkled her nose.

"Yes. No sex. Just chillin. Learn what each other likes and dislikes are. Goals. Etc." Victoria got to her feet. "Don't over think it, but consider the concept."

Victoria did a double check on the boob tape, ensuring Maxine was basically strapped in before they made their way downstairs.

She was going over what Victoria had suggested as they walked down. Friend dates. Sounded interesting.

"Oh my fucking God!" Cherisse exclaimed.

"Oh, hey." Maxine didn't realise anyone else was still here.

Remi and Sanaa had left earlier, before Maxine had got dressed and she just assumed everyone else had already gone over to the other villa.

Keiran, who was sitting next to Cherisse, gave Maxine a thumbs up. "Damn, you out to kill 'em tonight, sis!"

"Alright, calm down."

"No, no way. Look at you in this." Cherisse whipped out her phone and took a photo.

"What the hell?"

"Oh, she's gonna die." Cherisse chuckled.

Maxine had no doubt who the *she* in question was. "Stop! Don't you dare send that to her. I . . ."

Cherisse got to her feet, brow raised. "You?"

Maxine's face heated, especially with her brother still in the room. Dammit, how was she supposed to say this with a straight face? That she wanted Remi's reaction to be when she saw her for the first time and not because she was prepared for it beforehand. God, she needed to get a grip, seriously.

"She'd rather have her see this live and direct," Victoria said. "Don't ruin the effect."

"Oh." Cherisse nodded. "Gotcha."

"Soooo, I guess we're all just aware that this is happening?" Keiran asked. "We about to have three Kings on lock down?"

"Hush you!" Maxine scolded. "Nothing is happening. Can we just go?" Maxine couldn't take any more of these annoying grins. So much for them not addressing this directly to her face.

"Hope she's not drinking anything right now." Keiran linked his arm with Cherisse. "Wouldn't want her choking."

"Shut. Up." Maxine pushed her brother out the door to speed this along.

Her stomach was churning, and she almost stumbled in her heels when she felt Victoria's hand on her back.

"Relax and have fun tonight. Don't pressure yourself about anything," Victoria ordered as she rubbed soothing circles into Maxine's back.

Easier said than done. She did plan to have fun, but that didn't stop the butterflies working overtime. She took a deep breath as Keiran and Cherisse walked around the back of the villa.

"Oh wow, it looks so pretty." Cherisse waved at the décor.

It really did. The lights added a dreamy romantic quality to the pool area. The balloons had actually remained intact and were lazily floating around the pool, adding a classic vibe to the whole area. Nice.

"Oh my God, honey! Look at you!"

Maxine tried not to cringe at her mother's loud voice, which made every damn body look over at them. Great. Maxine didn't see Remi though. Maybe she was inside.

Her mother came over and cupped her cheeks. "You look so *so* beautiful honey."

"Thanks." Had her mother already started on Reba's drink's stash? She looked way too happy to see her.

"Let me get a shot of you to send to your aunt."

"Wait, why . . .?"

Her mother didn't wait, pressing their faces together and angling her arm so she could take their photo together. She showed Maxine the phone and, okay, they did look really good. Her mother was wearing a teal, long-sleeved sequined number that stopped a bit above her knees.

"Okay, go have fun honey. Leah's being supervised by the Daniels until her bedtime so don't worry about her. You have fun!" Her mother swished away and Maxine shook her head, but she located her daughter with Remi's parents.

Leah was busy dancing with Remi's mom, giggling as Mrs. Daniels twirled her around. She assumed her brother had set up a playlist to run until he came back over. He was way too possessive of his equipment to let anyone else deal with the music. And yup, Keiran was already sliding behind the table that was set up for his DJing.

Maxine turned back to Leah, a twinge of guilt that she'd spent precious time sleeping upstairs with Remi. She was still going to keep an eye on her until she fell asleep and they could carry her upstairs. She doubted her daughter would last until midnight. But at least she knew Leah could also have a good time tonight too.

"It looks even better from the back, god *damn*." The low voice near her ear made her jump, and then her body said *oh yeah I like that*, because she felt that tone to her core.

Remi stepped around her, grinning. Shit, well, she had wanted this, hadn't she? Remi's reaction?

"Hey."

"Hmm, yes, hi." Remi sipped the drink in her hand, eyes dropping right to Maxine's chest. "You look fucking gorgeous."

"Thanks." Maxine twirled, because why not enjoy this?

Remi bit her lip. "Fuck, Maxi. You look good enough to eat. Are you even wearing anything under this?"

No bra, but definitely underwear. She couldn't go full commando, not with this hemline already threatening to show the world everything. But she could let Remi wonder about that all night.

She shrugged. "You might have to find that out yourself."

She let her eyes run over Remi's outfit. A cute swishy silver dress with a neckline that was definitely not cute. The damn thing plunged almost all the way down to Remi's navel. The choker she wore had a piece that dangled right into the space created by that deep V, the silver a bright path against her warm brown skin.

Oh fuck. Remi and chokers were dangerous for her health.

"I need a drink," Maxine blurted out.

"Me too."

"You already have one." She pointed to the cup in Remi's hand.

Remi threw back the drink like it was nothing. "Look at that, now I need another. Let's go."

Maxine walked with Remi over to the bar setup. Reba had labelled all her concoctions, so they knew what it was called but not what was in it. Maxine just assumed everything had copious amounts of alcohol.

Remi pointed at a cooler. "Try the Jello shots first. Ease into it."

Jello shots were a safe starter, but the way Remi watched her as she sucked the shot out of the little plastic cup heated her up all over.

"You can't keep doing that." she said.

"What?" Remi's smile said she knew exactly what she was doing.

"Looking at me, like this."

"Like what? Like I want to bend you over this damn table?" Remi took one of the plastic cups from the cooler, sucked the shot out, tongue chasing the last bit of it from the cup.

Oh God, she wasn't going to make it to midnight. She had worn the dress to drive Remi wild and yet she was the one losing her damn mind.

Maxine tossed her empty cup in the trash bag provided for garbage. She could beat Remi back at her own game. "If there was no one here I . . . I might let you."

"Oh yeah?" Remi asked oh so softly, stepping closer, which meant that choker was well within her grasp. All she had to do was reach out and touch.

"Yes." Her hand twitched.

"Then what?"

"Mummy!" Leah's voice was a douse of cold water to her overheating skin. She came running over with a big grin.

Maxine cleared her throat before responding, "Hey sweetie, having fun?"

Leah nodded. "Uncle Devon said he'll help me light the sparkle stick thing if I want one."

Maxine assumed she meant the sparklers.

Leah grabbed her hand. "Can we go do one now?"

"Sure."

"Auntie Remi can take a picture of us!"

Remi disposed of her empty shot cup. "Sure. Let me get my camera. I should be taking photos for real. Got a bit distracted."

Distracted was an understatement as far as Maxine was concerned. Thank God for Leah's interruption. Maxine had almost forgotten where she was.

Talking about being bent over a damn table with her family around? She had truly lost it.

She let Leah lead her over to where Devon was sitting, frowning at his phone.

"Mummy wants to light some sparkles too."

Devon's expression changed immediately as he tucked his phone away, reaching to open a pack of the sparklers. No one could resist Leah's cuteness. Even Maxi's grumpy brother. It was funny to watch.

Devon handed them each a sparkler and told Leah to be careful as he used a match to light it. The sparkler erupted to life just as Remi returned with her camera.

"Oh, this is perfect," Remi said as she caught Leah in action, a huge smile on her face as she waved her sparkler around.

It really was. Maxine snapped her own photos with her phone as Devon held her sparkler. She then gave her brother her phone and asked him to take some of her and Leah.

Without thinking about it too hard, she even took a quick photo of Remi while she was busy doing her photography thing. Then another as she smiled over at Leah. She looked so beautiful. It was obvious how much Remi loved being behind that camera.

"Interesting," Devon noted from behind her.

Shit, she had once again zoned out and forgotten she wasn't alone in her perusal of Remi. Maxine stashed her phone back into her little bag and took her sparkler back from Devon. It was halfway fizzled out already.

"What?"

"Nothing, really."

Maxine rolled her eyes. "Don't you have a girlfriend to go dance with or something."

"Hmm, defensive. Intriguing."

"God, you're annoying with that thing you like to do. I've seen you with Reba and you're just a prickly marshmallow."

Devon frowned. "That makes no damn sense."

"*You* make no damn sense."

Her brother laughed, startling the hell out of her. "God, Reba was right. Is she ever wrong?" He shook his head, a fond expression on his face and Maxine glared at him.

"*What* are you talking about?"

Devon got to his feet, adding nothing to that cryptic comment, and simply walked away.

Leah came over with her burnt-out sparkler. "Can I have another one?"

"Of course." Maxine lit another for her and looked over to where Devon was now with Reba. If even Devon was partaking in his own brand of teasing, then she definitely needed to dial it back.

As the night went on, and they got closer to midnight, Maxine tried her best not to look at Remi too much. Difficult, when all she wanted to do was find out if the extended chain of that choker wrapped around her waist too. The way it didn't just dangle against her skin but disappeared under the fabric made Maxine consider it might be a whole-body chain thing. And if that was the case, she wanted to see it against Remi's skin, free of the obstruction of fabric.

"I think I had too much of Reba's Passion Punch thing," she admitted to Victoria.

They'd both had their fill of food and drinks and were now sampling Cherisse's desserts. Maxine had decided to over indulge a little tonight, so she'd needed to sit for a bit because she was buzzing. Her skin felt like she would spark if anyone touched her right now. Well, not just anyone. A pretty someone whose long hair had come undone from her messy updo a while ago.

Victoria nodded. "Haven't we all?" She waved over to where some exuberant dancing was happening.

Leah had been put to bed upstairs already so now everyone felt comfortable to let loose. Maxine hadn't danced yet. She'd been too busy covertly checking Remi out, being aware of exactly where she was in any room.

Like right now, while she tasted Cherisse's decadent champagne-infused Panna Cotta, she tracked Remi as she danced up a storm with her bestie and Reba. Remi's dress swirled around her legs as she moved her hips.

If Remi could dance with them, so could Maxine, right? Just a bunch of gals having fun. Nothing to it. She got to her feet, slightly wobbly. Yeah, it was time to have some water, but first she needed to go do a thing.

"I'm about to make a bad decision," Maxine muttered, resting her half-eaten dessert on the table next to her.

"Finally!" Victoria giggled. "Go get herrrr."

Oh, she sure would.

The music lowered for a brief moment for Keiran to shout, "Alright people, twenty minutes before midnight!" then the beat was back up.

Maxine danced over. "Hi!"

Remi pulled away from Cherisse and Reba to give Maxine her full attention. "Well, hello beautiful."

"Don't you start." Maxine wagged her finger at Remi who just grinned back and slowly twisted her hips in time to the beat.

"What you want me to do? I can't help myself when you looking this good." Remi spun around and did a slow roll against Maxi's front.

Oh God. She was aware of everyone around her, but they were all busy having a good time. Why couldn't she? This should be a safe space. The parents would just think this was two friends having some tipsy fun, wining on each other. They wouldn't read anything else into it.

She gave into her impulse and placed her hands on either side of Remi's hips, pulled her back. Remi was taller, especially so in her heels, but she dipped low and threw her ass back, head turned so Maxine could clearly see that smirk on her lips.

The song switched to Rihanna's *Only Girl In the World* and Maxine's head jerked over to Keiran. There was no damn way he had purposefully done that, right? Her twin gave her a quick salute and went back to the turntables. This fool.

Remi's finger on her chin turning her head to look back at her gave her no choice but to focus on the stunning woman in silver again. Who was—oh shit—singing along to the lyrics as she raised her hands over her head and danced.

"You are out of your mind," Maxine whispered in between giggles. She couldn't help it. The alcohol was definitely making her feel less nervous about this.

"For you, yeah."

"You can't just say shit like that!"

Remi grabbed her hands, swinging their arms between them as she danced. "Why not?"

"B—because," Maxine sputtered, not really having a coherent thought after that.

"Get your drink, if you haven't already!" Keiran called out again. "We have a minute to go!"

"We should go grab one of those glasses of wine," Maxine suggested.

"Maybe," Remi agreed, making no move to release their hands. Instead, she kept them swaying along to the music, never breaking eye contact.

Maxine's heart was legit racing. What was Remi thinking right now? They couldn't just stand here all night. The countdown would start soon.

"Okay, here we go!" Keiran signalled. "Ten!"

"Nine!" the others shouted back.

"Remi." Maxine could easily tug her hands out of Remi's grasp, but she was too buzzed to think right now.

"Eight!"

"C'mon," Remi said finally, dragging her away from where everyone was too busy counting.

"Seven!"

She let herself be tugged because why the hell not? She couldn't do what she wanted out there anyways. Remi kept leading her through the living room, then upstairs. They could still hear everyone's shouts clearly as they walked up to the next floor where the bedrooms were.

"Four!"

Remi pushed open one of the doors to whoever's bedroom, Maxine didn't know. It wasn't the one she had put Leah to sleep in, that was all that mattered.

"I'm not letting another second go by without kissing you." Remi closed the door behind them.

"Two!"

Maxine nodded, giving in to her urge to hook her finger around that choker—finally—and pull Remi to her. "Ditto."

"One!"

Remi bent her head and captured her mouth in hers just as the shouts of "Happy New Year!" erupted downstairs.

The year was off to a great start, with Remi's hand on her ass, massaging her flesh, her tongue thrusting against hers. Maxine nibbled on Remi's bottom lip. She dragged her hands up Remi's skirt, feeling the barely-there string of her underwear that disappeared between her ass cheeks.

"We can't . . . someone's going to come looking for us soon," she groaned, but arched into Maxine's touch.

"I know." She did know that very well, but they had some time. "Just a little more, please."

"You beg so prettily. How am I gonna say no to that?"

Remi took her mouth again, deepening the kiss as she pushed up the back of Maxine's dress, hand caressing her skin.

"Ah, so you did have underwear on." She pushed the lace aside and Maxine's entire body jerked as Remi rubbed at her.

"You just said we can't."

"But you asked for more," Remi countered. "So, more it is. Quickly, of course."

Maxine was so turned on it probably wouldn't take much for her to detonate, especially with the pad of Remi's finger rubbing at her like that.

"So wet, damn." Remi sucked on Maxine's lip as she pushed her finger in a bit more. In and out as Maxine's hips chased after the motion.

"Oh fuck, please." Maxine wrapped her leg around Remi's waist, giving her easier access, opening herself up more.

A few more thrusts of Remi's finger and Maxine was groaning into her neck, grinding down on Maxi's finger.

"Happy fucking New Year to me," Remi said in her ear.

Maxine sighed, content. "Yeah, same."

They needed to get back downstairs before someone realised they were missing, but neither of them moved. They just kept breathing in sync, gazes locked.

The serotonin coursing through her body right now had her relaxed and the drinks she'd had made her feel loose. She hadn't planned to mention Victoria's idea, but words were tumbling out before she could think.

"I have a thing I want to try. New year, new ideas, right? We can't keep crashing together like this with no definitive end, you know? But there's a thing we can do to see if this makes sense. To see if we make sense without all this." She waved between them.

Remi's brow furrowed. "I don't follow."

Of course she didn't; Maxine was rambling. She was too tipsy for this. Her body was ready to slump against the nearest flat surface because that orgasm had her body, and brain, a bumbling mess.

"This wasn't the best time," she muttered. "Sorry. I'm so all over right now. But when we get back, I'll be able to put this into actual words better. I want us to know each other. Because all we do is sex right now, which I like but . . . would you do dates with me? That are not *date* dates but hang-out dates. I don't know."

Remi brushed some of Maxine's hair behind her ear, her gaze way too fond for Maxine's fragile state. "*Okay*, definitely tell me more about these dates when you're sober and we're back home, alright?"

"Yes, okay. Happy New Year again. Best I've ever had really."

"You're so cute when you're tipsy." Remi placed her hands on her shoulder turned her towards the door. "Let's get back down there."

"Yeah." She let Remi lead her back downstairs, allowed her to steal one more soft kiss before she went ahead of her to rejoin the others.

Maxine took her time to put on a neutral expression. One that didn't scream she had just gotten finger banged into the new year.

CHAPTER THIRTEEN

REMI
JANUARY

Maxi: 😫
Remi: *that bad huh?*
Maxi: *I swear my father just loves doing shit to see my reaction. Now he's telling me last minute about some photo shoot??? I swear I'm suffering vacay withdrawals. Take me baaaack*
Remi: *is that so? You'd prefer to be back in Tobago hmm?* 😜

Remi waited for Maxine's reply to that. The three dots were doing a whole lot of bouncing, but nothing was being sent. She chuckled to herself, picturing Maxine's face as she tried to come up with a response to that.

Remi couldn't help it. She wanted Maxine flustered. Their return to Trinidad had been tension-filled after their midnight kiss. Luckily, they hadn't got busted by anyone and had returned downstairs unnoticed. Remi had been buzzing all over to get Maxine alone again, but that hadn't been easy at all. Instead, she'd settled for covert glances as the festivities wore on into the early hours, and during the boat ride to Trinidad later the next day. She *had* said they would talk about whatever this "date" idea was once they had returned.

Did Maxine want to date Remi? What was all that about? She had been waiting since new year for some sort of clarity. Since then, their texts had been pretty light, no flirting, more focused on trying to determine a schedule for Remi to teach Leah some basic photography skills. Not a peep about the *not date* dates. Remi tried not to let that consume her, but she might have to outright ask if Maxine didn't bring it up.

Maybe she was having second thoughts about her idea. Whatever it was. Remi was taking her cues from Maxine and— she wouldn't lie—she had been a bit bummed to realise Maxine seemed to be keeping their conversations pretty generic, for now at least.

She had also been consumed with the idea of having Maxine in her gallery show. The timing hadn't been right to bring it up. Yet. But she was determined at least to ask. Maxine could shoot her down, but she would never know if she didn't bring up the topic. Keiran's best friend, Scott, was already on board and Remi couldn't wait to get him in front of her camera.

Cherisse had flat out said no, which was fine. There was no expectation for anyone to agree to this. It would open them up to vulnerabilities that most would prefer to leave in the dark. Besides, her bestie was way too busy with preparing for her store opening.

"We're almost there."

The voice next to her drew Remi's eyes away from her phone. Maxine still hadn't responded, but Remi didn't need her to, especially considering she was about to surprise Maxine, who hadn't a clue. She tucked her phone away as Ari pulled into the carpark. Ari Cole was one of the feature writers at

Island Bites magazine. Remi usually enjoyed working with her, so today's assignment should go smoothly.

"You all set?" Ari asked before she exited the vehicle.

Remi grinned. "Oh yeah."

Ari raised a brow at her. "What're you so happy for?"

Remi shrugged. "Can't a girl just be happy?"

"KKE big boss got a rep for being a smooth talker, and you know I detest those types. Plus, he didn't even want me to interview him for the feature cuz he's accustomed to Brent kissing his ass, so . . ."

So Ari wasn't exactly thrilled to be interviewing Maxine's father. Understandable, considering everything Remi had heard about him. But at this point she was looking forward to seeing Maxine's face when she realised Remi was here. She didn't give a damn about her father.

"Ah Ari, we both know you can handle this easy peasy."

"Whatever, let's just get this over with."

Remi saluted. "Sure thing, Boss Lady."

Ari wasn't her boss, but Remi loved to tease. Ari rolled her eyes and headed towards the building. Remi's phone dinged and she pulled it out to see that Maxine finally replied.

Maxi: *anywhere but here sounds good right about now*

A pretty basic response, but Remi didn't let that get to her. Soon, Maxine wouldn't be able to hide behind a phone and Remi grinned at the thought.

They walked up to the receptionist and gave their names. Ari went over her questions while she waited, running them by Remi who agreed they sounded thought-provoking without being prying. Their boss was friendly with Mr. King, but even Remi couldn't get away with her feature writer bringing up the man's scandalous affair. Ari had been given strict instructions to stick to safer topics.

"We're not Spotlight, so keep it strictly business. No sensationalism," Jackie had warned them both. As if Remi's photos would be scandalous in any way.

"What do you think of Mr. Head Honcho?" Ari asked. "I heard he got his daughter working for him now. I do love the sweet smell of nepotism in the morning."

"Uh." Remi didn't want to reveal to Ari that she knew Maxine. She probably should have, but she simply shrugged. "I mean, that whole blow up about his affair did *not* look good for him."

"Yeah. But we can't refer to that at all. I just hate guys like him you know. But I gotta be objective." Ari made a face. "Jackie insists on this for the music feature, but if they're friends, she may just be throwing him a bligh for some reason."

The receptionist came up to them then, letting them know they could go on up.

Remi felt her stomach flutter with excitement to see Maxine again. She pulled out her phone as they zipped up in the elevator.

Remi: *I would rescue you if I could*

Maxine's response came seconds later:

aww my knight in shining armour. Too bad you can't . . . 🙁
Remi: *stranger things have happened* 😉

"What are you smiling at again?" Ari asked.

Remi slid her a sidelong glance. "Nothing."

"Uh huh. I know that 'I'm basically swooning talking to this person' smile. But no need to spill to me. Gate keep it then." Ari pushed out her mouth.

Remi laughed. "You're happily married. You must have that all the time. Why are you even pouting right now?"

"Because I love new love."

"That's not what's happening here." But Remi's heart rate spiked at the mere thought. It wouldn't take much, would it, to allow herself just to fall?

"Hmm. If you say so."

The elevator arrived at the floor and they both exited. They were greeted by Mr. King's assistant, Tamara.

"Shall we?" Tamara asked, not even waiting for them to respond. She was clearly expecting them to follow her.

Remi took several slow inhales as they walked with Tamara. Now, she wasn't sure she *was* quite ready to see Maxine again—Ari's comment making her jittery—but she was excited to see Maxine's reaction.

~

MAXINE

MAXINE TUCKED HER PHONE AWAY AFTER REMI'S RESPONSE. IT WOULD be nice if she could come and whisk her away, but this was real life and there was no one to rescue her right now. She needed to focus on this morning's task, especially since her father had basically thrown her a curveball with this photo shoot business.

Her day had begun fine enough. She had been working in the publicity department since she had started, as, according to her father, she needed to learn different aspects of the business. She would be moving around to different units when the time came she supposed. Publicity was fine, challenging even, especially now as the Senior Publicist, Pauline Jones, was trusting her to take on more tasks with some of their artistes.

There was a music video shoot coming up for a newer singer, Shalini, who was featuring on veteran artistes' track. It was a way to introduce her to the world before her own album dropped in May. Maxine had a long to-do list for the shoot.

Although all of that was fun, A&R was really where she wanted to be, where she felt her innate talents would shine, but her father insisted she stick with Publicity for now. Fine. She would do the best damn job in this department, but she would also prove to him that she was good at spotting a diamond in the rough. She wanted to find talent waiting to be moulded.

She had done it before, even though her father had taken credit for it. Which still chafed.

She had still been a teen then, in awe of this woman who was performing her heart out at karaoke night at a community centre. Maxine had gone to her father so excited, letting him know she had found someone he should totally be reaching out to, to bring over to KKE. He had dismissed her, but the next week she had been shocked to learn he had used the bit of information she had on the woman, tracked her down and had convinced her to sign with them. Not a single word of thanks to Maxine.

When she had asked him about it, he claimed his team wouldn't care to hear that his teen daughter had been the one who had seen the woman's talent first. And that this was just how it worked in the corporate world. Who would believe a teenage girl over someone who had been in this business for years? Someone who had built his company up from nothing? No one would have taken *her* seriously, so what did it matter if he acted like he had found her first?

Maxine was still slightly toting about that years later, but whatever. She was going to show him she would excel in any team she was placed on.

Everything had been going smoothly until her father had intercepted her on the way to the kitchen.

"Maxi! Good you're back. Change in plans."

"What's happening?" she'd asked.

"You're with Tamara this morning. I have some people coming in to interview me and take some pics for my spread in *Island Bites* magazine. You'll be assisting Tam with that." He'd glanced down at his watch. "They should be here in the next fifteen or so. We're shooting in my office to start. She'll let you know what she needs help with."

"But I'm supposed to be with Pauline. We have stuff to work on for that music video," she had protested.

Maxine actually liked working with Pauline, who didn't seem to give a damn who her father was and didn't act like she wasn't supposed to have this job.

Tamara, her father's PA, was a different story all together. The woman didn't like Maxine, or that was the vibe she gave off. Maxine wished she could go back to Tobago, bask in the sun, sand, and sex. The last thought had made her flush as she'd switched destinations from the kitchen to head to her father's office to meet up with Tamara, after he had given her a hard look and said, "This job isn't cut and dry. Unexpected things come up all the time and you have to handle it."

This wrench in her plan was a test, obviously. If she couldn't hack it, she wouldn't get another chance to prove anything.

She wanted to show him she could do this, but damn if a part of her didn't crave still being on vacation. She didn't know what to do now that they were out of that cozy bubble. She had drunkenly introduced the date idea but hadn't brought it up since then. Remi had to be waiting for her to shed some light on her word vomit.

But she was chickening out now that her head was clear and they didn't have the sex haze over them anymore. Should they really try to date without sex in the mix? Would that ease her fears?

She got to the office and pushed all thoughts aside. She could figure out her tangled feelings when she actually saw Remi next.

She opened the office door and nearly stumbled in her heels. Tamara was in bossy mode, directing the photographer as to the kind of shots they wanted – which was rude as hell, as far as Maxine was concerned. Photographers usually knew how to do their jobs. And she knew first hand that this one did.

Her hair was twisted up in a messy bun, but Maxine would know Remi from behind on any occasion.

"What're you doing here?" she blurted.

It was obvious why Remi was here. She was the photographer for today's activities, but why hadn't she mentioned she was coming here today? Had Remi planned to surprise her?

"Oh, hey." Remi turned and Maxine didn't know what the hell her body was trying to do to her because her heart was definitely trying to bunji jump out of her chest, the way it was pounding like that.

How did Remi look so delectable in skinny jeans, a plain t-shirt, sneakers and not a bit of makeup on? That was entirely unfair of her.

"You didn't mention being here." She hadn't been prepared to see her this soon and definitely not at her job.

Remi grinned. "Sorry, wanted to surprise you."

"You two know each other?" Tamara asked, brow furrowed.

"Uh yeah, we do," Maxine replied.

"Okay, whatever. I'm going to get Mr. King," Tamara said. "He's not replying to my messages. Again. Hopefully your colleague should be back from the bathroom by then."

As soon as Tamara slipped out of the office, Remi's grin slipped into smirk territory. "You look nice."

What was she supposed to say to that? *Thanks, please go?* The problem wasn't Remi, it was her and her inability to act neutral around Remi.

"Thanks. I . . ." Maxine cleared her throat. "You do too."

"Me in this? Definitely can't compete with you in your work get up." Remi turned away to resume her set up.

"Thanks." Maxine stared at the stretch of Remi's t-shirt against her back. Maxine had dreamed about tracing all that lovely skin with her tongue right down to Remi's ass. Whether she would act on her fantasies was another matter.

Nope. Not doing this here at my office for, fucks sake.

"You could've told me you'd be here." So she wouldn't be this damn flustered.

She rounded her father's desk to face Remi, who was focused on her equipment. Remi glanced up, eyes briefly dipping down to the front of her shirt. Remi looked a bit dazed when her eyes flicked back up to meet Maxine's. "Focus, Remi."

"While you're wearing that shirt *and* skirt? Your ass in it is just plain rude."

"I know." It was her favourite skirt for that reason. Her ass did look amazing in it. "Look, I didn't expect to see you here and I do appreciate the surprise but a heads up would've been nice. I'm a bit thrown off here because I can't control what my body does around you, but that's on me, not you. And I feel like everyone can see that I . . ." Her face grew hot. There she went rambling again.

"You're so cute. Everyone can see what?" Remi prompted, an amused smile playing about her lips.

"That I want—"

"Let's get this show on the road!"

Maxine stepped away from Remi as her father burst into the office with Tamara and a short woman who Maxine assumed was Remi's colleague.

"Are you done daydreaming over there?"

Tamara was standing in front of her, hands on her hips, glare on full blast. She was older than Maxine, had been with KKE far longer, and as her father's Personal Assistant knew all the ins and outs of the company, but Maxine wasn't about to let Tamara make her out to be some delinquent who didn't know how to do anything.

"Actually, I was discussing with Remi about doing a couple shots outside the office. Show dad in motion, what he really does. Inside office shots are so overdone, don't you think?" Maxine smiled her brightest smile, as if Tamara wasn't trying to end her with that scowl.

"It's a really great idea actually," Remi piped up and Maxine wanted to give her a big old kiss on the lips for that.

"Sounds good to me." Her father nodded. "And you should be in some shots with me. I was thinking we can make this a sort of legacy shoot. My boys don't want anything to do with KKE, but my baby girl sure does." Her father laughed like that was the funniest thing ever.

What? That hadn't been what Maxine was suggesting. "Um . . . me?"

"Yes, of course. I pitched the idea to Ari here." He waved at the short light-skinned woman. "She's on board with it."

Ari stuck out her hand at Maxine. "Ari Cole. Looking forward to working with you. You were chatting with Remi, but I should properly introduce you."

Maxine shook Ari's hand. "Nice to meet you and no need. Remi and I know each other already."

"Oh." Ari cocked her head to the side. "She hadn't mentioned that. Great! So you should be comfy with her for the shoot."

At least that was one plus to this sudden idea. Maxine focused on Remi as she took some candid shots, while her father expounded on the up-and-coming artistes KKE was excited about. Remi was commanding without being over-bearing and was great at putting her subject at ease. It was amazing to watch.

"Maxine's been working with one of our emerging artistes, Shalini, so make sure to mention that in the article. Ready for your close up, Maxi?" her father asked.

"Um."

Her father frowned. "You want to take over some day, you're going to need to be prepared to be in the spotlight. But if you're not serious about this . . ."

Of course he didn't give a shit that he'd berated her in front of everyone. She didn't look at Remi. Didn't want to see any pity there. She would take this like a champ.

"Yes, I'm ready." What else could she say?

Even as she wished she'd added some flair to her wardrobe today, the simple white blouse and black pencil skirt was the easiest thing to throw on this morning. At least she'd washed and flat ironed her hair, and her bangs were on point. Vacation hair was long gone. She'd done some light makeup this morning too, but thanks to frolicking on the beach for a few days, she was sporting a nice sun-kissed glow.

Dammit, she'd left her favourite lipstick home. She wasn't sure about this nude colour she was rocking, and was her shirt *too* tight?

"Hey." Remi tapped her arm, gestured her over to a spot by the window. "Just want to test the lighting." As Maxine walked over, Remi asked, voice low, "You trust me?"

Maxine stared at her. On top of her panicking, Remi was asking her this now? She didn't know what to say. She'd trusted Remi with her body, but did that mean she *trusted* trusted her? And now she was just standing there way too long not saying anything.

Remi laughed, not looking offended. "I mean, do you trust me to make you look amazing? You already do, so I won't have much work. In fact, you'll probably outshine your dad in his own piece."

Oh. That's what she'd meant. "Yes, I do. Trust you. For that. Yes." Jesus, she was pathetic.

"You're beautiful. Amazing. Perfect." Remi smiled at the others. "She's ready for her close-up."

She wasn't ready. In fact, Remi's praises had left her a bit shell shocked, which she couldn't show, so she acted as if she was fine. And in a way, Remi did make the shoot as comfortable for her as she could – directing her as she took a couple snaps of them on the move through the office and in the studio, ensuring she saw every shot she took. Dropping random compliments throughout.

After a while, Maxine relaxed and things were going well, until Ari turned her questions on her.

"What made you decide to come on board with KKE now? A newfound interest in the music business?"

Maxine took a beat to collect herself. "I've always wanted this. To be a part of this business. My degree's in Music Management. When I went abroad to study, the plan was to come back to KKE. But life throws curve balls and it didn't quite work out that way." She wasn't getting into details about Leo, and their divorce. "So I'm back to jump right in. I've been around my dad and this business for years, so while I'm not exactly new to all this, it's exciting to get to learn the ropes and each facet of it, you know?"

"The Dynamic Duo." Ari nodded. "So you're being groomed to run the empire someday?"

Maxine looked over at her father. That was a hell of a loaded question. Her father could casually toss out words about her being his legacy, but he had resisted the idea for so long. He'd focused so much on the possibility of Keiran and Devon that he had never truly seen her as a viable option. It was a small miracle that he had agreed to take her on after she'd come to him with her pitch about working here.

"Well, my dad isn't going anywhere soon, and I have a lot to learn to catch up to him."

Her father laughed. "Roundabout way of saying yes. You're learning well. I for one couldn't be happier. At least *one* of my children care about KKE."

Maxine bit down hard on her lip to stop the heated defence of her brothers. The man couldn't just give a compliment without tacking that on, could he? She hated when her father acted like Keiran and Devon had abandoned him. They just wanted different things and there was nothing wrong with that. Besides, Keiran and her father working together on a daily basis? Wouldn't end well.

"Hmm." Ari drummed her fingers against her lips. "We'd love to run with that idea you pitched about a family piece. With all of you."

Had her father seriously brought that up? Maxine wished them luck in getting that off the ground. Keiran wouldn't want to be any part of that because he hadn't forgiven their father for his affair, and Devon would be ambivalent.

Maxine hadn't forgiven him either. How could she? He'd hurt their mother with his cheating. But he was a means to an end. And in the end, she wanted KKE. She was excited by the things she learned daily, but refrained from discussing work at home. It was hard to keep it all bottled inside but she had no choice. She didn't want to upset her mother by gushing about working with her asshole ex-husband.

"We'll see," her father said, like it would ever be a possibility.

While Ari wrapped up a few follow-up questions with her father and Remi packed up her equipment, Tamara came over to Maxine.

"I didn't know you had that degree."

Maxine raised a brow. "There's a lot you don't know about me. It's almost like everyone forgets I grew up with the great Alan King. I've been around music my entire life, but now you want to take me seriously because of the degree you didn't know I had?"

Tamara looked properly chastised. Good. Maybe now she could stop being a bitch to her. "Okay, that's fair. Can we start over?"

"Sure."

Maxine could hold a good grudge when necessary, but working with her father meant working with Tamara, and she did look genuinely apologetic.

By the time the shoot was over, it was lunch time. Maxine would have a quick lunch then get back to music video planning. This shoot meant she was delayed on her to-do list for today.

"Still interested in that dance class my friend runs?" Remi asked, after she'd packed away her equipment. "My friend just texted me some info about it, so I figured I'd ask."

"Oh, yeah." She'd forgotten all about that, but her initial interest had been genuine, and it sounded fun. "Can you send me all the details?"

"Of course." Remi tapped away at her phone. "Just did. It'll be fun."

"I'm sure it will be. Let me walk you out." She could spare a few minutes to see Remi off.

Ari had already taken some of the stuff to her car, so they had some privacy as they walked out.

"You can bring your mom too," Remi said. "It's a beginner class so anyone can join to get a feel for the vibe of it. See if it's something they'd want to pursue moving forward."

"I'll ask her."

"Cools. Well, I'll be in touch." Remi stopped a few inches in front a silver Lancer. The damn sun making her fabulous skin glow as she slipped on her sunglasses and threw a glorious smile Maxine's way. "You do have something to talk to me about still, right?"

"Yeah." Maxine's eyes traced the curve of Remi's cheek, right where the sun bounced off her cheekbone. God, she was beautiful and made her heart ache, among other things. She had to get back inside, before she did something reckless like reach out and trace the natural highlight the sun created on Remi's cheek. "Okay, we'll talk about *that* soon. Bye!"

"Hey, hang on." Remi chuckled as Maxine got ready to bolt. "I have to talk to you about something as well, so we'll make a nice convo of it, okay?"

"Uh, okay." What was that all about?

"It's nothing super serious, so don't look like that." Remi laughed again. "Promise. Just something I want to run by you."

"Alright. Well, I gotta go. See you." Maxine had to get out of here before her brain went into overdrive with all sorts of scenarios. She threw a quick wave and headed back inside the building, the feel of Remi's gaze scorching a path on her back.

CHAPTER FOURTEEN

REMI

THE DANCE STUDIO LOOKED THE SAME. IT HAD THE SAME WOODEN floors she and the other dancers used to skate across in their socks after practice was over, the same set of mirrors that stretched across the front. The only difference was that their old dance teacher, Ms. Ellis, wasn't in front of the class. Instead, her daughter, Kim, Remi's old dance buddy, was front and centre as her newest batch of students filtered into the room.

Remi's attention was divided between Kim, some of the others from their old crew, and the door, as people filed in. For the past few minutes, she'd been hoping to catch Maxine's familiar face. As far as she knew, Maxine was still attending the session, but Remi was antsy. Would she change her mind?

She tried not to make it obvious that she was looking out for anyone by shifting her body. Her back was to the door now, but obviously that was a ridiculous move because she could still see the door via the expanse of mirrors.

"Nervous?" Kim asked in between her stretches.

"Nah. Like riding a bike, right?"

"For sure." Kim rolled her neck, shoulder-length curls pulled up in a bun, her Ellis Dance Studio tee fit close to her curves thanks to it being knotted in the back. The black booty shorts she wore hugged her strong thick thighs and Remi chuckled as she spotted one guys' eyes widening comically after catching sight of Kim. Remi couldn't wait for Kim to run through their planned introductory routine. That guy was sure to lose it at the bouncing split.

Soca music filtered through the room via the hidden speakers and Remi ran through the routine in her head. Kim thought it would be a fun way to introduce the class to their styles by running through an old soca concert routine.

Remi was excited to get her body moving and shaking. She also wanted Maxine to see her in action. So when she spied Cherisse's glossy, bouncing pony tail and Maxine trailing in behind her, her heart triple-timed it.

She spun around as casually as she could and waltzed over to them.

"You made it!" She almost winced at her loud-ass voice. It was the furthest thing from a calm tone.

Maxine's hair was pulled back in a ponytail as well, her ever-present bangs pinned back to expose her forehead. She wore a slouchy grey crop top that fell off one shoulder, showing her sports bra underneath, and that gave Remi a delicious peek of her tummy. Plain black tights and sneakers finished the look.

"We said we'd be here, didn't we?" Cherisse quipped, smiling slightly. Her bestie must have sensed her nerves before Remi even realised that's what it was, because she yanked her into a hug and whispered, "You'll do great," before releasing her to claim a spot up front.

"My mom sends her apologies," Maxine said. "She had plans."

"It's cool," Remi assured her. As long as Maxine was here, anyone else could join whenever. "She can fall in anytime."

"Alright everyone!" Kim clapped her hands to get the class's attention. "We got a special class this evening because I finally convinced my old dance buddy to join us today." She pointed at Remi who waved as all eyes landed on her.

She hadn't been in the spotlight like this in some time. The last few years had been all about being behind a camera than in front it.

As a backup dancer, the camera operators had focused on them from time to time. She'd been splashed across some social media sites and papers. The buzz of the crowd at those events had fuelled Remi's energy on the stage and even with this class being significantly smaller, that same old feeling was coursing through her right now. Was it just because she'd missed performing? Or was the fact that Maxine was focused on her partially responsible?

No time to dwell on that because Kim was letting the class know that she, Remi and Kwesi would be running through an old routine to show them what their teachers could do.

"Let's do it." Kim grinned and Kwesi bounced on his toes.

Remi nodded as the familiar soca song blasted through the studio's speakers and she took her mark next to Kwesi.

"Like old times," he said.

"Let's give 'em a show, hmm?"

Remi put on her best performance, the old routine coming back to her easily as she took her cues from Kim and Kwesi. She was focused on her hip shaking and waist rolls, but caught glimpses of Maxine's wide eyes and open mouth as she took everything in. The finishing move was quickly approaching and Remi grinned at the others right before they all cartwheeled into a spilt and bounced in place.

The class erupted in cheers and applause and Remi, still in her spilt, leaned back to high five Kwesi, who looked smug and sweaty.

"We have to learn to do that?" someone asked from the back of the class.

Kim laughed as she got to her feet. "It's not a requirement of this class, but if you want to work up to my advanced sessions . . ." Kim winked and reached for her towel to wipe her face. "Now that we got your attention and did our warmup—."

"What the hell, that's the warmup?"

Remi chuckled at the incredulous look on one woman's face, but Kim assured her this was still a beginner's class and they'd work their way up to the fancy stuff if they wanted.

She hadn't realised she'd missed this. Going through the moves with the class in a teaching role was far different from being the one taught, but Remi was enjoying herself, especially watching as the class slowly picked up the simple moves they were learning today.

By the end of it she was truly drenched but not tired. That would come tomorrow, after she wound down from the excitement of dancing in front of others again. Why had she given it up completely? Yeah, the touring had got tiring after a while and she'd realised this path perhaps wasn't sustainable for her, but her break from dancing shouldn't have gone on for so long. She'd always been into photography too. She had so many amazing photos from tour that she had never really done anything with. She'd posted a few, but what if she incorporated them in her Inner series somehow? Get Kim and Kwesi on board to be a part of it, too?

"You good over here?" Kim asked as she came over.

"I'm having an epiphany. I need you and Kwesi."

"Tell me more."

Remi gushed about her idea. It wasn't even fully fleshed out, but capturing them in motion juxtaposed against some old shots from their past life. Holy shit it would be amazing.

"Girl, you're practically vibrating right now and I'm down for it." Kim waved at Kwesi who had been ambushed by a bunch of students gushing about how great the class was and how eager they were for next week's session. "I'm sure Kwes won't mind either. You're really helping us out here so tit for tat and all that."

"Thank you. I'll let you know, yeah!"

Remi had a few students coming over to her as well. She high fived a couple of people who'd asked when they'd be learning the split bounce.

"Baby steps," Remi said, joking with them until they said their goodbyes.

Cherisse and Maxine came over as Remi was wiping her face with a towel and guzzling water to rehydrate.

"Damn, you still got it." Cherisse bumped shoulders with her, and Remi grinned and buffed her nails against her shoulder.

"Obviously."

"The class was amazing." Maxine was glowing, her cheeks rosy as she shot Remi her fabulous smile. Remi focused on that instead of the way her now sweaty top was clinging to her chest. *Simmer down girl.* Maxine stretched until she was up on her toes, then came back down and Remi was proud of herself. Her tongue didn't actually unfold out of her mouth like that cartoon wolf. "My body's probably not gonna love me tomorrow, but so worth it," Maxine continued as if she hadn't just robbed Remi of breath with that casual move.

"I bet a good massage would do wonders right now."

Cherisse looked amused and Maxine blinked at her once. Twice. Oh wait. She hadn't meant to imply that *she* was offering to massage Maxine. She'd only meant in general. She wouldn't outright tease Maxine in public with Kim and Kwesi around like that, knowing how uncomfortable Maxine could be.

Cherisse had given Remi massages after a lot of her performances in the past and that was what she was getting at.

"I wasn't . . ." she cleared her throat. "I didn't mean me. I meant in general?"

"Oh. Right." Maxine fiddled with the ends of her t-shirt.

"Yup."

"Cool."

Cherisse rolled her eyes. "I give good massages if you're ever in need."

"She really does," Remi added. "Like damn, after you're just drifting on a delicious cloud." Maxine's gaze turned speculative and Remi could guess where her thoughts went. "Strictly platonic. No happy ending or anything." God, she needed to stop talking and get out of here.

Cherisse snorted and Maxine flushed even more. Her ears were legitimately turning red. Remi had never actually seen that happen in person. To anyone. It was cute.

"I wasn't implying anything," Maxine said.

"Yeah, of course I didn't think you were. Not really."

"Okay, we should go." Cherisse gave Remi a pointed look, just shy of her usual you-need-to-stop-talking-now look.

It usually worked. Cherisse was great at reeling her in. But this time Remi chose not to exit this slowly escalating awkwardness. Maxine *did* owe her some explanations about her date ramblings, and the way she was on a high with her show ideas, she needed to ask Maxine if she would be a part of it.

"Dinner? Would you like to get some? With me?"

Cherisse sighed.

Maxine bit her bottom lip, her teeth worrying the plump flesh as if she was truly pondering it. "I mean I *am* hungry. What do you have in mind?" Maxine turned to Cherisse and

Remi knew she was about to recruit her bestie in some sort of chaperone mode, but Cherisse wasn't her best friend for nothing.

Cherisse let loose a loud, jaw-cracking yawn. "I better get going. Enjoy your dinner!" She tossed them a wave and breezed out the studio before Maxine could even get a single word out.

Remi did a mental fist bump of glory, which was short-lived as she realised Maxine might not want to be alone with her. "If you don't want it to be just us, I can invite Kim and Kwesi," she offered.

She craved alone time with Maxine always, and in her estimation, a casual dinner didn't have to be made into a bigger deal than it was, but Maxine's feelings, whatever they may be, were valid.

"No, it's fine. Really. I'm not scared to eat alone with you or anything. I didn't mean to imply that. You just make me nervous. Not in a bad way," she added. "In an 'I keep thinking about you in a sexy way'," she said, voice lowered so it wouldn't carry beyond them.

"Oh."

Maxine's smile was shy. "Yeah."

Satisfaction sizzled through her entire body, but Remi remained calm. "We'll just get food and go our separate ways then, okay? No pressure to do anything else. We can talk about both our ideas, too?"

"Yeah, I did just drop that on you then didn't say a thing, huh?" Maxine sighed, a soft sound that went right to Remi's heart and spoke of how much this was weighing on Maxine. "I don't know how to do this."

"Simple really. We decide on what food we want and we order it."

"Not what I meant." But it earned her a smile.

"You're steering this ship, Maxi. I'm taking my cues from you."

Maxine shook her head. "That's a lot of power to give me."

Remi closed the space between them a fraction. "I am *100%* okay with you taking the lead. Any way you want. Understand?"

"Yeah." Maxine sounded breathless. "I get you. I'll . . . keep it in mind."

"Good." Remi stepped back. "Now, what're we gonna eat?"

CHAPTER FIFTEEN
MAXINE

THEY'D DECIDED ON SUSHI AND SOMEHOW ENDED UP BACK AT MAXINE'S house. Somehow. Right. Like her brain hadn't figured this dinner would be easier at home because her family was there. Less chance for her to do something reckless like straddle Remi on the couch.

Her mother was in her room. Leah was sleeping—Maxine had peeked in on her when they'd arrived back to the house—and Keiran was holed up in his studio. But her so-called plan had backfired. Regardless of the house not being empty, this was still too cozy – lounging in Maxine's living room with the sushi and some random Netflix movie on that neither of them were watching because they were both too busy talking about the class.

"I still can't believe I never knew you could dance like that. You all were so damn good." Maxine had been enthralled watching Remi. Everyone was good just as she'd said, but Remi was so captivating.

"Thanks. I shouldn't have given it up totally."

"Why did you?"

Remi shrugged. "Touring isn't easy. It gets tiring and I didn't think that's what I wanted for a full-time career. I just sort of fell into it. So when I took my break, I never went back to it professionally. I fell back on something else I was good at and figured would be more sustainable. Dancing and touring like that isn't easy on the body."

"It blows my mind that you had this whole other skill I never knew about."

"Well, we didn't really allow ourselves to give a damn about each other outside of always fighting," she reminded her.

Wasn't that the damn truth. Maxine's younger self would never have imagined they'd be sitting talking in her house like this.

"Do you think they still have the cricket club?" Remi asked, dipping her sushi lightly in soy sauce before bringing it up to her mouth, chopsticks never faltering.

Maxine shouldn't be surprised by the question, but her heart raced all the same. Any discussion about their school days automatically steered the conversation into potentially discussing the night that had changed their relationship forever.

Danger danger danger

Maxine shook away the imaginary sirens. Friends did this all the time. Discuss fond memories of school. Except they'd been rivals in school. Not friends. And then the lines had become wobbly, which had made everything confusing.

They hadn't taken the time to learn truly each other. Victoria's question came back to her again: *How well do you two know each other?*

Not well enough yet, a tiny voice in her head taunted. *Because you're too busy having sex to do that.*

Now was a good time to introduce the idea she'd been mulling over ever since Victoria's suggestions. But she wasn't sure how to bring it up, even though Remi was clearly curious and waiting for her to say something about it.

"I don't know," she said finally. "Can't be that hard to find out." She pulled out her phone to Google their old school, and for something to do besides letting her nerves rattle her.

You're an adult. You can have dinner with the woman you've had sex with. People do it all the time. It's not that hard.

Except it was, especially when Remi scooted nearer to get a better look at the phone when Maxine held it up. They'd both showered at the studio and Remi smelled like the lavender body wash. Maxine tried to focus on the phone as Remi pressed more into her side to see the screen fully.

"She's still there!" Remi sounded surprised as a picture of their old coach appeared on the screen. "She always acted like we'd send her to an early grave, so I figured she wouldn't stay much longer."

"Coach loved us. Well, most times," Maxine added, ignoring that Remi was practically draped over her side, her unbound hair brushing Maxine's thigh.

She willed herself to be calm as she imagined turning to Remi. Their faces would probably be too close, given how Remi was sitting now. She'd play with a glossy curl and use it to pull Remi closer. Maybe.

"Hmm," Remi hummed. "We were terrible," she admitted.

Maxine nodded, keeping her gaze on the phone. It was true. They hadn't made it easy on Coach Lane at all. Especially since Remi and Maxine's respective crews were always arguing over some shit, their coach caught in between their squabbling. How they hadn't been kicked off the team was a miracle. Maxine figured Coach couldn't afford to lose good players—and they were that, no cockiness involved, just facts—so she'd swallowed her frustrations and not booted them.

"Yeah," Maxine said when she could find her voice.

"We should visit her sometime. Let her see we didn't turn out as horrible as expected."

Maxine turned to Remi and laughed, ready to make a joke about redeeming themselves with Coach, but all the words died away. Remi's face was just as close as she'd expected. It wouldn't take much for her to give in to this too-large thing simmering between them.

"We should." She echoed Remi's words instead. But she sort of croaked it out, because Remi's gaze had definitely dipped down to her lips. God. She grabbed up another Dragon Roll and popped it into her mouth. Anything to break the tension.

Remi's lips curved up. "It's a deal then."

She hadn't gone back to her space, she was still sitting too close, long legs stretched out, toes wiggling as she made herself even more comfortable.

God, even her toes are pretty, Maxine thought.

"Thanks. It's China Glaze Lubu Heels, my fave colour."

Oh no. She'd said that out loud? Heat rose up her neck and Maxine gripped her chopsticks, not looking at Remi. Perhaps her embarrassment would just engulf her entirely, let her go up in flames and blow her ashes right out the door so she wouldn't have to deal with this.

"I can loan you the colour if you want." Remi went on, acting like Maxine hadn't just made a fool of herself.

"Sure," was all she could manage.

Jesus, talk about being a mess. She should refocus on the TV because it was better than looking at Remi.

"It would look nice on you. You have pretty toes too." Maxine found herself leaning forward as if there was this invisible string between them. "Pretty everything really," Remi added.

"Remi . . ."

"Is that food?"

Maxine jerked back, heart pounding so frikking hard in her chest. They both peered up at Keiran who came shuffling into the living room, looking bleary eyed and dishevelled, his classic deep-in-the-studio look.

Maxine said nothing, sliding her remaining rolls his way, hoping to distract Keiran from noticing what he had almost walked in on. He gladly accepted it, eyes casually observing them as he chewed. Maxine gave him a warning look. Hopefully he understood how much he would regret making any annoying comments about Remi being here.

"So." He stuffed a tempura roll in his mouth, chewed, swallowed. "How was dance?"

"Cherisse didn't tell you?" Maxine narrowed her eyes, unsure what Keiran's angle was. She'd given him food but that didn't mean he wouldn't tease. She'd done enough of that with him and Cherisse a couple months ago. He had to be itching to reciprocate.

"I'm sure she did but I haven't checked my phone yet."

"Maybe you should."

"In a bit." He finished off his last roll and came to sit across from them on the chair, smile annoyingly cheerful. "So, class was good?"

"Yes, great. Super fun. Don't you have music magic to make?"

Keiran stretched and Remi released a tiny sound that sounded like a snort, but she couldn't be sure. When she finally allowed herself to glance over at Remi, her lips were rolled inward, not quite supressing her smile.

"I'm taking a break. I mean, I could leave you two to your . . . date?"

She was going to kill him. It would be nice not to have to share her birthdays anymore. Before she could *deny deny deny*, Remi leaned forward, smile oh so sweet, and said, "Keiran, may I remind you that I basically saved your ass with Cherisse? Don't play with fire here."

Keiran rolled his eyes but got to his feet and mumbled about needing to get back to the studio before leaving them alone.

Maxine's gaze swung to Remi. "*What* the hell was that?"

Remi leaned back. "I'm not saying I paid your bro a visit when that whole thing with Cherisse blew up in his face, but yup, I am. He owes me."

Maxine chuckled. "Keiran means well, but siblings. Always gotta be annoying."

"It's cool. I know this isn't a date anyways. Or you didn't want it to be a *date* date? And well, since we're talking about dates and all . . ."

Right. It was the perfect lead into her half-baked idea. "I . . ." Maxine faltered. She took a deep breath. "I think we should stop having sex."

"Oh. Hmm." Remi leaned away from her, maybe to give her space, because she thought her comment meant she wasn't comfortable being that close now. "That's . . . okay. Can't say I expected that."

"This is what I was trying to explain in Tobago. I want to see if we can actually get to know each other. Without sex clouding everything. I can't just keep fooling around without considering if we could be serious."

Remi blinked at her and, oh God, Maxine was ready to expire on the spot. Had she read too much into this? What if Remi had only wanted sex from her, and now, here Maxine came talking about being serious.

"Of course, if you didn't even want it to go there, just pretend I never said anything." Maxine covered her face. "Oh God, I'm literally going to . . ."

She felt Remi's hand on hers, gently trying to tug her hand away from her face. "Hey."

She let Remi pull her hand away so she could see her face. The smile she saw on Remi's face reassured her a bit.

She knew she had surprised her there with the no sex comment.

"Talk to me."

She inhaled deeply again then released in all in a big whoosh before she took the plunge. "I think we should try dating. Going on dates. See if we are compatible outside the bedroom. We know we connect physically, but that can't only be it. That could fizzle and then what do we have? *If* we wanted this to go further, that is."

"You want us to date? Why would you think I'd be against that?"

Maxine shrugged. "I don't know; we didn't talk about it at all. We just kept . . . you know." She wiggled her hand to encompass everything they had done since she'd come back.

The kissing. Touching. Getting each other off.

Remi nodded. "I get you. You have more at stake here than I do. But what will these dates entail? Can they be romantic? Or just like friend dates?"

Maxine nodded. "I was thinking we decide on a number of dates that can show a side of each other that we may not have known about. So, they can be a mix of friend and romantic, but without the physical intimacy aspect of it. Maybe we can try it out until the Sweethand opening so it gives us time to do this. Would you *want* to do that?" she asked.

Remi popped her last roll in her mouth and smiled. "With you? Of course. Especially since we got that year-long membership pass from Ava's wedding. Spa dates are the best date."

"Yeah, but there's more." Maxine didn't know how Remi would react to this part, but it was a requirement to prove they could do this. "If we give in and do get physical during that time, the dates get reset. So, if we're at number three and we uh . . . kiss . . . we're back to one. If we get to our deadline and haven't met the required amount of dates, it means we failed at this."

"Damn, Maxi, you're not going to make this easy."

"It shouldn't be."

"True. But how many dates would we do?"

Maxine hadn't settled on that yet. The opening was in May, which gave them about four months. How many dates was enough for them to know they were ready to do this for real? "Ten? Twenty? That would be five dates each month?"

"That could be doable," Remi agreed. "But we can decide to revisit that as we go along. There's actually a Sip and Paint coming up in Trincity. Ava told me about it. Could be fun."

Maxine had always wanted to do one of those. That did sound like a good time. "I'd be down for that."

She also wanted to learn more about Remi. They'd missed years of each other's lives and Maxine was eager for every little thing Remi revealed about herself. And what better way to do that than dates? Hopefully they could do this without any resets. They hadn't been the best about resisting each other thus far. But there hadn't been a countdown hanging over their heads either.

"Okay it's a date," Remi winked. Her accompanying smile was glorious as always. If only Maxine could bottle that smile and pull it out whenever she got sad or way into her head. But how did one capture a ray of sunshine like that?

They didn't. Besides, it could never compare to the real thing, could it?

"I'll text you details." Remi rose to her feet. "I should get going. Early morning gym session before work."

"I don't know how you do it."

Remi curled her arm. "These guns don't craft themselves," she said.

Maxine tried so hard not to stare at her toned bicep. She'd never felt the urge to bite that particular curve of muscle before, but she was beginning to realise Remi made her feel so many new sensations. She shook herself. She had to be stronger than this if they were going to succeed at this plan.

Maxine walked Remi the few short steps to the door. When Remi turned to say her goodbyes, she remembered Remi had also wanted to talk to her about something.

"Wait we didn't even talk about your thing."

"It's fine. We can do that at our first date."

"Well, see you then."

Remi gave her one thorough, scorching look before she took the deepest breath and said, "Yeah, see you." Before stepping out the door.

Maxine closed the door and leaned against it, gently knocking her forehead against the wood.

God and all the angels help her survive Remi Daniels and make it to May without giving into temptation.

CHAPTER SIXTEEN

REMI

HAVING TO STARE AT PHOTOS OF MAXINE FOR HER JOB WAS AN excellent way to start the day. Remi's fitness instructor had been extra brutal with her this morning and everything was deliciously sore. Looking over the photos from the shoot at King Kong Entertainment was a balm for her aching muscles.

Maxine had been so nervous about being photographed, but she had done well. The camera loved her, and Remi had done her best to make sure she was at ease. Maxine had relaxed after a while and her natural beauty just shone through all the pictures. It was tough to keep a neutral mask firmly in place as she scrolled through the reel on her work computer.

She would love to bring out another side of her for the gallery show. They would definitely talk about it at their first date. A little thrill ran through her at the thought. She hadn't anticipated Maxine's plan at all. Dating Maxine—even if there was a no sex allowed rule and no guarantee that she would agree for them to be a couple at the end—was exciting. She had to consider every activity she could plan for Maxine that would help her see who Remi was and that they *could* fit together.

"Oh, damn, *who* is that?"

Remi whirled around at the intrusion. "God damn, don't you knock?"

"I did?" Mackenzie, one of the layout designers for *Island Bites*, and the most annoying co-worker she'd ever had the displeasure of working with, leaned closer to the screen.

"It's polite to wait for someone to actually acknowledge you and give permission to enter."

"What's the big deal? Not like you were watching porn. Although," he smirked at the screen, "those lips are sinful."

Remi counted to three. She was working on her reactions where Mac was concerned. The man just didn't get personal space was a thing. "Don't be gross."

"Who is she?"

"Alan King's daughter. We're putting her in the feature as well."

"You think she's single?"

"Not for you." Remi was so close to saying that she was dating Maxine and telling Mac to fuck off. But that wasn't his business.

Mac cocked a hip against her desk and folded his arms. Remi was so close to stabbing him in the leg with a pen, but she needed this job and also didn't fancy jail time. So deep, calming breaths it was.

"Why not? You called dibs?"

Yeah, she fucking called dibs, but that would be a shitty thing to say. "She's an actual person. Not property. You can't just call dibs. Plus, she has standards."

Mac clutched his chest, pretended to be wounded. "Wow, you really don't like me, do you?"

Don't answer that, don't answer ...

"I have to finish narrowing these down." She waved at her screen where Maxine was still displayed next to her father. She'd had a pen in her hand and it had, at some point, reached her mouth as she appeared deep in thought. Remi hadn't been able to stop herself from capturing that. She wasn't certain they'd use it for the feature, but she'd planned to save it and send it to Maxine. Or just keep it for her personal stash.

"Whatever. Look, I came in here in the first place because Jackie wanted to meet with you."

"Why didn't you say that when you came in here?"

Mac waved at the screen. "Got distracted. Anyways, she's in the Sunflower Room."

Getting distracted by Maxine wasn't something Remi could usually fault anyone for, but Mac was too fucking annoying of a person for her to brush that off.

"Next time, deliver your message and get out." She locked her computer—no telling if skeevy Mac might actually try to steal photos of Maxine off there to do God knows what—and got to her feet.

"So rude."

Remi towered over Mac. "Don't care." She gave him the staredown until he swiftly exited, then she made her way to the Sunflower Room, named for the bright yellow colour of the walls. Each room was named after some kind of flower and reflected that in the chosen paint colour.

Jackie Lane, their editor-in-chief, was busily typing away on her laptop when Remi entered. She looked up. "Have a seat. I'll just be a sec," she said as her fingers flew over the keyboard.

Remi sat opposite and waited, thoughts ping-ponging around her skull. That Sip and Paint event was coming up. Her first date with Maxine. It consumed her.

"Remi." Jackie was done typing, and observed her with those shrewd eyes that Remi always felt saw everything.

Maybe she did. Jackie had been head of this magazine a long time and had been a journalist before that. She had various connections in the media/publishing world and Remi was grateful she wasn't stingy with her expertise. Remi truly enjoyed working at *Island Bites*. While she didn't have anything to do with the copy-editing side, she always listened when Jackie spoke about publishing in general. It couldn't hurt to soak up some of that knowledge.

Jackie tugged on her headwrap then leaned back in her chair. "Ari tells me you're friends with Maxine King?"

Huh, okay, she hadn't anticipated that line of questioning. What did Maxine have to do with anything. "Yeah, we are."

"Good, Alan has agreed to give us exclusive behind-the-scenes of promo activities for one of their new artistes, Shalini. Apparently, Maxine is working closely with her. I want you on this project so Maxine would feel comfortable being a part of the shoot too."

"Oh?" Well, this was interesting. "Shouldn't the focus be on the new artiste? What does Maxine have to do with this?"

Jackie propped her chin in her hands. "She intrigues me. Alan and I have known each other a long time but he never mentioned his daughter studied Music Management. I had no idea. If she's set to take over after her father retires, I want to get ahead of subtly positioning her as an up-and-coming player on the scene, before someone else scoops us. The focus will still be Shalini while we get the public familiar with Maxine."

Remi didn't know how Maxine would feel about this. She hadn't been excited to be a part of the shoot with her father. "Her father is going to advise her of this I assume?"

"Oh yeah. I just need you to be your charming self and soothe any nerves. Since you two are good like that. I'm firming up the timelines with Alan so you'll get an update when I do. I believe he mentioned an album launch in a few months too."

Any opportunity to work with Maxine was a plus as far as she was concerned. Remi was good at what she did and would make sure she got the best photos of Maxine, and, well, Shalini of course, who was really the focus.

"Sounds good."

"Excellent. How're the pieces for the show going?"

"They're going." Not the most confident-sounding response but she hoped Jackie would just think it was her being coy.

"The gallery is pretty excited about it and expect a good showing. I know it'll be amazing."

She appreciated Jackie's support and definitely needed to get her shit together because she couldn't let Jackie down. Besides, her boss' reputation was on the line too, since she had been the catalyst for all of this. And the gallery was going on her word that Remi wouldn't be a flop.

"I already have a few pieces done and some other shoots scheduled." Not to mention she needed to convince a certain King to pose for her. "As for today's shoot, I'll send you my photo picks out of the batch."

"I trust your eye, so I'm sure we'll be on the same page." Jackie went back to her laptop and Remi exited the room.

She tried to settle back down to stare at the photos for Alan's feature. She had been too engrossed in Maxi's, when she wasn't the main feature. She needed to choose the best ones with her father.

Her focus didn't even last a minute because her phone chimed and Maxine's name popped up on her screen.

Maxi: *Hiya! So . . . I know it's super last minute but Leah wants to have a photo session with you this Saturday. I don't know what your plans are but I told her I'd ask. She says she'll personally prepare a whole picnic for us at the Botanical Gardens if you say yes. She wants to know what kind of cupcakes you like?? LOL*

Remi couldn't help but smile at that. Pretty convenient since she was free anyhow.

> **Remi:** *who's making these cupcakes?* 👀
> **Maxi:** *apparently she's already asked Cherisse to help so you're safe. I swear I had no idea she was such a lil' planner* 😂
> **Remi:** *hmm, tell her to surprise me on the cupcakes. I trust my bestie with my life*
> **Maxi:** *oh you'll do it? You sure you're not busy?*
> **Remi:** *if this is like a pre-date date then I'm definitely free :P*
> **Maxi:** *it's not one of our dates ma'am. It doesn't count. Don't try to cheat the system* 😉
> **Remi:** *fine *pouts**
> **Maxi:** *okie. Thanks for being so accommodating. Enjoy the rest of your day* 😊
> **Remi:** *thanks you too. See you Saturday* 📷

Well then. Looks like the universe was on her side. Her fingers itched to type more but Maxi had effectively ended the conversation. It was still a workday after all. She was probably busy, and Remi really shouldn't be getting unfocused like this.

"Okay, girl, get your ass in a gear. She's all yours on Saturday," she muttered to herself. It wasn't a romantic picnic, but she expected them to have a great time. Just being in Maxine's presence brightened her day.

She grinned at what Leah's potential picnic would entail. And she was definitely going to get some cute photos of Maxine too. A win for her, really.

CHAPTER SEVENTEEN

MAXINE

"So, THIS ISN'T A DATE?"

Maxine choked on her tea as Cherisse watched her, amused. "No. Why would you . . .? Did *she* say it was?"

There was no doubt in her mind that Remi had shared their date plan with Cherisse. Why else would she ask that? Maxine told Victoria because it was her plan after all. But she hadn't mentioned anything to Keiran yet because what if they failed spectacularly at this? Maxine would rather see how the first few dates went before she said anything to anyone else.

"Well, no, she didn't." Cherisse waved at the cupcakes cooling on the counter ready to be popped into the picnic basket with the rest of the items. "But this is pretty cute for a *not* date."

"That's all Leah. I didn't do any of this."

Cherisse didn't look like she was buying it. If it had just been the two of them going to the Botanical Gardens with a whole picnic vibe, Maxine could see how anyone would get the wrong idea. But she truly hadn't even thought of a picnic. It was Leah's idea,. It *would* have made a cute date for her and Remi, though. Maybe they could still have one, just the two of them.

Leah had put a lot of thought into this. She'd asked Maxine to arrange with Cherisse to come over early to help her do the cupcakes. Leah had looked extra cute in her little apron, following Cherisse's instructions exactly. The cookies-and-cream cupcakes they'd baked were Remi's favourite, according to Cherisse. Maxine hadn't known that, so thanks to her daughter she had a new thing to file away about Remi.

Cherisse raised a brow. "She did mention you two would be doing *friend* dates, though, so this isn't that either?"

"Well, I mean, I wouldn't say it is? It's really about Leah learning some photography tricks and tips. It's not about me at all."

"The way she was tearing through her wardrobe looking for the perfect outfit says otherwise, but I'll take your word for it. Although, I probably shouldn't have told you that."

Oh, Cherisse was good. No wonder Keiran was such a goner for her. She had built her entire baking business around her sweet persona, but she truly had a little calculating streak under there. She had to know mentioning that Remi had been frantically trying to decide on what to wear would pique Maxine's curiosity.

Maxine sipped her tea, refusing to take the bait. She had dressed quite comfortably in denim shorts and a t-shirt. Cute and comfy. No makeup. Now, she wondered what Remi had decided on. Should she have made more of an effort? Maybe she had some lip gloss in her bag somewhere that she could put on. God, was she going to make it through this photography lesson?

Maxine drained her tea, rinsed out her mug and placed it on the drying rack. "We should probably get going?"

"Isn't Remi picking you up?"

Right, shit. She couldn't even recall why she had agreed to that. "Uh, yeah. I forgot. So used to driving myself."

"Can't relate," Cherisse said laughing. "But Remi's a good driver, so don't worry."

Maxine didn't doubt it. Was there anything Remi wasn't good at? Photography. Dancing. Fitness stuff. Driving Maxine out of her damn mind without even trying. Yeah, that last one. She was *so* damn good at that.

Cherisse leaned against the counter, lips quirked up in a tiny smirk. "Also, it's very date-ish of her to be picking you up, but what do I know?"

Leah bounced into the kitchen, stopping Maxine from responding. "Mummy, Auntie Remi is here! Let's go!" She reached for the basket, but Maxine shooed her away.

"I got it, sweetie. I'll add the cupcakes and we'll go, okay?"

"Okay. Thank you Auntie Cherry for helping!"

Cherisse beamed down at Leah. "Anything for my lil' bestie."

"Excuse me, are you trading me in for someone younger already?" Remi walked in, holding her hand to her heart for dramatic effect. "Damn, that hurt!"

Leah giggled, just as as Maxine paused in the middle of adding the cupcakes to the basket. Remi looked super cute in short denim overalls with a white sleeveless top underneath. Her thick curls were confined to a long French braid down her back.

Maxine hoped Remi was too busy pretend pouting at Cherisse to notice that she had almost dropped one of the cupcakes. This look was also casual and cute. Just like her own. So why was she acting as if Remi had just strutted in here naked?

Cherisse grinned. "She's cuter than you, so . . ."

Remi shook her head. "Can't even argue with that." Her gaze swung to Maxine. "Hey."

"Hi."

Cherisse looked back and forth between them. "You're matching. Well, isn't that just adorable. You should take a selfie together or something."

Maxine closed the lid of the basket. "Don't you have a boyfriend to go harass?"

"Nah, not today. I have to be at the bakery with the workmen and Keiran is in music cocoon mode." Cherisse leaned across the island. "Right now, I'm totally free to bother you two."

"We should get going anyhow, so good luck with that plan." She wasn't going to stick around any longer for Cherisse to have fun at her expense.

"Yes!" Leah agreed.

Remi pointed at the basket. "Want me to take that?"

"No, no. I'm good. My muscles may not be as big as yours, but I got it." She mentally face-palmed herself. Had she really just said that?

Remi laughed and then proceeded to flex said muscles. Damn, Maxine had never wanted to bite into a bicep this much. Lord, she needed help.

"Me and my muscles are here if needed. But alrighty, let's roll. Later, C."

Maxine waved at Cherisse who was giving them a wide grin that was way too similar to her brother's for her liking. She knew couples did end up mimicking some habits over time, but she wasn't liking this one damn bit. They hadn't even been together that long. How annoying.

Conversation on the way to the gardens was mostly Leah's excited chatter from the back seat while Remi threw occasional smiles at her. As they drove around the Queen's Park Savannah, Remi nudged Maxine.

"I'm curious about what's in the basket? Since you wouldn't even let me touch it."

"It's not about that. I know I'm not Miss Fitness buff over here, but I can carry a picnic basket," Maxine whispered, careful that Leah didn't hear their conversation.

"Ah yes, me and my big muscles."

Maxine's face got hot. She was hoping Remi would strike that moment from her memory, or at least have the decency to pretend it hadn't happened. How was she supposed to redeem herself here?

Remi chuckled. "Hey, don't stress. Feel free to appreciate my muscles anytime. I work hard for them."

"Yeah, no kidding. Just thinking about your workout routine makes me sweat." In more ways than one. Her brain took her back to that bathroom when Remi lifted her up on that counter. Oh so effortlessly. "I'm sure it's really hard and advanced," she added, unnecessarily. Just in case that came off like an innuendo or something.

Because they should be dialling back on the flirting.

Remi found a place to park outside the gardens and tossed her a blinding smile, whispering, "I can show you how I build up that sweat anytime."

Maxine didn't get a chance to say anything before Remi got out the car and opened the door for Leah to hop out.

The Botanical Gardens wasn't packed on a Saturday. There were people around at the zoo next door and those coming from their early morning walk up Lady Chancellor Hill. They had their choice of where to set up. Maxine spread the blanket under one of the trees that were blooming these pretty red flowers. She had no idea what type they were, but she snapped a photo as soon as she set down the basket. It would make for a lovely Instagram post.

Remi took off her sneakers with one hand, her camera in the other.

"Mummy can I take off my shoes too?" Leah asked.

"Sure." That didn't sound like a bad idea so Maxine did the same.

Remi wiggled her feet as she looked around. "I like to get down and dirty when I'm shooting. Which I should have told you, actually." She eyed Leah speculatively. "But she should be fine in her jeans and that tee if we have to lay on the grass to get a shot. But your call."

Maxine opened the basket. "It's fine. Do your thing. You want anything from here before you get down to business?"

Leah bounced up and down. "I made mini sandwiches and there's some fruit. And pineapple chow, which is also a fruit but different from the other fruit cuz no spicy stuff on it. There's water and juice too. And the cupcakes Auntie Cherry helped me make! Your fave ones."

Remi plopped down next to Maxine, legs outstretched. "I'm definitely trying something before we start. Gotta have our energy up."

"Yes!" Leah answered excitedly.

They munched on their sandwiches and fruit. Maxine suggested they leave the cupcakes for after the session to have something sweet to finish on. She noticed Remi glance at Leah briefly before looking away, as if stopping herself from saying whatever it is she wanted to say.

Maxine couldn't help her chuckle. Remi probably wanted to reply with some innuendo-filled statement but with Leah around . . . yeah, no.

Thank God, because she was trying her best here. Even though they had agreed to try this friend thing, she was only so strong, and had needs, dammit. Could she really be blamed if they tossed their agreement out the window?

It also didn't help that her father had told her on Friday that he had given some exclusive access to Shalini's activities to *Island Bites*. He'd also explained that she was to be included in behind-the-scenes photos as well. He hadn't said a thing about who the photographer was, but Maxine could ask Remi. She seemed to be their main when it came to shoots, but given they would have schedules that overlapped, she obviously wasn't the only one.

If she was the one working on this project, apart from their dates, they would be working together as well.

Remi cleared her throat and got to her feet after finishing up her fruit. "Ready to roll when you are."

Maxine would ask her about it after. This was Leah's moment. Leah jumped up excitedly, following Remi as she explained again how to hold the camera before going into some basic tips. Remi's teaching style was easy to follow. She would explain, then show Leah on the camera and have Leah repeat what she showed her, to ensure she understood what Remi was explaining.

And Remi was patient. Whether she knew it or not, her style was definitely effective with Leah, who was excited to hold the camera and put everything into practice. Maxine was a bit anxious about Leah using Remi's camera because it was probably very expensive, but if Remi wasn't fussing, she shouldn't be having mini panic attacks about it.

"Remember how I said the different shutter speeds will affect how your image will appear?" Remi asked. Leah nodded. "Great. It's also one of the things that affects the brightness of your photo. Let's take a look at how all these things will come together with a subject that moves." Remi looked over at her. "Maxi, if you don't mind being our muse for a sec?"

"Sure." She got to her feet. "What do you want me to do?"

"Just move around. You can do like you're dancing maybe? We're going to test the long shutter speeds and see our results."

Maxine felt heat rush to her face. This was to help Leah learn. So what if it would be awkward to prance around and pretend to dance in front of Remi? She did this kind of silly thing with Leah at home all the time. They'd had their own little dance parties and pretended to be ballerinas on numerous occasions. Besides, Remi was probably used to this. Maxine assumed she had to instruct her subjects to do odd things all the time.

She started off swaying gently, hyper aware of Remi showing Leah how to do whatever thing they had to with the camera to test shutter speeds. Eventually, she picked up the pace, starting twirling and jumping around for real.

"That's great!" Remi called out. "Keep doing that."

"Very good mummy. You're doing great!" Leah's voice joined Remi's and Maxine giggled.

She didn't mind the praises one bit. She'd continue to be silly, just to hear the compliments. She eased up on the twirling so she wouldn't make herself too dizzy, using the opportunity to properly focus on her photographers. Leah was showing Remi her results, and Remi was nodding back. Maxine was curious now.

"Can I take a look?" she called out, her motions now down to her just swaying gently side to side.

"Of course."

Leah showed her the camera and Maxine raised a brow at the image on the screen. "It's kinda blurry, isn't it?"

"Yup! It's motion blur," Leah said confidently, grin wide.

"If your shutter speed is long, subjects moving in your photo will appear blurred along the direction of motion." Remi pointed to where Maxine's arms were a blur in the photo. "See?"

"So that's how you do it. Now we know your secrets." Maxine winked playfully.

"Hardly a secret. Just a basic photography tip, but feel free to wink at me any time." Remi waggled her brows.

Maxine placed her hands on her hips, shaking her head. "You promised."

"Hey, *you* winked at *me* first. I have a weakness for winking women. Or maybe it's just you, I don't know." She shrugged, which didn't make her words land any softer. Seriously, how could she just say stuff like that?

"Remi . . ."

"Anyhooo," Remi interrupted, tossing Maxine a grin. "Lemme get back to Leah."

Maxine went back to the blanket and picked up her phone. She had a few messages from different people. She decided to reply to Victoria first.

> **Victoria:** *so how goes it?* 👁️👄👁️
> **Maxine:** *the combination of these emoji are creepy, you know that right?*
> **Victoria:** *I don't give a damn. tell meeee how your non date date is goiiiiing? I'm booored*
> **Maxine:** 🙄 *you and Cherisse are the same. Smh! What do you expect to happen in the botanical gardens huh? With my daughter here?*
> **Victoria:** *so you're telling me you're both being super chill. Zero sexual tension or flirting? You're taking this friends date pact seriously? #disappointed*

That wasn't entirely true, but Maxine didn't feel like getting into it at the moment. They could have that discussion face to face next time they met up.

> **Maxine:** *you make it sound like I have no control. We're keeping it cool as cucumbers.*
> **Victoria:** *god you are such a mom. Who says cool as cucumbers??* 🫠

Maxine: *whatever, you have no faith in me*
Victoria: *not true. I mean I know I suggested it but now I'm like past Victoria why did you even say this when your friend could be getting her* 🐱 *ate on the regular??? It's one thing if you didn't know how Remi's tongue game was but you already know so . . . have fun missing out on that I guess* 😏
Maxine: *YOU ARE A TERIRBLE FRIEND*
Maxine: **TERRIBLE*

"Hey."

Maxine fumbled her phone, heart racing as she looked up at Remi, who was watching her, amused.

"I'm letting Leah do her thing without me hovering, so if you don't mind my company?" Remi gestured to the phone in her hand. "Or I can come back."

"No, no I'm good. Was just talking to Victoria."

"Tell her I said hi."

There was no way in hell Maxine was returning to that conversation with Remi around. "Later." She tucked her phone away in her bag and gave Remi her full attention. Putting all thoughts of anything getting eaten way in the back of her mind. "I did want to ask you something."

"Yeah?"

"I had an interesting convo with my dad yesterday." She plucked a blade of grass out of the ground, twirled it around. "He said *Island Bites* will have the exclusive on some behind-the-scenes of one of our artistes, Shalini. We're getting ready to do some promo for her debut."

Remi smiled. "Mmhmm."

"You don't look surprised." Maxine narrowed her eyes.

"Cuz I already know. I do work there," she said, clearly playing coy. Remi's grin was filled with amusement.

"It's you, isn't it? The photographer on the project?"

"Guilty. I didn't want to say anything until I knew your father had told you."

Maxine brushed the piece of grass against her thigh. "He didn't say who the photographer was, but I'm glad it's you. Again, he wants me to be in the actual photos, so it helps to have a familiar face to work with."

"I'll make it fun, don't worry," Remi promised.

"Oh yeah. Shalini's so talented. We're preparing for a music video she's doing with a veteran singer. She's featuring on his new song. I won't say who yet."

"C'mon, don't I get some date perks?"

Maxine mimed zipping her lips and shook her head. "Nope. Sorry. Maybe when we're on our actual date I'll drop a hint."

"Fine. Be that way. I wanted to ask something too, but I'll leave that for our date as well."

Maxine folded her arm. "Now that's not fair."

"It's nothing, really."

Maxine didn't believe that for a second. Remi actually looked nervous as she reached up to fiddle with her braid, but she kept her eyes trained on Maxine. "Really? Unless I have something on my face, you're staring me down pretty hard for just nothing."

Remi shrugged. "Have you seen your face? Who could blame me?"

"Don't be cute. You're deflecting. Tell meee."

Remi looked around, moved closer to Maxine as if she didn't want anyone to overhear. "Nope," she said, making Maxine push her away playfully. Remi busted out laughing.

"Alright fine, don't tell me." Maxine pouted. She leaned in close too. "You know. I have my ways of finding things out."

"Hey, this is playing dirty."

"Mmmhmm. Don't you like that? When I play dirty?"

"This is really unfair . . . what the hell, Maxi?" Remi looked over at Leah who was still busy having fun with the camera.

Maxine grabbed the buckle of Remi's overalls, tugged gently so she would focus on her. "Leah's fine. You sure you don't want to tell me now?"

"This is a breach of our deal."

"Is it?" Maxine kept tugging on the buckle.

This was playing with fire. She knew she could easily slip from having the upper hand to being the one getting all hot and bothered. But it was too much fun to see Remi flustered. Maxine didn't do this enough. Remi could stand to be a little unbalanced every so often.

"You are a cruel woman," Remi whispered.

Maxine released her hold on Remi just as Leah came over. "I can be when it suits me. We'll talk about this *nothing* later, yeah?"

Remi didn't get to reply as Leah handed her the camera and said they should have some of the cupcakes now.

Maxine grinned over the top of her cupcake. Remi would tell her whatever this "nothing" was soon enough, but in the meantime, she could make it a teensy bit harder to keep mum about it. She had to channel her frustration over not giving into her desires somewhere. What better way than a little harmless teasing?

CHAPTER EIGHTEEN
REMI
FEBRUARY

Maxine: *might I offer this cute puppy in exchange for the nothing you didn't want to tell me last week?*

Remi grinned down at her phone. Maxine had been sending her cute gifs and photos all week, but she wasn't budging. Tonight was their Sip and Paint date. She would bring it up then with the help of a little wine. But that would be later. Right now, she was a bit frazzled trying to sort the photos for her show that she had already taken into some sort of cohesive theme.

She had a few months left still, but somehow February had creeped up on her and she felt like she didn't know what she was doing. She didn't want to screw this up.

She reached for her phone to reply to Maxine, figuring she would get back to sorting as soon as she texted, but her eyes widened as she saw Maxine's latest message.

Maxine: *ok, what about this one? So nice and fluffy. I knowww you wanna pet her right??* 😊

Included with the message was a photo of Maxine, and Remi swallowed hard. Fuck. Red lace and skin, practically in her face. Yeah, she wanted to pet the lace-covered pussy that was right there because *Jesus fucking Christ.*

> **Remi:** *fuck this is . . . really playing dirty O_O*
> **Maxine:** *oh shit shit I didn't mean to post that. OMG. Wrong pic!! I was supposed to send this dog pic not this one.*

Before Remi could reply, Maxine had deleted the message and Remi hadn't even gotten to save the damn photo because she had been too shocked. Now it was replaced by a fluffy puppy with its tongue hanging out its mouth. Cute indeed, but Remi wanted the other photo back, dammit!

> **Remi:** *so why do you have that photo hmm??? You deleted but it's burned into my mind cuz god damn you're gawjus!*
> **Maxine:** *this is embarrassing! Luckily it was you I sent to by accident. I bought a new set and took a pic of myself in it. Shit I should delete from my phone in case . . .*
> **Remi:** *wait you telling me you have sexy pics like these on your phone??*
> **Maxine:** *I will not confirm that.*
> **Remi:** *wear it later*

She hadn't meant to make that sound like a command, but fuck, if she couldn't help herself. The lace surely would have done the trick because she had been ready to call Maxine right then and beg her to be her muse.

> **Remi:** *I mean you should if you want to you know. Sorry. That was too much right?*

Maxine: *it made me a little hot, not gonna lie but let's move on from my underwear please. Focus on the puppy*

Yeah, that wasn't happening. No damn dog was going to make her forget what she saw. The lace prettily covering everything she wanted to touch and taste. Even though she couldn't—because they had agreed to focus on learning each other. She wasn't opposed to that, but fuck, this was going to be challenging.

She had to get back to choosing her photos and calm herself for this evening.

Remi: *I'll leave you be after you nearly gave me a heart attack. See you later. Nothing shall be revealed until then. :P*

She placed her phone away from her and manoeuvred her mouse over to the folder where she had uploaded Leah's photos from last Saturday. Another thing she hadn't gotten to yet. Maybe a quick peek couldn't hurt before she got back to her work.

Leah had really taken to the lessons, so she wanted to give real feedback and show her that she was taking this seriously, even though she had insisted it was free of charge. Maxine had been trying to fight her on that, but Remi wasn't budging.

Remi stopped as she came upon one she hadn't even known Leah had taken. It was of her and Maxine sitting on the blanket looking at each other. Wow, Leah had captured the moment when Maxine had grabbed the buckle on Remi's jumper. Leah had probably thought this was just them goofing around, but anyone else could probably—definitely—tell some flirting was going on here.

This one was going in her private not-to-be-posted-anywhere stash. It was so candid and sweet it kind of hurt.

She'd send it to Maxine as well, but it would have been perfect for her "Inner" series if she had set up the shot herself. There was so much damn emotion on display here.

"That's cute."

Remi jumped, nearly toppling back in her chair. "What the heck? When did you even get here?" She pressed her hand to her chest.

Cherisse grinned down at her. "Not too long ago. You were clearly too busy swooning over this to hear me."

"I wasn't swooning," she protested weakly because they both knew she was.

"Tell me again why you're doing this trial dating count-down thing when you're both looking at each other like that?" Cherisse waved at the evidence on the screen. "Just date for real."

Remi sighed, watching Cherisse as she took her stuff into the kitchen. She had returned from a meeting with a client for a catering gig. Something to do with providing the desserts for an exclusive fete. Remi couldn't recall which one. With Carnival coming up in March, Cherisse was booked and busy.

"I don't want to pressure her into anything when she's trying to figure stuff out. You know that."

"I know," Cherisse said from the kitchen. It was an open floor plan so Remi could see her from here. "Look, I'm not a part of the community, so I don't know what she's going through, but I can't help worrying for you, you know. I know how much you care about her, and I know what you want. But does *she* know?"

"That's the whole point of the dates. To figure out if we can really do this. If it's more than just lust, you know? I know what I feel but we haven't tried actually dating. I want to prove to her that I'm taking this seriously and show her I'm the right choice.

THE DATING COUNTDOWN 193

That I'm not just someone good for sex. It's fine, really," she added, because Cherisse didn't look convinced.

It wasn't totally. Remi was worried that at the end of the dates—or even before they got to that point—that Maxine would realise doing this with Remi just wasn't worth the potential hassle. Cherisse saw through her bullshit, but what was she supposed to do? Get down on her knees and beg Maxine to be with her romantically? No, she was going to use these dates to seduce her in another way. Show her how good they could be as a couple.

Cherisse tsked. "Okay, if you say so. I love you and I just don't want you to get hurt. That's all."

"I hear you."

She got Cherisse's concerns, but was it so bad that Maxine wanted them to get to know each other without all this tension and lust overshadowing everything? She didn't think so.

She looked at Leah's photo. She hoped for a particular outcome from these dates, but she couldn't force Maxine's hand. What *would* she do if Cherisse's concerns were right and at the end of this Maxine decided they were better off as friends?

These thoughts were bumming her out. As much as she kept saying to Cherisse she would roll with whatever, the truth was she wasn't sure she could. But that was her problem, wasn't it?

"What you wearing to this friend thing later?" Cherisse asked. Her bestie knew her well. The change in topic was meant to take her away from spiralling.

Remi drummed her fingers against her lips, her mind cycling through her closet. "Maybe not something white since paints are involved and all."

"Pretty sure you get aprons, but I guess better to be safe than sorry." Cherisse snapped her fingers. "Don't you have that red top? Could be cute. We're in the heart month after all."

"Hmm." Her brain flashed back to Maxine's accidental photo. Would she actually wear the sexy set tonight? Not that she would get to see it, but . . . "I'll figure it out. What're you and Keiran doing for your first V-day?"

Cherisse shrugged. "I don't know. I've been so tired with the planning for the opening and all these gigs. By the way, I got comps to one of those fetes. Maybe you and Maxi can tag along? Perfect place to test the friendship with a bumper backing up on you." She grinned as she started singing one of the songs on a riddim Keiran had produced.

Remi rolled her eyes. "In spite of your lack of support here, yes, I'll take the comps. Even though I'll actually be sent to some fetes on assignment for *Island Bites*. You know I don't say no to free ting. Now lemme go sort out my outfit."

By the time evening rolled around she had decided to go with simple but chic. Skin-tight jeans with a sleeveless black body suit tucked in. She left her hair down because she didn't want to wrestle it into an updo. Besides, she knew Maxine loved when her hair was wild and free like this. She had caught onto that fact early on. She was all about respecting Maxine's wishes with the date thing, but that didn't mean she wasn't subtly going to use her charms on her.

Her phone beeped and Remi smiled at Maxine's message that she was five minutes out. Maxine had told her she was picking her up tonight. Fine by Remi. She hadn't had the chance to be driven by Maxine yet and she was looking forward to it. It was their first date after all.

She was about to put her phone away when a WhatsApp came through from Sanaa:

> *enjoy your date! *Non-sexy time seduction mode on**
> **Remi:** *please find something constructive to do tonight*
> **Sanaa:** *already got plans* 😉

Remi: maybe you should try a non-sexy time seduction plan
Sanaa: LOL no I'm good. I'm not depriving myself of pussy cuz your pathetic romantic ass is in love and agreed to this doomed from the start plan. But enjoy!
Remi: wow you suck
Sanaa: tonight I plan to yup 😊

Remi exited the chat. Excitement and nervousness bubbled in her chest. She didn't care what Sanaa said. This wasn't doomed. They were going to do this. She wasn't some sex-crazed person who couldn't go without for four months. She would succeed in this. Even though she couldn't help the natural flirting that came out around Maxine, that didn't mean she was incapable of resisting.

She had just finished lacing up her boots when Maxine texted again that she was outside.

"Hey." Maxine greeted her, gaze lingering as Remi got into the passenger seat.

Remi smiled. "Hey yourself. You look nice." Maxine was wearing a yellow dress with red flowers on it, and she couldn't wait to get a better look at it when they arrived at the Sip and Paint session. She'd be able to appreciate how it clung to Maxine's curves mmhmm.

There was no rule against appreciating how amazing Maxine looked in this dress.

"Thanks." Maxine drove away from the apartment complex. "Hope it works for the country club vibe."

"Oh, it definitely works." The event had actually been organised by Ava's mother-in-law, who was rolling in money, so it was being held at the fancy-ass Millennium Lakes Golf and Country Club.

Remi had never set foot in this particular club and was intrigued. Thanks to Ava they'd been getting to experience these places.

"Considering it's Carnival time, it's super busy." Maxine pursed her lips. It would take them at least an hour to get to the venue, so conversation naturally flowed to discussing work.

"But everything is a learning experience. It's been fun preparing the artistes for their various interviews and gigs."

"Cherisse got some comps to some fetes, but I imagine you would be getting some as well. I might also work some of the events, so I'm sure we'll get to play as hard as we're working."

"You done know!" Maxine reached out with her palm up and Remi high fived her. "Gotta have some perks for dealing with my father who is annoying as hell most days. He's all about the tough love." Maxine's hands gripped the wheel. "But you know what? It motivates me to prove to him, even more, that I can do this."

Remi reached out, lightly patted Maxine on her shoulder. "Don't worry. All this work-week stress is gonna be painted right out."

"The wine's gonna help too." Maxine pointed.

"Thought you didn't drink much?" It was the one thing she had noticed about Maxine while they had been in Tobago.

"I don't overindulge much, but wine is a weakness."

"Mental note to stock my apartment with more wine," Remi joked. "But I feel you. A glass of wine is magic after a tough day, yeah?"

Maxine nodded. "Definitely."

It would also do wonders in boosting her courage to ask Maxine to be her muse. Apart from the date jitters, that had been an additional concern. Should she bring it up tonight? What if it ruined their date? Remi looked ahead as Maxine took the turn off to head to Trincity. She would assess how things were going then decide if she was going through with this or not.

Ava met them at the entrance of the building looking gorgeous and glowy as usual. Married life clearly suited her.

"Hey ladies! Look at you all. So cute!"

They exchanged hugs and followed her around the side where Remi could see some long tables set up in the spacious garden area. The lights strung overhead gave everything a romantic ambiance. There were a few other persons milling about, chatting, inspecting the table décor and set up.

"You're looking amazing yourself. Must be all that good loving and money," Remi teased, winking as Ava giggled.

"Well, it sure doesn't hurt. But don't let my mother-in-law hear that last part." She led them over to say a quick hello to Eric's mom before guiding them to their seat. Each person had their mini canvas, brushes and paints set up for them. Remi supposed the sip part would come once they started.

"I hope the painting isn't anything too hard." Maxine picked up one of the brushes, turning it over in her hand. Under the soft glow of these lights she looked so enchanting.

As Remi had expected, the dress kissed Maxine's curves as she walked, the bottom of it swirling around her wedges. Remi's eyes had zeroed in on the subtle slit at the side of the dress.

"We'll be failing together if it is. I don't have a single talent for this sort of art." She picked up her phone. "Want me to take a pic of you with the lights? It's a perfect shot right here."

Maxine smiled. "Sure. Send it to me after. We can take a selfie too if you want." She brushed down her bangs, even though they were perfectly in place, then posed with a slight smile.

Remi took several shots, because one was never enough, before moving her chair closer so they could take the selfie. She didn't know what scent Maxine was wearing but she smelled amazing. She always did.

She took some more photos of the decor. She would post them on her socials later as the teacher was getting ready to show them what they would be working on tonight.

Halfway through the session and a few glasses of the fancy wine later—white for Maxine and red for her—Remi couldn't help the loud snort that escaped.

"Oh shit, this is bad."

Maxine looked over at her painting. "It's not that . . . terrible."

Remi pointed her brush at her. "You hesitated. Why aren't my colours blending like yours? It's all . . . hmmm . . . how to even describe this mess?"

"Remember the teacher said everyone can make it their own, so it doesn't have to look like the original." Maxine dabbed some colour onto her canvas.

Her flowers looked great. Remi's looked like unrecognisable blobs.

"Eh, we'll just say it's an abstract representation. Anyhoo, I'm ready to satisfy your curiosity and ask you the thing." It was now or never. If she waited too long, she might never work up the courage.

Maxine put down her brush and picked up her wine glass. "Ask me."

Remi leaned in and said softly, "But first, tell me. Do your undies match the flowers on your dress?"

"Remi!" Maxine's tone strove to be a warning, and yet she was biting her bottom lip.

"Sorry, sorry. You know I'm a curious sort and *whoo* this wine is potent. But okay, real question time now." Maybe she should have some water before she did something foolish like blurt out her feelings or something. "I have a gallery showing coming up. My boss got me the in, and while I have some photos I know I can use for it, I'm still looking for that main something. My muse. I think it's you."

"*Me?*"

"Yes, you. You're everything I want." Remi took a long drink from her glass. "For the, uh, show, I meant. Obviously."

"Okay."

"Okay yes? Or okay this is really fucking weird?"

"I don't really know what to say. Why me, other than the obvious reasons?"

Remi frowned. Things were a bit fuzzy at the moment. They had brought out some finger foods to soak up the wine but that wasn't doing much for Remi at this point. These fancy places and their artfully prepared food wasn't going to fill anybody. She had still captured the dishes to post later, because when would she get to set foot in a place like this again? Unless it was for work.

"What do you mean? Why not you?"

Maxine slid her hand over her bangs again. "You don't have to include me in things just because you want to sleep with me."

"Wait, now *hold* on. Even if I didn't want to fuck you, I'd still think you'd be perfect for this." Remi didn't like what Maxine was blatantly assuming at all. "If I only cared about sex, why would I even be here? Doing this? It's our first date and that's what you're saying?"

Maxine's nails tapped against her wine glass. "Sorry. You're right. I'm a bit on edge, I'll admit. I haven't been on any kind of date in a while. That was unfair of me but . . ." Maxine shrugged. "I'm just me. I'm not exactly muse-worthy."

Remi knew without a doubt that damn ex of hers was to blame. Maxine hadn't mentioned him, but Remi could bet everything she had in her bank account that Leo had told Maxine some shit along the way that had her like this.

"You are exactly who I need for this. Real talk. No pussy-tinted glasses or anything."

Maxine sputtered and looked around to ensure no one had heard that. Remi didn't care at the moment.

"God, you are so . . ." Maxine shook her head, but at least she was smiling now. None of that sad look in her eyes.

Remi grinned, reached out and gave Maxine's thigh a friendly reassuring squeeze. She didn't think about how she wanted to swipe aside that slit in the fabric so she could have a nice view of her soft thigh. Nope. Nothing to see here. Just your average friendly, platonic touching.

"Say yes. Maybe?"

Maxine went back to her painting. "I'll think about it. It would be outside my comfort zone, but maybe that's what I need. Do I have to show my face?"

Remi kept her gaze on Maxine's profile. Her own painting was a lost cause anyhow. "I have some suggestions, but I don't want anything to look too directed. If you get what I mean. So, you don't *have* to show your face if you don't want to."

"Hmm, okay. We'll see."

It wasn't a yes, but it also wasn't a hard no. Remi wanted to do a little dance, but kept it cool. When the teacher came over to ask how things were going, Remi couldn't even suppress her smile.

"The art is questionable, but it's a nice night all the same."

"Beauty's in the eye of the beholder, isn't it?" the teacher said, and Remi didn't know about that where her painting was concerned, but for her maybe muse? Oh yes, definitely.

She was going to ensure that if Maxine said yes, every single eye that looked upon whatever result she got from her was going to see her beauty. If Maxine didn't see how amazing she was, Remi was going to make it her personal mission to make her aware.

They finished up their paintings and the teacher corralled everyone into a group shot while holding up their art. Remi was going to find somewhere in the apartment to stash hers—far away from anyone's eyes. She couldn't have this poor attempt clashing with her photos that she had framed and up on her walls.

"It's really not that bad," Maxine insisted. "Besides, it was fun, wasn't it? Learning that we are both not good at this?"

Remi snorted. "Yeah, no. *I'm* not good at this. Yours is pretty."

Maxine twirled her canvas round and round. "Do you want to take a photo of us with our masterpieces? We've never posted anything together on any of our accounts."

Remi paused. "You'd be okay with that?"

"Yeah. Why not? It's just a photo."

True. It didn't mean it was some sort of declaration. Anyone seeing it would simply think it was two friends out having a fun time together.

Instead of taking it themselves, they asked Ava to help. Remi made a funny face while pointing to her painting. When she checked the phone after Ava handed it back to Maxine, she couldn't help her laugh. Maxine had also made a face in one of the photos. Cute.

"Do any pass your professional eyes?" Maxine asked as she scrolled through.

"Use the one with the cute face." It was the perfect memory from their first date.

"Alright."

Maxine showed her the caption she wanted to use and the hashtags. ***When the art is questionable but the artists are cute. #SipAndPaint #WeTried #TheWineWasPerfectThough***

"Oh, that's good."

Maxine beamed at her before going back to her phone to post and tag Remi. Remi couldn't help her responding grin. Their night was quickly coming to an end and she was trying to think up an excuse for them not to have to part ways.

She was too silent on the ride back to her apartment. The music in the car was the only sound as Maxine drove away from the club. But her mind was racing. She considered the date a success, but she didn't know what Maxine thought. She could just ask, but damn, she was afraid of what the feedback would be.

Maxine hummed along to the music and Remi just basked in that until she pulled up to her apartment and they both got out.

"Thank you for inviting me tonight. It was nice," Maxine said as she walked beside her to the door.

"You didn't have to walk me up."

"What kind of date would I be if I just let you out and drove off?"

"Do you want to come inside?" Remi wished she could take back the invitation the moment it slipped out. Maxine fiddled with the ends of her hair. Dammit, she probably thought Remi was asking her to come in with the hope that it could lead to fooling around.

"Not to *do* anything. Just if you wanted to, you know . . ." she trailed off.

"Thank you, but no. I don't think it's a good idea." Maxine's smile was gentle. She didn't appear upset, but Remi was mentally kicking herself.

She had simply wanted to go in so they could keep talking. But Maxine was right. Probably not the best idea at the moment.

"Maybe next time?"

"For sure."

Maxine threw a thumb over her shoulder. "I'm gonna go."

"Yeah. Message me when you get home." She watched her walk back to her car and didn't close the door until she was sure

Maxine was safely in and buckled up. She popped her horn once then drove off.

Remi shut the door and shook her head. She had fumbled that. Had she always been this pathetic at dates? Definitely not. But this was different. She felt it. This wasn't just any rando she had chosen to go out with. It was Maxine.

"You are such a loser, my God," she chastised herself.

She made a promise right there and then. She was going to be better for the next one. Use her words. Actually be clear on what she was saying, because obviously she couldn't have expected Maxine to know what her motive was. Geez.

She went about her process of organising for bed, reminding herself that she couldn't fail at this. Too much was at stake.

CHAPTER NINETEEN

MAXINE

SHE HAD MADE A MISTAKE.

When Remi had asked her to be her muse at the sip and paint, she had been shocked. What could she possibly have to offer Remi for her series? Even after Remi had told her a bit more about what she wanted to achieve, Maxine still didn't think she was right as her muse. But in the brief moments she got to breathe during the hectic workday, it was the only thing she could think about.

Remi had made it sound like she was worthy of the title, even as doubt crowded her mind—even as she could hear the remnants of Leo's snarky voice asking her why she felt she needed to be anything other than a mother?

But she did contain multitudes. She could be a mother, a rising somebody at King Kong Entertainment and now maybe Remi's muse.

She'd agreed to do it, but now she was in Remi's studio, she wondered if she had bitten off more than she could chew. They'd agreed to do some test shots before getting into it so Maxine could feel comfortable in front the camera. The studio venue thankfully gave them some privacy. She wouldn't feel comfortable doing something in a public space. But it was *not* going well. She was tense as fuck and even though Remi wasn't making her feel bad about it, she could see a bit of frustration bleeding through her patience.

"Alright wait, I have an idea." Remi drummed her fingers against her lips. "The series is about no barriers, showcasing the most organic you. When do you feel the most uninhibited, like you can just let go without a single care in the world?"

"After a few glasses of wine," Maxine joked.

Remi's eyes narrowed as if in deep thought. After about a minute, she refocused on Maxine. "Okay, hold on a sec, I'll be right back."

Maxine blinked as Remi left her in the room. She hadn't been able to focus on the photos around her when they'd arrived, only on the fact that she was really doing this – posing for Remi. It had felt too intimate, even as she couldn't get herself together enough to produce any good results.

But now she wandered over the giant blown-up shots of a woman in motion. It was only as she was right up to the photo that she realised it was Remi, in various dance poses. Some had the blur effect she had been showing to Leah. But still her dance lines showed through.

There were several of her in just a simple pair of boy shorts and sports bra, the muscle beneath her thighs, stomach and arms flexing as she moved, but the ones that really caught her eyes were of her in a sari. The skirt flared around her, one leg raised while the other was planted firmly. The look on her face was pure bliss. Maxine wondered what she had been thinking in that moment.

It was clear that Remi loved dancing. Maxine lamented that she had never known of that love when they were teenagers. Even though they hadn't been friends then and were always bickering, she wondered what knowing a Remi who was passionate about dance would have been like. Possibly for the best. She might have developed a crush if they had been closer, which would have made it harder to leave.

She drank in every aspect of the photo. It was a stunning shot, so much so that she couldn't help herself from getting her phone and snapping a photo of it.

"Don't go sharing that anywhere. It would ruin the surprise for the gallery showing," Remi's voice said from behind her.

Maxine jumped and spun around. "Sorry, I didn't mean to . . ."

"It's okay. It's my fave too." Remi raised the plastic bag she had in her hand. "I brought liquid encouragement and snacks. I took these shots myself. Just put on the timer and I pretended the camera wasn't there. I want to experiment a bit with something similar for you."

She removed a couple bottles from the bag and Maxine's eyebrow went up.

"You tryna get me drunk?" she asked, spying the wine.

"We'll both be drinking, so I guess, yeah? I've never shot anything tipsy before, so we'll try both things, the timer shots and me shooting. We'll both be loosened up and see how it goes. You down for experimenting?"

It sounded unorthodox as hell and a terrible idea. Did Maxine want to risk lowering her inhibitions? It might be great for getting her to relax enough not to be nervous about being photographed, but could she resist throwing herself at Remi?

The potential for a date reset was greater with wine. She never thought they would be here. Hell, Maxine couldn't have fathomed she would be divorced either, which just proved life could only be planned to an extent.

"Let's see how it goes," Maxine said, cautious but willing to prove she could do this. "What snacks you got?"

The salty snacks didn't do a damn thing to curb the tipsiness. By the time they were one bottle down, Maxine was a whole lot looser and was doing her thing in front the camera that Remi had set up with the timer on.

She didn't know if Remi was getting anything useful because she wasn't saying much, just silently watching, but Maxine didn't care. She felt great and kind of warm. She reached to tug down the waist band of her shorts.

"Wait! Hold on, you sure about this?" Remi finally spoke up.

Maxine shimmied out of the pants. "Hmm, yes, just angle it so you can't see my face."

Remi came over to adjust the camera. Why the hell not just go for it? She giggled as she tried to kick her shorts away, but they got stuck on her foot. "Oopsie. You know I've never done this. Leo tried to get me to take sexy photos and videos but I've always been paranoid they'd get out somehow. He didn't think I was being very adventurous, but look at me now!"

"Yeah, fuck, look at you." Remi's voice was low, but it carried.

"I heard thaaat," Maxine sang as she turned her back to the camera, ass fully on display since she was wearing a thong today. Remi was seeing everything, but so what. People did tastefully sexy photos all the time and they didn't have any problem being professional. Her ass was nice, wasn't it? If Remi tried to grip her cheeks, all her dimpled flesh would be overflowing in her hands, wouldn't it. Remi had nice strong hands.

Maxine giggled at her not very platonic thoughts. She looked over her shoulder to where Remi was just standing there. Staring. Oh yeah, she liked that. She enjoyed the way Remi looked like she wanted to come over and do exactly what Maxine had been imagining. Touching and squeezing. Maybe a little nibble or two.

Damn, she felt her core throb at that. She turned around. "I feel hot." Her finger dipped below the waist band of her thong.

"Yeah, you are. So fucking hot like this."

"I like you watching me," she admitted. Remi wanted her inhibitions lowered, so here they were.

"Maxi, maybe we should take a break. Drink some water. Regroup for the next . . . oh *fuck*."

Maxine smirked as the curse fell from Remi's lips. She had lowered herself to the ground and spread her legs wide. Her thong was definitely clinging to her core obscenely.

"I can't use this. Any of it. It's too . . ."

"Explicit?" she asked innocently.

Remi stalked over to her. "I didn't reset the timer, so it didn't go off anyhow, but no, I'm not sharing this with any damn body."

"Oh?" Maxine looked up at her, pouting. "But why? You wanted this from me, yes? Not to think too much. Be more relaxed."

Remi's grip on her thighs wasn't exactly bruising but it wasn't gentle either. Maxine was supposed to be guiding them back to safer ground. The friend dates had been her idea, right? But damn if she cared about anything else except the way Remi licked her lips just then.

"I want to taste you, so fucking bad."

"Yes." She tugged the crotch of her panties to the side and Remi groaned, closing her eyes briefly.

"We're both high right now. We shouldn't. We just agreed to your plan."

"I'll do it myself if you don't want to." She rubbed at her clit. "I'm so wet you can probably hear me if I just finger myself huh? Wouldn't that sound nice?"

"How the fuck did we get here?" Remi muttered but she opened her eyes and watched as Maxine pleasured herself.

She didn't stay a silent observer for much longer though, going down to her knees and gently removing Maxine's hand so she could replace it with her tongue.

"Mmm, yes." She spread her legs as far as they could go, giving Remi all the access she needed.

How had they gotten here indeed? With Remi licking her way inside and Maxine moving her hips to meet every feel of her tongue.

"Oh fuck," she whispered as Remi's tongue went deeper, fucking into her so damn good.

She imagined a photo of them like this. Remi on her knees, Maxine's head thrown back and panting as she wriggled her hips. Wouldn't it be an interesting representation of "Inner" indeed?

Not that she would actually do that, but the thought of it made her hotter as Remi continued to eat her out vigorously, alternating between licks and her tongue moving in and out of her. She completely lost it when she felt a finger rubbing at her puckered hole right before just the tip dipped inside.

She shattered completely, clenching down on Remi's tongue and finger as she came. She was on Remi before she could say anything. Moving so she could straddle her.

"Whoa, easy there." Remi chuckled but Maxine just wanted to kiss her.

Remi licked her way into her mouth and they both groaned as Maxine reached under Remi's top to knead at her tits.

Maxine pulled back a bit. "Let me go down on you please?" She hadn't done it yet, but she wanted to now. God, she wanted.

"You sure?" Remi asked.

"Yes, so sure. I want to taste you." She kept up her gentle squeezing at Remi's flesh, thumb moving over her taut nipple too.

Maxine moved down Remi's body, kissing at her stomach, licking at her skin before going for her pants. She had never done this before, but she was so turned on and wanted to make Remi feel good too. Plus, her curiosity had been getting the better of her. She hadn't told Remi, hadn't told anyone actually, not even Victoria, but she'd dreamt about this. Kissing Remi down there, tasting, making her come all over her face.

Fuck. She was so close to where she wanted to be. She tugged Remi's sweatpants down until she got to the simple black underwear beneath. She rubbed her thumb over the damn crotch. Oh yes, Remi was wet. Perfection. She peeled the underwear down slowly, looking up to catch Remi's reaction. She was watching her intently, teeth pressed into her bottom lip.

Maxine grinned. "Keep watching," she said as she rubbed at Remi's bare flesh.

"God damn. Maxi."

They were so far across the platonic line right now, but Maxine couldn't muster up a single care. She was too buzzed and horny to remember why she had agreed to that plan in the first place. She leaned in and licked at Remi, cataloguing the feel and taste of her against her tongue. Remi's hands found their way into her hair and she thrust her hips up, legs spread even wider. Maxine wanted her to come undone, shatter into a million pieces knowing she had done that.

She alternated between licking and thrusting her tongue inside that warm, wet flesh, drinking up the moans that fell from Remi's lips.

"Please, please, please," Remi chanted above her, and luckily for them both Maxine knew just what she needed.

She brought a single finger in to play along with her tongue, pushing it in and out slowly as she kept flicking her tongue. Remi's grip on her hair tightened.

"Fucking hell, that's so . . . fuck. I'm gonna . . ."

"Mmm, yes, all over my tongue and finger. Do it." She didn't know if Remi actually heard what she said. She hadn't removed her tongue as she spoke so she supposed she may have sounded muffled, but she didn't care.

Remi ground down on her finger, hips moving faster now. "I—I need more."

Maxine added another finger and Remi shattered around her, pussy clenching around Maxine's finger so sweetly. She lapped it all up, making a big show of licking her lips.

"You're the actual devil," Remi groaned, leaning back, chest rising and falling. "I'm convinced."

Maxine laughed, crawling over to where Remi lay, eyes closed. "Nah, just determined."

Remi smiled but didn't open her eyes. "Determined to fucking ruin me."

"I feel so relaxed now. Ready for some more shots?" She brushed Remi's hair from her face.

Remi cracked open one eye. "You can't be serious."

"Shouldn't let this feeling go to waste. I'm probably as open now as I'll ever be today."

Remi sighed but leaned up. "Where are my panties? I'm gonna need a minute. Or ten."

Maxine couldn't help the little thrill than ran through her as Remi tried to catch her bearings. She had done that – flustered her to the point of malfunction. Maybe she shouldn't be enjoying this so much given the fact that she'd detonated her whole plan, but it made her feel powerful. Knowing that she could do this to Remi.

"Take all the time you need." She got to her feet, shimming back into her underwear and pants as Remi still sat there, looking up at her, dazzled.

Remi shook her head. "You look so damn smug over there. You do realise we have to reset now? Back to number one."

"I know. Sorry." She was still too buzzy from her orgasm to truly mean that.

Remi went over to check the camera, either to look at the footage she had captured or to restart the timer. Maxine couldn't be too sure. "So we're back to square one. Are we ever gonna make it to ten?"

Maxine shrugged. "We just gotta try harder."

Remi looked over at her as if she wanted to argue, say something to counter that, but she just looked back to the camera. "Right. You expect me to be the strong one here? Say no if you're stripping in front me like that. Not really fair now, is it?"

Okay, she was right. It was shitty of her to ask for this and then detonate the entire thing so soon. Remi was now probably wondering why Maxine continued to insist they do this if she was going to be the one self-sabotaging.

"Do you want this to succeed?" Remi asked, all the playfulness from earlier gone.

"I didn't mean to get carried away. I swear. I guess the wine was not a good idea. I'm not blaming you," she added quickly. This was on her. "I could've said no and tried harder to relax, but," she pressed her hands to her eyes. "I fucked up. I'm sorry."

She was apologetic for real this time as she came down from her orgasmic high.

"Maxine." Remi sighed her name as if she was tired of all of this.

"I know. Can we just please try again?" She practically begged. She didn't want just to give up, call this a lost cause because they hadn't actually tried.

"Whatever you want," Remi said.

Remi's words didn't make her feel all that powerful anymore. Rather, a bit guilty. But if she didn't want to try again, she would just say so, right?

CHAPTER TWENTY

REMI

THE SUN WAS OUT IN FULL FORCE AS REMI MADE HER WAY ACROSS THE expansive grassy area where people were having a time and dancing to the music. The DJ was playing the current soca for the season and everyone was vibing.

Remi didn't usually work breakfast parties. The thought of getting up that early never appealed to her. But Maxine's artiste, Shalini, was doing a performance of her song with Chris Garcia so it was the beginning stages of the joint project with *Island Bites*. Remi had been given the backstage access to get her behind-the-scenes shots and she was intrigued for the actual performance.

Shalini seemed really sweet and excited about the entire thing, which helped Remi get some genuine photos of her and Maxine as they prepped for her turn on stage. The song and music video had dropped a few days ago and Remi was already vibing with it. She and Chris played off each other well and the fun song was perfect for the season.

Cherisse, Keiran, and Scott were also here, since Keiran had secured them some tickets. Once she did her job, her boss wasn't fussy about her having some fun with her friends. She limited her alcohol intake all the same because that didn't mean her boss would want her being messy on the scene while working.

"Hey, number one stunner," Scott called out as she came over to them.

"Look who's talking." She gestured to Scott's bare chest that was visible via the deep V of his colourful shirt. He was also showing a whole lot of thigh in those coral shorts. Perfect. Just the kind of thirst traps Remi wanted for the online version of their magazine. "Lemme get a shot of you."

She didn't even have to direct him to pose; Scott knew the best angles to show off his enviable cheekbones and catch the light on his dark skin and that glittery nose ring perfectly. She couldn't wait to photograph him for her series.

Her mind went back to her session with Maxine. That had gotten pretty damn intimate. She had some gems in there she could use, but the aftermath of getting them tipsy and Maxine . . . fucking hell . . . she had been so hot like that.

It sucked that they hadn't even made it past the first date before they had to reset, and Remi did wonder if Maxine was setting them up for failure. But why would she? Maxine could have easily just told her she didn't want anything serious with her and they could have kept this strictly to fucking. Or stop altogether and be friends, so it didn't make sense that the studio session had been some sort of set up to prove that they couldn't stick to the dating pact.

She was going to chalk it up to the wine and Maxine getting too into the moment. Remi hadn't stood a single chance with saying no. Perhaps she should have tried a wee bit harder to steer then back to safer ground, but she was a weak woman when it came to Maxine.

By the time she had gotten her hands and mouth on her there was no turning back. Fuck, Maxine had looked so stunning like that. The sounds of her moans, the way her hips had moved when Remi had . . .

You're at work. You need to focus on that. Not how good she tasted and sounded!

Ugh, couldn't she multitask? Work and lust? People did it all the time.

She gestured for the others to join Scott. Keiran and Cherisse were cute as ever in their sort of matchy couple wear with the shades of green they had going on. Cherisse kept playing with her hair as she stood next to Maxine who had joined them for a bit while Shalini relaxed in the artistes' room. Her bestie was nervous about something. Remi just assumed it was Sweethand's opening-day jitters. May felt far off, but with the way time could just creep up on you, the opening had to be on her mind. Especially since this had been her dream for so long.

And maybe she was a bit too caught up in trying to act casual with Maxine that she didn't think too hard about the way Keiran was rubbing Cherisse's back like he was trying to reassure her. Maxine was just there looking an entire goddess in a crop top and high waisted flowy pants with slits at the sides, so of course there was a lot of leg going on there.

"Okay, you all ready?" Remi asked, going into professional mode instead of dropping to her knees in front of Maxine and begging her just to ditch this entire trial date thing and date her for real. But a public place was definitely not ideal for her to humiliate them both like that.

"Yeah," Keiran said, just as Scott yelled out, "Hold the fuck up, is this Cherisse?!"

"Huh?" Remi didn't immediately get what Scott was going on about or why Cherisse was grinning sheepishly like that until Scott said, "Listen! Don't you hear those background vocals?"

Well, holy shit. He was right. The song playing now was

one she hadn't heard for the season yet, and that was very much her whole best friend's voice on it.

"What the hell?" She narrowed her eyes at Cherisse because she had not been aware that any song was going to be released with her on the track.

"Uh, surprise?" Cherisse shrugged like it was no biggie. "Keiran convinced me finally to let him use the vocals I recorded sooo long ago as a backing to this new track and . . . it's not bad, right?"

"Bad?" Remi shook her head because, seriously, Cherisse was just so ridiculous sometimes. "This sounds so damn good! I can't believe he actually got you to agree."

"I can be very persuasive." Keiran smirked and Maxine punched him in the arm.

"Stop right there. I don't need to know. None of us want to know, but yeah, what Remi said, cuz this is a vibe."

"Okay, can we just get back to the photo taking and move on?" Cherisse was definitely blushing with all the attention, but Remi would let it go, for now. She was going to make a bigger fuss of this after.

The crowd was definitely feeling the groovy vibe of the song.

"I'm making this my ringtone. Keiran, you better send me the audio," Scott said, and he busted out a small wine in front of Cherisse who laughed and danced back.

Remi left them to enjoy the fete while she made another round to capture some more of the fun. Events like these, she liked to get a mix of photos. People who were just there to pose and be seen and those who were the bacchanal section. Those were her favourite. They came out in their best fits—a requirement for all-inclusive fetes—but didn't give a damn about behaving. They were going to be wining low even in a cute dress and heels.

She found just such a group and immediately got a few spontaneous shots before asking them to do some fun poses for her. They were all too happy to oblige. Most fete goers loved to be photographed. They didn't get this dressed up for nothing.

Remi continued to roam around, capturing shots that would tell a story about this fete. The writers would put their word magic to her photos, but she always had a narrative in her mind when photographing at events like this. In her last round before she decided to take a little food break, she saw Maxine chatting with a woman in a short pink romper that dipped low in the front showing off her ample cleavage and thick legs.

"Damn," Remi muttered, because together the mystery woman and Maxine looked absolutely delicious. "Hey," she approached. "Can a grab of shot of both you lovely ladies?"

"Sure," Ms Pink Romper answered before Maxine could say anything, but she turned to her and asked, "You good with that?"

"Yeah, this is my friend Remi who's working on the exclusive with Shalini." Maxine gestured to Pink Romper as Remi counted down to ensure they were ready to take the shot. "This is Pauline. She's a senior publicist at KKE."

"Oh, yes, I've seen your work in the magazine. Amazing stuff!"

"Nice to meet you," Remi said, laughing as Pauline hammed it up for the camera, encouraging Maxine to do a Charlie's Angel-type pose.

Maxine went along with it, giggling. Clearly, she and Pauline got along. Remi was glad, since Maxine had expressed how working at KKE was a bit stressful with her being the boss's daughter and all. The staff would surely have their preconceived notions about her, but Pauline seemed cool.

"Can we see the photos?" Pauline asked. Remi showed them both and Pauline nodded. "Pretty and talented."

Hold on, was Pauline flirting with her? Remi looked over

at Maxine, who didn't say a thing, simply watched the reaction with a neutral expression.

"Thanks."

"Did Maxi tell you about Shalini's album launch?" Pauline was eyeing her contemplatively.

"Jackie, my boss, mentioned it briefly, but I haven't gotten the full details yet." What Remi had seen of the plan so far showed that KKE had a lot of marketing activities planned for Shalini. Performances, interviews, and now this launch Pauline mentioned. She supposed KKE would give them the full run down soon.

"That's fine. We're still fleshing out some things, but I have Maxi on point with that so you two can chat," Pauline said. "I want really nice shots for Shalini's event. It's her debut album so we're gonna do it up big."

"Sounds fun. I can't wait to hear her perform today. The little bits of the practice I heard sounded so good."

"Oh yeah, we were lucky to grab her up." Pauline pulled out her phone. "Which reminds me, I need to send an email about some launch details. Maxi, ensure you both get some shots just before Shal goes on stage. I saw you already did some teasers on our socials, so keep it up."

Maxine saluted. "Will do, boss."

"Great!" Pauline's phone buzzed. "Let me get this." She walked off to find a quiet spot for her call.

"She seems cool and she called me pretty so –" Remi grinned as Maxine rolled her eyes.

"You're so easy. One lil' compliment . . ."

"Jealous? I only have eyes for you."

Maxine sputtered. "What the heck was that?"

"We're kinda dating. I should make an effort with my pickup lines, no?"

"If *that's* what you're coming with then absolutely not."

Remi slung her camera strap over her shoulder so she could put her hands on her hips. "I will have you know that I had the ladies swooning with my lyrics back in the day."

"Oh really?" Maxine's raised brow said she wasn't sure if she believed that.

"Yeah. I could pull just about anyone. If I really turned up my charm." She waggled her brows because she knew it would make Maxine laugh. "You better watch out Ms. King. I'll have you falling for me in no time."

Maxine played with her bangs. "Is that your masterplan then?"

Remi leaned in. The music was loud, so chances of anyone hearing them was slim, but she didn't want to chance it. "Yeah. I'm serious about showing you that I'm more than my pussy game and my sexy body."

Maxine nodded, teeth digging into that bottom lip. Was she remembering what happened at the studio too? "I'm sorry again for *that*. I . . ." she sighed. "I just need to be sure we're not just in a lust haze you know? And then if we do decide to be something it all just falls apart because it's nothing more than that. This would be a big step for me. I can't just do whatever."

Remi squeezed Maxine's arm lightly to reassure her that she understood. "I get it. I do. But don't ever think I just want your body. I like you too. As a person. I know we have a lot to learn about each other. We've missed out on some key years, but I'm down for knowing all of you."

"Thanks. I'm struggling so much here." She laughed. It didn't sound joyous at all. "Anyway." She took a deep breath. "I don't want to bring down the vibe. We should check on Shalini and Chris." She looked towards the stage where the DJ was running through tracks to keep the crowd entertained until the next performer was up. "They're on in a few. The song's been doing well, gaining traction, so hopefully everything goes as it should for the live."

"Chris Garcia was a vibe back in the day, so I'm sure that little bit of nostalgia will help. And Shalini brings a fresh take to the track. They play off each other so well. And that part in the music video that's like a call back to his Chutney Bacchanal video? Hilarious."

"You really watched it." Maxine seemed genuinely surprised.

"Yeah, why wouldn't I? I'm interested in what you do, you know. And I can tell you really enjoy doing this." Maxine was practically glowing today as she ran around ensuring everything was going well for Shalini.

"I really do." She sighed. "I mean, I prefer to work with the artistes in a different capacity, in A&R, that's Artists & Repertoire by the way, but learning all of this is actually so interesting and fun. And while I hate to admit it, my dad was right about me needing to learn all facets of the business."

"What does A&R do exactly?" Remi had no clue.

"They're in charge of talent scouting and creative development of artists."

"That sounds exciting. Go get it girl!" Remi nudged Maxine's arm. "You'd be such a sexy CEO, damn."

Maxine reaching her full potential would be even sexier than she was now. Remi could just picture her in all her leadership glory.

"Thanks for the confidence." Maxine gave a shy smile. "I'm nowhere near CEO level yet, but I'm going to work hard to ensure I make it there."

She tugged on the ends of Maxine's hair. "Hey, you wanna get something to eat before you have to head backstage? Gotta keep your energy up."

Maxine didn't comment on Remi touching her hair like that, but she didn't seem phased by it. "I had a bit earlier, but yeah, I could eat. The spread looks nice."

They made their way through the buffet lines trying to

sample from each different type of food. Remi looked at her loaded plate and realised she would probably have to make a second round to try other food stations and come back for dessert.

"These small plates are really not cutting it," she noted once they were settled away from the more crowded areas. "You're good here or you want to get back to the crew?"

"Here is fine, for now. Just two pals vibing." Maxine grinned as she swayed to the smooth sounds from the DJ.

"Hmm, right." Remi ate her food, dancing along as well.

She and Maxine had a great time as they ate and danced, until Maxine signalled that they should get a move on. Remi documented as much as she could of Maxine chatting with Chris and Shalini. When they got the countdown for them to head on stage, Maxine and Remi gave them a thumbs up, cheering along with the crowd.

Maxine was busy recording on the company phone and Remi couldn't pass up the chance to capture her too. The way her mouth curved as she danced along while Shalini sang. She looked happy. Remi had to get her in her element.

It was nice, even though Cherisse's words kept swirling in her head. Remi was aware she could get hurt. Of course, that possibility existed, but she was seeing this through to whatever end may come.

Maxine was still focused on the stage, cheeks bunched up as she smiled so hard while singing along with everyone else. She would give anything for Maxine to say yes, she wanted to try, but that wasn't up to her. She also refused to add any pressure when she knew Maxine was going through a lot.

The waiting game was on. Until then, she was determined to enjoy the time she got to spend with her.

CHAPTER TWENTY-ONE
MAXINE
MARCH 1ST – CARNIVAL FRIDAY

SHE WAS GOING TO THROW UP. SERIOUSLY. IF HER STOMACH DIDN'T stop burbling like this she might have to run to the bathroom for real.

She shot a glance at Remi who was busy clapping along with the rest of the crowd to the current performer on stage. The bar was buzzing since it was Carnival Friday and people were eager to be out and about before the big celebrations on the road Monday and Tuesday.

Maxine hadn't been sure about her date. Karaoke at a bar in Arima didn't sound on the same level as the Sip and Paint, but she tried to stop second guessing everything. They were supposed to be getting to know each other with these dates and music was something she enjoyed. While karaoke held both amazing and not so great memories—after her father had taken credit for her talent find—she wanted to share that love with Remi.

"Damn, he is so good!" Remi said, whooping as the guy on stage continued with his rendition of Lenny Kravitz's *Fly*.

Maxine smiled and turned back to the stage. The guy was pretending to do an epic guitar performance while he sang along to the words on the screen. Remi was right, he was good. Not everyone who got up there had been this great, but it was about the fun and not so much the vocals—although Maxine kept an eye and ear out for anyone who caught her attention. She wasn't officially on the A&R team, but that didn't mean she wasn't going to do what came naturally to her. She had to think that a win for KKE was a win for all of them, even if history repeated itself and she didn't get the shine for it.

"He's giving Lenny a run for the money for real," she agreed.

"This was a good idea. I'm thoroughly entertained."

Maxine felt the nervous fluttering in her stomach ease a bit. Remi having a good time was all she wanted.

"You think you could get up there and do it?" Maxine asked. She had never heard Remi sing before so she didn't know what she was working with.

Remi scrunched up her nose. "Negative. I leave that to the professionals."

"Not everyone who gets up there is a professional, though."

"I mean, I'm not a wailing cat like your brother, cuz damn I still have nightmares about that terrible serenade he gave Cherisse at the wedding. It must be love, because how did that even work?"

Maxine couldn't hold back the snort that escaped. Keiran *had* been bad. "I'd do it with you if you're scared."

"Oh no no no. I'm not falling for those eyes."

Maxine widened the eyes in question, because what did Remi mean?

Remi groaned and shook her head. "Those eyes. We're gonna get reset, I just know it."

"Hey, I'm not doing anything!" Maxine was thoroughly confused. She knew when she was being naughty to tempt Remi, but she really was just standing there.

"Girl, you really underestimate your charm, don't you. You got Bambi eyes."

"Um what?"

Remi chuckled. "You really don't know, do you?" She gestured to an empty table that had luckily just been vacated. "Let's sit and I'll explain."

Maxine slid into her seat, brow raised. She couldn't contain her curiosity. No one had ever told her she had Bambi eyes. Whatever the hell that meant. "Well . . ." she waved at Remi to continue.

Before Remi could get into it, their server came over to clear away the bottles and food debris left from the previous occupants before swiftly returning with the fries and wings they had ordered earlier. Finally. They had been enjoying the entertainment on stage, but Maxine was hungry. She had decided to stick to something soft tonight—she needed all her faculties around Remi—so she ordered another shandy while Remi asked for another Corona.

Remi reached for a fry. "You got these gorgeous brown eyes that do this doe-eyed thing without even realising. Makes it a bit hard to say no to you."

The bottle paused near Maxine's mouth. "Oh. Damn, is that where Leah got it from?"

Leah was a good kid, but she knew how to turn up the cute and Maxine and most of her family members were helpless against that. It was surprising to know she was capable of the same thing, unknowingly.

"You seriously didn't know?"

"Nope, I swear." Maxine grinned because this was an awesome power to have.

"Oh God. I think I made a mistake letting you know this."

Maxine leaned forward, fingers laced. "Don't worry, I'll go easy on you."

Remi's throat flexed as she swallowed a fry. Maxine was going to have so much fun with this. Within reason of course. She didn't want to ruin their pact. Again.

"So, would you get up on stage with me?" she asked, because while she didn't have a Cherisse voice, she enjoyed singing and loved a fun karaoke song.

"Uh," Remi paused. "To be honest, I don't think it's my thing really."

"But it's so fun!" Maxine tried to give maximum Bambi eyes. She wasn't sure if she could intentionally do it, but Remi shook her head and covered her face, so maybe she had succeeded.

"No. Stop that. I will not be doing any serenades as a cute gesture. Sorry, nope."

Maxine nudged Remi's knee with hers to get her attention. Remi's hand slid from her face. "I'm kidding. I'm not trying to use my power for evil. Yet." She winked and reached for a fry. "It would have been fun, but I know it's not everyone's thing. I'll give it a try, though."

"For real?"

"Yeah, I'm no wuss."

"Hey!"

Maxine blew her a kiss to show she was only teasing. The look on Remi's face was going right into her forever memory bank. The fond smile on her face. For once there wasn't this urge to drag her off somewhere to kiss the shit out of her. Maxine just felt a warmth blooming in her chest. It wasn't that it hadn't always been there. If she was being honest, it was usually overshadowed by the too enormous lust that kept distracting them from everything else. That was what she wanted to hone into, bring out more. She wanted to see if that could be sustainable rather than the attraction that made them act like horny little bunnies.

She got to her feet. "Any special requests?" she asked. She was serious about getting up there.

She had no desire to be a singer, that wasn't where her goals lay, but the adrenaline rush she got from karaoke was unexplainable. And she thought Remi would enjoy seeing her perform.

"Surprise me," Remi said.

Maxine already had her choice in mind as she went up to the DJ. Her heart thumped against her chest. The song choice wasn't random. She had carefully chosen it with Remi in mind. Was she doing too much for their second date? She hoped it wouldn't make things awkward, but the DJ nodded to her and she walked up there with the mike clutched in her hands.

The crowd was lively and immediately started cheering as the opening *lalalalas* of Rihanna's *Only Girl in the World* started up. She found Remi at their table and the smile on her face was just beautiful as Maxine belted out the lyrics and added some dance moves and strutted across the stage. She wondered if Remi was remembering the Tobago trip. She had side-eyed Keiran for playing that song then, but now she wanted to call back to a moment that was just for them.

The bar patrons sang along with her, and Maxine wished so badly she could walk down to Remi and serenade her directly. But she didn't know the reception she would get, and she didn't want to risk it for either of them. Damn, maybe she was no better than her brother, because now she was thinking maybe she needed to do a private serenade for Remi. Except she would actually sound good.

She finished off the song, bowed, and walked back to Remi who was standing up clapping.

"You were so good!"

Maxine took a sip of her drink. "You sound surprised."

"I never knew you could get down like that at karaoke!"

"Lots you don't know about me yet, but you'll learn." Remi's gaze became heated, but she cleared her throat and looked away to the next performer coming up on the stage before she could really lean into it.

Maxine smiled. In spite of them staying clear of sex and any overt flirting, it never got old when Remi looked at her like that.

Remi leaned back after a few moments. "What else don't I know? What are Maxine King's dating go tos?"

"You looking for ideas? The point of these is to get to know each other, so don't go trying to just impress *me*," she teased.

Remi's pursed lips were so adorable that Maxine was this close to leaning in to steal a kiss, but not only would she have to lean too far over the table for that—giving Remi a chance to figure out what she was up to—there was no way she would do that with all these people around.

"Not what I meant. I don't know your dating history, but there's gotta be something you like doing constantly, *so por ejemplo*, I like tucking random hair behind my date's ear if the hair type or length allows for that. It's a cute thing," she explained.

"Oh." Maxine definitely had that, but did she want to share it right now? She took another handful of fries to stall.

Stop being a loser and just tell her.

"I, um, want to try something. It's my thing." She felt like the sun was engulfing her face as Remi's gaze turned curious. It wasn't that big of a deal, but she still felt a bit shy about it.

"Tell me."

"Can I hold your hand? I know that's a little weird, and please tell me if it's not something you're into, but I like that little connection. When I'm out, I like to do that even if we're not seated next to each other. And no one will notice if we did it here under the table, so it's not too obvious, and yeah . . . okay, you think it's weird."

Oh God, why was she just so not suave? Remi was saying nothing, just *looking* at her as she threw all of that at her.

"Sorry, forget I said any of that."

"No, *no*, I'm just processing. You really want to hold my hand here?"

Maxine bit her lip, nodded. "I wanted to try? Just to see how that would go." And gauge whether she would freak out about doing something that she considered a couply thing, with Remi.

"Yeah, I want that. Bring your cute self over here." Remi didn't wait for Maxine to get off her chair and move over, she simply grabbed the side of the chair and dragged it closer with her still on it.

Holy shit, every time Remi showed her strength like that, Maxine felt like she was going to combust. Did she have a strength kink this whole time and not know it? Jesus.

"Well, hi there."

"H-hey," she stammered, glad the dim lighting in the bar was a good mask for the blush that was surely staining her cheeks. "So, um, I can just go ahead?"

"Yes, doll, I'm waiting."

Doll? What the hell was that? Was Remi trying to kill her with that and the intense staredown. "Nope, you gotta dial that charm right the hell down."

Remi pulled back, hands up. "Okay, I'll behave."

"Hand, please," Maxine asked politely, and she knew Remi wanted to say something that would not be appropriate for the parameters of their date, but she didn't. She just allowed Maxine to take her hand.

Remi looked down at their joined hands before facing her again. "Sorry my hands aren't the softest."

"It's fine."

They discreetly held hands under the table while the next person gave a terrible rendition of a love song. It felt nice to be

able to do this again after Leo, even with the anxiety of someone seeing them like this and having a problem with it. But
most people out tonight were too busy enjoying the vibes of
the bar and the music.

Maxine tried to level her breathing as Remi's thumb rubbed
against the back of her hand. Remi was focused on the stage, so
she didn't know if that was a subconscious action or deliberate.
Either way, it added to the butterflies battering away at her
stomach.

But she liked it. A lot.

"You on the road Monday and Tuesday?" Remi asked,
thumb still stroking.

"Mmhmm. With Pauline and Shalini on a truck."

Remi slid her an amused glance. "Ohhh nice. Didn't see
that on my official schedule. But we can link up if you want?"

"Sure." The idea of seeing Remi in a skimpy costume was
so damn appealing. She took a big inhale then let it out before
squeezing Remi's hand. "Thanks for indulging me."

"For you? Anything."

She didn't respond to that. What could she say? That the
thought of that was scary because, damn, she didn't know if she
wanted to have that power over someone?

Stop overthinking and enjoy it.

Yes, she would try. It was only officially date two, eight
more to go. The number wasn't that daunting, but she
wondered if she could make it to May without wanting to jump
Remi, again.

CHAPTER TWENTY-TWO

MAXINE
MARCH 5th– CARNIVAL TUESDAY

MUSIC BLASTED AS THE SEA OF REVELLERS JUMPED, WAVED, AND wined down low until they nearly touched the ground. Maxine shook her hips as Shalini belted out her song with Chris grooving by her side. The crowd was eating it up, singing the words right back at Shalini.

Maxine grinned and captured it all to update KKE and Shalini's accounts. She even posted a quick selfie to her Instagram with Shalini and Chris in the background of the shot. She had been focused on getting lots of content for work, so she hadn't posted a thing to her own accounts.

Calling it now. big things on the horizon with @shalinivale 👀 *#TheSongTooSweet*

She took a minute to look at the comments, wondering if Remi would see her post. She had checked her Instagram, but apart from a few shots of some revellers in their glee, there was nothing. No post with her in a costume or anything, which made sense since Remi would be busy doing her job, but Maxine was curious. She scrolled as her phone started to buzz with responses to her photo.

@keiranking buh check you nah. Take a wine for me!
@queenvictoria umm we need to see the full costume??
@cherrygoody nice 😊

Remi: *hey tell that truck don't move I comiiiiiin*

Maxine grinned at the message in their chat. There she was. Maxine couldn't dictate the movements of the music truck, but it was moving at a slow enough pace that wherever Remi was, hopefully she could catch up.

Maxine: *where are you?*

Remi must already be on the move because her message remained unread. She stared down at the colourful crowd of people on the street. There were so many people it would be difficult to spot Remi, but she still scanned the bodies. She caught sight of Pauline, who chipped by the truck waving at her. Maxine gave her a thumbs up to let her know everything was going well. Pauline had gone down into the crowd to say hi to her friends and Maxine assured her she had it handled.

Pauline smiled up at her and twirled her finger in a circle to let her know she would be back.

"Was that Pauline?"

Maxine turned to look at Shalini, who was taking a break while the DJ pumped out some other soca.

"Yeah. You good? Need anything?" she asked going back into work mode.

Shalini still look put together in her costume, even after all that exuberant jumping and waving she had been doing while performing. Her short black hair was still stick straight.

Shalini raised her water bottle. "I'm good. Feeling so energised! Can't wait for the next single to drop."

They had planned for the next release to be after all the buzz with this one. "It's gonna be amazing," Maxine assured her. Outwardly, Shalini didn't look nervous, but the art of this job was being a hype person for your artiste regardless.

Shalini went back over to the DJ to get on the mic, and Maxine felt her phone buzz against her hip.

Remi: *I spy with my little eye something sexy*

Remi had sent her a photo of herself on the truck. She looked back down into the street and spied Remi waving up at her. She was right alongside the truck as she chipped along, camera in hand. She had actually found her.

Maxine's eyes went right to the costume she was wearing, a skimpy bikini adorned with orange and blue gems that caught the waning sunlight as the afternoon headed to evening. The back of the costume sported feathers in the same orange and blue. Instead of a big headpiece, she had a simple headband that was decorated with the same gems on her costume.

She looked amazing. Maxine had opted for something with a fuller coverage, but no less pretty with its beads and feathers. King Kong Entertainment had comped them the costumes and she had chosen one that also didn't have a big annoying headpiece, but a smaller, more subtle one like Remi's.

"Hey!" Remi called up. "You been on this truck all day, haven't you?"

How did she know that? "Maybe." Maxine shouted back.

"I haven't seen a single photo of you on the road, so I'm thinking it's definitely not a maybe."

"*Maybe* I just plan to post them later."

Remi shook her head, small smile playing about her lips. She clearly didn't believe Maxine. She waved her phone at

Maxine, signalling that she would message her. Easier than shouting back and forth like this.

> **Remi:** *meet me at the Socadrome for las lap ok? Save a wine for me* 😊
>
> **Maxine:** *sure thing!*
>
> **Remi:** *later gawjus. I'll msg when I'm there. Can I get an official photo of you up there? I'll get a full length later when we meet up.*
>
> **Maxine:** *lemme strike a pose then*

Maxine checked her makeup in her phone camera before she put the phone back into the bag. Her face has been professionally done by Scott—the early-morning appointment had been worth it because he had done the damn thing—and while she hadn't been down in the crush of people on the streets, the day had been hot. She still wanted to look cute.

"Ready!" she called down to Remi, who did her thing.

As the truck made its way closer to the Socadrome, where most bands would converge to have the final fun before the day's festivities officially ended, Maxine felt her mood shift. She became more on edge. She tried to busy herself and not think about the meet up with Remi.

Pauline was kinder to her than most other employees, but Maxine was under no illusion that Pauline would let any screwups slide. Boss's daughter or not. She wasn't about to fail this crucial test.

As the sun set and night drew in, the revellers got even more hyped up as they knew the end was coming. Pauline returned to the truck somewhere along the way and Maxine noted pieces of her costume were missing.

"Yeah, wined that off, oops! How was it up here?"

"Great."

"Okay, you need to get down there. Is Las Lap! No excuses. I need to rest my feet up here."

Pauline shooed her away just as Remi texted.

Remi: *I see your truck. I can meet you there?*
Maxine: *sure thing. I was just coming down* 😊

"Well, look at you. Feet finally touching pavement?" Remi teased as they met up.

"Hey, I had my fun. Don't judge me. It's not like I've never played mas before."

"Sorry, but Atlanta Carnival isn't the same as a Trini vibe." Remi's eyes swept up and down her body. "May I?" she lifted her camera and Maxine nodded. Remi's smile was playful as she lowered her camera. "Need to capture it all now cuz you're going to get sweaty."

"Says who?" Maxine placed a hand on her hip, pretending she didn't notice the way Remi's eyes naturally followed her hand movement.

"Me. I just need to stash the camera with my co-worker, then we are going to have a time!"

Maxine followed Remi to where a tall, serious-looking guy waited.

"Kobi, this is Maxine. He's our production manager for the magazine."

"Hi," Maxine said.

Kobi nodded. "You two have fun."

Remi took Maxine's hand and guided them through the crowd, both of them dancing in time to the beat. Remi moved Maxine to stand in front of her and placed her hands on Maxine's hips. Maxine let her body do what it wanted. She didn't think, just bounced her ass up and down to the fast-paced soca song.

Remi's lips brushed along Maxine ear. "You're good, right? It's Carnival. No one cares."

It was the only reason Maxine wasn't giving a damn about how close they were right now, her ass so snug against Remi's front as she ground back on her. Everyone around them was too busy being caught up in the beat of the music. Besides, no one would really look too closely at two women dancing like this for real. It was the norm during Carnival. Expected, even.

Remi brushed away the hair from her neck and Maxine shivered, remembering what Remi had told her about that lil' hair-tuck move she liked to do. It wasn't the same, but close enough. "This is what I wanted to do back at Shades."

Maxine bit her lip as she took Remi's hand and put it right back on her hip. Remi's hand brushed against the bit of skin exposed by the cutouts in her costume. The closeness of the crowd and the buzz of the music made her not want to over-think this. They weren't in breach of their deal, yet. Maxine felt her core throb as Remi's finger made swirling motions against her skin.

Fuck, she wasn't going to survive this.

"Okay?" Remi's soft voice came in her ear as she rolled her waist behind her. "Dancing is what I wanted, but this might be a bit of a danger zone here."

Maxine's hand covered Remi's. It would be so easy to guide it down until her finger could reach up under the curve of her bathing suit bottom. She could continue moving her hips along with the music while grinding down on Remi's finger. No one would know. Anyone who saw her face would just think she was wasted, and high on the music too, not about to come from being finger fucked in the middle of this party.

Ah, shit, she had to get control of her wayward thoughts.

The song changed to a groovy soca and Maxine stepped away, gripping her hair with her hand to get it off her neck.

Remi kept watching her, swaying along to the sensuous beat. She needed a cold-ass shower right now.

"It's so hot," was all she could muster as Remi kept her gaze focused on her, tiny smile flitting about her lips as if she knew the dilemma Maxine had been in during that dance.

"Cold shower needed." Remi was for sure making fun of her now. Maxine narrowed her eyes, but Remi shrugged. "I'm just agreeing it's hot."

"Uh huh."

"What else could I be referring to?"

Oh, she had her there. If she said anything, she would be admitting she had been turned on while they danced. She was not going to do that. It wasn't a competition, but she refused to be made out to be the one struggling through this when it had been her damn idea. No way.

"Nothing."

"Wanna keep dancing. Seems we in a groovy mood for a bit." Remi leaned in. "Unless you don't think you can handle it. Or maybe I won't be able to. You dancing front to front with me. Corrupting me by rubbing that hot pussy all over mine?"

"God, don't say shit like that," Maxine whined.

"Why?" Her breath washed against Maxine's ear, hand on her hip to draw her closer. "Are you feeling hot, hmm?"

"I said I was, but not like *that*," she insisted. "Are you tryna get me back for the studio thing?"

Remi laughed. "No, I'm just wondering. But if you're all good we can get back to dancing, or . . ."

She placed her finger under Maxine's chin and gently turned her head towards a bunch of women gyrating against each other like there was no tomorrow. Someone was basically on the ground being dry humped. Good for them. Maxine couldn't dance with Remi like that because she would literally come. The constant friction between them was enough to start a damn fire.

"They seem to be doing just fine."

"There is no way . . ." Maxine muttered.

Remi was still close enough to hear that. "I hear yuh. I wouldn't last very long, but don't worry. I have plans for our date."

"What?" Maxine's curiosity perked up.

"It'll be all innocent fun, I promise. But let's just enjoy the rest of this first."

They somehow ended up liming with the same group of women who were all on the ground previously. The wildness didn't give Maxine much time to focus on her horniness, but when Remi's hand pulled her leg up around her waist, all bets were off. Maxine could tell Remi was caught up in the rowdy fun, especially when the way she was gripping her leg high on her thigh made her hand brush right against Maxine's core.

"Oh shit, sorry," Remi said, just as someone bumped into her, jostling them so she almost fell.

Remi's grip tightened on Maxine's leg, but Maxine was a bit off balance now and used her other leg to steady herself. She hopped around and grabbed onto Remi's shoulders, which Remi didn't expect, almost pitching backwards.

"Oh crap!" Remi exclaimed. She released Maxine's leg and latched onto her too. They ended wrapped around each other.

Maxine stared at Remi wide-eyed before they both busted out laughing. "Damn, we both would've gone down, and not in the not fun way. Geez."

"Def not how I would've wanted to end the night. You good?" Remi asked.

"Yeah." Maxine was still revved up, but the almost-fall was the smack to her system she needed. Lord have mercy, she was seriously on the verge of losing it.

"No more leg-off-the-ground moves. Promise." Remi's smile was cheeky as hell.

Maxine narrowed her eyes. "Holster those fingers ma'am, cuz they should be registered as deadly weapons."

Remi held up all ten of her fingers and wiggled them. "That was a mistake. I swear. What're you doing tomorrow? Beach?" she asked casually.

"With the whole rest of the island?" Maxine wrinkled her nose.

On Ash Wednesday, the island's beaches were usually packed with tourists and locals who wanted to cool down after all the Carnival fun. She didn't like the beach when it was overly crowded.

It was still a workday, but some people took an unofficial day off and just didn't go to work or school. Maxine would be expected at the office as per usual.

"I see your point. But my family's having a lil' thing up Mayaro side for my grandmother's birthday, if you'd be down for playing hooky and coming with me."

"Oh." Maxine had only met Remi's parents. She didn't know about meeting her extended family when this thing between them was so . . . volatile. Of course, she would be going as a friend, so it wasn't an odd invitation. She just didn't know if she should. Besides, she didn't think now was the time to be ducking work when so many eyes were on her.

"Your mom and Leah can come too, so it won't be us alone. If that's what you're worried about."

"I just think it's too early for me to be ditching work."

"Ah yeah. Makes sense. I know my job's a bit more fluid that way."

They resumed dancing for a bit but kept it PG-ish – as PG as anything at a las lap fete could be with the gyrations going on around them – until Remi decided to leave before the official end to the party.

"Mayaro's a long drive so I need to be up early. I'm the chosen driver, since no one else wants to."

Maxine gave her a thumbs up, which felt ridiculous after how they had been carrying on, but the tiredness was starting to seep in and she needed to get back to Pauline, who was her ride home.

They found their way back to where Kobi was still stationed, and then he walked with them to drop Maxine at the truck. Pauline waved at Remi as she saw them.

"You two look like you had some sweaty fun," Pauline said, smiling.

"Yeah. Well, laters." Maxine stood there awkwardly, not sure if she should give Remi a goodbye hug or just do nothing. She decided on the latter. "Message when you get home."

"Will do. Bye."

"She really seems cool," Pauline noted as they both watched Remi and Kobi walk off. "I had a lil' chat with her after you sent over the album launch details."

"Oh?" Maxine hadn't been aware they had spoken details. It wasn't like she had to go through Maxine to talk to Remi. It would be ridiculous of her to assume that because she and Remi knew each other, Pauline would be totally hands off.

"I know you got point on this, but I like to get to know the supplier's we're working with. Might set up a lunch with her sometime."

"Just you two?" Maxine regretted the question the moment it left her mouth.

Pauline's brow popped up. "Yes, is that an issue?"

"No, I just . . . shouldn't I be there if you're going to talk about the project?"

"Just so we're clear, this isn't me micromanaging. You two already know each other, so it's essential for me to craft that relationship. I can see us working with her exclusively for something else again. Her work is amazing."

Of course it was about work and nothing else. It made this all the more awkward if these dates meant them ending up in a relationship. Maxine didn't think she would have to disclose her private life to Pauline. She was definitely getting ahead of herself here. Maxine had to rein in her messy thoughts.

"Right. Sorry. I didn't mean anything by it. Was just wondering."

"Okay, now that we've established I'm *not* going after your woman . . ."

"W-what? That's not . . . she is not my woman. We're friends. I'm not . . ."

Pauline patted her shoulder. "Calm down, King. I was just teasing. I swear you were giving me some heavy jealous girl-friend vibes, but my mistake if that's not the case, as you said." She yawned, then clapped. "Okay, let's get some of that free Nescafé they got over there and then go."

Maxine stared as Pauline started to walk away, but caught herself before she was totally left behind. Right, Pauline was joking. But Maxine had clearly been giving off some sort of attitude for Pauline to tease about it. She was going to need to simmer that down, because, damn, she couldn't be called out like that when she was trying to be incognito about her feelings.

CHAPTER TWENTY-THREE

REMI

ASH WEDNESDAY

"Why're you looking at naked dudes in your grandmother's living room?"

Remi turned to look at her brother Akash who was leaning over the back of the couch to stare at her laptop. His long curly hair was unbound and hanging almost in her face.

"Ugh, can you not?" She swatted him away and he came around the couch to slide in next to her. "I'm not watching naked dudes."

He gestured to the shiny bare torso on her screen.

"It's for my gallery showing. And it's just Scott's bare chest. Relax." She zoomed out so he could see the entire photo of Scott, who was in his tight boxer briefs, his sinewy muscles in his chest, arms, and legs fully on display, his eyelids shimmering with gold eyeshadow.

"Oh."

Remi turned towards her brother, who she'd never heard that sort of tone from before. Interesting.

"Stunning, isn't he?" It was the usual reaction to Scott, but Akash falling prey to it as well was surprising. Her brother never seemed charmed enough by any other human being to sound like that. She supposed Scott just had that effect on everyone.

"Yeah. I suppose," he shrugged, and there was his usual nonchalance. "But anyone could have come in here."

Unlikely. With food and drinks flowing, her relatives were definitely too busy to notice she was missing. "Eh, they're all busy liming outside. Besides, they might jump for joy thinking I'm hetero now."

"Being attracted to guys doesn't make *you* hetero."

Remi slid a glance at her brother and laughed at his confused expression. "We know that. Because God forbid the lil', maybe, 20% attraction I feel for anyone who's not a woman negates my pansexualness."

Akash sighed, as if he understood her dilemma where their family was concerned. She had no clue if he did. Her brother had never brought home anyone to introduce to them and she had no inkling if he had ever been in any sort of romantic relationship.

Luckily, her parents never questioned or pressured him about it, unlike their extended family who were always asking when he would be bringing home a girlfriend, and badgering him about why a thirty-two-year-old man wasn't married yet.

"They're exhausting," he said finally. "Regardless, you probably shouldn't be doing this in here." He waved at the screen.

Remi closed the top of the laptop. Akash was right. It wasn't the best place for this, but her relatives had launched into a conversation that had her itching to go off, so she had come in here to calm down by looking at pretty people. Her parents had tried to switch the conversation to something less likely to ignite her ire, but with alcohol in their system, the talk had swayed to politics and to harassing Remi about when she was going to find a good man to settle down with.

Her response of "or woman or gender non-conforming person" had not gone down well with certain family members.

"You can blame Uncle Ricky. He's had a few drinks, so . . ."

"Ah." Understanding dawned on Akash's face. "They need to stop inviting him to these things."

"I did ask mummy if he was coming, but I guess she didn't know. Luckily, Maxi declined my invitation."

Remi would've loved it if Maxine could have made it, but she also knew she shouldn't try to monopolise all of Maxine's time outside of their dates. They had work and other shit going on and she supposed it turned out for the best because she would have hated if Maxine had been uncomfortable because of something her Uncle Ricky said.

"What's the deal with that, huh? You and Maxine?"

Remi rolled her eyes. "Nothing."

"Sure. I might not be experienced in relationships like you, but I can see when someone is whipped."

"We're friends."

"Who fuck," Akash stated matter of factly, and Remi couldn't help the laugh that busted out of her.

"Wow, just dropping that like it's hot, huh?"

"Am I wrong? I'm here if you wanna talk about it?"

Yeah, no. She and Akash only had two years between them and got along well enough, but they didn't talk about her love life in any capacity. They weren't the sort of siblings who were all up in each other's personal business. Akash had never been that older brother that liked to tease. They looked out for each other and hyped each other up work wise, which reminded Remi that she did want to talk to Akash about something.

"I'll pass, thanks." She patted his shoulder. "That's what Cherisse is for, but I do have a gig opportunity to discuss with you."

"Yeah, what?" And there was the usual excitement she was accustomed to. Most of Akash's high emotions were left for anything music-related or that dealt specifically with his band.

"My gallery showing. I convinced the owner that A Roti and A Red Solo would be perfect entertainment for the launch of the show."

Her brother's band had been gaining popularity over time. Since she had casually mentioned her show to Pauline, when they had spoken about the album launch, Remi was hoping she could get Akash's band in front of someone who might be inclined to mention an up-and-coming band to Pauline's music exec boss. Remi hadn't wanted to bring that up with Maxine since she didn't want it to seem like she was using their connection to get her brother an in with the company.

"Sounds good to me. I'm sure we'll be able to. When is it?"

"Two months away."

Akash raised a brow. "And why am I now hearing about this?"

Remi's phone trilled and she used the interruption as an excuse not to answer Akash. The truth was, she was extremely nervous about her first real gallery showing. While she had mentioned it to her parents, she had been sort of shy about saying anything to the wider family. And her brother. Which was silly, because those who wanted to support her would come. Those who didn't just wouldn't bother.

Maxi: *how's it going? I wished I had run away*

Maxine had attached a photo of her pouting at her desk and Remi couldn't help but smile.

"Hey, don't ignore me for your girlfriend."

Remi rolled her eyes. "Hush. She's not my girlfriend. Just gimme a sec, please."

Remi: aww so cute. It's fine here. Lots of food.

She switched to her camera and leaned closer to Akash to snap a selfie of both of them.

"Hey!" Akash protested.

Remi: my brother says hi
Maxi: lol. He did not look like he wanted to be in that pic. Wow. The lush hair really runs in your fam huh?
Remi: sure does. Mummy used to have hers really long too but she prefers the short cut. I'll send you one where I cut mine short a few years ago too. Never agaiiin
Maxi: I'm sure it was cute. I can't deal with all that unless I put in some braids or something. Which I don't do often.
Remi: well you'd look good with any style I'm sure 😉

"You seriously got me third wheeling out here right now?" Akash grumbled.

Remi: okkk so my bro is pouting now. hope you can get off work soon. Let me go back to giving him attention. I am trying to get his band to play at my show so guess I shouldn't ignore him huh?
Maxi: oh. cool. The elusive show that I don't even know the actual date of even tho you're gonna use my pics for it?? 👀
Remi: LOL sorry it's just so personal to me. I've been keeping everything so close to the chest. I'll send all the info. Later. Gotta go butter up my bro now. byeee

"Ugh, people in love are so sickening."

Remi tucked her phone away and laughed at Akash's scrunched-up face. "Shut. Up. Maybe your time will come or not but don't be hating on me. Anyhoo, for context, the showing is called 'Inner' and the photos are going to showcase various persons revealing sides of them they usually keep hidden or just don't outright show the world. The feeling I want for this is smooth, groovy. Which means I need your honey voice for that."

Akash nodded. "You know I got the range."

"Facts," she agreed.

His vocals were something else. Akash seemed so shy and reserved usually, but on stage he became someone else who could go from smooth crooner to sensual rock god. She didn't know where he got those personas from, but it was why she had tried to get him to participate in her show.

"Maxi'll be there I presume?"

"She's got photos in the show, so yeah. I know you always bring your A-game, but if Pauline, who's a publicist for KKE, comes and is wowed, who knows. You guys could be signed with Maxine's dad's company! Exciting, right?"

"Right. I keep forgetting who her father is. Okay, okay, yeah, the guys would be excited about that. We're in for sure." Akash nudged her shoulder with his. "Guess I gotta be nice to you since you have all these connections now."

"I'm not using Maxi's proximity to KKE to get you a deal, but who knows what could happen. Just don't suck," she teased.

"I don't suck. We're just that good."

She knew they were, but what sort of sister would she be if she didn't drop some occasional picong?

"Here you are. And a two-for-one special too."

They both looked up as their father came into the living room. He took a seat across from them.

"Uncle done being an ass out there?" Remi asked.

"He's currently passed out in a chair, so yeah." Her father leaned forward, face serious. "I'm sorry he went in on you like that."

"You don't have to be sorry. I know you didn't fist fight him because of us. But some bigoted fool isn't going to make *me* feel bad about being myself." She shrugged. She really wished they would stop inviting his ass to things, though.

"I know. Still doesn't make it right."

"Exactly," Akash chimed in. "Imagine him telling me my hair is too long and if I tryna be a girl? Like? It's just hair? Why's he trying to kill my Chris Garcia vibe? He don't know this is my money maker or what?" Akash swung his head around as if he was in a shampoo commercial.

Remi and her father laughed.

Remi tugged on one of his long curls. "I thought your selling point was your voice?"

"Can't a man be a multifaceted thirst trap?"

"Boy, you better stop." Her father was laughing so hard.

Remi felt a bit better. At least she knew her small circle had her back. They didn't care who she chose to love as long as she was happy.

"So, daddy, I have a question. Hypothetically. If you like somebody and they're obviously attracted to you too but they're being cautious—rightfully so—how long would you wait for them to figure out what they want? What if they decide you're not worth all the potential hassle?"

Her father's warm brown eyes landed on her and Remi was certain he saw right through her supposed hypothetical. She hadn't brought up her "thing" with Remi, but they were observant people. She was sure they suspected something there.

She hadn't kept her relationship with Sanaa from them and in fact they had met her many times when they'd been dating. Their only concern had been the age difference, since they figured she and Sanaa were on different paths in their lives, which had turned out to be true. But they had never treated Sanaa with anything but respect.

While the entire point of the dating pact was to figure out if Maxine and Remi were compatible beyond the bedroom, Remi couldn't help but have anxiety about the entire thing. She couldn't control the outcome, only what she showed Maxine and hope that she could wow and woo her.

"Hmm, that's a tough one. You don't know what they'll decide in the end, but if you think they're worth the wait, then I say go for it. But," he raised a finger, "I don't care who it is . . . don't let anyone string you along indefinitely."

Remi nodded. Solid advice, but a lot was riding on her faith in Maxine choosing her in the end. Remi sighed. "I hear yah."

Her father came over to place his hand on her shoulder. "I know you may feel like it's all or nothing when feelings are involved. But sometimes the timing isn't quite right and that's okay. Just don't bury how you feel as well to please someone. I don't think they'd want that either. If they really cared about you."

"You went through that with mummy?" she asked. Her parents were her inspiration for what she wanted in the future. They were still so much in love to this day, which didn't mean they didn't have issues, but they worked on them together.

Remi and Maxine's potential relationship would be that much harder, given those asshole relatives, but she had experience being in a relationship with a woman and being subtle about it around her extended family. Maxine didn't. Would she trust her enough with something like that?

"I mean, not really. Your mother was down bad, as you say, from the earlies." Her father chuckled. "So I didn't have to do much convincing."

"Excuse me, what?" Remi bit her lip to stop laughing as her father's eyes got wide at her mother's voice. "Curtis Daniels, what lies you telling these children here, eh?"

"I was only joking with dem," her father started.

Remi exchanged looks with Akash. "Yeah, I gonna get something to eat." She got to her feet and saluted her father to give him strength and rolled out the room with her brother not too far behind.

"That is what you want to look forward to with 'she who shall not be named'?" her brother asked as she stashed her laptop and ventured into the backyard again.

"Hush lil' bit, nah man." She pushed him out the way and he just laughed.

Maybe she did want that with Maxine. It seemed like an unattainable dream the way things were going, but she was no quitter.

She would see this through to whatever end may come.

CHAPTER TWENTY-FOUR

MAXINE

THURSDAY 14TH MARCH

MAXINE STARED INTO THE BATHROOM MIRROR AS SHE TRIED TO CATCH her breath. The meeting was about to start in a few minutes and she was having a mini meltdown. It wasn't a great start to her day, especially as Pauline had also asked her to take point on today's updates.

Pauline usually handled things for the department during their weekly catchup meetings. She always tossed things to Maxine if she wanted her to add anything else, so of course Maxine had to be on top of what was going on at any given moment, but today it would be all her.

"Okay, you know what you're working on. You got this," she murmured to her reflection.

If she flubbed a simple thing like this meeting, everyone would think she truly was a "just here because of her last name". It was fine. She knew everything they had going on. She'd even thrown in her own ideas for the launch that Pauline had approved. There was no reason for her to stumble.

She checked her phone, sending a message to her chat with Remi:

please wish me luck and that I don't look a whole 🐶
Remi: *meeting day today??? You're amazing! Beautiful!*
Smart! Sexy (not related to this but it's truuuuue!!) Good
luck!! Give em the 🐮 *eyes!*

It took Maxine a minute to decipher that emoji and catch that Remi was talking about her doe eyes superpower. Doubtful that would work in the meeting, but it made her smile and Remi's compliments gave her a mood boost.

Remi: *lemme know how it goes. We can do lunch maybe if*
all goes well?
Maxine: *is this part of the dating countdown?*
Remi: *nope. just regular lunch if you want. I got bigger*
and better planned for number 3 😋 *now go get em!*
Maxine: *ok. Text you after*

She stashed her phone away, reapplied some of her red lipstick for fortitude and made her way to the meeting room. The worst thing ever was showing up late, so she ensured she was early—even Pauline wasn't in the room yet—and went over her carefully crafted notes. The key event they had on their schedule was Shalini's promo activities, especially the album launch.

Eventually, the other teams started shuffling in. Pauline slid into the seat next to her and squeezed her arm, round cheeks bunching up as she smiled at her. "All set?"

"Yup!" Maxine tried to sound confident and not like she was quaking inside. Remi's support had helped a bit but the nerves still battered her.

"Awesome. You'll do good. It's literally just a rundown of everything we're working on currently. But be prepared for him to ask questions too, as you know."

"Right." Her father wasn't the type of boss that would purposefully try to trip you up into making a fool of yourself, but he wasn't here to coddle anyone either. Least of all her. If he had a question, she'd better be ready with a response or indicate that she would find out and get back to him on it ASAP.

He strolled in with Tamara by his side, talking nonstop. She was probably updating him on a million things he had to do just today alone. Maxine didn't envy Tamara at all.

"Alright everyone, I know we're all busy. Even with the post-Carnival comedown you know a bunch of our artistes are now prepping to head overseas for tours. No rest for the wicked, eh." He chuckled as he slid into his seat, eyes scanning the various faces. "A&R team, what do you have for me?"

Maxine listened as the A&R manager spoke briefly about some promising new acts they were eyeing.

"There's this one group that's so fresh and versatile. A Roti and a Red Solo. Even the name is fun and plays up the local vibe while having this great potential regional and international appeal."

Maxine perked up at that. So the company did have Akash's band on their radar. Awesome. She itched to text Remi, but this was all confidential stuff. She couldn't talk to her about this even if it was her brother's band. The A&R team had their protocols. She couldn't overstep because, even though they obviously recognised the band's talent, if her father didn't see them as any sort of product he could mould into making profits for KKE, she would just be giving them false hope.

The A&R Manager pointed at the projector set up. "Have you all heard of them? They've been rapidly gaining an amazing following on YouTube."

Her father stared intently at the clips where the band did their thing in an intimate setting, then at smaller venues and shows. Damn, Akash was good.

She had always seen him as quiet compared to Remi's charming personality, but this guy was a different person in front of a mike.

"Isn't that your friend's brother, Maxine? What's her name again? The photographer."

Maxine jolted out of her thoughts as all eyes shifted to her. "Uh, yes." She cringed, as she sounded so unsure answering a simple question.

Her father's brow rose. "She *was* the one who did the photos of my interview, yes? I remember seeing her in one of his videos and made the connection."

"Yes. Correct. It's her brother," she said.

"Excellent. They have something there, as the team pointed out. I'd love for you to make the connection for us so we can possibly have a chat with them."

Maxine's eyes grew wise. "Me?" she couldn't help the shock.

"Yes. It would be more receptive coming from someone they know than some exec. Or is that a problem?"

"No, of course not." She cleared her throat. It was time to show her worth. "In fact, Remi is the photographer for the *Island Bites* exclusive with Shalini *and* I have it on good authority the band will be playing at Remi's gallery showing. A perfect example for the A&R team to get a taste of what they can really do live. I can wrangle an invite."

She hoped that was true. Remi's show was personal and she might not want her father's team there trying to scout her brother's band, but Maxine didn't let her resolve waver. She didn't think Remi would refuse this chance for Akash.

"I love it. Make it happen," her father said. "While we're on Shalini, what's new there? How's all that going?"

Maxine took her cue and ran with everything they had already checked off their list for her next set of radio interviews and the album launch, as well as what was left to do, which was still a lot, but things were going smoothly. "We've also tapped into some local influencers who have already begun their teaser spots for the launch. The RSVPs are rolling in and based on the numbers we anticipate a good crowd."

Her father nodded as she continued to talk, her nerves dying away as she ran down her list. Pauline was also nodding along beside her, which couldn't have made her happier.

The meeting ended on a high note as her father actually seemed happy with all the updates. He asked her to stay back a bit while everyone went about getting back into their regular work day.

"Jackie, the editor of *Island Bites*, seems to have taken a liking to you. We've known each other for years so I appreciate her judgement. The behind-the-scenes exclusive will be good exposure for you."

Maxine waited, wondering where he was going with this. Was his friend's interest in her finally making him wake up and see her worth? It should irk her that he couldn't see that on his own, but Maxine would take anything at this point.

"Yeah," she agreed.

She had been iffy on the idea when he'd presented it to her, but she knew how this business went. Her father wasn't some hidden CEO. Everyone knew exactly who he was and what he had done for this industry. His scandal aside, he was one of the major players in the local music scene.

"So, here's what I'm thinking. By the time the exclusive issue comes out, if all goes well with that band, maybe you could have yourself a new role in A&R, if you want it. We could highlight your transition in there too. Not to take Shalini's shine, but a small footnote."

Holy shit, was he being for real? Her heart was racing, battering against her chest so hard. This was what she wanted.

How the hell had he even figured that out? He was practically dangling her dream right in front her face.

She should have known his casual mention of Remi and asking her to make that initial connection with Akash's band hadn't been some random request. It was another test.

"It would," she agreed. "I would love to dive into a new challenge like that."

"Well, you know what to do."

Maxine reached for her phone to text Remi as soon as her father dismissed her.

> **Maxine:** *can I call you?*
> **Remi:** *yeah sure*

Remi picked up immediately. "To what do I owe an entire phone call?"

"My father's interested in your brother and his band." She jumped right in without any preamble.

"What? Are you serious?" Remi screeched. "Sorry, no, everything is fine," she said to someone else.

"Are you at work? Sorry, I just dived in there, but . . ."

"Hold on, Give me a minute. I'm with Cherisse helping her with some last-minute bakery planning stuff."

Maxine waited as Remi got somewhere she could talk and get excited without disrupting anyone.

"Now, say that again. Slowly."

"At the weekly meetings, each department shares what's going on in their respective area, and A&R mentioned Akash's band. I didn't even know they already had A Roti and a Red Solo on their radar! My dad knows we're friends so he may have asked me to make the initial connection for us, which is wild because he's trusting me with a lot. And I basically sort of invited the A&R team to your show cuz I know Akash would be playing?"

"Oh."

"Yeah, I know I should have run that by your first, but I got so excited." She didn't mention that her securing a new role was also riding on this. "If that would be weird, I can just let them know . . ."

"No, no it's fine. I mean their band getting eyes of a company like KKE on them like this is amazing. He's gonna freak the fuck out! I had actually wondered if something like this could happen when Pauline mentioned she might come to the show. Let me know how many invites you need, I'll sort that out."

"You already invited her?" Maxine didn't want to make this seem like a thing. It wasn't. Not really. Except, now that Pauline had cracked that little joke, Maxine was so hyper-aware of how she needed to act around Remi when work was involved.

"Yeah, we got to chatting about the project and it just came up. I didn't get to mention it. Would that be weird for you? Considering your piece and everything?"

Maxine hadn't even considered that angle of it. The photos Remi had taken wouldn't show her face, so Pauline shouldn't recognise her. "No, it's fine. It's your show, you can invite who you want."

"Okay. Have dinner with me tonight. Lunch would be time constrained because we'd both have to get back to work, but dinner would be better. My apartment. Low pressure. We can talk shop with Akash one time so he knows what to expect."

That made sense. They could be relaxed and not feel rushed. "Sounds good. Text me the time etc, okay?"

"Yeah. Let me talk to Akash *and* get back to Cherisse before she pulls any hair out. May is shaping up to be a busy month for us both with the opening and my show."

Maxine was curious how her pieces for the show were coming along. She could find out about it later. "Tonight, then."

She ended the call and almost did a celebratory shimmy down the hall to her department, but kept herself in check. Just barely. At least something in her life was going the way she wanted.

CHAPTER TWENTY-FIVE
REMI
TUESDAY 19TH MARCH

"So, tonight isn't one of the dates either?"

Remi rolled her eyes. "Nope."

"You sure?"

"Yes, it's a business dinner basically. Akash'll be there too."

Cherisse tilted her head as Remi lifted another outfit option to the screen. "Hmm, then why do you care about what you wear?"

Remi surveyed the mess on her bed. Why indeed? It didn't matter that she wanted to look good. Her bestie was supposed to help, not interrogate. Cherisse was at the bakery late again, with Keiran, observing the progress that had been made so far, so Remi had video called her. Remi didn't make it a big deal she hadn't been home to help her.

"Can't a woman just look good?" Remi asked as she yanked another combination from her closet. She could do casually cute. She didn't want Maxine to think she had made an extra effort.

"Hmm," Cherisse said again.

"Okay, fine! I want to look cute for her alright? Is that a crime?"

Cherisse grinned. "That's all you needed to say. All this pretending . . . such a waste of energy."

"Just *help* me," Remi whined. "What says 'I just casually threw this on and not at all had a meltdown about what to wear'?"

"You are so down bad, oh my God." Cherisse chuckled. "But I love you, so those leggings that make your legs and ass look amazing. With that crop top. Leave the hair down. Her business is with Akash. You're just the additional cute cupcake on the side reminding her, subtly, that this is what she could have if you two stop playing."

Remi laughed, but she couldn't help defending Maxine. "She's not playing. You know that."

"Eh." Cherisse shrugged just as Keiran appeared in the frame.

"Hey, Remi. A lil' birdie told me you're hanging with my sister tonight?"

Remi sighed. She appreciated that her friends were on team Remine or Maxmi—Scott had sent those names to the group chat one day randomly, claiming every good "ship" needed a combo name, which was ridiculous—but their enthusiasm made the situation even more frustrating for her.

She picked up the leggings Cherisse had suggested. "Is the birdie a cute pastry chef by chance?" she asked, brow raised.

Cherisse raised her bare wrist as if consulting a watch. "Well, look at the time. We gotta finish up here. Enjoy your business meeting!"

Remi shook her head but waved as they ended the call. She had to get herself ready and sort out dinner, not that she had much to do. She'd ordered a pizza, which was on the counter. Cherisse had given her so much side-eye when Remi had suggested attempting to make her own, since Cherisse knew Remi's culinary skills were minimal. All Remi had done herself was to throw together a little salad for the side. Nothing too fancy. It wasn't a date.

She'd laid out an assortment of drinks, ensuring she had her brother's favourite soft drinks since he didn't drink alcohol, and had put a bottle of wine to chill, just as an option. It was supposed to be all about business tonight, so she didn't know if Maxine would want to have a glass, but the choice would be there.

Her phone chimed as she was taking down the ice bucket.

Maxi: I'm here 😊

Remi took several calming deep breaths. It was just a normal meeting, nothing to have her heart suddenly racing like this. Yeah, she was truly down bad as Cherisse had said. Lord help her just to act casually.

Maxine stood on the other side of the door in a cute orange dress with thick straps that hugged all her curves deliciously. It ended right above her knees. The material was the clingy kind of knit that rode up every time you sat down. Great. She was going to be distracted by *that* the entire time.

"Hey, come on in. Akash isn't here yet."

Her brother had texted when the pizza had been delivered that he was on his way, so it shouldn't take him too much longer to arrive.

Maxine took a seat on the couch.

"I just gotta sort out some stuff." She tossed her thumb in the direction of the kitchen and the abandoned ice bucket that she'd left on the counter. "You can make yourself comfy."

"Need any help?" Maxine offered.

"Nah, I'm good. The pizza already came so just sorting out some ice here, but do you want a drink in the meantime? Water, juice, something stronger?"

"Water's fine."

Remi got Maxine's drink and handed it to her when she returned to the living room.

"Thanks. Those photos are yours?" She pointed to the ones hanging up around the wall.

"Yup." Remi was proud of her work but had Cherisse to thank for it being displayed. She had done it as a surprise for her when they had just moved in.

Remi sat across from Maxine on the single armchair not wanting to crowd her on the couch. She was looking way too cute tonight and Remi's brain was telling her to curl up next to her, but that was something a couple would do. They weren't quite there yet, but she was determined they *would* get there.

"They're so good. You really see things differently. I like your tee," Maxine pointed to the cropped top that announced *I* ♥ *Burpees . . . Said No One Ever.* "Perfectly captures my feelings about burpees."

Remi chuckled. "Oh yeah. I don't know a single person that enjoys those. Pull-ups, however, I actually like."

Maxine's brow raised. "Only you would love those. But your upper body strength is ridic cuz you lifted me so easily that . . . uh . . . one time . . ." she trailed off.

Remi couldn't help her smirk. Oh yeah, she wasn't forgetting that bathroom moment, ever.

"Sorry, I shouldn't have brought that up." Maxine fanned her face with her hand, clearly flustered, as the AC was on.

"No big. I'm not gonna pounce on you just because the memory of that is flashing through my mind now. We're adults. We can talk about this without succumbing to lust, yeah?"

Maxine rolled her eyes. "Now you're just teasing me."

"You make it so fun."

Remi's phone beeped. Akash was here and Remi jumped up to open the door.

"Wow," Maxine grinned as he walked in. She gestured around her head. "The hair is really doing the damn thing with you two, isn't it."

Akash's hair was pulled back in a low ponytail, but the curls were popping.

"The results look good, but washing it is a chore." Akash indicated the spot next to Maxine. "Okay if I sit here or . . .?" He looked over at Remi who was seriously going to beat his ass if he said anything irritating.

"Oh yeah, feel free." Maxine scooted over to make space for Akash, either not picking up on his not-so-subtle teasing or simply ignoring it.

She was there for business, so maybe she was too focused on that to notice.

"You want to eat while you talk?"

They both nodded and Remi went about plating the pizza, after they had chosen their preference. She had ordered a meat and a veggie option.

She let them do their thing. It was important they get to know each other. Akash didn't know this business side of Maxine—neither did she to be honest—so she was curious how Maxine would handle this. Remi was just there for moral support and, as Cherisse said, to look cute, too.

"KKE has been rolling out some heavy hitters for years." Akash took a bite of his pizza. "But if we came on with you all, would we still have input in our sound? I know your dad's got a business to run and may have a certain direction he would want us to go, but I want to make sure we don't get railroaded and have no voice. And before you ask, yes, I have the go ahead to speak on behalf of the band."

Maxine nodded. "I feel you. You've worked hard to get your music out there and it's not easy to trust a big company. I get that, but I can say we would definitely make sure you have a say in your artistic direction. Before we do anything, our A&R team will come to Remi's show to get a feel for you live, and we'll just move from there." She leaned back, pizza in hand. "Trust me when I say the team already sees you're destined for great things. Just be your amazing selves and should be all good."

"Don't worry about that; we always do," Akash said confidently. He had the skills to back it up, so Remi was certain the band would handle their stories at the showcase.

She was more worried about the actual show and whether anyone would come. Of course, she had her close friends and family, who would for sure be there, but it wasn't an intimate "by invite only" event—which, thinking about it now, why hadn't she done that first? —but open to the public too. The ads had been posted to the gallery's social media, which meant she had to buckle down to get everything in perfect order.

It was nerve-wrecking as hell to have people who didn't know her coming to judge her work. She always tried to bring her flair into the shots she took for *Island Bites*, but this was more personal. This time, the entire thing was her own story being told from start to finish.

"Earth to Remi, you still with us?"

She blinked over at Akash and Maxi who were eyeing her as she had gone off into her own overthinking. "Yeah, fine. Just so much to get done still for the show."

"You'll do great. Let me know if you need help with anything," Maxine offered.

Remi wanted to hug her for the offer, but she maintained her calm since Akash had a lil' gleam in his eyes as he watched the two of them interact. "I'll let you know what exactly, but I'll definitely accept the assistance."

Akash pumped Maxine full of questions and she answered flawlessly, no bias or anything. Maxine definitely knew her shit, which made her even more attractive in Remi's eyes.

"Well." Akash got to his feet. "I got the basics. So, you all come to the show, check us out and we go from there." He tapped his chin. "You also get an invitation to our rehearsal for an exclusive sneak peek if you like? Just you, though. The other A&R people can wait 'til the show."

"Oh yeah?" Maxine looked excited about the prospect. "I'd definitely love that!"

Akash gave her a thumbs up. "I have to say it was nice meeting you like this and seeing you two actually get along. I remember Remi literally ranting about this King girl back in the day."

Heat crept up her neck as Akash happily recounted how she would come home and go on and on about "that girl". He wasn't wrong, but did he have to drop her files like that?

"Okay, you had your fun. Get out."

Akash laughed. "Hey, you're both cool now, right? I can officially reveal these secrets." He laughed again as Remi playfully dragged him away and shoved him towards the door.

"Hush! Nobody want to hear none of that. Just go home, nah!"

Maxine was full-on doubled over laughing when she returned. "You used to vent about me, huh? That King girl. Guess I was living in your mind 24/7, hmm?"

"Don't you start. I'm sure you did the same when we left school for the day."

Maxine wiped at her eyes. She had laughed until she was actually crying. "Nope. Didn't give you the time of day outside of school."

Remi leaned forward from her seat, their legs slightly bumping. "I don't believe that for a second. C'mon, you can admit now. We're grown."

"Nope. Never happened."

"So that's how it is? I'll just ask Keiran. He owes me."

Maxine tugged at the hem of her dress that had ridden up since she had been laughing so hard. "You wouldn't."

"Oh doll," she drawled, "I *so* would, and I will. He'll do anything for me since I basically convinced Cherry not to blank him." She leaned back in the chair, hands laced over her stomach, bare foot almost brushing against Maxine's leg. Maxine had scooted into the spot Akash had vacated so she was that much closer.

Maxine looked down to where Remi's foot was bouncing. "I see how it is, Ms Daniels. I thought we were gonna keep this on track. No dirty tactics, but if you wanna go there." She tilted her head up, gaze locking with Remi's. "Do you want to reset again?"

That look was challenging, her tone slightly scolding, but still light enough that Remi didn't feel chastised. It was more teasing than anything. This entire thing had to be stressful for Maxine, but she was clearly trying not to get overwhelmed by it.

"Well, this *is* your show, doll. But as hard as this is for me to say with you looking like that, in that dress—and we have a whole house to ourselves?" The struggle was real, but she was going to keep them on track, dammit. "I don't think we should purposefully reset."

Maxine sighed. "You're right of course, but . . . damn those fricking leggings." She muttered the last part, but Remi heard it.

"What about my leggings? They're pretty comfy."

Maxine shook her head. "Yeah, you look very relaxed. Anyhoo . . . I should go."

"You don't have to. We can chill, watch a movie. See what Netflix got going on?" Maxine raised a brow and Remi grinned. "Not like that ma'am. I legit mean just watch a movie. But maybe some other time when I'm not wearing the leggings of distraction that make my ass look grabbable."

Maxine rolled her eyes but got to her feet. "Your entire existence is a distraction. But yes, let's have a movie night some other time."

"Alright."

Remi walked Maxine to the door, being a perfect lady by not letting her eyes dip to Maxine's ass. Barely. God, she loved clingy dresses.

"I'll text you the date details."

Maxine's smile was sweet. Remi hoped she was looking forward to it as much as she was. "Sure. Goodnight."

Remi watched her walk down to her car and ensured she was safely in and off before she closed the door.

This was getting harder with each passing day, that countdown clock to ten always at the back of her mind. In spite of her worries about what the end date would bring, she was enjoying this wooing. With Sanaa they had gone from intense hooking up just to falling into being a couple—until they weren't. Anyone after that had sort of followed the same way. Make out with some random at a party. Keep doing it. Try to date for a while or just enjoy each other for sex until one or the other moved on. Damn, she did have a pattern, didn't she? Maxine had been right to want to see if they could do this.

Hell, she and Maxine had started that way as teens too, from that first kiss to going further during the holidays as they prepared to graduate. They had never brought up dating during that time because it didn't make sense. Even though Remi had been deep into her feelings, she had never said anything, since Maxine was leaving. Plus, Maxine had probably been freaking out about everything. They never actually talked in depth about it.

What a mess. She was determined that history wasn't going to repeat itself. She was pulling out every romantic tactic she knew. Anxiety be damned.

CHAPTER TWENTY-SIX
MAXINE
FRIDAY 29TH MARCH

THE COOL NIGHT BREEZE WAFTED INTO THE CAR AS MAXINE MADE HER way to the dance studio. Remi had offered to pick her up, but Maxine had ended up working a bit late that Friday so she told her she would meet her there.

Her mind was going a mile a minute trying to guess what they could be doing for their date. The studio location suggested it could be dance-related. Was Remi going to teach her some moves? It was a logical assumption and a great way for Maxine to get a solo viewing of that side of her character.

Remi had told her to dress up and Maxine had gone right for a flirty red dress, heels to match. If they were going to be dancing, she wanted to have a swishy dress on so she could get the maximum date vibes in.

Girl, you think you living in a rom-com or what?

Was it so wrong to want some razzle dazzle? In her excitement to capture the perfect look—she had even switched up her hair and done some soft curls—she totally forgot that this would send out the bat signal to her mother, who didn't know about her dates.

Her mother had raised a curious brow when she saw her all dolled up. "Something you need to tell me?" she'd asked.

"Nope. Just heading out."

"Dressed up like that? I know you said you were going out but you don't have to be shy about telling me it's a date."

"It's not a d—"

She hadn't even finished the sentence when Leah had come into the living room, rubbing her eyes. "Is mummy going out with Auntie Remi?"

"I thought you were sleeping?" She tweaked Leah's nose as she giggled. She had been dozing in her grandmother's lap while Maxine had been getting ready.

Maxine was not about to admit she was out here like this because of Remi. Too many questions could follow, and tonight wasn't the time to get into it. Leah, of course, had no idea what she may have clued her grandmother into with her innocent question.

Her mother was watching her, waiting for her to answer either of their questions. Too bad, wasn't happening.

"You should be in bed, missy." She placed a kiss on Leah's forehead. "Bye, love you."

She should have been prepared for the questions, but she hadn't considered them when she was getting ready. She'd only wanted to dress to impress. A thrill ran through her as she anticipated Remi's reaction.

She was moments away from seeing just that as she pulled into the studio's designated parking area. All thoughts of the interrogation she was going to get tomorrow from her mother were pushed to the back of her mind.

Tonight was for them. Nothing else was allowed.

Remi told her she would buzz her in and she was heading up the stairs within a minute of texting her that she was here. Maxine had tried to picture the type of scene Remi would set, but she had not expected anything like what she walked into.

"Holy shit," she whispered as she looked around. The simple studio where she had done another class just last week was gone. The mirror that allowed the students to see themselves was totally covered with a black drape and shone with several strings of fairy lights. Clipped to the lights were a bunch of photos. Some Polaroids were included in the mix. Maxine knew Remi was trying different types of cameras to capture her subjects.

She didn't remember the other fancy camera names, but Polaroids were easy to identify.

Standing in front of the pretty backdrop was Remi in some sleek palazzo pants and a tight-fitting waistcoat worn like a top, with nothing under it that Maxine could see.

Oh God she looked good. Those toned arms could lift her so easily again.

Nope, do not go there.

"Welcome." Remi smiled and beckoned her forward. "I wanted to show you a little sample of your photos for the show."

"Oh my God!" The photos were all her. They were the ones taken when she was too tense to relax. The ones Remi had captured after they had both loosened up a bit. "It's me. Really me."

Her eyes slid over the sensual shots, neck getting warm. Those were stunning, but she hadn't expected Remi to include the shots she had considered a failure. Seeing them all like this, she grasped the story Remi was telling here. It showed a progression, from her struggling to being more open to the experience.

"I hope it's okay I use the first set. I know you didn't think it was working, and I thought so to at first, but "Inner" is about showing sides we may not want others to see." Remi tapped one of the photos. "Or parts of us others don't know. We so heavily curate everything these days. Our feeds. Our emotions. I felt like to not have these shots where you're clearly frustrated would make it lacking."

Maxine touched one of the Polaroids where she remembered being *oh so done* with everything. She wanted the process to go smoothly and had been overthinking it, getting annoyed with herself when she felt she had been doing a terrible job. Seeing it here now, raw like this . . . "I love it. You're so good at this. Seriously. It's perfect."

Remi smiled. "Thanks. Your approval means a lot. So, this is just part of it. I wanted our date to be here because we didn't get to dance like we wanted to. Just us. No prying eyes." She reached out her hand. "Would you dance with me?" She gestured off to the side where a bamboo mat was displayed with a pitcher, glasses, and some food containers. "We can work up an appetite."

Maxine's throat felt tight. Remi had truly done all of this, for her. Did she deserve it? Deserve her? All she'd done was make them do this pact to satisfy some need to prove that they had something more than their fiery attraction.

"Yes, I'll dance with you." She took the hand Remi offered and allowed herself to be reeled in, right into Remi's space.

Remi took her phone out of her pocket and used the thumb of her free hand to press something. Soft Latin music filled the studio and once she tucked her phone away that hand went right to Maxine's waist. It felt like it fit so perfectly there.

"Just follow my lead, okay?"

Gladly. Maxine didn't have the classic dance moves down like Remi, but she knew a thing or two from watching her parents back in their happier times. It was enough to follow along as they swayed around the studio, Remi showing off by spinning her around, then bringing Maxine in so she clung to her.

"I'm sorry again for ignoring you like that. That night." She felt the need to say it.

Remi pulled back, hands still on Maxine's hips. "Hey, no. Nothing to be sorry about. You weren't comfortable to dance with me there. That's fine."

"I like this. Dancing with you. A lot."

Remi tucked a wayward curl behind Maxine's ear. "You sound surprised. Did you think you wouldn't?"

"Oh no, I knew I would. Too much. I love going out and dancing. I just never had any anxiety attached to it before, you know?"

"Yeah."

Maxine allowed herself just to enjoy the moment, not overthink it. It was easier since they were alone rather than out in public. She rested her head on Remi's shoulder, inhaling her fresh lavender scent. She wanted not to care about what anyone would say. But she couldn't shake it off. There was a difference between two female friends who were fooling around on the dance floor for fun, or getting into the spirit of things during Carnival, and two women who were a bit more intimate enjoying the feel and movements of each other. She was certain people could tell.

"I want to be braver," she mumbled. "I really do."

"You already are," Remi's voice sounded in her ear. "Deciding who you want to be and what you want to do, on your terms, is already extremely brave. Don't let anyone chain you up to think you have to express any part of your identity in a specific way. I'll kick their ass if you need me to."

That made her laugh, easing some of the tension. She suspected that was exactly what Remi had been aiming for.

Maxine leaned back. They were still swaying slowly, in no hurry to untangle from each other. This close, she could lean in and brush her lips against Remi, but she wouldn't, not yet.

They had done this in reverse—had sex, then were trying to see if they fit together outside of that.

Why are you punishing yourself like this? Just date her for real and you can pull up to the all-you-can-eat buffet whenever you want.

"Hungry yet?"

Maxine almost choked at the question coming right after her less than innocent thoughts. "Yeah, let's eat."

Remi didn't let her go. "I wish I knew what was going on in that head of yours. Seems like you were thinking something else, something more . . . fun."

"Nah. You really don't wanna dive into this mess." She tapped her forehead. "This place needs some sageing or something."

"I love a dirty-minded gal, so don't go spring cleaning on my account." She took Maxine by her hand, leading her over to the bamboo mats.

Maxine took off her shoes to get comfortable as Remi went about pouring them drinks and plating up the food which smelled delicious. The drink also looked pretty, with its grapefruit, lime, and peach slices. The mint leaves added a nice touch.

She had taken a photo of the spread before they'd dived in but hadn't posted anything yet, still indecisive about the caption. What if she just said fuck it and went with #datenight? That would definitely stir up some questions.

"You made all of this?" Maxine asked as she sipped her drink. It was refreshing and delicious. "Oh, this is really damn good."

Remi's smile made her entire being glow. "Reba helped me with the drink. She's good at these random combos that just work. Never would have thought of Grapefruit Peach Sangria. The food was all me. I tried not to make anything too complicated."

Maxine nibbled on the crusty bread that was smothered in

some sort of cheese and topped off with diced seasoned tomato that was just the perfect combination as well.

"This is yum." Her mouth was full, but Remi just laughed. She probably had chipmunk cheeks going on right now, but damn this was too delicious.

She didn't care. Remi had to know what she was getting into with her and when it came to food she didn't hold back.

"Glad you're enjoying. I'm not the best cook. Not gonna lie, I considered just ordering everything, but I can handle simple things. Full disclosure, though. I didn't make this bread. I am *not* good with baking shit."

"Your whole bestie is a baker. I'm sure she can give you some tips if you wanted them."

"Yeah, nah." Remi picked up a skewer that was layered with some perfectly grilled meat and veggies. "Cherisse says I'm unteachable and I'm banned from using her oven."

"Damn, what did you do?"

Remi shrugged. "You almost catch a thing on fire once and you're blacklisted for life."

"Remi, noooo." It was funny to picture that. Remi was so good at everything that she did. Fitness. Photography. Dancing. Being sexy.

"Unfortunately, yes."

An idea was beginning to formulate. "Cooking or baking together can be fun. If you ever wanted to try it. No pressure of course."

"I'd love that actually. I don't think Cherisse has the patience for me, but maybe you do?" She raised her glass, gesturing for Maxine to complete the toast. "To me, not destroying your kitchen because Cherisse will never agree to doing this at the apartment."

They clinked their drinks together and Maxine felt a bubble of excitement in her stomach. She would love making dinner for

Remi. Cooking was something she enjoyed but rarely got to do these days. Her mother was a bit possessive about her kitchen, but Maxine could swing this as trying to help a friend out.

"I promise to get us out of there unscathed."

They ate the rest of the meal, drank some more sangria, and just talked about whatever came to mind. By the time they had finished half of the pitcher, Maxine felt light and carefree. Not because of the drink—Remi had been courteous enough to make it a virgin one as they both had to drive home—just by being in Remi's presence.

She was telling Maxine stories about her dance tour day, how she intended to use some of her old photos in the show, and she looked so happy recounting her memories that Maxine couldn't help feeling dazzled. She didn't hesitate when Remi jumped up to show her some of the old routine, trying to copy the moves as they both slid around the studio barefoot.

"You have to twirl like this, so you're really just doing it on one foot, the other tucked up." Remi did a flawless spin, her curls flowing around her like a black curtain. Maxine tried to follow but ended up stumbling.

Remi moved fast, catching her. "You've got to stop falling for me like this," she joked as she helped Maxine up.

"Damn, I can't even blame the alcohol since we've had none."

They were in each other's arms again. That seemed to be the norm for this dance date. Maxine didn't pull away. Just enjoyed Remi's eyes roving over her face.

"I like you so much, you know that right?" Remi brushed away curls from Maxine's face, fingers lightly grazing her ear as she tucked the hair away.

She could ignore the comment, make a joke, switch gears to something far lighter than this, but she didn't want to. Remi deserved her honesty.

"I know." Of course she did. Remi's actions said a lot. She still felt like they had missed out on ten years of each other and it could make things better if they fixed that. They were different people now. "I like you too," she admitted.

Her skin felt heated after her confession. The curving up of the corner of Remi's mouth didn't help matters. If she hadn't basically put them in time out, now would be the perfect time for her to lean in, seal her words with a kiss.

Then release yourself from this misery.

"But I have to be sure."

Remi nodded. "I know. Just know that regardless of what the tenth date brings, I'm here for you always."

"Thank you." That meant a lot to her. She hadn't realised it but part of her was scared of losing Remi if she chose not to pursue anything romantic with her.

Her mind was a jumble of should she or shouldn't she? But she was going to see this through. "Please bear with me. I know it's kind of unfair and I hope you don't think I'm just stringing you along. I really just need to figure this out."

Remi kissed the top of her head. "I know. One more dance for the road?"

"Yes, please."

Her heart thumped a drum beat in her chest as they swayed to some Sade. She could get used to this. If only she could release her fear and just say yes.

CHAPTER TWENTY-SEVEN

REMI
SATURDAY 6TH APRIL

> *Maxi: ready for later?*
> *Remi: you got home insurance right?*
> *Maxi: it's gonna be fine. Seriously lol. You're that worried?*
> *Remi: >>*
> *Maxi: you literally just cooked for me!*
> *Remi: some grilled meats and veggies. Done on a small portable grill we have. Store-bought bread. The tomato topping didn't require me anywhere near the stove . . .*
> *Maxi: I promise I'll take good care of you.*
> *Remi:* 😬

Maxine had been reassuring her since they'd left the dance studio date that Remi would do well. She wasn't so sure about that, but if Maxine wanted to show her how it's done, she wouldn't back out, even if she totally bombed at this.

They had both been busy with work so they had been communicating by texts as usual. But nothing beat face-to-face time together. With Shalini's album launch and Remi's show next month, there was a lot going on between them. Remi was determined to make the efforts for the dates.

Today was going to be quite interesting too since Maxine's family would be there. Remi assumed Ms. King didn't have a clue about what was going on between them so she would have to be on her P's and Q's this afternoon.

Not too hard considering she would be more nervous about screwing up the cooking lesson than Ms. King getting any vibes off of them.

She threw on some sweatpants and a comfortable slouchy top. On impulse, she stopped at the grocery store near her apartment to grab something for Maxine. She stared at her gift tucked away safely in the passenger seat and wondered if this was too much, but decided not to overthink it.

Hopefully it wouldn't cause too much fuss.

All second guessing was tossed out the window when Maxine's eye lit up upon opening her front door and seeing the bouquet of flowers in Remi's hand.

"Hey."

"Are they for me?"

"Yup," she said, trying to sound casual, as if she wasn't having heart palpitations over Maxine accepting the flowers. "Sorry, if this is too much. I didn't think. I just wanted to get you something because it's a date. So . . ."

"Hey, no take backs! I haven't had flowers from anyone in a while. Thank you." She took them, cradling them gently in her arms as she told Remi to come in.

Remi felt like she was walking on cloud nine now that Maxine hadn't thrown her impulse buy back at her.

"I'll get something to put this in."

Ms. King entered from one of the side rooms just as they were heading to the kitchen. Her gaze landed on the flowers. "Well, that's sweet of you, Remi."

"It's a thank you in advance to Maxi for risking me in the kitchen." She tried to play off the gesture as nothing but friendly appreciation.

Maxine rolled her eyes. "Seriously, we'll be fine." She continued towards the kitchen area.

"You're in good hands. Just don't mess up my kitchen," Ms. King told her, wagging her finger in her direction, but she was smiling, so Remi didn't feel too worried about it. She trusted Maxine would ensure things went the way they should.

"You girls have fun. Keiran's got Leah down in the studio showing her some stuff to keep her distracted so you can focus. I'm heading out in a few with a friend to check out the farmer's market."

"Uh huh. We have yet to meet this friend you keep going out with," Maxine called out as she filled a vase with some water and arranged the flowers. "Hmm, where should I put these?"

"Dining table can work," Ms. King suggested, pretending as if she hadn't heard what Maxine said about her friend.

Remi chuckled but didn't add her two cents to that, joining Maxine in the kitchen as Ms. King went about her business.

Maxine pulled out her phone. "Thank you for these. It was really sweet. Let me capture them before they wither."

Remi watched her type up a caption before clicking to post. "I really am grateful for you taking your time to do this. I've never had a cooking date before."

Maxine tossed her a smile before she looked around the kitchen. There were ingredients laid out, but Remi couldn't fathom what sort of dish they were making. "It's a great way for people to bond and get to see what the other's made of. Can you handle the heat, or do you need to get out the kitchen?"

"How long have you been waiting to say that?"

Maxine played around with her phone until the smooth vocals of Kes' *Hello* started playing. "Okay, busted. I'm a sucker for pun-filled dialogue on those cooking shows. Random fact, I do like pretending to be one of those hosts while cooking." She pressed her hands to her face, shaking her head. "I'm sorry you're on a date with an actual, real-life dork."

Remi removed her hands from her face. With her bangs pinned back and her hair pulled in a ponytail, Maxine looked as adorable as ever. "I like cute dorks; you're good. So what're we making today?"

Maxine clapped her hands. "I told you seafood would be involved, just to be sure you're not allergic to anything, but today we're keeping it simple. Eggplant florentine with fire-roasted tomato sauce and toasted ciabatta, lobster ravioli, and to finish off a candied walnut and pear salad."

"Uh." Remi stared at Maxine. All of that sounded fancy and complicated. "That's . . . wow . . . okay. And lobster?" That shit was expensive. She definitely didn't want Maxine going out of her way like this just for her.

"I make cooking fun. I promise. And I got that lobster as a gift for helping somebody out."

"Hmm." Remi narrowed her eyes. "It was from a guy, wasn't it?"

Maxine poked her in the arm playfully. "No jealousy allowed. He's like sixty and he and his partner have been quite happy for many years. C'mon. We'll start with the eggplant."

Maxine was right about making it fun. She talked Remi through everything she was doing while they both followed the recipe, dancing around the kitchen while Remi studiously prepared the tofu ricotta for the eggplant that was already in the oven roasting away.

"Always set a timer," Maxine instructed. "I can't tell you how many times I put something to cook and got caught up with Leah or something else and ruined a whole dinner. Trial and error are all part of it, but it doesn't hurt to mitigate disaster. Being a stay-at-home mom for years, I couldn't afford to be redoing stuff because I got distracted."

"I don't know what your ex did for work but did you have to be entertaining a lot?" Remi had been so curious about Maxine's life back in Atlanta. She had gathered certain things from her social media over the years but the way people curated their lives to only show the good, she didn't know if that was any real indicator.

"Eh, sometimes."

She hovered close by as Remi prepared the saucepan. Maxine tossed in the minced garlic and Remi inhaled the delicious scent as it sautéed.

"Good, good," Maxine assured her as Remi added in the fire-roasted tomatoes with some salt and pepper.

That simple praise made Remi feel even warmer than she already was from being this close to the bubbling sauce.

"At least he was good about giving proper notice in advance. Some of the other moms would randomly get a text saying their husband was on the way with so and so asking if they would whip up something quick." Maxine shook her head. "He knew I would've murdered him for that." She laughed as if remembering something. "I won't ever forget the time I burnt dinner because I was busy taking in some show while putting Leah to sleep. I literally ordered something and pretended I made it because I didn't have enough time."

Remi shot her a sidelong glance. "Really? No judgement, but that's hilarious."

"Aye, I wanted to make a good impression too. But desperate times and all that. Let's taste this now."

Remi got a spoon, dipped it into the sauce and brought it up for Maxine to taste.

"Oh yeah, that's good." She practically moaned in pleasure. "Good job!" She high fived Remi who was trying to ignore the tingling in her stomach over Maxine's tone.

That's how she sounds when you go down on her. Or finger her. Or touch her anywhere . . .

"Thanks." She took a taste herself to keep her mouth busy from vocalising just that.

They finished up the spinach and got the ciabatta ready and worked together to assemble the eggplant.

It felt domestic and almost like Remi was seeing what their future together could be like. Sashaying in the kitchen to some tunes while they prepared a meal. Stolen kisses and playful banter in between monitoring the stove or oven.

"Damn, we really did that." Remi snapped several shots of the first course of the meal. The eggplant were stacked atop each other with the ricotta in between, and the sauce and spinach finishing it off looked divine.

Flavour exploded in Remi's mouth as she took a sample. "Oh shit, that's good."

"See. Easy, but really tasty and satisfying."

"Where do you even find these recipes?"

"Online. Pinterest mostly. I got boards upon boards for everything in my life basically. Alright, onto the ravioli."

By the time they had completed all parts of the meal, Remi was buzzing. Maxine's words and little touches of encouragement had her entire body on high alert. Learning that Maxine was way more tactile than she had thought was a double-edged sword, because every press of her hand to her arm, or teasing poke to her side to get her attention, was just too much.

Going from giving into their urges to fighting hard not to was giving Remi's vibrator an extra workout these days. All these light touches meant Remi was one-brush-of-a-finger-anywhere-near-her-body away from pressing Maxine against the counter and kissing the breath out of her.

She watched Maxine bend to capture different angles of the dishes. Remi didn't think, she moved closer to Maxine's side. "Try this," she encouraged, gently guiding her hand to angle the shot differently. She grabbed a handful of leftover walnuts and sprinkled it on the counter near the dish.

"Oh. That's nice," Maxine agreed. "You're so good at this."

"Yeah." She leaned back, tugged on Maxine's ponytail and, oh shit, the way her neck followed the movement and her back automatically arched. She had meant it as a playful gesture. Why the hell had Maxine responded like that? She didn't want to think anything sexual in the moment, but fuck, Maxine would look so good getting railed from behind. Ass and tits bouncing.

Remi stepped away before she ran her hand down Maxine's back to cup her shapely ass in those shorts. "We should go eat before it gets cold."

Maxine turned around to face Remi, back pressed to the counter. "Mmmhmm, yup, let's do that. Thanks for the photo tip."

"Anytime." They both didn't move. "Fuck, I'm in trouble," Remi couldn't help admitting.

Maxine inhaled deeply, then exhaled with a small laugh. "We can't be this pathetic."

"We most definitely can, because you don't know what I want to do to you right now."

"What do you wanna do?" Eyes heavy lidded, head cocked to the side, Maxine was the picture of decadent. Yeah, she was casually dressed, but the way that move had bared her neck? Remi wanted to press her hand right there.

Maxine's tongue swiped across her top lip and, god dammit, it wasn't supposed to go this way.

"I wanna eat, but not all this fucking delicious food we just made. You like having your hair pulled." It wasn't a question because there was no doubt how Maxine had reacted to the innocent gesture.

Maxine tilted her head back. "Yeah. There's just something so sexy about it." She crossed her legs. Remi's gaze dropped down to her fleshy thigh. "This is part of getting to know each other too, you know. We can talk about this without acting on it."

"You're stronger than me cuz I'm two seconds away from putting my damn fingers up your cunt."

"Okay, that's." Maxine shook her head. "Dammit. Can we just go eat?"

Remi smirked. It was mean of her to do this but she was so deprived of Maxine's taste and touch right now. She moved into Maxine's space.

"The food. I meant the food. I can't think about anything else getting eaten right now." Maxine's chest heaved up and down as Remi curled her hands at her side to stop from actually touching her.

"It's alright. I won't go down on you in your kitchen in broad daylight."

A cough made them both jump and they turned to see Keiran standing there looking extremely chagrined.

"Yeah. I'm gonna just grab these juices for me and Leah. I was never here. I heard nada. Carry on. Well, *don't* carry on with your . . . uh . . . plan . . . cuz I am still here. In the house. So maybe don't do that."

"We're gonna eat. The lunch," Maxine added, and Remi laughed in spite of the awkwardness.

Keiran quickly took the drinks from the fridge and practically fast walked out of the kitchen. Maxine pressed her hand to her forehead. "Remi, whyyyy?"

Remi gave her a side hug, while still cracking up over

Keiran's terrible timing. Or maybe it was the perfect intervention. Things were getting too hot in here. "I'm sorry. Let's eat the food. For real. I don't wanna ruin all your hard work. We can discuss preferences as we munch."

"We are not resetting again. I swear to you Remi, I will . . ."

Remi started stacking the plates and dishes on a tray so they could take everything outside. "What you gonna do, hmm?" she taunted.

"Making me so damn turned on I almost . . ." she huffed. "You know what? You wanna tango? Let's tango, Remi Daniels." Maxine stalked out the room with the wine-and-juice-infused drink they had prepared.

"Oooh, full names. Should I be scared?" Remi was so tempted to kiss away Maxine's pouty glare but she simply sat across from her smiling.

She was satisfied with herself when she had no right to be, but she was having a great time. She reached for her fork to cut a bite of the ravioli just as Maxine said in the sweetest tone, "There's just something about back shots where you don't even take everything off. Just push your underwear to the side so you see it all, but it's a bit constricted by the fabric. Oh, this ravioli is perfection."

Remi choked on her food, started coughing as she couldn't even swallow her bite properly after that. Maxine pushed a glass of water towards her. "Don't die over there. I haven't sat on your face yet."

"Fuck, Maxi, what the *fuck*?" she said when she could catch her breath, "You really tryna kill me over here?"

Maxine continued eating, slowly licking the sauce off her fork, eyebrow raised. "Not at all. We're just having a friendly conversation, aren't we?"

The hell they were. There wasn't a damn friendly thing

about a visual of Maxine on her knees as Remi went to town with her strap-on. Or Maxine riding her face, moans falling around them like the sweetest music.

Remi had made a mistake. Maxine was going to torture her until *she* was on her knees begging her to let her fuck her, wasn't she? Her plan had totally backfired.

CHAPTER TWENTY-EIGHT
MAXINE
TUESDAY 9TH APRIL

THE MIRROR REFLECTION OF HERSELF LOOKED BACK AT HER, EYES WIDE as she took in her body in the black lacy number. Her ample curves were overflowing everywhere. She grinned as she turned around to get a view of her ass in this. Damn. She looked so good. She hadn't meant to try this on. Today's shopping was about finding something to wear to Shalini's launch and Remi's showcase.

But she had seen the sexy lingerie and a light bulb had gone off in her mind. She had told Remi she wasn't going to let her teasing slide. Her reflection smirked back at her as she took some shots and sent the photos before she could stop herself.

Her notifications went wild, and Maxine grinned.

Remi: TF!
Remi: YOU DID NOT
Remi: wait, are you in a public dressing room like this?
Ass out. Tits just . . . WTF!
Maxine: good day to you too 🙄
Remi: this is what you get up to on your lunch time??

Remi: push the panties to the side and let me fucking see you. I'm going out of my mind here!!!!!!!!

Maxine contemplated. Could she be that bold? She was tucked away in the dressing room away from any eyes so what she did in here would be for her alone. Her phone pinged again.

Remi: sorry, sorry. That was *not* very polite. I shouldn't be demanding anything but . . . I am a weaaaak womaaaan. This is not in keeping with the dating rules ma'am!

Maxine: I did warn you about tangoing with me didn't i? 😉

She could picture Remi wherever she was—she wasn't sure if she was out on assignment or in her office—having a melt-down. Either way, she didn't care. Remi might have thought she was joking about payback, but she wasn't about to be the only one suffering.

They had got through the cooking date on Saturday with no further almost incidents. Conversation had moved from any talk of sex to other things—safer ground—which Maxine didn't mind. It helped her calm the hell down and she enjoyed learning more about Remi, sharing things with her they hadn't spoken about before.

It felt . . . nice. The word didn't truly capture it, but she had missed that part of dating – getting to know someone and their quirks; their likes and dislikes.

And now all her curiosity about Remi over the years was being fulfilled.

During their time in school, there was no desire to know anything about Remi other than she was Maxine's competition and the most annoying person ever. Then it became about simply getting off and not looking too closely—or at all, to be honest—at why they were fooling around when she wasn't staying. They were just going with it until it all imploded, as she should have expected.

Their teen selves had channelled their antagonistic relationship to sex. It was a terrible idea, but they hadn't been thinking anything beyond how good it all felt.

God, they really were a bitchy mess back then. Maxine grinned in spite of how cringey the memory was.

Now, they could create new memories. Maxine recalled the sweet kiss Remi had given her on her cheek after they had finished the meal. It had left her so fluttery, she hadn't known what to do with herself. Keiran and Leah had come up for a breather after and her brother had been shooting her amused grins the rest of the afternoon.

Another message came through from Remi:

I'm sorry I was being a brat then. Please ease meeee uuuuup

Maxine took once last photo and sent it. There would be no easing up. Remi could enjoy the explicit shot she had sent and think about her all day long.

The knock on the dressing room door almost made her drop her phone. "How's it going in there?"

Ah shit, she had totally forgotten that she hadn't come on this shopping adventure alone. Scott had agreed to meet her to help choose her dress and some new makeup.

"Great. One sec!"

Now she had to figure out how to sneak this lingerie out of here with the rest of the clothes without him knowing. She had basically grabbed it off the rack when he hadn't been looking and ducked into the room.

Scott had known her too many years because of his friendship with Keiran. He was for sure not going to act like he didn't see the scrap of cloth if he caught sight of that, not that she had made up her mind she was buying the sexy thing. It might be better to come back for that at a later time.

She slipped it between the dresses she wasn't going to take and breezed out the room. "These two for sure." She raised her arm where the hangers dangled on her wrist with her options.

"Definitely the two I liked the most on you. Now onto the makeup?"

She casually handed the bundle of clothes to the lady who had been helping her since they had arrived and quickly paid for her dresses, then she followed Scott over to the makeup section.

"I can't wait to get my hands on you and Remi for your events."

She had agreed to let Scott work his makeup magic for the launch as well as Remi's show. Having done the bridal party's makeup for Ava's wedding, she knew he was damn good at this. If she was going to be one of the people featured, she better put some more effort into it, even if guests wouldn't know it was her in the photos. Victoria had offered, but Maxine wanted to get something a bit more dramatic than usual and that was definitely Scott's vibe.

"Which dress goes with which event?" he asked as he scanned the individual eyeshadow selections and the palettes. The girl working this area kept staring at Scott, but he didn't seem put off by it. With a face like that and skin that basically glowed, he was probably used to it.

He smiled at her. "Love these new baked palettes. Pops on most of my clients."

"You're a makeup artist?" the girl asked.

"Model. Makeup artist. Creative Director. Beauty is my life, baby. I love the look you got going on right now." He drew a circle around the girl's face. "Fresh and fun. That yellow is doing it for you!"

Maxine held in her giggle as the girl looked positively dazzled by Scott's attention. Today, he wasn't even in full Scott mode, his eyelids bare of any colour. Just his nose ring was adorning his face.

"But back to you, Max. The dress options?"

"I'm thinking the flashier one for Remi's show. The launch is still a work event so the other can look cute but not too much?"

"Gotcha."

Maxine listened as Scott went on about her options. She wasn't totally hopeless with makeup, but when it came to doing elaborate stuff, she didn't feel the need to dedicate so much time or energy. So she was happy to have someone knowledge-able at least guide her about colours that would stand out more and some that were subtler, for everyday use.

The girl at the booth had even offered to do a little demo on Maxine's face, but she had to get back to work.

"So, how'd your shoot with Remi go?" Scott asked as they strolled away from the makeup to head to the food court. Since she knew she was going to be out at lunch, she hadn't bothered to walk with food. They were going to grab something quick then head back to their respective jobs.

"Trying to get spoilers?"

"I meaaaan she didn't say a thing about it when I did mine so. Was curious."

Maxine mimed sealing her lips and tossing the key. "Stay curious then."

Scott peered up at the board with the food selections. "Ugh. I hate when you and Keiran do this to me. He's like Fort Knox when working on new beats. Aren't I supposed to have best friend privileges?"

"But your nose gets all scrunchy when you're annoyed. It's fun."

"I thought you were the cooler twin." Scott shook his head. "I was wrong. So tell me about your dates at least?"

"And what dates are you talking about exactly, hmm?" She hadn't told Scott about the deal with Remi, but Keiran definitely knew. She swore those too just couldn't stop gossiping.

"I mean, I'm not gonna rat my source out but . . ." Scott shrugged. They both already knew who his supposed source would be. "Besides, you two been posting cute shit on IG, you think I wouldn't figure something out? I gotta live vicariously through somebody while this dry spell hits. Not a prospect in sight."

"You? On a dry spell? How?" It didn't seem possible.

They paid for their food, heading to the exit on the side of the mall where they had both parked. Scott was so charming and damn good looking. He should have guys running him down left and right.

He shrugged. "Know any single queer dudes out there looking for a good time so I can get over my unrequited crush?"

Maxine unlocked her car, stashing her bags in the back. "Wait. You still got a crush on A—"

Scott waved his hands around. "Shh! Don't even say the name out loud. It's too absurd to even voice out loud since he's never even given the impression he knows I exist."

"I can put in a good word for you?" She bounced her brows up and down and Scott shook his head.

"Right, cuz you got an in with his sister? Nope. Don't even. I'll deal with this my way."

"So basically, you mean do nothing and hope he'll come around to falling in love with your fabulous self?" she teased.

Truth be told, Scott wouldn't have to do much, but no one in their little group knew what Akash was about where romantic relationships were concerned, even after all these years. Not that she'd had any sort of conversation with him until recently. Remi's brother was this sort of cool enigma. She could see why Scott was into him.

Scott rolled his eyes. "I don't wanna be hitting on some straight dude by accident. So I've been trying to feel him out. But that man is a mystery."

Maxine nodded. "Eh, maybe just ask him outright."

"Is that how you do it?" Scott asked, brow raised.

"Absolutely not. I'm a mess." She tried to keep it light, play it off as if it wasn't a big deal, but Scott's expression changed from teasing to concerned.

"You're not a mess. You're doing what you need to. Giving yourself time to figure this all out."

"I just . . ." she sighed, leaning against her car door. "How do I navigate this if I decide to give *us* a try? How do I just *be* within my family who might look at me differently?"

"You worried about your parents specifically. Or your whole fam?"

"Leah, daddy, mummy . . . I don't know what I'd do if mummy looked at me some type of way for dating Remi." God, it felt awful even to voice that, but it was a legit fear.

"The same mom who let me stay with you all after my own family kicked me out?"

He had a point there. Her mother hadn't hesitated to offer Scott a safe space, but she knew for some that didn't always extend to their own children. And how about Leah? "Maybe I'm just overthinking it, but I have no clue how any of it will go, so I'm spiralling, I guess. How do you do it? Be yourself without fear?"

Scott laughed. "Girl, you think I still don't worry if today's the day some homophobic asshole's gonna lash out because he thought I breathed near him? I do, but I refuse to let anybody dampen my shine. Didn't you see how I thrived after getting out that toxic environment? I've always been fine, but the super glow-up was real!"

Maxine laughed. Scott really was a trip. "Okay, yes, being your authentic self did give you this very specific annoying glow. I've never seen you take a bad photo once."

"Facts, but hey, don't beat yourself up about it. I'm here to chat about this with you anytime. Just maybeee not in this hot-ass sun when we both have to get back to work, hmm? Call me and we'll talk. I'll be your queer mentor."

"I got Victoria for that as well, but alright, yes. Thanks for all the help today." She gave him a big hug. She was truly grateful.

"My pleasure. Stay sexy and ease up on your girl a bit. She's just a mere human." He winked and waited until she got into her car to wave and walk away.

She hadn't even been given the time to rebut that "your girl" statement. Her friends seemed to be casually throwing that around. A lot. As if it was a done deal.

She's not my girl.

It's not like that.

You basically are dating, just like he said . . . so what is the truth?

She was beginning to sound like a broken record to herself now. All her worry and fears were there alongside her budding feelings for Remi. She couldn't deny that part anymore. And even considering whether it was worth it to take the risk and try with Remi felt terrible.

She knew she would have the support of her brother and friends, but as she'd told Scott, the thought of telling her mother especially gave her heart palpitations. She would be heartbroken if it didn't end positively. But should that fear ruin her chances at an actual relationship with someone, regardless of gender?

Head too full of all her thoughts, she went to the kitchen when she got back to the office to eat her lunch. She hadn't noticed a whole conversation was going on about her until she heard: "He wants to give her A&R now? Like for real? As if she deserves that. Pure nepotism in effect."

"Where you hear that? Isn't she working with Pauline now?"

Maxine froze. She was already all the way into the kitchen when the second speaker saw her, as she was facing the door.

She considered her options. Back the hell out the kitchen and go eat in her cubicle. Just eat her lunch and then leave the room, acting as if she heard nothing. Or confront them for even talking about her like this.

She wasn't about to starve for anybody and she didn't feel like eating by her desk. They would just have to deal with her presence. She was tired of people talking behind her back.

"Good afternoon," she said as she placed her food on one of the tables, because she had manners, even if they didn't deserve niceties from her.

The woman with her back to Maxine turned around and responded. "Oh, hey, afternoon!"

Jameela's chipper tone grated on Maxine's nerves. She was just going to act like she hadn't been questioning whether Maxine deserved consideration for A&R? How had they even found out about that? That wasn't something her father would share with just any employee. Someone had definitely over-heard something, and decided to run with it.

She could call them out on it, but she didn't want to ruin her lunch with this bullshit. She had way too much going on already to add getting into some heated argument with other employees. Instead, she would be damn good at her job to shut up the haters.

She munched on her food and decided to give her time to other things—like, if she was going to be ready to say yes to Remi's unasked question. There was no pressure from her side, but even though she claimed she was fine with waiting, Maxine also didn't want to string Remi along.

She would make a decision one way or the other.

CHAPTER TWENTY-NINE

REMI
SATURDAY 13TH APRIL

"Oh my god."

"I know."

"It's . . . literally your dream come to life."

"I *know.*"

Remi and Cherisse looked at each other then squealed as they hugged, jumping around. Sweethand, Cherisse's new store, was shaping up to be a real place. Remi had heard Cherisse talk about having a physical space for ages, and finally it was happening. Next month, Cherisse would officially open and begin selling her goodies. No more having to do the bulk of stuff in their apartment.

"So proud of youuu," she sang as they released each other so Remi could continue taking photos. She had promised Cherisse she would be documenting every step of the way with progress shots.

"I feel like I'm running on bare energy, but we're almost there," Cherisse said. "Thanks for coming by before your date. You didn't have to."

"I made a promise. You were here first, you know." Remi nudged Cherisse with her shoulder.

"Yeah, but I don't think I can compete with Maxi's, you know . . ." Cherisse cupped her hands in front of her chest and Remi laughed.

"They're pretty magnificent yes, but besties before breasties. You know this." Remi moved around, taking a few more shots.

She couldn't wait for the grand opening next month. All Cherisse's hard work was paying off. Plus, she had been stress baking and trying new recipes that would be exclusive to the store, so Remi also benefited from sugary goodness.

Cherisse had given her a variety of baked goods for her to take along on today's date, which involved a road trip to a beach near Salybia. Maxine would be meeting her here in a bit. Keiran had offered to drop her off so they could ride together.

Remi might have chosen the beach because she hadn't seen Maxine in a bathing suit since Tobago, but she wasn't admitting a damn thing. It wasn't the only reason, though. Maxine had mentioned the conversation she'd overheard in the lunch room and Remi decided they both needed to relax.

Work stress. Life stress. It could all take a little backseat while they frolicked with some sand, sea, and sun. Besides, next week was the Easter long weekend and every beach on the island would be too crowded. So today was perfect. Maxine also had to take Leah to some Easter party thing and Remi didn't want to get in the way of mummy/daughter time.

"The Kings have arrived," Keiran announced as he and Maxine walked into Sweethand.

Maxine rolled her eyes, looking around. "Ignore him. Wow, this looks great."

Cherisse bobbed her head. "Yup. Yes. Right? But they still have to finish up the final painting, and the lil' floral wall section where people can take pics." She blew out a breath. "Almost there."

"Can't wait to see the final thing."

Remi observed her as she chatted with Cherisse. Maxine was in a little yellow sundress, her colourful bathing suit peeking out from the top, a portable red cooler in her hand. Remi couldn't tell if it was whole suit or two piece, but she was eager to find out.

Maxine turned to her. "Ready to go?" She lifted the cooler. "I just brought some water and soft drinks as you said we'd get eats on the way and at the beach."

"Sounds good. Cherisse gave us goodies too. Let's go." She grabbed the container with the baked goods.

"So where exactly is this beach?" Maxine asked as Remi chose a station for some good trip tunes.

"It's a little ways after Salybia. It's really nice. There's a fishing village too so we can get fresh fish if you want. But we'll stop for some doubles in Arima first. Then there're places on the Valencia stretch to get some fruits, chow, honey."

"Is this our own lil' mini food tour?"

"If you wanna look at it like that, then sure."

They cruised up the highway with both of them singing along to the songs on the radio. It was the most carefree Remi had felt all week. While she couldn't put everything on the back burner forever, for a few hours her attention was on Maxine and not worrying about her site visit to the gallery next week, or going over the full set-up in her mind.

She wanted to be fully present in this moment. They were at date five, halfway there, and she was no closer to knowing if Maxine would have a favourable response for her at the end of this.

"What do you mean you never had doubles at the side of the road?" Remi gasped as she put in their orders with the vendor. Four with slight pepper and sweet sauce. Two for each of them. "How you get to your age and never done that?"

Maxine shrugged. "We always just took it to go."

Remi couldn't stop gaping at her as she was handed the first doubles, which she passed to Maxine. "That's shocking." She dug right into hers as soon as the hot wax paper hit her palm, using her hand to break off pieces of the barra and scoop up some channa.

It was perfect. No wonder this guy had so many people stopping here to grab a quick breakfast before they were on their way. They finished up theirs in no time, washing their hands at the sink setup off to the side.

"Well, how was it?" Remi asked as they got back onto the road. They would stop for some honey when they got into Valencia.

"Delicious. Was a lil' cumbersome to eat it standing up, but nothing I couldn't handle."

"You really learn something new by dating a person."

"Hey, don't make it sound like that," Maxine huffed. "You gonna revoke my Trini card now?"

"Nah, that bumper is too real to be anything but Trini."

The teasing continued as they stopped to get their bottles of honey and some pineapple chow to munch on as they still had about an hour and a half before they could get to the beach. Remi enjoyed the fresh breeze blowing around them. She kept glancing over at Maxine who was smiling and grooving along with the music as they talked.

It was already the perfect day, and Remi anticipated it was going to get even better when finally they parked and took their stuff down to the beach.

"How did you even find this place?" Maxine asked, tossing off her dress and stuffing it in the backpack she'd brought with her.

Remi shimmied out of her shorts, watching as Maxine sprayed on her sunscreen. Her bathing suit was a one piece but with some strategic cut outs.

"One of my uncles took us here when the beach near

Salybia was looking a hot mess after the rainy session one year. Never knew about it before then."

"Need any?" Maxine shook the can at her and Remi gladly took it. She sprayed her arms, legs, and stomach. "Can you get my upper back?"

Maxine nodded. "Sure."

Remi's hair was rolled up into a high bun so it wouldn't be whipping all in her face on the drive. Maxine was easily able to spray her back and rub in the sunscreen. Remi relished the feel of her hands on her skin. Too soon the touch was gone, but she couldn't expect Maxine to give her a full massage right here on the beach.

"Thanks. There's some food people who do BBQ under that tent we passed, so whenever we're feeling peckish again we can head over there."

"Sounds good." Maxine pointed to the water. "Last one in is sponsoring lunch!" she shouted, taking off down the sand.

"Hey, that's cheating!"

Remi chased after Maxine, but of course with Maxine's head start Remi got to the water after her. Maxine splashed her with water, sticking out her tongue.

"Bit of advice. Always stay ready around me."

"Is that so." Remi grabbed Maxine around the waist. She squealed as Remi dunked her in the water.

Maxine came up soaked and sputtering. "No fair!"

Remi cupped her hand to her ear. "What was that about staying ready?" she ran out into the water and dove before Maxine could throw her in.

The waves weren't too bad today so they were able to swim without getting tossed about too much. After a while, they retreated back to the shore.

"Next time, I'm bringing Leah. She'd like it here." Maxine plopped down on the blanket they had spread out.

Remi stretched out next to her, grabbing her towel to dry off. "You could've brought her."

Maxine sat with her legs out, arms propping her up as she turned her face up to the sun. "I wanted it just to be us for this one. Like a real date."

Remi unravelled her hair, rubbing at her curls with the towel. There was definitely sand in there, which meant a proper wash when she got home. "Hey, just for future, I have no problem with Leah tagging along on a date. In case you thought that was an issue."

Maxine rolled her head in Remi's direction. "You're really okay with that?"

"Why wouldn't I be? I love spending time alone with you, but I don't mind doing the same with Leah."

"She likes you. Everything is 'how cool Auntie Remi is with her camera'. And 'would Auntie Remi like this shot?' Now that she found out you dance, too? She's suddenly wanting to know about that as well."

"Oops!" Remi laughed as Maxine reached over to tug one of her curls out before releasing it to watch it bounce back.

"How can I compete with Auntie Remi, hmm?"

Remi buffed her fingers against her shoulder. "Sorry, you can't. I'm really too cool."

"Ah, well. Can't be helped. I've never been the cool sort."

Remi bundled her towel, turned to lay on her stomach. "Maybe you'll never be my brand of cool but you're really hot in my eyes." She waggled her brows for effect and Maxine tossed her own towel over Remi's head.

Remi kept most of the towel around her head, peeking out to grin at Maxine's look of exasperation.

"How can she think you're cool with those corny-ass lines?" She shook her head, laying down to mimic Remi's position so she was on her stomach too.

"You love it."

Remi saw the flash of panic at her careless words. She hadn't meant love with a capital L. She was just talking casually. Before Maxine could freak out about it, Remi jumped up. "My tummy is saying it's food time. Ready?"

She stretched out her hand for Maxine to take, and Maxine grabbed it, allowing Remi to help her up. But Maxine held onto her hand a beat longer than necessary. Remi wasn't going to be the first one to pull away, so she just swung their hands between them, mumbling, "Just gals being pals," which made Maxine snort.

This was exactly what she wanted. No nerves or awkwardness was going to spoil their day.

"Just a bunch of scissor sisters."

"Oh you did not."

Maxine gave her hand a squeeze before she extracted hers. "A couple of cunt connoisseurs."

Remi choked. "Stop iiiit!"

"A pair of pussy . . . uh . . . professors? Okay yeah I don't know about that one."

"You fucking nerd." She linked their arms, dragging Maxine over to the lunch tent. "Let's go. No more ridiculous alliterations."

"Oh wait . . . one more. Coochie consultants."

"Alright, that's it." Remi unlinked their arms and reached down to scoop Maxine up in her arms.

She flailed, holding onto Remi for dear life. "Wait, no! C'mon, that was a good one," Maxine cried out as Remi ran down to the beach, heading for the water.

She didn't care if people were watching them. Maybe they would think they really were just two gals playing around, but she was having too much fun.

"Waiiiit. Pleaaaase," Maxine begged.

Remi paused in the calf-deep water. "You promise to stop?"

Maxine pouted. "Fine. Yes, but I just have one more thing to say." She leaned in and whispered in Remi's ear, "Vagina virtuoso."

Remi had slackened her grip on Maxine, so she wiggled right out of Remi's arms and swung her leg out to off balance her, then pulled Remi down into the water with her.

Remi sputtered, pushing her mass of wet hair out of her face, looking over at Maxine who was laughing so hard everything was jiggling. "Oh, you're gonna regret that."

Maxine blew her a kiss then dissolved into giggles again. "*So* worth it."

Remi couldn't agree more. They were both wet, sun-kissed, and happy. What more could she ask for?

"Can we for real go eat now?" Remi's stomach was making so much noise she felt as if everyone on the beach could hear the damn thing.

Maxine nodded. "Yes, let's. I do have one more, but I'll save it for the ride back." She winked, getting to her feet.

Remi groaned. "Figured you ran out." She got to her feet too, wringing her hair out.

"Want me to braid it for you? I can do the fancy fishtail one?"

Remi's stomach did a little flip. She didn't know why the simple offer made her feel so warm and fuzzy. "No one's ever done that for me," she admitted. "Except my mom when I was little. She let me do my own thing once I got to secondary school."

"It's part of the girlfriend package." Remi blinked and Maxine cleared her throat. "I meant like friends who are girls. You know, not necessarily saying we were *girlfriend* girlfriends, or anything like that."

"Yeah. Well, let's eat, then you can braid it after it air dries a bit," said Remi.

"Sounds like a plan."

Remi chuckled to herself as she followed Maxine out of the water and up the sand. Girlfriends. Yeah, she liked the sound of that.

CHAPTER THIRTY

MAXINE

FRIDAY 3RD MAY

Remi: *muff magician is on the way. Be there in a few*

Maxine bit her lip so she wouldn't let out the laugh she was holding in. On the way back from their beach trip a few weeks ago, she had told Remi the final alliteration. Since then, she'd been dropping them in conversation randomly.

The beach trip had been so needed. Even though the weeks after had been hectic, Maxine had clung to those memories, pulling them out at random moments to get her through a particularly difficult day. Victoria had started referring to Remi as her "emotional support hottie".

Maxine couldn't deny that. Remi had become an important part of her day. Her life, really. That was terrifying, especially when she caught herself randomly re-reading some previous conversation and smiling like a besotted fool.

"Got a sweet joke to share there?"

Maxine slipped her phone into her purse and looked up at Pauline. "Nope. Just Remi saying she's on her way."

"Perfect!" Pauline clapped her hands, surveying all their hard work. The album launch event was finally tonight.

Maxine felt like she was running on dregs since the setup had gone later than expected last night, but the place looked spectacular and Shalini was ready to wow everyone. She would make her appearance when more guests arrived and run through a few of the tracks from the album. Of course she'd be performing some live too.

"You did a good job."

"Me? It was a team effort." Maxine had come up with the concept, sure, but they had both been instrumental in fleshing out the idea, and selling it to everyone too, especially her father.

"Granted, but trust me. The powers that be definitely noticed your hard work."

Not that he'd said anything to her face. Yet. The night was just getting started, so hopefully he would have some positive feedback.

Shalini's album was a mix of genres that showed her versatility as an artiste, but since the album was called *Game Play* Maxine had pulled the old school arcade aesthetic to bring that concept to life.

The invitation had mimicked the tickets you got at the arcade when you won a game. Guests could have fun with all the favourite vintage games placed throughout the venue, while Shalini's vocals greeted them upon arrival. Large screens also had her latest music video for the solo single that had dropped after Carnival.

It had all come together just as she'd visualised.

"I'm gonna miss you when you go to A&R," Pauline sniffed, pulling a sad face.

"We don't know if that's happening." Even if she succeeded in convincing Akash's band to sign with them, what guarantee did she have that her father would follow through on that?

"Oh, it's happening," Pauline said confidently. "Let's see if Shal is prepped and ready for her greeting."

Shalini was supposed to welcome her guests officially within thirty minutes, so Maxine ensured she was calm and ready. Once Shalini said she was good, Maxine made her way around the venue to get a feel for how the event was being received by the guests and to capture content.

Guests hadn't been required to dress on theme, and Pauline had assured her she could wear what she wanted, so she had chosen the purple wrap dress.

She was filming something with Shalini when she spotted Remi walking through the crowd. Remi saw her and waved, raising her camera to get a shot of her with Shalini, causing Maxine to smile.

"Ooh, whose got you smiling like that?" Shalini grinned.

"Uh. Just Remi. Let's get some pics before you head up to the stage to start?"

"Of course!" Shalini's bubbly personality had taken some getting used to, but that was just how she was.

"Hey, this all looks amazing. Congrats on the album launch," Remi said as she came over, looking delectable in a black jumpsuit.

"Do you mind capturing some shots of Shalini?"

"Not at all. That's what I'm here for."

Shalini did her best poses, dragging Maxine into a few as well, even though she wanted to protest. She had to remind herself that this was all part of it.

"You deserve some shine on you. You did a great job putting this together," Shalini insisted as she moved her head along to the music.

Her usual sleek black bob was replaced by an added-on piece that allowed her to fashion her hair into a long, neat French braid. Shalini had decided to channel Lara Croft since she was the star of this show and felt she should at least go all the way with the vintage game look. She had finished off the look with a crop top, some tight pants, and boots. The black bands around her thigh made her look legit.

She approved the shots Remi took then told Maxine she was ready to head up to the stage.

Shalini killed the greeting as expected. She wasn't shy when attention was focused on her, which meant she had everyone relaxed and ready by the time the listening segment was cued. Maxine catalogued the reactions. Guests and media seemed to be enjoying what they were hearing so she was hopeful for good reviews.

Social media was buzzing about it too. Thank God. Maxine felt a bit more comfortable to switch to a somewhat more relaxed mode where she could search out her brother and Remi while still casting an eye to ensure there were no hiccups.

Keiran and Dax had been invited since they'd worked on a few tracks for Shalini. They had their own in-house producers, of course, but it was normal to use ones not in the company as well. And it was a known fact that anything Keiran and Dax touched turned to gold.

Her brother found her first, coming over, a huge smile plastered on his face.

"You hearing this? Track five sounds like a hit, boy. I wonder who suggested we start off this song with that Mario dying sound huh?"

"It's aight." This track was actually her favourite, but she was obligated as his sibling to give him a hard time. The song beginning with that sound was genius, since this track, *Game Over*, was about a failing relationship.

"Ha, ha," he deadpanned. "So, how you doing? The party looks like a success." He swept his arm around where guests were having a good time, drinking, enjoying the hors d'oeuvres being passed around, actively playing the games.

A woman in a fancy short dress was busy blasting away enemies at the Terminator game.

Maxine had been worried guests might just pose with the games and not actually use them, but luckily they were getting into the gaming spirit. It was one less thing for her overworked brain to get anxious about. "Tired. Sleepy. In need of a foot rub after this probably." These shoes had a time limit on how long she could walk around in them.

"Well, you got someone who can take care of that foot massage easy," Keiran pointed out.

"I do, don't I?" It wasn't as if she didn't know that. But hearing it put so plainly made her realise that she had been wasting so much time being afraid.

What if she just said eff every*damn*body who might have an issue with her dating Remi for real and just . . . did the damn thing?

"You've got lightbulb face on." Keiran took her by the shoulders and turned her so she could see Remi across the room, laughing it up with a group of people who she was arranging for a pose. "A wise woman once made me come to my senses. Maybe you should have a talk with her too."

"But what if we don't work out?" She couldn't help but ask.

"This isn't easy for you, I know that. But don't go into it thinking the worst right off."

It wasn't the right place to have this conversation, but Maxine felt as if she would burst if she didn't say something to Remi. It was as if time was running out, which wasn't true. *She* had set the timeline of ten dates. But did they really need to go through all that when . . . she felt like this?

What if Remi decided she was tired of waiting for her? What was all this time doing but giving her a chance to talk herself out of a good thing? And hadn't Remi been showing her that? That she was willing to go the extra the mile for her?

"Okay, okay. I can do this."

"Go get your girl." Keiran gave her a slight push and Maxine almost stumbled in her heels. She shot him a glare and he backed away. "Hey, I'm helping here."

"Me or her? Since you owe her one?"

"Um, both?"

She gave him a quick hug then took a deep breath. She waited until Remi looked to be on a break from photographer duties then snagged her arm.

"Come with me please."

"Hey, what's going on?"

Maxine took her into one of the rooms in the venue that would have the least foot traffic. It was a storage space for the decorators' things, so they'd have some privacy from potential prying eyes.

"I don't want to do this anymore," she blurted before she could chicken out. "We should stop and . . ."

"*Oh.* Oh wow. I didn't think . . ." Remi inhaled loudly. "I was so sure I'd be fine with whatever you decided, but fuck I'm . . . I didn't expect this."

Maxine frowned. Wait, what did Remi mean?

Remi started pacing the room. "We're only on date five. So you're saying you decided not to bother getting to ten then? You don't see us being anything more?"

Oh shit, she had fucked this all up. "Remi, wait *no.*" She grabbed her arm to stop her agitated movements. Damn, she couldn't even make a romantic declaration right. "That's the opposite of what I'm saying. I'm saying I don't want to keep doing this countdown thing. I don't need to get to ten. I want to try for real. Now."

"Really? Shit! Can a heart just literally jump right out your chest, because *Jesus* Maxi." She moved Maxine's hand to her chest and sure enough the thump against her palm was so strong.

"I'm sorry. I should have worded that more carefully. I'm a mess. I can't stop thinking about you all the time. And honestly, this may crash and burn spectacularly, but I want to try for real." She was determined to make sure Remi understood her this time.

"Shit, yes. I'm allowed to kiss you now right?" Remi tugged her closer. "Please say yes."

"Yes."

Remi crashed their mouths together. Gentle wasn't even an option. Maxine had deprived them both for too long. She could kiss her girlfriend how many times she wanted? Oh damn, they were girlfriends now. They hadn't actually talked about having that title, but later. As far as she was concerned, that's what they were.

She didn't know how they would introduce each other though. My gal friend? Partner? Did they even have to say anything to anyone who wasn't in her carefully crafted circle?

Before she could panic about that further, Remi's hand roamed down to her ass, cupping her, squeezing. "God, I missed this ass."

"Stop. Don't make me laugh. This is supposed to be sexy," Maxine chided against Remi's lips.

Remi tugged on Maxine's bottom lip with her teeth. "I aim to please." She flicked her tongue against Maxine's and her core throbbed.

Remi's hand moved up under her dress. "Mm, the pussy professor is about to get a lesson in . . ."

"I will literally strangle you."

"By sitting on my face? Yes please?"

Lord, this was her own fault. But she forgot about every single alliteration she had created when Remi pulled her panties to the side and rubbed at her clit with her thumb.

"Oh, fuck," she breathed as Remi kept kissing her like she had an unquenchable thirst. Sipping first at her lips, then diving in, turning it deeper, wetter, nastier. Tongue thrusting in and out like the finger she had just slipped inside Maxine.

Maxine raised her leg to wrap it around Remi's waist, which pushed them back against the door. Hopefully, no one needed to get in here right this minute because while it was wild to be doing this at her work party, she didn't care.

She wanted this. Wanted it all.

Remi stroked her slowly. It wouldn't take much, really. She had been so pent up, release wasn't far off. She pressed her face into Remi's shoulder, moaning as she ground down on her finger.

"Mm, yeah. That's it. I love those sounds you make. I've missed it so much. And now you're all mine."

Remi slipped another finger in, pressing in so deep. Maxine shattered, unable to hold back anymore, core clenching.

Remi slid her fingers out, "Look at this. Look what you did."

Maxine shouldn't have looked. She didn't need to see Remi's fingers glistening like that.

"Were you this wet all night?"

Maxine shook her head, cheeks burning. "Oh God, *stop*."

Remi cupped her cheek, brought her in for another kiss. "We'll get through this night then we can continue this."

"Yes, please."

She was floating on a cloud as they exited the room. Maybe that's what made her reel Remi in for one more kiss right there in the corridor. A reckless move, but she wanted to savour what was hers before they joined everyone back in the main location.

Remi gave her a big grin and salute before going back to work. Maxine couldn't help smiling to herself about everything. No regrets.

"There you are." Pauline approached. "Shalini's insisting she needs to big up the team so she's requesting us front and centre."

"Uhh." Maxine did *not* want to go up there, but she followed Pauline, hoping it would all be over soon.

"Okay everybody. I need to big up these ladies right here from KKE who made everything go so perfectly. They've taken really good care of me through this process!" Shalini gestured for them to come up and Maxine hoped she didn't look as much of a deer in headlights as she felt.

Being in the spotlight wasn't something she willingly did. She'd avoid that at all costs if she could, but realistically, she couldn't be trying to get her father to see her as a serious contender for running the company if she shied away from things like this.

The glow from her moment with Remi was still there, magnified even more when she saw Remi cheering loudly for her as she was introduced. Her girlfriend. She was going to have to get used to that. And shit, she had to tell her mother. And Leah.

One thing at a time there girl. Get through the night first.

After the brief spotlight moment, it was time for Shalini to perform some songs.

The guests were eating it all up. Maxine was singing along when she felt a tap on her shoulder. Thinking it was maybe Remi, she turned, huge smile ready, but it quickly slipped away as she saw her father standing there.

Oh boy. She hadn't seen him all night. She'd briefly wondered if he would even show up, not that she had dwelled on it too much. Now that he was here, she wondered if he was about to point out some supposed oversight.

"You did well," he said, causing her to blink at him.

"Thanks."

"Keep it up with your next task and you'll get exactly what you want." He turned and walked away.

Well alright then. His delivery could have been better, but she'd take it. Nothing was ruining her mood tonight.

Things would wind down eventually and Maxine was counting down the minutes until she could get out of here, go to Remi. She didn't expect Remi to stay back late with her but it couldn't hurt to ask. She texted, not sure where she was in the crowd that didn't seem to want to leave.

> **Maxi:** *will you wait for me? Or should I meet you at the apt?*
> **Remi:** *I'll wait. let's leave together*

It was the response she wanted, so she was thrilled to hear it.

"Your friend is really dedicated to her job," Pauline observed as they started winding down for the night.

The decorator had already returned and was packing up his stuff with his staff. The people who had rented them the games would come back in the morning. They had already arranged with the owners of the venue to meet them for collection. The few stragglers who didn't seem to want to leave were given takeaway boxes with whatever food and treats were left over.

Once the bar people said they were closed off, most of the guests who had been lingering left—probably in search of another place to continue liming.

And while all that was happening, Remi flitted around still taking photos of it all.

"She is. Besides, these shots will be useful for the exclusive."

"That they would."

Pauline came over and thanked Remi as soon as they got everything done for the night. "Make sure my girl gets home safely, yeah? She's a valuable commodity at KKE."

Remi nodded. "For sure."

They both walked Pauline to her car, then Remi followed Maxine to hers. The plan was for her to follow Remi back to her apartment to spend a little more alone time. She couldn't stay over all night; her mother would definitely get suspicious. They would get a lil' sexy time in, then she would head home.

"You sure you don't want to spend the night? You'll be so tired to drive back."

"Just don't work me too hard." Maxine shot her a playful look as she got into her car.

Remi lingered by the window. "I can't promise that." She leaned in and Maxine met her halfway for a quick kiss, then she followed Remi back to the apartment, anticipation building in her stomach. She was getting everything she wanted. Sleep be damned.

CHAPTER THIRTY-ONE

REMI

THEY WERE ON EACH OTHER BEFORE REMI HAD EVEN CLOSED THE front door. But Remi still fumbled to ensure the door was locked. Cherisse would kill her if she left it open because she was too busy having sex. Cherisse was probably already asleep, but safety first and all that. Besides, Remi didn't want to do this in the living room. She wanted to take her time with Maxine.

She was all hers to debauch tonight and Remi wasn't allowing anyone to interrupt that. She took Maxine's hand, led her to the bedroom and closed the door.

Maxine peeled her dress off before Remi could do anything and she looked so delectable. Red. Fucking red underwear.

"Did you plan this seduction?" Remi rasped out.

"No. Happy accident." Maxine reached behind her and released the clasp on her bra.

Remi watched it fall to the floor. Still not moving yet. Maxine wanted her to watch. She would watch. She shimmied out of her underwear next and Remi barely contained herself. All that bare skin was hers to touch. Hers to taste. To devour.

Maxine gave a slow spin, bending to retrieve her under-wear and treating Remi to a full view of her ass and her pussy.

"We don't have all night since you insist on not sleeping over," she gritted out. Yeah, her patience was about to be gone.

Maxine looked over her shoulder. "Aww, there'll be other times for sleeping over. Girlfriend privileges."

Remi came up behind her, palmed her ass. "Yeah, girlfriend privileges. That includes me telling you to get on the bed, on all fours, right?"

Maxine stood up, turned around, sly smirk on her lips. "Sure. But first, take all of that off."

Remi didn't bother with a slow striptease. That was for another time. She was too horny. She wanted to fuck her girl-friend quick and dirty. "Strap-on tonight? Or my tongue and fingers."

Maxine leaned in, brushing her lips against Remi's. "All of it."

God dammit, and she expected Remi to let her leave here at all? Allow her to reach home in time? She would just have to be fast about it.

She had Maxine a wet, moaning mess in no time. She hadn't lied about being a muff magician. Maxine was making so much noise, grinding back on her tongue that Remi's face had to be a sticky mess. She didn't care. She wanted Maxine inco-herent by the time she got that dick all up in her. She had put on her strap-on as soon as Maxine had gotten on all fours. There was no time to waste.

Next time she would go slow.

She pressed down on Maxine's back, wanting her ass higher. Then she did what she had wanted to do since their cooking date. She took a hold of Maxine hair, tugging her head back as she thrust in.

"Oh fuck, please, Remi."

"Yes, gimme all of it. Everything." She thrust in harder, enjoying the way Maxine's ass practically clapped around the dick. "Fuck yeah."

Remi didn't let up on her hair, pulling it a bit more as Maxine panted, thrusting back. Heavy breasts bouncing. She looked so good. Remi wished she could capture this. Frame it so everyone could see Maxine was hers.

The sounds falling from her mouth were so hot.

"Taking it oh so good, hmm? Keep going," she urged. She could feel herself getting wetter too.

"I can't . . ." Maxine whined.

Remi released Maxine's hair. She needed to feel more of her. Gripping Maxine's waist she pushed her hips forward, harder, faster until Maxine was begging.

"Please please please." Maxine panted. Remi dug into one ass cheek, drinking in the way Maxine moved, chasing her pleasure. "Shit, I'm gonna . . ."

Remi revelled in Maxine's moans as she came. Her own pussy clenching just from the sounds.

She took off the strap-on, which she would need to clean, but later. They both fell into the bed boneless. Maxine's hand was thrown over her face.

"Might have died and gone to heaven. I dunno," she said.

Remi laughed, traced her finger over Maxine's stomach. "Rest a bit."

"Not too long. But yes." She turned on her side, hands propped under her head.

"Good?" She looked a sweaty mess just as much as Remi felt, but she was oh so beautiful like this.

Radiant. Glowing. Remi hoped she could keep her like this always.

"I'll live." Maxine moved her fingers over Remi's clavicle, down her chest to her breast. She cupped her gently before brushing a thumb over her nipple. "You're so pretty. Do you know that?"

"They're barely a handful," she joked.

"I'm serious, Remi. We're so different, but we fit."

Remi shivered as Maxine passed the back of her fingers down her abs, circling her belly button. "Mm. Yeah. Yes. Glad you think so."

"What's it like wearing that strap?"

"It's fun. I've used it with a guy before too." Her attraction leaned more towards women, but she had been with a bi guy who was open to pegging. "Wanna try sometime?"

Maxine patted her pelvic bone. "Yeah, maybe." She was open to trying whatever Maxine was comfortable with. "Not this minute though. Tired. But I want to make you feel good too."

"Nap first, then we do a quick round two." Remi wanted Maxine to keep touching her, but she needed her rest, too.

"'Mmmkay."

Maxine still reached down to stroke her. Remi wanted her to nap, sure, but she wasn't going to say no to some good fingering.

"So soft. So wet," Maxine murmured, finger moving slowly in and out while Remi tilted her hips up to meet it.

She kept up those languid movements, Remi's leg falling open more as Maxine kept praising her for just being her. Oh, she could get used to that. She didn't think she had a praise kink, but those soft murmurs were doing something to her.

"So, so good. Good at everything, aren't you?"

"I like to put my best forward y-yeahhh," she groaned as Maxine used her thumb on her clit too.

"I know."

Remi pressed her lips together, not sure why she was trying to keep quiet. It was too damn late for that. Maxine sucked her own finger clean and Remi felt her core clench again.

"A nap so I'm not too tired to drive, and then I really have to go." Maxine burrowed into her side and Remi held her close.

Sounded like the perfect end to the best night ever.

CHAPTER THIRTY-TWO

MAXINE

THE SUN WAS STREAMING IN AND MAXINE SQUINTED AS SHE wondered why the hell her blackout curtains weren't shielding her from all that brightness as usual. She squinted at the unfamiliar room. Where the hell . . .?

She definitely didn't have tasteful scenery shots on her bedroom walls. Her plan when she got her own house one day was to have some framed photos of her favourite musicians around. As a teen, she would plaster her walls with artistes from the centrefolds found in the Showtime newspaper.

Her mother had not been pleased.

She felt something move next to her and everything came rushing back. Remi. Remi's apartment. Oh my God, had she spent the entire night?

She bolted upright. She had meant to take a nap only. Clearly, that hadn't happened. She looked for her phone and found it on the dresser. 6:30am. *Shit.* She had also meant to set an alarm to ensure she wouldn't oversleep but had been too busy cuddling Remi to actually do that.

Her mother was definitely awake by now. It was a bit strange there was no text asking where she was, unless her mother assumed she was still asleep. Given that she knew how much work Maxine had been putting into this event, it was likely that her mother expected her to sleep in late.

That would work in her favour. Except, if she noticed Maxine's car wasn't in the garage, things would go a bit differently. She had to get home and get inside somehow without alerting anyone. She didn't have a change of clothes, so coming home in this same dress was a walking flashing neon sign that she was just getting in.

Remi's clothes wouldn't fit her, so that plan was out. She just needed to get to the house and she would figure something out.

"Remi." She shook her lightly, not wanting to startle her too much.

Remi cracked open one eye. "It's the weekend. Why?"

"Notice the sunlight streaming in here? On that note, I need to get you some blackout curtains cuz nope. But yeah, it's morning. Like *morning* morning."

"Oh." She didn't look too concerned. "Oops?"

"Yeah oops. I'm too old to be doing a walk of shame."

Remi wiggled her toes against Maxine's leg. "Are you ashamed?"

"No." She wouldn't change anything they had done.

But she had wanted to have a chat with her mother about it and now there would be questions. Ah well, maybe it was better they had that conversation sooner rather than later.

"Good. Because you're an adult and you can sleep out if you want."

"Not if mummy is watching Leah and I didn't tell her I was doing that."

"Oh, yeah, damn. Okay, let's get you off then."

"I slept in my makeup. I just need to brush my teeth." She touched her hair, which probably looked like a whole nest right now. "Fix this hair and I'm good. Do you have an extra toothbrush."

"You look gorgeous." Remi grinned up at her.

Maxine's stomach did that swooshy thing even as she rolled her eyes. "You're a whipped mess, so can I really trust your judgement on that?"

Remi wrapped her arms around Maxine's stomach, mumbling something into her chest that she couldn't understand.

"Remi."

Remi leaned back. "Fine. I release you."

Maxine freshened up as much as she could. Remi brushed her teeth too, then sat on the bed, grinning at her as she slipped back into her dress.

"Stop looking at me like that."

"Like I think my flustered girlfriend is cute? Not gonna happen." Remi pulled her in for a kiss, hands kneading her ass.

"We are not getting back into that bed; I have to go!"

"Then go."

Maxine melted into that touch because she was soft and weak-willed. Remi walked with her downstairs and started giggling the minute they both spotted Cherisse on the couch. She had frozen with her coffee cup halfway to her mouth.

"Well, good morning. Didn't know we had a guest."

"Yeah, yeah, good morning. No time for teasing, I gotta go." Maxine breezed out the apartment with Remi's laughter following her.

"Message when you reach home, please."

"I shall." She waved, not wanting to risk a kiss in the full daylight outside when any of Remi's neighbours could be watching.

Her hope for an easy entry into the house without being noticed was dashed as soon as she got in. Her mother was enjoying some tea on the couch. She looked up. "Well, good morning."

"Morning. Sorry I didn't message, I was . . ."

"With a friend. Yeah, don't worry Keiran already told me you were hanging out after the show. Didn't think you would be so late though."

"I fell asleep. Sorry. Was so tired but they wanted to celebrate the launch being a success." It wasn't a lie really. She had celebrated in her own way. With Remi. She would have to thank Keiran for covering for her, but as she stood there watching her mother sip her tea, she made a decision. "I want to talk to you about something, but let me shower first."

"Sure thing, sweetie. Want me to get you some tea too?"

"Yes, please." She would need to calm her nerves.

She showered and took time to wipe away her makeup, wash her face, and pat on some toner, finishing it up with her usual moisturiser. She felt refreshed and a teeny bit ready to talk to her mother. She checked in on Leah first, who was still asleep. It was Saturday after all. There was no need to bother her to get up early.

"Okay, you got this. You can say what you have to say. Easy." Maxine gave herself a pep talk in the bathroom mirror.

She returned to the living room, heart thumping, nerves jittery as hell, but she tried to keep her face neutral. Maxine slid across from her mother, hands cupped around the warm teacup. "So, I *was* at a friend's last night. Just as Keiran said. I was with Remi."

"You two got really close since you got back," her mother noted. "Never thought I'd see that." She chuckled. "I didn't know all the details, but you two didn't get along in school, right?"

"We were always competing for everything, but yeah, since I got back, we've been close. Um . . ." She took a sip of the tea and made a quick decision not to draw this out. Rip the band aid off. "We're together. As in dating. Well, as of last night, we're officially dating so . . . that's where I was. I really did fall asleep by accident, though," she rushed out.

Her mother raised a brow. "Oh. I see."

"Yup."

She waited for her mother to say something. Anything.

"Well, that's nice honey. Maybe we can double date. Or triple. Or quadruple? Not sure how that would work with Keiran and Cherisse and Devon and Reba, but bring her over for a Sunday lunch. I have someone I want you all to meet too. It's time, I think."

Maxine's mouth fell open. "I knew it! But wait, wait before we get to that. That's it? That's nice? You're not . . ."

"What? You think I'd make it an issue because Remi's a woman?"

"Well, I don't know. We've never had to deal with anything like this before. I mean I'm still figuring myself out. How I want to ID, but I'm dating a woman right now, so yeah."

"Sweetie. I still love you. Why would that change? Once she treats you right, I'm good and minding my business. And I've seen how she is with Leah too. Why wouldn't I be okay with it?"

"I don't know. I was so scared."

"Aww honey." Her mother got to her feet, coming around to her side of the table. "Come here."

Maxine rose, allowing herself to be wrapped up in the hug. She was so glad but so overwhelmed too that tears started falling. "I'm sorry I ever thought you'd be weird about this. But I was terrified, not gonna lie."

Her mother stroked her hair. "Hey, it's okay. I'll fix anybody who tries to bother you two. Although Remi looks like she could good punch somebody out. So you safe."

Maxine laughed through her tears. It wasn't going to be easy for sure, but at least she had her support system.

Her mother released her from the hug and wiped at her tears.

"But now," Maxine said, "what's this about you dating? Who is it? How long?"

Her mother actually flushed right before Maxine's eyes. She was so curious who this guy was. Who had her mother like this? She had suspected, but she was clearly meeting this guy away from the house since Maxine hadn't seen anyone around. Maxine raised a brow, and her mother waved her hand.

"Sinclair," her mother said.

"Sinclair? As in your friend Sinclair? Wait, wait, wait. Hold up." Maxine took a big sip of her tea because this morning was shaping up to be full of surprises.

Sinclair was her mother's friend from so long. Hell, he had been her father's friend too, up until her father's cheating-ass ways and whole other family had been revealed. Sinclair had been there for her mother, but Maxine would never have considered them in anything romantic. They had never given a single inkling of anything.

Come to think of it actually, she hadn't seen him around in a while. Now it made sense why. They would probably have been busted in no time.

"Yeah. We were just friends for so long until one day things changed. I won't get into the details, but yes, I'd like to introduce him as my boyfriend this time. It's only been a few months."

"I like him. For you."

"Thanks, sweetie. I like Remi for you too."

She would cry again if they kept this up. She needed to tell Remi how the talk went.

Leah came into the room, rubbing her eyes. "Morning."

"Good morning, baby!" Maxine gave her a quick hug.

Leah patted her face. "Is mummy sad?" she asked.

Ah right, her tears. "No honey. It's happy tears. Mummy wants to talk to you about something, okay?"

"Okay. Can I get pancakes for breakfast?"

"Sure thing. After our chat, alright?" Leah already adored Remi, so she didn't anticipate any lasting issues, but she wanted to have that talk regardless.

She led Leah over to the couch while her mother gave her a quick thumbs up and said, "I'll go start the pancakes."

Maxine took a deep breath. "You like Auntie Remi and all the photo stuff you've been doing right?"

"Yes! She's so fun. I love her!"

Maxine smiled. "I'm so glad, sweetie." She fiddled with the hem of her top, anxiety eating away at her insides. "How would you feel about Remi and mummy being . . . uh . . . girlfriends? You know how daddy and I used to be together as a couple? Not quite like that but . . ."

"Auntie Remi's going to live with us?" Leah asked excitedly.

Oh Lord, Leah would have them walking down the aisle before Maxine could catch herself. "No, sweetie, but we'd be in a romantic relationship. So we'd go on dates and stuff. And we'd all get to hang out more together. Would you be okay with that?"

Leah nodded. "Okay, yup. Cool. Can I have the pancakes now?"

Maxine laughed pulling Leah into a hug. "Of course. Go help grandma in the kitchen."

Maxine figured she would definitely have to circle back on the parameters of her relationship with Remi because she didn't want Leah to think marriage was on the horizon, but she felt more at ease. She checked her phone, seeing that Remi had already messaged.

Remi: *you're home?*

Maxi: *spoke to mummy, and Leah, about us. Crisis averted. She's dating one of her old friends??? Quite the morning I'm having . . .* 😩🌀

Remi: *I'm glad! Oh who mummy dating??*

Maxi: *Sinclair. Someone both my parents have known for ages. It's just . . . idk . . . strange but she deserves someone who will treat her right*

Remi: *This Sinclair guy a silver fox or??* 👀

Maxi: *wait, is that your type in men???* 🫤

Remi: *lol noooo. I'm just playin. So what you doing today? I miss you already* 🥺🥺🥺

Maxi: *resting since someone wore me out.* 😮‍💨 🫣 *Might just have some family time. Lounge in the inflatable pool with Leah for a bit. ttyl maybe we can do lunch tmrw?*

Remi: *sounds good, I'll be finishing up my stuff for the gallery. Lunch sounds great. D-day is soooon!!*

Two weeks away to be exact. Maxine was proud of Remi. She had promised to help but hadn't been able to yet with her own commitments. They could have lunch tomorrow and she would make the time to assist. Her mother wanted them to have a Sunday lunch together, but it didn't need to be that soon. She wanted to see her and Sinclair in the same room together now that she knew, but that could be whenever. She wanted some more alone time with Remi before everyone found out and descended with the teasing and questions.

She should also let Victoria know what had gone down. In fact, she sent her a voice note asking if she wanted to come over and have a chill day in the pool.

Victoria: hell yessss I'm in! what I need to bring?
Maxi: just yourself. I got something to tell you.
Victoria: 👀 👀 👀

She left her in suspense and decided to let her mother know the plan.

"I'm doing nothing but relaxing in that blow-up pool later," she announced.

"Sounds good to me. Remi coming over?"

Maxine should have known that would be the next question. "No, Vee is though."

"Alright, you all have fun."

"You're not going to be home?"

"I have plans." Her mother took her cup of tea to the kitchen and Maxine didn't even need to ask who the plans were with.

She shook her head. That sit-down lunch was going to be either super awkward or fun. She wouldn't be too hard on him, but if both of her brothers were invited, then poor Sinclair.

Victoria arrived around noon just as she had filled up the pool and tossed in a few of Leah's toys. Maxine had put some meat on the little outside grill, too. They were going to make a fun afternoon of it. She had done some garlic baked potatoes to go along with the BBQ and that was cooling inside.

Leah greeted Victoria, then asked, "Is Auntie Remi coming too?"

"Wow. Good thing my ego is more than intact," Victoria joked. "You got some competition there as Remi's number one fan."

"Nah, I know the hierarchy. I'm number three at best. Cherisse is number one."

Victoria tossed off her cover-up and settled into the pool with one of the lime slushies Maxine had whipped up. "Once you know! But anyhoooo, how you been? Looked like everything went well with the event last night. I was macoing the KKE page. Everything looked so fun and amazing."

"It *was* amazing. Shalini was a star and Pauline sent me some early good reviews. My dad even told me I did well."

"No wonder you look so happy." Victoria sipped her drink. "Oh, this is just what I need. So what we gotta talk about, hmm?"

Maxine glanced at Leah, who was splashing about next to them, enjoying herself with her toys. "Well, Remi and I are official."

"Whaaaaaaat?!" Victoria screamed, causing Leah to watch her as if she had lost her mind. She went back to playing and Victoria lowered her voice. "Oh my God yessss. Finally, regular pussy on deck."

"Shut up, my God." Maxine splashed her with water, but Victoria wasn't going to be stopped.

"Tell me how that all went down and then if anyone, you know, went down." She waggled her brows.

Maxine expected this sort of response over the next few weeks as their official status became known to their friends and close family. Her anxiety around it hadn't fully disappeared, but she was prepared to deal with it.

"Well, I realised something. I'm afraid, yeah, but should that stop me from being happy? The ID stuff is still all over the place too, but I just want to be with her."

"I love you so much you lil baby queer." Victoria tweaked her nose causing Maxine to laugh. "Take your time. No one is pressuring you to choose an ID, okay? And if they are I know a 5'11 hottie who will make them regret they ever looked at you wrong."

"Why does everybody think Remi's gonna fight somebody for me?"

"Remi's strong. She's practically an MMA fighter with the way she trains. She could kick some ass. And look so hot doing it." Victoria pretended to swoon.

Maxine poked her in the side. "Hey, no lusting after what's mine."

"Oooh possessive Maxine is hot too."

"Lemme go check on the meat." She came out the pool to give the chicken a quick flip and additional basting with the sauce before drying her hands so she could check her phone too. If she was anticipating a message from Remi, so what? She was allowed. Remi had sent her something—a cute selfie with Cherisse and Keiran doing who knows what in the background. Maxine hadn't known Keiran would be there helping out today.

> **Remi:** *this is NOT the cute King I ordered* 😞
> **Maxi:** *poor thing. Tmrw I promise.*

She took a selfie as well, capturing Leah and Victoria in the back.

> **Maxi:** *pool day with you next time* 😊
> **Remi:** *definitely! somebody better come get K2 before I kick him out, he's distracting my helper! But let me not take up your time. Tmrw then :D*

She had just seen Remi a few hours ago but couldn't wait to see her tomorrow. She was such a sap for her. Maxine got back into the pool. She could already picture a cute cozy lunch with the two of them lounging in here after.

"Oooh now you two can come to the fun queer parties as the new hot couple on the town." Victoria interrupted her thoughts.

"I guess?" It wasn't on her must-do list, but it would be some sort of comfort knowing that, when she did choose to go back, she had Remi by her side.

"Not that you need to, but I know some fun ones. Sanaa and I are going to one next month."

"You two planning dates ahead that far?"

"It's not a date. We're just having fun. Sexy fun," Victoria clarified as if that wasn't already obvious. "Sanaa isn't looking for anything serious and I'm just happy to be getting what she's dishing out. We're not exclusive."

"Well, have fun. I'll ask Remi if she wants to go."

"Aww look at you. Asking your girlfriend to do things. So cute."

"You are as ridiculous as you're short."

Victoria splashed her and Maxine caught a face full of water, which was more refreshing than annoying. Who really was the winner here?

She settled back against the pool, feeling content. She had her friends to do things with—that wasn't going to change— but there was something about having a partner to do stuff together as well. She had missed that.

She was excited to see all the fun they could get up to. Nervous too, but nothing was going to dampen the buzz she had going on.

CHAPTER THIRTY-THREE

REMI

TWO MORE DAYS. TWO MORE DAYS. TWO MORE DAAAAYS.

Remi was freaking out. Logically, she knew everything was going smoothly. Her photos were being installed. The stage would be set up tomorrow so Akash and his band could come in and do their sound check the day before and on the day of the event. He was meticulous about these things. In fact, Maxine was with Akash right now, getting that sneak peek at their rehearsal he'd promised.

The installation time unfortunately clashed with the rehearsal, so Remi was missing out, not that she hadn't seen the band do their thing numerous times. She had wanted to be there to see Maxine's reaction, but she needed to be at the gallery more. She wouldn't leave this part to anyone. She had a specific setup in mind and needed to be sure that everything would be as she wanted it.

Maxine had sent her a short video of the guys practicing earlier, though, so she knew things were going well.

Maxine: *wow think I'm a Roti and a Red Solo stan now!*
Remi: *it was inevitable*

Maxine had also included an excited face selfie that had Remi smiling. They hadn't been able to chat much since Remi was running around directing. She knew she needed to calm down, but her nerves were all over the place. *Two more days.*

God, she was going to throw up. Her stomach bubbled and she took several deep breaths. If she was like this now, what sort of mess was she going to be on the actual day? Would she be able to explain calmly what the inspiration was for the series. Or would she sound like a bumbling mess.

She had been practicing potential interview scenarios with Cherisse and Maxine, but was it enough?

Remi hadn't sent up any SOS to Maxine, simply saying that all was going well when she had asked because their relationship was so fresh. A week old. She didn't want to get too clingy just yet. Maxine had a job to do. She would come here soon. She had been with Remi as much as she could while she finished up her pieces, offering moral support and sweet kisses.

They messaged each other every day, so even though she couldn't hog all her time, she was grateful for the check-ins. But God, she was getting anxious as the hours ticked by and the larger, blown-up photos were carefully being hung.

"Hey." Cherisse came over, placing a hand on her shoulder. "Stop freaking out. Your work is amazing."

"How do you know I'm freaking out?" It was a foolish question. Cherisse knew her better than anyone. Without saying a thing, of course she would know that Remi was silently having a meltdown.

Cherisse folded her arms. "Not gonna dignify that with a response. How can I help?"

Bring me my girlfriend, was on the tip of her tongue but she clamped her mouth shut, not sure how that would go over. Maxine wasn't a replacement for Cherisse but right now that's what she wanted.

"I just . . . it's so intimate, isn't it?"

She had been of two minds about putting everything up, wondering if she should keep Maxine's photo specifically for herself. But she had her permission. It was an integral part of the series. She couldn't hoard it away because she was nervous.

Maxine was sure that no one who knew her would recognise her from these. Her face wasn't shown in any of them, and the only person who could know her body like that—apart from her—was all the way in Atlanta.

Remi made a face at that thought. She didn't need to be thinking about Maxine's ex right now.

"That's the whole point of the series," Cherisse reminded her gently.

"I know. But . . . why did Jackie even agree to let me do this? Why did *I* think I could do this? Who am I to even think that? I don't know if I can really pull this off."

"Do I need to call Maxi?" Cherisse asked.

And this was exactly why Cherisse knew her too damn well. She didn't look any type of annoyed that Maxine was what Remi might need in this moment.

"*No.* Do *not* call her. It's been a week. I can't be calling her every time I have a meltdown." She blew out a long breath. "I don't wanna be a burden already."

"You won't be. She'd come if you told her you needed her, you know. That's what partners do." Cherisse gave her a pointed look. "And you keep saying it's been a week. Officially yeah. But you two have been circling each other for months now. You don't think that counts for something?"

"I know she would if I asked, and technically, girlfriend status is what's so new. Even though we've been intimate before and went on dates, it's different now. Just . . . don't call her, okay? She'll be on her way here soon anyhow. Let me handle this." She patted her stomach, where the nervous sensation was lodged.

As much as she would love for Maxine to walk through the gallery doors, she had to suck it up. She shook her arms out walking around as she surveyed what they'd put up already.

She stopped at the one with Maxine. That one she had wanted installed first. She couldn't help herself from returning to it over and over since it had gone up. She didn't have favourites, or so she had planned to say if asked. All the photos told their own story. But to herself, she could admit this one photo of Maxine, showing the sensual curving of her body, was the one that stood out.

This one was the showstopper. She had told them to place it at the centre so it dominated. The other smaller photos went around it like a spiral to show the progression of where they had started out to the final centre shot. She should ask them to drape this one now.

Maxine had seen all the photos of herself, but not the final arrangements. Remi wanted that to be a surprise for Saturday's show. She should find the gallery worker who could help with that.

She was going to have to channel nonchalance on show day. How was she supposed to act as if this piece wasn't more special than the others? She wanted guests to be curious, yes, but not to the point where they noticed her feelings and all the love to be spilling out everywhere.

Love, yes. She was there, but she wouldn't say it to Maxine yet. Now wasn't the time for declarations that could scare Maxine off. Besides, that was a very private thing between them. She would show her with every savour of her body, instead, until she felt it was time to say it out loud without Maxine running for the hills.

"What's the story for this one?" Cherisse came to stand beside her. "I know you're not about to tell people this is your girlfriend seducing you."

Remi shot Cherisse an epic side-eye, not that it did any good. She was beyond being affected by Remi's stares anymore. "We weren't together then, so no, that's not the story. This one remains anonymous, but it's about embracing your inner sexuality and sensuality. Opening up to new experiences with your body. Learning the power of it."

"Damn, you're good. I almost believed this wasn't before you two bomchickawowwow'd all over that studio."

"Don't you have a bakery to be at?"

"Keiran's supervising the final touches. I'm here for however long I want to beeee."

"You trust him to do that?"

"He's been checking in so it's all good. You're not getting rid of me that easy."

Remi rolled her eyes, but she was grateful for her best friend. Always. "Lucky I love you, you silly goose."

"Ditto."

She went back to her phone to see if Maxine was on her way. Nothing. No message. Which was fine. The rehearsal was probably still going. No biggie. She would be less on her way to meltdown mode if she focused on what was going on in front of her and what was left to be done.

The gallery owner came by to check on her. Remi gave her a smile and claimed, "I'm all good yeah. Just can't wait to see it all up."

"It's brilliant!" Jody shook her head. "You got a great eye. I know it's going to be a sensational showcase. I'm so glad Jackie brought the idea to me."

Remi asked for the drape to cover Maxine's photos, trying to channel some of Jody's confidence, taking some teaser shots for her pages. It didn't hurt to drum up some excitement. She had just posted on her feed and to her story when she noticed Maxine had also posted a story a few hours ago.

Remi felt her stomach flutter as she saw Maxine had shared her promo ad with the caption *Come check out this very special inner series!*

She had been hyping up the show the last few weeks, but it never got old to see another new post of her doing that.

Her phone rang and Remi was surprised but delighted to see Maxine calling. They usually messaged via the chat rather than call, but Remi couldn't say she wasn't eager to hear her voice.

"Heyyyy, you on your way?"

"Hey, sorry no. I can't make it anymore. I . . ." she trailed off.

Remi's nervousness ratcheted up. "Maxi, what's wrong?"

She sighed. "Leo sent me a photo. Of us from the event. I'm *so* pissed off. Someone sent it to him. I didn't even see anyone there. Not that either of us would have noticed since we were kissing, but . . ."

"What? I don't understand. What is happening?"

"I sent you the photo."

Remi switched over to her WhatsApp, because what sort of photo could someone have sent Maxine's ex-husband that would have Maxine sounding upset like this? Her brain supplied her with the worst-case scenarios. She hoped it wasn't some invasive shit because she was going to kick someone's ass.

The photo of them embracing and kissing was clear as day. Who the hell would have taken that?

Remi returned to the call. "What the hell? Who sent that to Leo?"

"Some woman he knows who was obviously at the party. I don't know. He just sent it to me and asked, what the hell is this? I want to come, Remi. I do. But I need to have a proper conversation about this shit. Because I'm not going to let this slide."

"Do you need me to come to you?" She would drop everything here and go to Maxine if she said yes. She didn't give a damn.

It was one of Maxine's main fears come true. Someone had taken away the chance for her to have this conversation with Leo on her own terms. Now, she was forced into it. It was a goddamn violation of her privacy. Granted, they had been at a public event, but that didn't matter. That person had obviously recognised Maxine and had taken that photo and sent it with malicious intent.

"No, stay. Finish up there. I need to deal with this. But thanks for offering. I'm just so fucking angry. And . . . I don't know. I just need to talk to him now. But I wanted you to know why I'm not coming anymore."

"Hey, don't worry about that. Do what you have to do. Take his ass to task because this shit is not okay."

"Thanks. I'm sorry."

"*You* have nothing to be sorry for," Remi assured her.

"I'll let you know how it goes."

Holy fucking shit. Remi was about to trip off. But she couldn't. Leo wasn't even in the same country right now. But that woman was. Not that she had any way of finding out who she was. Even if she did, Maxine wouldn't want to cause a scene.

Cherisse took one look at Remi as she stalked over to where Scott's photos were being set up. "What's wrong?"

"I'm about to trip off and I can't because I need to focus on this, but Leo sent Maxi this photo someone else sent him and . . ." she shook her head. "She said she'll take care of it, but all I want to do is go to her and make sure she's okay."

"Wait. Hold on. Leo? As in Maxi's ex? Explain it all to me slowly."

Remi did and Cherisse's eyes grew wider and wider. "Holy fucking shit. That's fucked up. I'm so sorry Remi."

"I'm worried about Maxi because this is what she was scared would happen. Well, maybe not this exact thing, but . . ."

"Yeah." Cherisse nodded. "I get you."

"It's been a week. Just a week and we were happy and now."

"Do you think this will scare her off?"

Remi shrugged. She didn't know. Maxine had sounded upset. Pissed. As she should be. Remi couldn't discern anything else from her tone. She had said she would update her after she'd spoken to Leo, but Remi had no way of knowing what that would mean.

"I'm just going to have faith she won't go running. I can't do anything else 'til we talk." She scrubbed her hand over her face. "Ugh, let's just . . . I need a distraction. Can you help me do that, please?"

"Yeah, of course." Cherisse wrapped her arms around Remi. "I love you and it's gonna be okay. You'll see."

"Yeah."

She let Cherisse drag her over to where they were setting up another one of her subjects. It was going to be fine.

CHAPTER THIRTY-FOUR

MAXINE

SHE STORMED INTO THE HOUSE, HEADING STRAIGHT FOR KEIRAN'S studio downstairs. She was grateful her mother and Leah were probably watching TV until it was Leah's bedtime. She didn't want either of them seeing her like this.

She had called Keiran after she'd spoken to Remi. She had needed privacy to chat with Leo, because she sure as shit couldn't do it at the gallery.

She had been ready to leave Akash after the rehearsal and about to message Remi that she was on the way. She had been looking forward to getting a sneak peek of the installations when the message from Leo had come in. Now, her evening was ruined.

She hadn't been sure of what she was seeing. Even as the photo was right there, plain as day, she calmly said bye to Akash and had taken several deep breaths before calling Remi. She needed to be the first to know since it involved them both.

The way her hands had been shaking, she hadn't been sure she could forward the photo, but she had. Then, after she'd hung up with Remi, she had called Keiran, and now she was here.

It was a miracle she had made it home in one piece, because the anger that was coursing through her felt dangerous.

Keiran turned around in his chair as she stalked down into the room.

"How you feeling?"

"Like I want to kick Leo's ass, but I'm ready to call him. I need to do it now. I don't want this to linger past today. He needs to know how fucked up this is!"

"Agreed. You need anything? Water? A shot?"

She waved Keiran off and dialled Leo's number. "Maybe after. I just need this motherfucker to pick up!"

"You want me to leave you alone?" he offered.

She could tell he had work to do, but she could use the support.

"Could you stay? Damn, he better pick the hell up."

The call connected and Leo's deep voice rumbled in her ear. "You want to talk about this now?" was how he greeted her. She didn't give two shits what he was doing. Fuck yes, they were doing this now.

"Yes, Leo. Since you sent it to me now. I want to talk about how fucked up it is for your friend to send *you* that invasive photo of me."

"And her," he added.

"Yes, and Remi."

"So, you don't want to explain why you're out there kissing some woman?"

Maxine paced the length of the studio, her free hand clenching into a ball and unclenching. "Why do I need to explain a damn thing? I need your friend to explain why she felt the need to even take that photo and send it to you. Like some sort of gotcha moment. Who gave her the right?"

Leo sighed. "Look, she sent it to me because she thought I

should know. She assumed I didn't, and she was right, wasn't she?"

"What business is it of yours? If someone sent me a photo of you and your girlfriend before you got to tell me anything, would that be okay? You'd be cool with that?"

"Well, I mean I'd feel some type of way, but . . ."

"But nothing, Leo! I wasn't even afforded the courtesy to talk to you when *I* was ready. Because your fucking friend took that from me."

"So, tell me this, then. Was our relationship even real? Or was that just about pretending you were someone else."

Maxine rubbed her forehead. "Oh my God, I swear I'm going to fucking scream. Seriously? Not that I need to explain anything to you, but yes, you and I were legit. Me being with Remi now has nothing to do with our past. *You* ruined us, so don't you dare insinuate otherwise."

"Okay, fine."

She didn't give two shits if he believed her. He wasn't going to throw that back at her, not after everything.

"And what about Leah? How do you think this is going to affect her?" he asked.

She had been waiting on this line of questioning. He was so predictable. Of course, he would also try to act like all of this was warranted, as a concerned father.

"Leah already knows. I had a chat with her as soon as we realised we were going to officially date. And she literally just said cool. She already likes Remi, so there's no issue."

"No issue?" Leo scoffed. "And what's going to happen with school stuff. She's gonna be coming to PTA meetings with you now? You don't see how that would look?"

"You're a fucking jackass," she spat out. "We literally just made this official a week ago. Did you afford me the right to ask you any of this shit when you started dating? No, you fucking didn't. You just told me, by the way, after Leah already spilled the beans, so don't you dare come at me with this. Listen to me very carefully, Leo. Tell your lil' friend that this shit was unacceptable."

Leo sighed as if he was so exasperated with this entire thing. He wouldn't want to sit around while she shouted at him, but too damn bad. He was going to deal with it.

"I handled that already. Yes, you're right, okay? She should never have taken your photo, but don't worry, it's not like she going to post it anywhere."

"I should hope the hell not. In fact, you should give me her name."

"What? No damn way. For you to go do something unhinged? No."

"I'm not going to do anything drastic. I think I'm well within my right to ensure she never attends another KKE event again. It's only fair, hmm?" she asked sweetly.

"I'm sorry, Maxi, but no. I can't be sure you won't do something else with the information."

She breathed loudly through her nose before replying. "Well aren't you just loyal. For all the wrong fucking reasons. Whatever, keep your lil' friend's name."

She would probably never find out, but if she did, that person was getting blacklisted from their events for life. She hoped Leo had truly spoken to her, because Maxine didn't want to feel uncomfortable wondering if something like this could happen again.

"Is there anything else?" Leo asked after a while.

This conversation wasn't totally over. They would definitely talk about it again. But Maxine was done. She was tired. Drained. She should have been with Remi giving her the support she needed. Instead, she had to deal with this shit.

Her head was pounding now. "I've said everything I need to for now."

"You know, I should have guessed from Tobago. I felt like I got a vibe off her—that she didn't like me and was sizing me up or something."

Maxine laughed and Keiran's brows went up, probably wondering if she was having a breakdown. "You're pathetic, I swear. Don't ever ask me shit like that again. Just don't talk about my girlfriend, period. Ever. I'll afford you the same courtesy with yours. Fuck you very much."

She ended the call and plopped down on the couch. "That shot sounds good right about now. Just bring a bottle. Anything."

Keiran got to his feet. "You sure? I know you don't really drink much."

"You can't be offering then taking it back. I'm sure."

He squeezed her shoulder "Talk to Remi before we start on the drinks."

Yeah, solid advice. She didn't want the first message she sent to be some drunken ramble.

Maxine: *hey is now good to talk? I'm done with Leo.*

By the time Keiran returned with the drinks—a bottle of white wine and tequila—Remi still hadn't responded yet. She must not be able to at the moment.

Maxine: *call me when you can*

She tossed her phone, nearly losing it when it almost bounced off the couch. She caught it at the last minute and safely tucked it away. She didn't need a cracked screen on top of everything else.

She eyed the bottle of tequila. "I didn't get on to Remi, but hopefully by the time she gets back to me I'll be sober enough." She pressed her head back into the top of the couch. "Why did this have to happen?"

"Cuz there are fucked up people in this world." Keiran rolled over a little trolley he had set up in the corner. She supposed he had his moments where he needed a drink break too.

"I'm sure she's wondering if this means I'm gonna chicken out. I want to let her know I'm not. This threw me, I won't lie. Knowing that someone would do that?" She shook her head. "*Did* do that."

Keiran held up the bottles. "Pick your poison."

She pointed to the tequila. It wasn't the best choice, but she didn't want to feel this burning rage anymore. She felt as if she would do something reckless. She could just be numb for a little bit, then tomorrow she would compartmentalise, because Remi needed her too.

Keiran prepped their shots, then they clinked their glasses before both downing the drink.

"Damn."

"Yeah," Maxine echoed. The burn felt good though. Her phone chimed, showing a call coming in from Remi. "Hey."

"Heyyyyyyyyyyyyy, my pretty doll. How are youuuu? Did you verbally kick his ass? If you need me to, I will, too. He's far, but I know a site that sends people these glitter bomb things."

"Uhh," Remi sounded tipsy as hell. What the heck was going on?

"Whoa, hey, who are you talking to?" That was clearly Cherisse.

"My girlfriiiiieeeend," Remi sang out.

"Gimme the phone!"

"But she told me to call herrr."

"Hey, hiiii Maxi." Cherisse had clearly gotten the phone from Remi.

"Cherisse, what the hell? Why does Remi sound drunk?"

"You see, what happened was this." Cherisse sounded sheepish. "She wanted me to give her a distraction cuz she's stressed out as fuck about this show, so I convinced her to come to a nearby bar for a bit. But then things sort of escalated."

"You're supposed to be helping! Not drunkening her when she needs to be monitoring her installations." Maxine had never experienced a drunk Remi. She sounded cute as hell, but seriously, now wasn't the time for any of this.

"I know! But she was worried about the show. Worried about you. Freaking the fuck out, so I didn't know what else to do, okay! I didn't know she'd get this wasted this fast."

Maxine pressed her fingers to the bridge of her nose, trying to alleviate the pressure building. She didn't want to shout at Cherisse, but what the hell? This wasn't what Remi needed right now. "And what was your plan exactly?" she asked as calmly as she could manage. "Ensure she's so intoxicated that she's no longer freaking out?"

"Not exactly, but she's not freaking out anymore, so . . ."

"Right, but now she's also in no shape to get her shit done. Which means when she does sober up, she's going to freak out even more."

"I just wanted to take her mind off things for a bit."

Maxine sighed. "Where's this bar exactly?"

"Wait, no, you don't need to come here. I got this. I've been taking care of her a long time. Sorry about what happened to you all by the way; that shit sucks. Fuck that guy."

"Thanks," Maxine said dryly. She was definitely not getting drunk anymore. "But I'm coming."

"You really love her, don't you? I was worried you would be running."

"Cherisse, we got past all that bickering bullshit from our teens. I know you're watching out for your bestie. Or I thought you were, but respectfully, you fucked up. I'm coming to get my girl. Please don't let her drink another drop of alcohol."

"Yes, ma'am. I'll send you the location."

Keiran got to his feet. "So, I'm guessing drinks are on pause."

"Maybe I'll just end up drinking there, who knows. Or maybe I'll shout at your girlfriend, too." Maxine shrugged. "The evening is young and ripe for more mess."

"Yeaaah, maybe don't get into a fight with Cherisse. I'll be your designated driver then. What do we tell mummy?"

That was a good question. Hopefully, by the time they got upstairs, they would figure it out. Maxine hugged her brother again. She was so grateful for him. Truly. But now she had to go pick up her tipsy girlfriend. This one week of being official was not going the way she would have expected.

CHAPTER THIRTY-FIVE

REMI

Remi: I'm so sorryyyy. I'm embarrassed. I was such a mess. Did I say anything weird?
Maxine: hmmm, well you threw yourself at me the moment I got into the bar and you said my pretty pretty doll is here
Remi: >.< yeaaaaah I'm moving to Alaska. I can't face you
Maxine: you'll be fine. Get up cuz we have to get your installs done. Oh, you also uh said you loved me but we can talk about that later lols BYE

Remi blinked down at her phone. No. She couldn't have been that wasted to confess that. Maxine must have been teasing. She had really been a mess last night. It was a blur, but *shit*, bits and pieces were coming back as she lay in her bed feeling like her head was about to explode. Like how Cherisse and Maxine had been arguing while Keiran stood awkwardly by, and Remi had sat there drinking water, beaming up at her girlfriend, who looked a beautiful goddess, even as she and her best friend had been going back and forth.

Remi wasn't upset with Cherisse. She had been trying to distract her like she asked. Remi had just overdone it trying to drink her stress away.

She remembered now, how she had practically slurred. "I'm good. We can go back to the gallery."

Maxine had been adamant about that being a terrible idea and they could return as early as possible the next day. Which was today.

God, she better get her ass up like Maxine had said. She checked her phone again.

> **Maxine:** *I'm coming in 20 be ready! I'm bringing hangover soup so don't eat anything.*

Yeah, she had to get ready. And damn it was so cute that Maxine was going to make sure she was okay. She had to have been annoyed last night. Well, actually, she had been, because, yeah, she was bickering hardcore with Cherisse, which Remi hadn't thought she would ever see again. She thought that was left behind after graduation, but oops, guess not.

Cherisse was pacing the living room when Remi came down. She stopped, rushing over to her and peering at her face.

"How you feeling? You're good? You can get through today at the gallery, right?"

"Relax. I'm not dying."

"I fucked up."

"It's *fine*." She wasn't going to make it a big deal.

"Maxine was so pissed off at me."

Remi grinned. "Oh yeah. It was magnificent. Sanaa really was right about that."

Cherisse shook her head. "You're hopeless."

"So hey, I apparently said some things last night? To Maxi."

She cleared her throat. How did one go about asking their bestie if they confessed their love to their girlfriend in some random bar?

"You sure did."

"Oh God." How was she supposed to face Maxine in—she checked her phone—less than fifteen minutes?

"You'll live. You should have seen her face though." Cherisse chuckled. "Priceless."

"It's too early for love confessions."

"Maybe? But just get through your show and you can talk about it after."

"Ugh."

Her head pounded even more, but Remi just guzzled some water and hopped into Maxine's car when she messaged that she was outside.

"You look a hot mess," Maxine said, leaning over to plant a small peck on her check. "The soup will help."

"Thanks. I'm sure it's tasty." Remi stared straight ahead as they drove to the gallery. She was making it awkward by being so silent, but she didn't know what to say.

"Are you okay?" she finally asked. Remi had been too out of it to even ask Maxine for details about her call with Leo.

Maxine's jaw clenched. "Yeah. Mostly. I still want to wring that woman's neck, but . . ." she shrugged.

"Sorry you then had to deal with my drunk ass on top of that."

Maxine reached over and took Remi's hand in hers. "I'm here, okay. Just know that. You would've done the same for me. You may have to since I didn't get to have my drunk moment."

Remi winced. "Sorry. Again."

Maxine squeezed her hand before removing hers to place it back on the wheel. "Make it up to me."

Remi could think of many ways to do that. Even though

the dating countdown was effectively stopped, that obviously didn't need to stop them from going on dates.

They got to the gallery before eight. Maxine had apparently swung by last night to beg the owner to allow them to come back super early to finish up. God, how was she supposed to not fall in love with this woman?

She had done all of that when she had been dealing with her own stress. No wonder she had blurted it out last night. The alcohol had just helped loosen exactly what was being guarded inside her.

Maxine walked around observing the pieces they had managed to set up. "Oh, wow. This is amazing! Where's mine?"

"Nope. you can't see it until tomorrow."

"Oh c'mon. After everything I did last night?" Maxine was in full Bambi-eyes mode, but Remi refused to relent.

She sipped her hangover soup, shaking her head. "Can't ruin the surprise."

The rest of the day continued like that. Maxine tried all how to persuade Remi to give in, but she wasn't having it. Maxine could easily have peeked, but she was being respectful of Remi's wishes, which she adored her for even more.

By the time they had finished all the installations and put up the stage, Remi was ready to keel over. She would need to rest up early tonight. As much as she wanted to take Maxine back to the apartment and show her just how grateful she was for her, she couldn't even muster that energy to flirt.

Akash and his bandmates had come through, done their practice, and now it was just Remi, Maxine and the owner left. Well, just Remi here in the main showing room right now, with the photos illuminated by the warm lighting. She had a different feel she wanted for the evening part of the showcase.

Maxine had disappeared a little while ago saying she had to

go collect something and Remi wondered what that could be. A small noise sounded behind her, and Remi turned to see Maxine walking towards her juggling a cake box, a bouquet of flowers, and a gift bag on her wrist.

Remi's mouth dropped open. "What's all this?"

Maxine placed the box and bag on the small table in front her and handed her the flowers. "I wanted to have a lil' mini celebration before everyone monopolises you tomorrow. Just us."

"Maxi, you didn't have to do this."

"I know. But as your girlfriend, yeah, I wanted to." She smiled and flipped up the cake box to reveal a mini cake with the words *I'm so proud of you!* written on the front.

Remi's nostrils burned. This was too much. She clutched the flowers in her hand.

"It's a cookies-and-cream cake too. Oh, and one more thing." She picked up the gift bag and handed it to her. "Happy almost showcase day."

Remi removed the kite paper-wrapped item and slowly opened it, revealing a framed photo. It was the one Leah had taken of them at the Botanical Gardens.

"I love it so much," Remi whispered. *And you. I love you.* Remi blinked rapidly, trying to dispel the tears that were welling up. "Thank you."

Maxine grinned. "No, thank you, for not giving up on me while I kept you waiting."

"It wasn't that long of a wait." It felt like forever, but they were here now, she didn't need to rehash all those emotions.

"Please, you were struggliiiiing not to ask me why I was putting us through this."

"I didn't want to pressure you! I was being a good friend."

"Yeah." Maxine tugged on one of her curls. "And you're an even better girlfriend. I know you said, uh, some words last night that we still haven't addressed . . ."

"Hey, we don't have to. I was really a mess."

"Did you not mean them?"

She wouldn't lie. "I meant it."

"Okay, I'll get there. But I'm going to hold those words close, okay, if you don't mind."

Remi leaned in. "Yeah."

"I care about you a lot," Maxine said, leaning in too.

"I know."

The kiss was sweet. They weren't trying to make it any more than that. They had all the time to share all sorts of kisses, as they pleased.

Remi leaned back, took Maxine's hand in hers. "I've liked you for a long time. Ever since we fooled around back then, in school. It's why I acted an entire fool when you were leaving. Not that my feelings made that right, but adult me would like to apologise."

"You told me I was using you to experiment."

Remi cringed. "Yeah, God I was a bitch."

"I actually didn't take it to heart. I was too focused on leaving."

"Well damn, I'm hurt." Remi clutched her chest. If Maxine had told her that back then, she wouldn't have taken it well.

"Doesn't matter now. You've got me."

Hell yeah, she did. "It's our take two."

"Hmm, I like the sound of that." Maxine got to her feet, held out her hand as music filled the quiet space.

Remi looked around then back at Maxine, who was looking so smug. "How the hell . . ."

"I got my ways. Dance with me?"

Remi took her hand, allowed Maxine to pull her in. "You trying to show up my dance date or what?"

Maxine swayed with her. "If it's nice, you do it twice."

"Oh really?" Remi hooked her hand around Maxine's waist. "I'd like to do you more than twice, actually."

"You're too tired."

"I know, but I just need a hit of sugar from my cake and I'm good as new." She was joking, of course. She really was too tired, but she couldn't help herself.

"No sleeping over. Early bedtime tonight. After this."

This being them whirling around the gallery like no one was watching. Jody probably was, but if Maxine wasn't bothered, neither was she.

It would take baby steps to get Maxine comfortable enough to do this in a public setting, but Remi didn't need that. She had everything she wanted right in her arms.

And while the countdown itself had been put on hold, their moment was just beginning.

EPILOGUE

MAXINE

THE BUZZ OF THE GUESTS AS THEY WALKED AROUND, DRINKING IN each and every photograph, had Maxine on a high, as if this was her work. She was so happy for Remi. Every bit of conversation she had eavesdropped on sounded positive.

"I love this one especially. So raw. Wonder if the model is here tonight? Wouldn't it be fun to figure that out?"

Maxine flushed as the elderly couple stood in front her photos. The model was indeed here, but no one was going to know that. It was an interesting experience seeing herself up there, hearing people talk about her like this.

She was glad she had done it. Remi truly was a genius.

"You're the photographer?" the old woman asked as Remi walked over.

"Yes, hi." Remi glanced over at Maxine but just smiled.

"I really think this one is my favourite," the older woman said. "Love the progression of it. Whoever she is she truly came into her power by the end of it."

Remi nodded. "That she did."

"Wink once if she's here tonight. This is just some woman!" The man nudged the woman's arm with his shoulder.

She shook her head. "Behave," she scolded, but there was no real heat behind it.

"All I can say is, she is quite the woman indeed," Remi explained.

"Are you not selling these?"

Remi smiled. "Sorry, no. This one's all mine."

"And what do you think about it, young lady?" the man asked, turning to Maxine.

Maxine startled. "Oh. I love it, too. Very provocative and powerful."

The couple nodded and wandered off to the other side to view some more photos.

"Provocative and powerful, huh?" Remi brushed at her dramatic sleeves. "Sounds about right for my muse."

"Muse, eh?"

"Yeah. I need to stockpile a private collection. For my eyes only. If you would be into that."

Oh, the idea appealed. In theory. She didn't know if she could actually go through with it. But posing for Remi's eyes only sounded so hot. She knew Remi would make her look beautiful.

"We'll try some time," she promised. "See how it goes. How're you feeling, though?" Maxine had given Remi her space, not wanting to crowd her.

Their friends and Remi's family were here too, giving their support, oohing over the photos as most of them wouldn't have seen the full series.

It was Remi's time to shine, and Maxine was just glad to be a part of it.

Pauline and the A&R team were here too, and soon Akash and his band would be on. She knew what she wanted that outcome to be, but she didn't want to overstep there either.

"I'm overwhelmed, but in a good way?" Remi replied. "It's a lot, but everyone who matters is here."

"Yes, and we'll keep being here," Maxine assured her. She had kept assuring her of that.

She knew after the photo drama that Remi must have had doubts. Maxine had decided to provide that casual assurance as much as she could.

"I'm not going anywhere."

Remi leaned in, lips brushing her ear. "Except to my bed later."

Maxine shivered as Remi pulled away, but not before she grazed her ear with her teeth.

"Wait for me." Remi patted her side, then walked over to some other guests who were staring up at Scott's magnificent photo.

Oh yes, she was most definitely going to wait. She wasn't running anywhere except into Remi's arms.

ACKNOWLEDGEMENTS

Wow, I can't even believe we are at book 3 of this series! Remi and Maxi have been simmering in the background of books 1 and 2 and finally I get to fully show them off to everybody. I hope you, dearest reader, fall in love with them as I did, again, while writing them.

To Jen as always for giving me constructive feedback and keeping it real with me! You are truly the BEST friend and supporter a girl could have. Love ya lots! We are gonna make it to a BTS concert *together* someday. I am manifesting iiiiit (looks to 2025 👀)

To my agent Lauren who's always there to explain things to me when I come asking random questions about publishing things lol. Thank you for your patience and for all that you generally do.

I must give a shout out to the Little, Bown / Piatkus team who took a chance on this little series of mine. Many thanks to the editing team, Eleanor Russell, Emma Beswetherick and Tanisha Ali, Narges in production, Rebecca Lee and all who had a hand in getting my book ready for your eyes!

And in case you were wondering who did my gawjus cover, that was all Monika Wiśniewska. Monika, it was a pleasure working with you. You captured that scene so beautifully and I look forward to working with you in the future (I better get started on book 4 then hmmm?? :D)

As always, to the romance community, the readers, authors and bloggers who have cheered for me and shown their support in so many ways. I appreciate you all. Much Love!

Until the next book ☺

Do you love contemporary romance?

Want the chance to hear news about your favourite authors (and the chance to win free books)?

Kristen Ashley
Meg Cabot
Olivia Dade
Rosie Danan
J. Daniels
Farah Heron
Talia Hibbert
Sarah Hogle
Helena Hunting
Abby Jimenez
Elle Kennedy
Christina Lauren
Alisha Rai
Sally Thorne
Denise Williams
Meryl Wilsner
Samantha Young

Then visit the Piatkus website
www.yourswithlove.co.uk

And follow us on Facebook and Instagram
www.facebook.com/yourswithlovex | @yourswithlovex

PIATKUS